ISBN 13: 978-1-940014-36-4

Library of Congress Catalog Number: 2014952752
Printed in United States of America
First Printing: 2014
17   16   15   14   13   5   4   3   2   1

Cover and interior design by Aurora Whittet

Wise Ink, Inc.
53 Oliver Ave S
Minneapolis, MN 55404
www.wiseinkpub.com

To order, visit www.itascabooks.com or call 1-800-901-3480. Reseller discounts available.

This is a work of fiction. Names, characters, places, and incidents either are the product of the author's imagination or are used ficticiously, and any resemblance to actual persons living or dead, businesses, companies, events, or locales is entierly coincidental.

Bloodrealms

Endorsements

"*Bloodrealms* will transport you to a fantasy world full of glamour, excitement, and the romance between Ashling and Grey will whisk you away!"
— **C.A. Gray, author of *Intangible* and *Invinvible***

"Full of intrigue and tension, *Bloodrealms* will leave you panting for the next installment in the series."
— **Juliann Rich, author of *Caught in the Crossfire,***
** *Searching for Grace,* and *Taking the Stand***

"Fans of adventure and of paranormal romance will delight in the epic saga that is *Bloodrealms*. Ashling Boru is an engaging and fiery heroine."
— **Wendy Delsol, author of *Stork, Frost, Flock,* and**
** *The McCloud Home for Wayward Girls***

"*Bloodrealms* simply sparkles!"
— **Jami Brumfield, author of the Winters Saga, Mystery Springs**
** Series, PBI Case Files, and Ghost Connection**

"A one of a kind, must-read for all paranormal romance lovers."
— **Emily Fay, blogger for *Hooked in a Book***

Bloodrealms

Aurora Whittet

We never know the destination of our path
until we have the strength to pursue it.

To my sweet son Henry;
you are my happy thought and my sunshine.

Contents

I

Good-bye

"Why bloody not?" I said. "Why can't Grey come?"

"It's not up to us. If Lord and Lady Kahedin don't invite the House of Killian to the wedding, he can't go—it's disrespectful," Mund said.

"Don't pretend this is okay, because you know it isn't," I said, pushing myself off of Baran's kitchen counter. I was on the edge of losing my mind. We had barely gotten home from the Rock of Cashel, where my father forced three unwanted suitors on me, and my family was already trying to pull Grey and me apart again.

I knew how delicate the balance was within my family and among our allies. Each day, sides were being chosen. Baran, Mund, Tegan, Quinn, Gwyn, and Mother had all chosen my side—some more publicly than others, but it was obvious they belonged to me. Flin had made it abundantly clear that he was on Father's side. My brother Felan was unknown; he seemed to favor Father, but possibly out of fear.

Each of our strongest allies had offered a son to marry me. Lord Kingery offered Channing, Lord Kahedin offered Brychan (whom my father had already tried to marry me off to years earlier), Eamon offered himself as King of the Dvergars, and Grey offered himself with Mother Rhea's help. Each family wanted to "win" me, and the losers could riot. The entire betrothal process could start a war. I was to fulfill Calista's prophecy, and the wolf who claimed me at Carrowmore would rule our people with me. I was a prize to all of them, all of them except for Grey. To him, I was Ashling.

If Grey didn't beat all three of them, he would not win my father's choice. My options would be to submit and agree to marry whomever the victor ended up being or abandon my family and life to be with Grey anyway. If I chose Grey, it would split all the packs apart. The true victor would align with Father, and the other two losing families would have to choose between me and Father. Only an Elder God like Mother Rhea could rule over Father, but even then I wasn't sure Mother Rhea would let me chose Grey. I was trapped in their game, and Father knew it. He had me right where he wanted me, in a cage. My choice didn't truly matter, not by our laws, but many of my family members still backed me. They would all fight for me . . . of course, that meant they might have to die for me.

I felt so helpless. There was nothing I could do. Everything rode on whether or not Grey could win.

"This is crap," Baran said.

"I don't care what is proper, Mund," I said. "Grey and I need to be together. He's coming to the wedding."

"Ashling . . ." Mund said.

My body shook with anger and fear. My soul had already begun binding with Grey's, and physical separation would tear away at our strength. Grey wrapped his strong arms around my shaking body and lightly kissed my ear.

"We'll be okay," Grey said, but his reassurance didn't calm the fear that raged through me.

"Please?" I begged Mund.

"We can't dishonor the Kahedin House," Mund said. "And it's

Gwyn and Quinn's wedding; they need us to support them."

My brother Quinn was marrying the love of his life, Gwyn Kahedin, in Wales. As much as I loved them, I didn't want to go without Grey.

"This is Pørr's doing, isn't it?" Baran said.

"I don't know," Mund said.

I shook my head, but the fury still loomed in the back of my mind like a black fog. I couldn't stand having decisions made for me . . . which, unfortunately, was what my father did best.

When Grey and I were together, I felt whole; the pain and hate that still lingered from Adomnan's attack would just drift away. I felt free with him. When we were apart, the disgusting reality that Adomnan had touched me would fill my mind once again. I was filled with self-hate, doubt, and guilt, and though I logically knew that none of it was mine to bear, the feelings from being under Adomnan's power still ate away at me. I reached out and touched Grey's hand, and my panic eased. I took a deep breath, filling my lungs with his scent.

The deeper Grey and I fell in love, the harder it was to deceive everyone else. With three other suitors, our love had to remain a secret, but being apart for that long would show on both of us. I just didn't know how painful the impact would be, or if others would see right through me and realize I had already bound my soul to Grey's.

"I know it's going to be awful," Mund said. "I'm feeling the same pains now. I haven't seen Tegan and Nia in a month; it wears on me, as it will wear on both of you. But we must all make sacrifices for our family." I knew it pained him to be away from his wife and daughter, but he did it for me. I could see it in his dark eyes and the tightness in his jaw.

"I'll be here waiting for you," Grey said to me. He held my face in his strong hands as he kissed my angry tears. "We'll be back together before we know it."

I took another deep breath to calm my panic. Grey was trying to be strong for me, but I could see his fear. His bright green eyes always gave him away, and I could feel his emotions as though they were mine. I knew just how scared he really was.

"I love you," I said.

"And I you," he said.

"How long will we have to stay?" I asked Mund.

"You will spend a fortnight at the Rock of Cashel. Then, you and Mother will travel to Castle Raglan in Wales and stay through the Lughnasadh celebration," Mund said.

"The entire summer?"

Mund nodded.

My shoulders sagged as I thought about it. Three months sounded like an eternity. I hadn't felt separation pain for that long before, only a day here or there. This would be agony that wouldn't end until we entered the Bloodrealms on Lughnasadh. Of course, a new kind of agony would begin in the Bloodrealms.

Grey would have to fight my three other suitors in the Bloodrealms. Brychan was a skilled warrior and Tegan and Gwyn's brother. Channing's body rippled with strength, and he had spent years training for battle. Eamon was also extremely powerful, and, since he was Adomnan's brother and a participant in my abduction months earlier, he scared me half to death. I also had the feeling that there was more to him that he was concealing. I just didn't know what it might be. Grey would have to beat them all in the fighting pits to win my father's choice for my husband. I could never accept any mate other than Grey. I would rather die first. Maybe that's what my father had been hoping for all along. Maybe he never wanted me to fulfill the prophecy and unite the packs; maybe Father wanted to steal my power. It would surely give him great pleasure to be able to lead in my—a woman's—place. Of course, Calista Vanir's prophecy hadn't said anything about my father's role as a leader.

The prophecy told of a girl with crimson hair and snow-white skin, who would unite the wolves and bring balance among the humans. After Adomnan Dvergar kidnapped and tortured me, and I had to kill him to protect myself, I wasn't so sure I was strong enough to lead anymore. I felt weak and self-conscious, and though I knew I was internalizing his abuse, my feelings couldn't quite catch up with my brain. I always drew strength from Grey when I was with him. He was my rock, my center—and I was his. When we were apart, it was hard for either of us to feel right. When I already didn't feel quite myself due to the trauma from Adomnan, I dreaded the emotional repercussions of being away from Grey—and reliving Adomnan all over again.

My ragtag pack had a new member in Odin Pohjola, who had been the guard to Lady Calista centuries earlier. He had tried to protect me when I had been in the Netherworlds with the Dvergars; now, Odin had sworn his alliance to me. I still wasn't sure what he wanted from me; I could sense that he was yearning for something, but I just didn't know what it was. At this point, I hoped his yearning was in alignment with my own: I yearned to fulfill the prophecy and come into my own as a leader, and to have Grey—the man I had chosen by my own will—by my side. In one year, we'd have to travel to Carrowmore for my eighteenth birthday under the Bloodmoon, so I could be claimed before Old Mother, fulfill the prophecy, and take my place as the leader of our people. Only at Carrowmore could I end this constant battle against my father, our allies, and our enemies and truly begin living my life with Grey.

I glanced from the kitchen at Odin sitting in the living room smiling at me. He always looked oddly amused. I was endlessly annoyed by his smirk. At least I was finally able to convince him to stop wearing that dreadful wolf carcass everywhere he went. I felt like its vacant eyes watched my every move from the afterlife.

"We leave tomorrow at dawn," Mund said. "I'm sorry Grey, I wish I could do more."

"We'll escort you both to the plane," Baran said.

Baran and Mund walked away to Baran's office discussing travel details, leaving Grey and me sitting in the kitchen. Grey held me tightly against him like he was trying to absorb me.

"This is so stupid," I complained.

"I hate this. But I will endure any pain for you, my love." His mischievous smile always broke through my sadness, and I couldn't help but smile back at his handsome face. I lightly brushed my lips over his. The sensation was erotic, and it burned through every inch of me, making me want all of him.

"Come on. I want to show you something," he said, pulling me to my feet.

Odin stood to follow us. Grey stopped at the doorway and turned to him. "Why don't you take the day off?"

Odin looked irritated, but his expression softened. "I'm here to protect mi' lady."

There was always a lot of tension between Grey and Odin. I wasn't sure what it was all about, but it was clear they didn't trust each other. I thought Odin was quite pretentious to think we would pick him over Grey, but I knew Odin didn't like the Bloodsucker in Grey. I couldn't blame Odin; it scared a lot of wolves.

"We won't be needing your services today." I smiled.

Odin's expression grew cold, but he nodded.

We hopped on Grey's motorcycle and headed south, leaving them all behind. The warm summer air whipped my red hair around my face and I clung to Grey's back, his warmth and scent filling me. I didn't know where we were going, but I didn't really care as long as I was with him. Since the day I met him at Baran's shop, I hadn't wanted to spend a moment without him. We were one soul in two bodies, and every time we touched it was like an electric current zapped through my skin.

We drove across the bridge from Newburyport to Plum Island. Grey and I often hid there among the wildlife and beach plums. We drove past a pattern of scattered houses to the grassy dunes and a dusty trail followed us to the wildlife refuge. We finally stopped at our secluded beach on the southern end of the island.

The coast welcomed us with lapping waves. Adrenaline pumped through my veins. I jumped off the bike pulling my shirt over my head, revealing my bra. Grey stared at me openmouthed. I could hear his pulse quicken with mine.

"What are you doing?" he asked.

"We didn't come all this way just to look at it." I smiled as I slid my jeans off, tossing them over the handlebars. I flipped off my shoes as I ran toward the ocean in just my bra and panties. A few feet into the water Grey grabbed me around the waist, spinning me into his arms. He crushed my lips into his. I wrapped my legs around his hips, devouring him. He stood barefoot in his jeans as the water splashed around us. His hard chest rubbed against my smooth skin and hunger filled me.

I leaned back, letting my hair dip into the water as he kissed my chest. Primal need flooded me, and all logic was gone. Our bodies rubbed as the waves crashed into us. I desperately wanted all of him and I could feel his need press into me. Every inch of my body tingled with desire. He lightly bit into the tender flesh of my neck and I moaned for him. We fell back into the sand and I straddled him as the water rushed past us in and out of the ocean. Our faces nearly touched as we panted for air.

"You're beautiful," he said. "Inside and out, every part of you is love."

His hands slid down to my bottom, cupping it as the ocean moved my body lightly over his. It aroused me even further. His intense green eyes stared deep into my soul.

"I want you," he said.

"You can have all of me," I breathed. My lip quivered with anticipation, and my cheeks burned red. I hid my face in the crook of his neck and tasted his skin. He rolled his body on top of mine, trapping me under his strong frame as he nibbled at my delicate ears. The wetness of his lips started a flame in my stomach, and I whimpered as his teeth bit my earlobe.

"I wish we could just elope," he said. "I don't want to stop."

"I'm not stopping you."

"We need to stop," he said.

"No," I almost begged.

"I don't want to dishonor your family," he said.

"I know," I said, accepting our standstill.

I ran my fingers over the scar on his chest, feeling the different textures of his skin. Touching him always got my blood pumping, but his scar was a bittersweet memory. When I was dying, after I had killed Adomnan, Grey had rushed in to save me. His fear and rage ripped through him and caused him to shift into wolf form for the first time. Before then, I knew that he was strong and half Bloodsucker, and that my heart belonged to him, but I had never known he was a werewolf. Watching him shift into a wolf the first time was out of a dream . . . a dream from which we were both lucky to wake up.

Grey scooped me up and carried me to the grassy dunes, where he sat down with me in his lap. He moved the wet curls off my face. Night was beginning to settle in all around us, and his beautiful green eyes glowed in the dark.

"Do you see that star, the tiny little blue one? That one, that's our star."

"Why that one?" I asked.

"Because its small but beautiful, and surrounded by an entire sky full of stars; that's our pack. That's how we know we can survive anything, because we have them," he said.

I snuggled into his arms, breathing him in deep. His scent filled my mind. I loved everything about him—his messy hair, bright green eyes, his seductive voice, and the way he strummed his guitar and was always writing new songs in his head. Sometimes he would accidentally hum them out loud, and I would become putty in his hands.

"I'm going to miss you," he said.

"All we have to do is close our eyes and feel the wind to know we still surround each other," I said.

He wrapped his arms around me, holding me tight. He rested the side of his face on my chest, and I played with his wet hair. My fear was creeping in around the edges of my strength. I didn't want to leave him behind; the very idea terrified me. Time marched on and the darkness settled. We both knew that the drive home would lead to my eminent departure, but neither of us dared speak the words. We just lay with our bodies intertwined listening to the rhythm of the ocean and dozed off to sleep.

The night sky was still filled with sparkling stars lighting our way as we began our journey home. I clung to Grey's back, silently begging him to turn around, but the burning sun began to rise off the ocean.

We pulled up in front of Baran's house and started walking toward the door. I noticed Baran peek out the front window. We had delayed the inevitable as long as possible, but reality waited for us on the other side of the door. I desperately grasped at Grey's hand. The good-bye I had to say was nearly choking me. How would I learn to endure this pain? We stood on the porch embracing one another as I buried my face in his chest and he ran his fingers lightly over my back.

"It's okay, love," he said. "This is nothing. Just a tiny, little piece of our forever."

"I know."

The door opened, but I didn't look up. I knew who it was. I could smell them. I could feel their emotions. They were my family and I had to leave two of them behind, and it was breaking my heart. I let the tears seep down my cheeks, hoping it would wash my sorrow away, but it didn't make me feel better.

"It's time to go," Mund said.

Grey scooped me up in his arms and cradled me to his warm chest, carrying me to Baran's Land Rover. I felt weak, but I didn't care. I just wanted him. We all rode in silence to the airport, but really, what was there left to say? I had fought this battle and lost.

We parked at the airport and Grey got out of the car with me still in his arms, but he set me on my feet and I wanted to scream. He wrapped his strong arms around my waist and rested his forehead on mine, letting our energy mingle once more.

"Baran, you know what you have to do," Mund said.

"I do," Baran said.

I didn't know what secrets they kept, but I wasn't interested in any of it. I just wanted to hold on to Grey a little longer. Though I knew no amount of time would ever be enough for either of us.

"Sorry, Grey," Mund said. "I will bring her home to you soon."

Grey nodded, but he didn't loosen his grip around my waist. I kissed his lips, letting his love pour over me like warm honey sticking to my bones. The energy of his kiss would have to give me strength for the summer.

"I'll meet you in my dreams," Grey said.

"I'm counting on it," I said.

We didn't say good-bye. It wasn't a word we knew how to say. I slowly followed Mund and Odin to the plane, but I looked behind me at Grey and Baran, longing to stay with them. Grey looked strong and confident, but even from there, I could see a tear escape down his cheek. Seeing him like this broke my heart.

"Damn this," I said and ran back, jumping into his arms. I crushed him with kisses. I could feel him smiling as I kissed him. "I love you, Grey."

"I love you, too," he said.

I leaned in close and whispered in his ear, "Please come to Wales. You might not be able to go to the wedding, but they can't stop you from being near me."

"I will find a way," he said.

"Don't make me put you on that plane kicking and screaming,"

Mund joked.

"No need," I said. "I just wanted one more kiss." Grey smiled so big I tripped as I ran back to Mund.

"See you soon," he said with a wink.

2
Return to the Rock

The flight was inconsequential; I had more important things on my mind. I knew Father would never let me leave Castle Raglan without some sort of protection, so I had to figure out who would help me escape to see Grey every day. I doubted Mund would be interested in breaking rules under the Kahedin roof, and Odin seemed pleased to have Grey out of the picture. Maybe Tegan would help me. I would have to find someone Mund would trust when we got to Castle Raglan, but for now I had to bide my time at the Rock of Cashel and find some way to stay out of Father's path. The last thing I needed was his unpleasant attention. The last time he chose to notice my existence, I ended up with three unwanted suitors.

We landed in Ireland at the Cork airport, where my brothers Flin and Felan waited for us. Neither looked too pleased to see me, but I couldn't say I felt any different to see them. Mund shook Flin's hand and gave Felan a hug.

"*Fáilte* Ashling," Flin said.

"Thank you. I'm so happy to be here," I lied.

We were silent on the hour-long drive to the Rock of Cashel. The drive was all familiar, the limestone and the ruins, but nothing about it welcomed me home. The last time I saw Flin, he threatened to kill Grey, and I hadn't forgotten. The tension vibrated between us.

As we walked slowly into the castle, the memories all flooded back through me. They didn't suffocate me as I thought they would, but it was still overwhelming. In York Harbor, I could pretend that it was all just a bad dream. But here . . . here it was all real, Father's unending, controlling hatred and Adomnan's assault.

"Mother wanted to see you right away," Felan said. "Follow me."

I was eager to see her. Not much time had passed since I'd last seen her, but I already missed her. I knew all the sacrifices she had made for me since I was born. She loved and protected me. She was so much a part of me.

"Are you happy to be back?" Felan interrupted my thoughts.

"I can't say that I am," I said.

He laughed. "I can't imagine why."

I pushed him and laughed. I barely knew him, but at least he understood my sense of humor. "Felan, what's going to happen here?"

He looked around the empty stone hall for any who might be watching us. "All I can tell you is Flin has plans for you."

"What plans?"

"He wants you to marry Lord Channing."

"Why Channing?" I said.

"I don't know," he whispered. "I just know he doesn't like Lord Brychan."

We turned the corner and I saw Mother's beautiful smiling face. I nearly leaped out of my skin to hug her. This place didn't feel like home to me, but her love did. I nearly crushed her in my embrace. She cried softly as she ran her fingers through my curly hair.

"*M' eudail*," she said.

"I missed you."

"Ashling, I think of you with every breath I take. I am so happy to have you back." She looked around. "Where are Baran and Grey?"

"What?" I said confused. "They weren't invited . . ."

"What do you mean?" she said.

"We were told that they were not invited."

"Your father must have something to do with this. Felan, what's going on here?"

Felan shook his head. "I'm sorry, Mother. I failed you."

"How could you have failed me, Felan?" she said, holding her arms open to him to join our embrace.

"I should have called Lord Killian myself," Felan said.

"Lord Killian?" Suddenly, Father's voice penetrated the air. "He isn't a lord."

His voice made my hair stand on end. I hated to admit it, but I was terrified of his power to ruin everything in my life. I watched him as he closed the space between us.

"Pørr, why did you not extend the proper invitation to Baran and his pack for Quinn and Gwyn's celebration?" I could see the anger on her perfect porcelain face despite her calm composure.

"This is a royal celebration, not a celebration of commoners," he said. I glared at him, wishing my hatred could burn a hole in his skin, but he never even looked at me. "Besides, *my* queen, it is none of your concern."

I could feel the icy tension in the room as they stared at each other, but Mother didn't back down. "You'll regret your actions, Pørr Boru."

He glared at her with contempt. "Or will you?" he said, turning his attention to me as I still clung to her side. "Ashling, I will require your attentions on Lord Channing while you stay here at the Rock."

"Oh, haven't you heard?" Mother said. "We are traveling this evening to help Gwyn prepare for the wedding."

"You will travel to Castle Raglan in a fortnight," he said.

"Gwyn has requested our presence at once. We have to help her prepare for all the festivities. It is our duty as the women of the pack."

Father ground his teeth together; it was a hideous sound. "I command you to stay to greet our guests," he said.

"I'm sure you can keep them well accommodated and entertained," Mother said.

"Cadence and I will welcome Channing and Cara," Felan said. "We will ensure they have a pleasant visit to the Rock."

Mund walked into the room. His footsteps echoed off the walls, fueling the tension.

"And you, Redmund?" Father asked. There was bitterness in his voice when he spoke to Mund. Father knew Mund had chosen my side and resented him for it.

"I will be meeting the Four-Claws at the border of our territory tonight to escort them to Castle Raglan. As they requested."

"You all think to betray your king? Your bloodline?" Father said. "We shall see who regrets their decisions."

There was a threat in every word he said. He was furious; I could smell it on him, but I wasn't as afraid of him anymore. He looked like an angry toddler to me. I watched as he stormed out of the room, leaving us to wonder what his plans truly were.

3

Castle Raglan

Mother and I traveled to Wales to Castle Raglan in the dead of night while Odin drove. To the human eye, not a soul stirred. But I saw them. Some were guards protecting our path, others just came to get a glimpse of the myth—me.

The stories that had circulated among our kind ranged from ridiculous to demonic. None were close to the truth. They described me as being a godlike creature with unyielding power and immeasurable beauty—laughable, to say the least. They described the battle with Adomnan as heroic—that I had beaten all of his guards singlehandedly, and the Dvergar pack was no match for my strength and skill. Of course, they were all wrong about what really happened. I'd barely survived that brutal attack, and the bad memories still haunted me. Others believed I really had died as a babe, and that my father had resurrected me. They thought my coming back from the dead was a bad omen. If ever I had felt like an outcast before, it was nothing compared to this.

"I'm sorry for your father. He does mean well," Mother said, interrupting my thoughts. "Most of the time."

"I doubt that."

We waited while all the cars parked behind us and our guard approached in formation. "Do you love him?" I asked.

She smiled at me. "Sweet one, of course I do. Love isn't always easy, and sometimes you have to work at it, but I think one day he will get it right."

I sighed.

We approached Castle Raglan. From the outside, it appeared to be just a decaying stone castle covered in vines. In the soft moonlight, the architecture still sang of the old world. I could almost hear the ancient songs echoing off the stone.

It was the family home of the Kahedin Pack. The outer structure no longer held true through the trial of time, but the underground home was a different story, I'd heard of its magnitude. The Kahedin pack still resided here, and one day Brychan would inherit it from his father, should he ever pass. The humans believed the Kahedins were the stewards of Raglan; in truth, the Kahedins lived below the city and watched the human generations pass, protecting the humans and their own family heritage.

Mund said most days the Kahedins and their visitors would come and go through a passage in the woods about a mile north, where a small home stood as a decoy, so as not to draw unwanted attention from the humans. Because my mother was queen of our pack, she had to be received with full honors through the main gates.

Mother and I slowly got out of the car as Odin held her door. Everyone was on alert; they expected someone to attack us, though I couldn't imagine who would. Fifteen of the Boru warriors walked at our sides with Odin as we approached the stone archway into the castle.

I couldn't help but notice how the soft light illuminated my mother's beautiful pale skin. She glowed with radiance. Her steps were light on the ground, not leaving a single footprint behind. Her long strawberry-blonde hair was expertly woven into braids that hung down her back, and a silver floral-filigree diadem encircled her head. Her gown shimmered with her every movement. She was a goddess to me. Even Greek mythology spoke of her; over time her name was lost, but she was a daughter of Rhea.

I walked a step behind Mother in my emerald gown. I had begged until she allowed me to wear my brown leather boots, though. I suppose she was just happy I wasn't wearing my usual scraps of leather. My curly red hair danced lightly in the breeze as we walked through the ornate gatehouse. The ruins were three stories high; despite being crumbling stone, they were impressive.

The perfume smell of frankincense filled the air as we entered the keep. The interior walls were crumbled sandstone surrounded by distressed archways. The grounds were beautifully green in the moonlight. Lord Bledig and Lady Rhonwen stood in their finest attire, surrounded by ornate pillars with copper bowls burning frankincense. Brychan stood to the side of his father. If it weren't for the fresh bruise on Brychan's left cheek, the stubble on his face, and the mischievous grin, he'd look the part of the refined gentleman. It struck me as odd that Brychan was Tegan and Gwyn's older brother. The younger two were elegant and refined; Brychan seemed to enjoy fighting. He reminded me of Grey sometimes in the way that he didn't seem to be afraid of anything.

They all bowed to Mother.

"Queen Nessa, we are honored to welcome you," Lord Bledig said.

Mother nodded in approval. "It is we who are honored."

"You are most welcome in our home," Lady Rhonwen said.

Lord Bledig and Lady Rhonwen turned to lead the way into the secret stairs below. Mother followed as Brychan offered me his arm. Duty dictated that I accept the gesture, but it felt alien to me. Odin walked quietly behind me; I could feel him there, always watching. I still couldn't decide whether or not it was a comfort.

I lightly ran my fingers over the bruise on Brychan's cheek, asking my wordless question. His chuckle was the only response as he led me down the dark, winding stone staircase. We reached a dead-end stone wall, and only a single light flickered on the rocks. The small room looked as though it was once used as food storage, and the crisp air bit at my bare skin. Lord Bledig put a key into a nondescript crack in the stone and it opened, revealing a passage. Cold air rushed past us, blowing out the light, but the light from within beaconed us inside.

We crossed a small stone bridge over dark waters to an exquisite stone staircase. At least thirty guards stood watch on the gatehouse above. I felt nervous under their scrutiny. Brychan put his hand over mine as though he knew. It was a simple gesture, but I noticed it. We climbed two flights up the stairs to an aged copper door that opened as we approached.

"Lord and Lady Kahedin," a deep, rumbling voice announced from within. Our hosts walked forward. "Queen Nessa and Princess Ashling of the Boru, Lord Brychan Kahedin."

The architecture was massive—stone pillars and large, raw wooden beams held up the structure deep within the earth. Antlers adorned the walls of the room. I stared in wonder at my new surroundings and stumbled as we stepped farther inside, but Brychan kept me upright. I had heard that the Kahedins' home was the size of a small village. Their family and the entire pack all lived there in separate homes within the underground fortress. There were more stairways and doorways leading away from the room than I could count with a glance. The room felt like the center of a maze.

"I've been waiting." Gwyn smiled.

Nia lay on the floor at Tegan's feet, digging her fingers into the course fur of an Irish wolfhound that licked her face. Nia smiled and giggled as I knelt down in front of her. Her laugh could melt my heart. She had a few ridiculously cute dark curls and big blue eyes like her mother.

"Brychan, stop hogging all of Ashling's attention," Gwyn complained. "It's our turn."

He messed up Gwyn's spiky blonde hair as he turned and lightly kissed my cheek, and was gone before I could say a word. His warm lips left a tingling sensation behind. At one time, I held such disdain for him. Now I looked upon him with neither fear nor resentment, which felt odd. In truth, he had always been kind to me.

Mother picked up Nia and sang her a sweet lullaby. Mother's voice always entranced me; even now it could have lulled me to sleep. Watching Mother with Nia made me realize the depth of her unending love for children. She was the brightest and most beautiful when she was caring for innocent babes.

Gwyn grabbed my hands. "Ashling, you simply must see my wedding dress. Tegan made it!" She didn't wait for my reply as she dragged me along with her up one of the many staircases. I glanced back where we'd come, trying to remember the way. The stairs suddenly turned and went down as we began to descend deeper into the earth. The banisters were adorned with antlers. Their pack deeply respected all creatures of the earth, and the stag was their Kahedin Bloodmark.

We passed ancient paintings that covered the walls. One in particular caught my attention. Framed in black glass, the painting featured two Viking ships sailing in different directions as a storm separated them. On one ship, Mother Rhea sat weeping with three girls by her side as she held the hand of another beautiful girl dead on the deck of the ship. I assumed the dead girl was Althea and that it was Faye, Calista, and my mother surrounding her.

The girl on the other ship I didn't know. Just looking upon her sent a cold chill down my spine. There was something sinister about her. Her hair was raven black and tightly bound into a hooded cloak. She wore a fitted black dress, but it was the black lettering in the language of the Bloodmoon tattooed on the left side of her face that made me shudder just to look at her. I felt like she was watching me.

"Gwyn, what is this painting?" I asked.

She glanced at it nonchalantly as she continued to pull me up the stairs. "It's called *The Parting*. It's always been there."

"Is that Mother Rhea?"

"Yes," she said. She stopped and turned to face me once again. Her expression grew somber. "No one knows why, but her daughter Vigdis broke her vows to the pack and disrupted the balance of the natural world. They say that Vigdis started the war, long before Uaid Dvergar killed Calista. She killed her sister Althea, causing the Vanir pack to shatter. Mother Rhea fled Vigdis's anger and sought refuge at the Rock of Cashel with her other daughters, but Vigdis pursued them during a terrible storm at sea."

"What happened to Lady Vigdis?" I asked.

"Her ship sank, but the Dvergars rescued her and she became one of them. It is believed that she died at the battle of Carrowmore and that her soul is trapped in the Bloodrealms in an eternity of darkness." She shook her head in disgust. "Now come. It's time for more pleasant things."

I followed Gwyn, but my mind remained with the painting. Was Lady Vigdis viewed as a family curse like I was? Was she evil or was there more to the story? I wanted to believe that every soul had goodness somewhere. Then Adomnan's hideous face hissed in my memory and reminded me that some souls couldn't be saved. I shivered at the thought, forcing him from my mind.

I needed to be with Grey. His presence always kept my demons at bay. Without him, I knew the nightmares would start again. I missed him already. I knew to some it was foolish, but I craved being around him.

Gwyn pulled me into an elegant room. I felt as though we had left the traditional Kahedin home and entered the modern world. Complete with a small kitchen, a living area, a few bedrooms, and a bath. The suite had her fashionista style with a contemporary, modern twist—unmistakably Gwyn.

On the side of the bed stood a dress form covered with a light lavender lace dress with a sweetheart neckline and capped sleeves. Just below the open center back was a beautiful lavender aconite flower; at first I thought it was made of iridescent fabric, but when I reached to touch it, the petals closed. The humans knew aconite as wolfsbane, and they used it as poison. The flower was toxic to mortal creatures; even traditional wolves could be killed by it. To us, however, it was the one plant that would cure us from silver poisoning. The sacred plant was a symbol of healing to our kind, but a flower like this was rare.

I lightly rubbed my finger on the edge of the bud and it opened wide; it was a glorious bloom, but it wasn't even the most exquisite part of the dress Tegan had made. The hand-stitched lace was stunning. It was clear Tegan had painstakingly planned every detail.

"Gwyn, it's perfect," I whispered.

She giggled and jumped around me in a circle. "I know, right?" She fell onto the bed. "Tegan is amazing. She made the maids' dresses too. Yours is in your room already. You're going to love it! Brychan said it was perfect for you, too." She sat up suddenly and studied me. "I hope you'll actually consider Brychan; he's wonderful. You could be really happy with him. He could keep you safe."

"Not you, too," I complained.

"He's not as passionate as Grey, but he's always loved you," she said.

"Gwyn, you know what Grey means to me," I said. I couldn't believe she was doing this. I loved Grey and only Grey.

"And I know what choosing Grey will mean for you when your father chooses another."

Tegan poked her head into the bedroom before I could respond. "Ashling, let me show you to your room."

I always thought Gwyn liked Grey, but I guess I was wrong to assume she'd think of him before her brother. I couldn't fault her for it, but it still hurt. And of all of my suitors, Brychan was the most likely to win the fights—he was a warrior.

I followed Tegan. "This is our suite, should you need anything," Tegan said, gesturing to a door as we passed. We continued past three more doors, finally reaching an arched door. "This will be your guest chamber."

She opened the door to a brightly lit room with antique brick. The room was filled with antique white-and-gold upholstered furniture that surrounded a white fireplace. She led me to the bedroom decorated in white, silver, and gold, but it was bare of furnishings—only a large bed sat in the middle of the room with an enormous crystal chandelier hanging above it.

"The bathroom is over there." She gestured to the doorway to the right. "All of your things should be up here shortly. This wing is for our family; the servants and other pack members sleep in other levels of our home. You'll be safe here."

"Thanks, Tegan."

"Get settled in, and I'll come get you when it's time for dinner." She smiled and gave me a hug before leaving me to my maze of thoughts.

I was twisted up about what Gwyn had said. Did everyone expect me to fall in love with Brychan, Channing, or even Eamon and simply leave Grey behind? Was my soul even capable of loving another when I'd already shared so much of myself with Grey? I couldn't fathom being without him. The idea of it made me want to weep. Grey was a part of me.

I didn't know how long I had stood and stared at the sparkling chandelier, but a quick knock at the door broke my attention.

Odin ushered in my belongings. "Mi' lady, are you well?" he said. He seemed genuinely concerned.

"Just a little travel fatigue," I said.

He nodded and then quickly placed my things in the closet. "Do you need anything else before I retire?"

"No. Thank you, Odin."

I watched him leave, but soon my mind was lost again.

From what little I knew about Channing, I already knew he would never be an option for me. His arrogance and elite status was too much for me to handle. He was nice enough to me, but he obviously held himself in high regard and lived a life of luxury that I found excessive.

And I could never love Eamon. Every time I looked at him, all I saw was Adomnan, and it filled me with hate and loathing. Even though he tried to protect me from Adomnan, I couldn't love him. I also wasn't sure why he was pursuing me now. I wondered if his motivation was a misguided idea to "make things right" between our families, but I would never accept him.

Brychan was a different story. If it weren't for Grey, I probably would have learned to love him. He was mischievous but humble. And I had to admit, very good looking. I found his dark eyes and his ruggedness to be very intriguing. He appeared to be about thirty years old, though I knew him to be much, much older. Had I accepted him when I was fourteen, we would have built a life together and he probably would have loved me, but it would have been desolate compared to my connection with Grey. He was the safe choice, but I didn't want safe. I wanted love.

Tegan interrupted my inner monologue as she stepped inside my room. Had the day already gone? "Ashling, you look worried." she said.

"Oh, I'm just a little nervous," I lied.

4
Intrusion

Tegan held my hand and led me down to dinner. I was certain I'd never find my way around alone. The Kahedin home was a labyrinth of passages and rooms; some of the hallways went into endless passages, and others led to secret exits. As an outsider, it seemed daunting, but Tegan knew them all.

I was seated next to Mother and across from Brychan on the dais. The entire large hall was filled with their pack. Many eyes watched me as they scrutinized my every move. Most watched me openly, but some had the courtesy to pretend they weren't staring. I was the potential future wife to Brychan; I couldn't blame them for being curious. I'm sure they'd heard the rumors about me and were trying to decide which ones were true. Was I reincarnated, a demon, or a goddess? It was almost comical.

There was tightness in my chest, and I felt overwhelmed by it all. I felt uncomfortable partly because of the room full of people watching me and the rumors they believed. But most of all, I was uncomfortable being away from Grey.

"Why didn't the Killian pack come with you?" Brychan asked.

"We were told they weren't invited," I said.

"Nonsense," Brychan said. "The Killians are a proud and honorable pack and our ally. Who told you they weren't invited?"

"Pørr can be misguided," Mother said.

Brychan nodded. "Well, I will call Baran on the morrow and see that they make the journey in time for the wedding."

"Thank you, Brychan," I said. I felt suddenly calmer, like I could breathe again. Knowing Grey would be by my side set my mind temporarily at ease.

"Do you like your room?" Brychan asked.

I nodded. "Yes, it's lovely. Thank you."

"My room is across the hall should you need anything. I would be happy to serve you," he said, smiling. He reached over and lightly squeezed my hand.

"Oh, that's not necessary. I'm sure I'll get by."

His expression changed briefly, but it was quickly replaced by his friendly smile once again. A flicker of disappointment maybe; I couldn't be sure.

I studied the food on my plate, trying to hide from all the eyes on me, when something bumped my leg. I looked up to see a wolfish grin on Brychan's face as his leg brushed mine.

"You should come with me on the full moon," he said.

"Brychan . . ." Tegan warned.

"Oh, Tegan, don't be so prudish," Gwyn said.

Brychan winked at Gwyn, but I had no idea what they were talking about.

"I'd be happy to chaperone," Mund said.

Brychan shot Mund a dirty look. "So what do you think?" Brychan said, bumping his leg into mine again.

I crossed my legs to the side, out of his reach. I could feel the dare in his question; there was something mischievous in the way he watched me. He was up to something. "I would love to be part of the celebration," I said. "Thank you for offering to escort me." I'd know soon enough if I'd made a mistake.

As dinner continued, Brychan found reasons to lean across the table and whisper to me, often secrets about the guests. I didn't need to know that this lady had a secret lover, or that gentleman was a hellacious drinker, or that Tegan was afraid of lightning. He was using the secrets as an excuse to be close to me. And every time he leaned in, his masculine scent filled me with a sensual blend of intensity and subtlety. His scent was stronger than I remembered . . . but of course, it was close to the full moon of Beltane.

Our scents were always the strongest during the full moon, and we were almost halfway to the summer solstice. As crassly as Baran would put it, we were "in heat." I never liked the term, but it was true. Our blood ran hotter between the spring equinox and the summer solstice. Sitting across from Brychan, I felt his scent fog my mind, consuming me.

The Beltane celebration would begin tomorrow with the great bonfires to mark the time of purification and herald in the season. I was eager to be a part of the festival. I had never been allowed to join in Beltane, even though the Boru heralded it. I had only heard rumors of the hunt and hand-fasting couples, and I was anxious to see it all and experience the sacred traditions. Gwyn and Quinn's wedding would be during the Feast of Beltane.

As I looked at them, it was easy to see they were in love. In the last year I had really begun to know them, more than I ever had before. I had always viewed Gwyn as a picture of the female tribute—unmoving, unflinching. But now I knew her to be feisty, flirtatious, and stylish. She wasn't afraid to tell anyone her opinion. She was so much stronger than I'd given her credit for.

Gwyn had really found her mate in Quinn. They were ever so much the same. Together they would be a strong pair. It was odd that a man as traditional as Lord Kahedin would allow his youngest daughter to choose her mate, but I suppose he couldn't have found a higher-positioned male for her. Quinn was a prince of the Boru.

Maybe that was why Father and Flin wanted to marry me off to Lord Channing, to strengthen our alliance with the Kingerys of Switzerland. We had plenty of strong ties to the Kahedins already, with Mund and Quinn.

"May I escort you to your room, Ashling? I'm sure after your long travels you'd like some rest," Brychan said.

He offered his hand to me as he waited for my reply. The table had been cleared around me, though I didn't even remember having eaten anything. I forced a small smile and put my hand in his, and he led me away. His presence was a much-needed distraction.

He lightly rubbed the back of my hand in lazy little circles, but it was his quiet demeanor that always intrigued me. We stopped in front of my door, and he kissed my hand before releasing it. His stare was intense, and his scent swirled around me as his pulse quickened. My body betrayed me, warming to his scent.

Panic swarmed in my stomach like bees.

"Should you need me . . ." he said. He smiled as he backed away toward his chamber door.

I nodded and quickly closed mine behind me, but his face was burned in my mind. I didn't want to think of him this way. It was just my body reacting to his during a full moon. It was nothing.

I crawled into my enormous bed still wearing my green dress and wrapped my arms around myself, wishing it were Grey's strong arms wrapped around me. I let the exhaustion take me into restless sleep.

I opened my eyes and I was lying on the deck of a ship. The water rolled and heaved. The sky was black and the rain poured down. The ship rocked back and forth in the storm, creaking and groaning. I tried to move, but my limbs were numb. I couldn't even blink. Was I looking at the world through dead eyes? Lady Vigdis stood over me. Her face was expressionless.

"You will die," she said.

The churning black water of the ocean ran over the deck, and the ship began to sink. I tried to sit up, but the cold black water covered my face and seeped up my nose. Her expression didn't change. I gagged and sputtered and water filled my lungs.

I woke from the dream lying on the floor next to my bed. My hair was drenched with sweat, and I had broken skin where I had dug my fingernails into my palms, four half-moon divots pooled with my blood. I curled into the fetal position and cried. I needed Grey. Whenever I was away from him, the bad dreams came. They always haunted me, but they couldn't reach me when our love surrounded me.

It was the middle of the night and the earth was still. This wasn't like my home on the cliffs of Ireland where the water crashed like thunder, or even Maine with the sounds of nature all around. This place was still. Not a sound came this deep into the earth. I slipped from my room and crept barefoot down the dark hallway with a candle to light my way.

I tiptoed up the stairs and sat down with my sketchpad in front of *The Parting*. I wanted to try to translate the words tattooed across the side of Lady Vigdis's face. It had to mean something. I studied her face and black eyes. A chill settled over me. The more I looked at her, the more I was sure she was seeing me too. It didn't make sense, but I felt it. Every time I looked back at her, I was sure she looked away. Was it possible that she was alive in that painting? Trapped there? Or was I letting my imagination get the best of me?

I studied the letters, but they were so small I could only make out some of them, and even those blended together. I sketched them in my notebooks so I could translate them, tracing over each letter to make them darker and more intense.

I woke the next morning still lying on the stairs with my notebook clutched in my fingers, but I had been covered in a wool blanket. I knew at once by the masculine scent that surrounded me that it was Brychan's. The bustle from the kitchens echoed up the stairs. I wrapped the blanket like a shawl and I crept back to my room.

I wandered into my bathroom and started the bath. I picked up a few of the herb jars. I chose eucalyptus oil and sugar and poured it into the bath, filling the room with its potent aroma. I stepped into the deep, steaming bathtub and the hot water surrounded me up to my waist. I let my dress slide down my body to my waist, exposing my skin to the cool air. I stood in the deliciously hot water enjoying the sensation. I closed my eyes, letting the steam swirl around me.

"I . . . um, I beg your pardon." Brychan cleared his throat.

Startled, I grabbed my dress from the water and clutched it to my chest as I looked over my shoulder to see Brychan staring openly at my exposed back all the way down to my waist.

"What are you doing here?" I demanded; my cheeks burned with embarrassment.

It took him several seconds to finally respond. "I am truly sorry for the intrusion, Princess Ashling. I did knock."

"If you did not hear a reply, you should not have entered."

I could hear his heart race and his scent filled the room, making my throat ache. I turned away, closing my eyes shut. Trying to close him out.

"Leave at once," I said.

He nodded and abruptly turned and walked out the door. I heard his footsteps fade away, but my cheeks still burned and my heart pounded. I was a little embarrassed, but he didn't see anything really. He'd only seen my bare back, but I still felt uneasy. He could have waited to be invited in, yet he chose not to. He invaded my privacy, and it annoyed me that he felt he was allowed in my room without permission.

I stepped out of my dress and lowered myself into the enormous tub, letting the water cover me up to my neck. I closed my eyes trying to block it all out, but all I saw was his face, and his scent still filled the room.

After my bath, I locked my door to keep Brychan out of my room. I didn't trust myself with him. There was something primal about him that my body responded to. It wasn't love or lust; it was the wild animal inside of me. It was pleasant torture, and it made guilt an unavoidable presence.

Lying across my bed, I pulled out my sketchbook and studied the letters I'd drawn. The words ran vertically, like rain. The characters from the language of the Bloodmoon were beautiful, but as I started translating the words, their beauty faded:

The walls will bleed with your crimson blood.
They will scream your name as they die around you.

I slammed my sketchbook closed, terrified. That couldn't have been for me. It was just an evil spell on Lady Vigdis's face to instill panic in her enemies. I wished Baran were here; he'd know what to do. Being without Baran and Grey was like losing my lifeline. I felt so lost without them.

I hid in my room the rest of the day, trying to get those words out of my head, but when the castle grew still and nightfall had come, I snuck out of my room with my sketchbook again. I crept down to the kitchen to steal some food. I passed a guard in the hallway, but he barely noticed me. In the kitchen, I pulled some dried spiced meat from the rack and bit into it.

I jumped at the sound of someone snoring. I looked around the butcher table and saw an old woman asleep with her head resting on the counter. Her wrinkled face was pretty in the light. I sat down and began to draw her face, every line and contour that defined who she was. I didn't know her, but by the time I was done drawing her I felt as though I did.

On my way back up the staircase to my room, I walked past the painting again. Lady Vigdis was just as unexpressive as I remembered her to be, but something had changed. Something was different in the pattern tattooed on her face. I opened my sketchbook to the drawing I had done of her the night before and studied the letters. The tattooed letters on her face didn't match the letters in my sketchbook. The message had changed somehow.

I quickly sat down and started drawing them, capturing her new message. Footsteps on the stairs forced me to hurry. I quickly sketched the last few letters and ran up the stairs before I was seen lurking about the castle. I slammed right into Odin as I rounded the corner to the hallway.

He steadied me so I didn't fall. "What are you up to this late at night?" he asked.

"I should ask you the same thing," I said.

"Touché," he said studying my sketchbook. "Well, I was doing my nightly rounds to check the guards and security of the castle. What's your excuse?"

I struggled for the right words. "Well, I snuck down to get some food, but I stopped to sketch . . ." I paused warily, "something."

"The painting?" he inquired.

I nodded.

Odin gestured for me to walk next to him as we continued back to my room. He was quiet and always watchful like he was waiting for a sign, but his company was comforting in a lot of ways.

"Have you noticed anything about it yet?" he asked.

"It changes. Doesn't it?" I asked.

"Depending who is looking at it, the message on her face changes to mirror the viewer's greatest fears. What did you see?" he said.

"That I would watch everyone I love die," I said.

He nodded, but his posture was rigid.

"Do you think it means anything?" I asked.

"The real question is, do you?" he said.

"No, it's nothing," I blurted.

"If you say so," he said, studying me. "Goodnight, then."

I hurried into my room and sat down on the floor right in front of my door and started translating the new message, daring to know what it said.

I see you watching me with your golden eyes filled with fear, but you have yet to feel my wrath.

I stared at the words on the crisp white paper and the threat that was hidden there. It was horrifying and obviously written just for my eyes. Somehow Vigdis was threatening me from the grave. It didn't make sense, but very little of my life made sense. I couldn't grasp why my own aunt would threaten me. It was crazy to fear a painting and even stranger to fear the dead, but it didn't stop me from worrying. I crept to my bed to cower under the covers.

From that point on, I avoided the painting. I didn't want to know what else she had to say to me. I avoided Brychan, too, but for a completely different reason. There was something far too alluring about him. I spent my days alone in my room, dreaming of Grey . . . but once night came and the castle grew silent, I would sneak from my room to draw the faces of the people I found throughout the castle. One night, I drew a guard who didn't see me hiding in the shadows. Another night, I sketched the evening's herald, who sung to himself by the fire.

Tonight while I was exploring the throne room, I found a young couple stealing kisses. They heard me enter and disappeared through a doorway, giggling. I was envious of their love; it made me miss Grey immensely. I missed his touch, the feeling of his skin on mine, the way my skin tingled when he kissed my neck.

Lord Kahedin's throne was smaller and simpler than others that I had seen. It was carved wood adorned with veins of carved antlers. It was intricate but simple. I ran my fingers over the surface, feeling the textures.

"It's beautiful, isn't it?" Brychan said.

I nearly leaped out of my skin, but his smile eased my fears.

"Are you following me around?"

"Nah, one of the guards told me you were in here," he said.

"Oh . . ."

"I will leave you to your thoughts." He turned to leave.

"Wait . . . would you mind escorting me to my room?" I said. "But you're not invited inside."

He smiled as he closed the distance between us. "Always. Of course."

As we walked, he lightly rubbed my back. His touch was strong and warm. I nestled into his side, enjoying the security.

"I haven't seen your pretty face in a few days," he said.

I blushed. "Sorry about that."

"Have you been avoiding me?" he asked with a wicked grin on his face.

I studied his strong jaw, stubbled chin, and a fresh cut on his cheek. His features were so mature compared to Grey's. I couldn't deny how attractive Brychan was, but his overly protective nature made me feel like a child in his presence sometimes. His deep brown eyes studied me with a glint of mischief, and my heart pounded as I looked up at him. I looked away, trying to pry him from my mind.

When we reached my door, I stood up on my tiptoes and kissed his lips. I didn't know why, but I felt drawn to him for some reason. At first it was just a soft kiss of appreciation, but the rough feeling of his lips set a fire in my stomach. Soon my lips had a mind of their own and the kiss deepened. His stubble-covered chin rubbed mine raw, and my pulse burned through my veins like wildfire.

I hated myself even as I was still kissing him, but he pulled away before I did anything else I would regret. My eyes filled with tears that threatened to spill over. It didn't have to mean anything. I tried to convince myself, but regret had already filled my heart. I'd betrayed Grey.

Lust had filled his brown eyes as he gazed at me. I quickly turned away from him. I didn't dare look into his eyes—I'd be nothing more than putty in his experienced hands. It was alarming how easy it was to be lost to him.

"I've always dreamed of this moment," he said, his voice rough. He softly kissed my cheek.

"I'm sorry I didn't marry you when you asked," I said, opening my door to escape. "I never meant to hurt you."

"You can still change your mind, you know. My offer still stands." I couldn't breathe. What had I done? "Sleep now, my sweet Ashling. I will keep you safe," he whispered.

5

Inhibitions

Over the next few days, my family arrived for the wedding. With the hustle and bustle of preparation, no one noticed I was hiding again. Except perhaps Brychan, but he didn't come to my door. I was still struggling with what I had done. I should never have kissed him. It only made everything more complicated. I often distracted myself from boredom and self-loathing by reading, but often my mind would wander to Grey.

As I lay on my enormous bed, I could feel Grey's sadness mixing with mine. The intensity of our shared pain was unreal. My bones ached from being separated from him, and every day it hurt more than the day before. Every time someone arrived I kept thinking it would be Grey, but it never was. Sometimes his emotions were faint inside of me, like a whisper, and sometimes they were so intense I couldn't tell them from my own. It was both intimate and lonely.

After days of hiding that I finally heard a knock at my door. I looked up to see Mund standing in the doorway laughing.

"What?" I grumbled.

"I've missed seeing your messy hair. It brings back my memories of you as a child," he said.

I ran my hand over my wild hair, realizing I looked something like Medusa herself. I hadn't bothered to tame it the last few days. I pushed the books under my covers, hiding my obsession, though I wasn't sure why.

"Good morning to you, too," I said.

"It's already afternoon. You've missed breakfast, but if you hurry, you can join in the festivities. And there will be the Beltane hunt and full moon tonight." He messed up my hair even more. "Now hurry up. I'm not leaving until you get up."

I limply slid off the bed, under protest, as Mund wandered out to the sitting room to wait. "What am I supposed to wear to all these festivities?"

"Anything you want. It's informal. I'll wait for you outside." He smiled and shut the door behind him.

I pulled out my leather skirt, wrap-top, and soft leather boots. I had missed the feeling of the soft hides. It was certain to get a rise out of the curious spectators. I figured if they insisted on staring at me, I might as well have some fun with it. I finished off my ensemble with the two-leaf, patinated necklace Grey had given me. I ran my fingers over the metal, missing him.

Mund smiled when I came out. "Should have guessed. It's nice to see you in your finest."

"Why thank you, Prince Redmund. Aren't you a peach?" I replied as he chuckled. "So what's on the list of festivities?"

He offered me his arm as we headed down the hall. "First I'll be dropping you off in the kitchen to do your part of preparing for the evening meal."

"What a delight," I said.

"It's tradition, and if you behave yourself, you'll get to participate in the hunt tonight." He winked as he pushed me into the kitchen.

There were three full kitchens, each filled with busy women preparing the enormous meal. Gwyn and Tegan waved to me from the farthest kitchen. They didn't even bat an eye at my outfit, but the other women stared as I slowly walked past them.

I heard a few of the women whispering as I passed. I didn't want to hear what they had to say about me; I didn't need to hear their judgment. Luckily they got back to their work slicing the meat from the carcasses when I reached Gwyn and Tegan. I busied myself laying the thin slices of meat on the racks to be smoked.

If the hunt were successful, we would also have fresh, warm meat served tonight. My mouth watered at the thought. I hadn't hunted since I'd been home in York Harbor. It was agonizing. Just the thought of hunting filled me with anticipation and a primal need for flesh and blood. Maybe feeding would help ease my longing for Grey and guilt from Brychan's kiss. I needed my four paws to center my uneasy mind.

"Finally finished," Tegan said with a sigh as she wiped blood from her hands. "It must be nearly dusk and time for the hunt. Are you ready, Ash?"

"What do I need to be ready for?"

"Stay close to us," Tegan said. "We'll explain."

I followed the women out of the underground home to join the men in the crisp air and the light of the setting sun. Large piles of burning branches surrounded Castle Raglan, some stacked as high as eight feet. At the center of the castle was a pile of sun-bleached antlers, a tribute to the hunt. The full moon lit the night sky in a false dawn.

My skin tingled with excitement. We gathered around the pile of antlers as Mother, Father, Lord Bledig, and Lady Rhonwen came forward to initiate the hunt.

"In the beginning, we hunted as one—one pack, one heart, one kill," Lord Bledig began. "Tonight we hunt as one again. The sacred pair awaits us, and a successful hunt is a good omen."

Brychan came and stood next to me, giving my hand a little

squeeze of reassurance as he studied my outfit. I blushed, remembering his lips on mine. He winked and I quickly looked away.

"In honor of their wedding, we look to you, Prince Quinn of the Boru and my fair daughter Lady Gwyn, to lead us in the hunt," Lord Bledig said.

Cheers went up all around us. We were split, men and women, to opposite sides of the runes to shift. I felt like a stranger among these people, but Tegan smiled as she walked by my side.

"I'm staying behind with your mother and Nia. Stay close to Gwyn and don't leave the pack," she said.

I nodded nervously as I quickly undressed in the light of the full moon, letting the radiant glow bathe my pale skin as we all shifted into our natural form. As soon as my four paws touched the earth, I felt the strength of the pack. There were so many of them; every one of their hearts beat with mine. I could sense them all; we were one. My red fur glowed in the dancing light of the fire. I followed Gwyn to the front of the female pack. She was unmistakable with beautiful white fur and black-tipped ears and paws.

The energy of the pack radiated through my blood as we waited. It was intoxicating. Finally, Gwyn spotted the stag and doe and started running with Quinn by her side. Lord Bledig sounded the ancient horn and we all began to run. My heart beat in rhythm with our footsteps as the entire pack raced after our prey. I tried to keep up with Gwyn, but her pace was much faster than mine. Fear struck through me like lightning as I lost sight of them. I was quickly absorbed into the crowded pack.

I tried to race faster and force my way closer to Gwyn, but my paws slipped on the loose rocks and I fell. My body hit the ground; rocks tore into my shoulder. Panic shook through me as the others leaped over me, trapping me on the ground.

An enormous grey wolf pushed me back to my feet before the pack trampled me. I looked to my side and saw Grey's beautiful green eyes and his thick, delicious scent swirled around me. He'd finally come for me. Seeing Grey as a wolf was utterly arousing. We'd never been wolves together. The raw emotions that flooded my veins stimulated every nerve in my body with need. This was a level of our connection that was intense and unexpected.

The pain of our separation lifted like it had never been, erasing all the agony and leaving only our love for each other. He ran with me to the middle of the pack. I could feel the urge to win within him, but he kept his pace matched to mine, protecting me, loving me.

We ran through the trees, dodging around them as we closed in on our prey. I could feel Grey's love pouring through me, and it made me love him even more. Our connection was more intense as wolves, and the rush of being connected to the pack filled me with adrenaline. In these moments, I felt truly free.

The hoofbeats stopped and I heard a deer scream, then the night was silent. Only the sounds of our breathing surrounded us as Grey and I slowly padded forward. Gwyn had taken the doe and Quinn had taken down the eight-point stag. It was the perfect blessing on their union. Quinn howled at the moon in celebration. Gwyn joined her voice to his in an eerie love song. We all howled with them, filling the night sky.

Grey and I padded back toward the castle with the others. The cooks came to collect the kill for the celebration. I returned with the women and shifted back into a human and quickly dressed. I ran over to meet Grey, with the thrill of the hunt and all my emotions for him still pulsing through my human veins. I felt completely uninhibited.

"That was amazing," I said.

"No, you are amazing," Grey said.

His green eyes were filled with so much lust that he looked almost pained. He grabbed my neck, massaging my skin as he pulled me to him. His lips captured mine as he shared all of himself with me in his intimate kiss. His tongue darted into my mouth like electricity.

His hand roamed shamelessly over my breast down to the bare skin of my stomach. His thumb circled over my skin as he lightly brushed under my top, rubbing my breast. I moaned and practically purred for his touch. I was so caught up in the excitement of his touch and the adrenaline of the hunt that I let myself get lost in the passion of his kiss.

It was an eternity before I finally remembered where we were—we were at my betrothed Brychan's home, and I was kissing Grey in the open . . . an action punishable by death.

6

Feast of Beltane

Had I lost my mind? I knew better than to expose our love here, to expose our bond. Grey would be killed if anyone knew our secret, and I had to protect him. I pulled away, my mind fogged with emotions. I took several steps backward, trying to create distance between us. The hurt in his eyes cut me deeply.

Mund barreled between us before I could explain. "Are you stark raving mad?" he snarled. He was angrier than I had ever seen him. He looked from me to Grey and back again. His anger filled me with bile. "Do you want him to die? Do you, Ashling? Because that is what will happen if you don't keep your hands off each other. Do you know where you are? You are in Brychan's home, and you dare to disgrace him and his family like this?"

"I'm sorry, Mund," I said. I knew he was right. I continually endangered Grey's life.

"Don't be sorry to me," he said. His voice was still uncharacteristically cold. "If you love him at all, you will keep your distance."

"I understand," I said.

"I'm not scared," Grey said.

Mund stared at Grey. "You should be," he said. Grey stopped smiling and I could feel his doubt. Mund shook his head. "The two of you will be the death of me."

"Please, Mund," I begged. I needed his forgiveness. I needed him on my side.

He pulled me into his side, giving me a squeeze. "Try not to get in any more trouble," he said. "You're both easier to love when I don't have to constantly worry about you. Just don't draw any more attention to yourselves. I don't think anyone else saw."

I ached knowing I had betrayed Grey before he arrived. Now I had betrayed Brychan in his own home. I hated the mess I had created. I wanted to turn and run from all the confusion, but I heard my name being called by Lord Bledig, and I was trapped by duty.

"Let us offer a dance with our Princess Ashling as the prize for the winner of the fights?" Lord Bledig said as he gestured to my father for his answer. He nodded in approval and everyone cheered. "Those who intend to fight, stand forward."

Lord Bledig and Father had just auctioned me off as the prize for bare-knuckle boxing fights. Yet another archaic tradition of our people. Women were not equals in our kind; though we were all ruled by Old Mother, the men always ruled over us.

"Oh no," I muttered.

Grey put his hand on my shoulder, trying to comfort me, but I could feel his frustration watching all the men line up to fight for their chance to dance with me. I felt nervous and sick to my stomach. Over a dozen men of various ranks and packs came forward, including Brychan.

Grey stepped forward to join the fight, but I grabbed his hand. "Please stay," I said. I didn't want him to fight.

He nodded. "Okay." The concern in his eyes was plain to see.

I wasn't ready to watch actual bare-knuckle boxing. I knew all the rules from Mund, but I'd never seen an actual fight. The opponents would face each other without any padding on their hands and punch each other until one yielded or was knocked out. And each winner would face a new opponent until only one was left standing.

"Let the fights begin," Lord Bledig announced.

As the fights began, spectators circled around to see. The brutality of bare-knuckle boxing was almost too much to watch, even though it was still considered civilized. The only thing civilized about it was that opponents weren't allowed to strike a downed opponent. Once someone was unconscious, the fight was over. I watched as men beat each other bloody, each swearing they would win for me. I knew they didn't do it for me, but for the thrill. One by one, the bloodied men were pulled off the field and given mead to heal their pride.

Only Brychan and a stocky man of lower status remained. I held my breath. The stocky man wasn't a lord, but he wasn't a servant. They were both covered in dirt and blood as they stood facing each other. The stocky man labored for breath as he lunged at Brychan, knocking him to the ground. He punched Brychan in the face repeatedly. I wanted desperately to scream for them to stop this nonsense, but no words came. I just stared in horror. I watched Brychan take blow after blow. The blood spilled from his lip in a red river down his face. I was disgusted and terrified, but there was something in Brychan's expression that made me pause.

Brychan maneuvered himself and gave the man one explosive punch to the face, knocking him out. The man's body fell, partially covering Brychan's, but Brychan easily shoved the man off. Brychan left him unconscious on the ground to be tended to by the healers. He closed the distance between us and knelt before me. Blood seeped from his lip as he bowed his head. Instead of publicly claiming me as his prize in front of Grey and forcing me to dance with him, he chose to give himself to me. I was thankful and let out the breath I'd been holding in.

"May I have this dance?" Brychan said, holding his hand out to me. There was a masculine tension between Brychan and Grey; I could smell it on them.

I carefully put my hand in his as nervousness washed over me. A woman began to sing an Irish love song, filling the night with its eerie tune. I could feel Grey's anger and jealousy, but I was the prize to the victor, and the choice wasn't up to me. I followed Brychan closer to the fire to dance.

"Why did you do that?" I asked as I wiped the blood away from his lip and chin with my hand. "Why did you fight?" I said again.

"Why waste years of boxing lessons?" he said with haughty cockiness. Then he whispered, "Besides, I got what I wanted: a dance with you."

I shook my head in disbelief. "You could have just asked."

"Aye, yes, I could have, but then someone else would have won a dance with you, and I was hoping to steal all of your attention tonight." He glanced toward Grey where we had left him. "But I think I have some competition."

I blushed and looked away from his intense eyes.

"Ashling, you should know that I have always loved you. From the first moment I saw you stand up to your father, I could see your strength to rule, but I have to warn you . . ."

"Warn me of what?" I asked.

"That you'll fall madly in love with me." His smile was disturbingly contagious.

I rolled my eyes. Castle Raglan was full of energy as he spun me around the fire. The warm crackle of the bonfire mixed with the packs' laughter and cheers created the perfect night for Beltane celebrations to begin.

Brychan kept his hand at the small of my back and lightly pressed me into him. Butterflies filled my stomach, and I knew every emotion that betrayed me would flood through Grey. I didn't know why

I was drawn to Brychan or how to stop it. It scared me to think I was allowing him to touch me so intimately, especially with Grey looking on. But my duty prevailed over my emotions, and I finished the dance without freaking out.

As much as I was beginning to adore Brychan for reasons I still couldn't understand, I loved Grey more. It broke my heart to have to hurt Brychan, but my life was with Grey. I just had to survive Gwyn and Quinn's wedding without my mind becoming more clouded by Brychan than it already was. Brychan's hand remained at the small of my back as he studied my face.

"You were meant to be in my arms. I'm not sorry we kissed the other day. It certainly wasn't the worst mistake I've ever made," he said.

I had to admit that I wasn't completely sorry either, but I was intrigued by his cocky answer. "Then what is the worst mistake you've made, Lord Brychan?" I asked, challenging him.

"Letting you walk away the first day I saw you at the Rock of Cashel," he said. "I should have stayed by your side. It should have been me who protected you."

I quickly looked away. He was right; had he stayed with me, I might have never met Grey, and my life would have been very different. Instead, he gave me the space to grow up and lost me without ever knowing me.

The song ended and we moved to the edge of the trees by Grey. He and Brychan stared at each other, and I could feel the tension in them both. Grey's jealousy was so heavy I felt like I was drowning in it.

"I think we'll all need a drink tonight," Brychan said. "Grey, why don't you help me?" Grey nodded and followed Brychan toward the kegs while I waited for them to return.

I watched as many of the pack began to dance naked around the fires to celebrate Old Mother, and I heard the hypnotic sounds of love-making from the edge of the trees. I was drawn to it . . . I wanted to get a closer look. I took a step toward the trees, trying to catch a peek of the revelers' passion, and I wondered what it would be like to lose myself in Grey's arms right here. I ached to finally feel all of him.

The stocky man that had lost to Brychan suddenly blocked my path. The front of his shirt was soiled with mead, and his angular face was still covered in dried blood. I took a step to the left, and he countered with a lazy smile, blocking my path again.

"Would you care for a romp?" he asked.

"And who do you presume to be?" I asked.

"My apologies mi' lady. I am Drystan Borooque, nephew of Lady Rhonwen," he said, slurring his words.

I studied his plain face: nothing more than average about his appearance, but his muscles almost rippled with a life of their own under his tight shirt. "It's a pleasure to meet you," I replied through clenched teeth.

"It would be both our pleasures if you joined me," he offered again.

I understood what he wanted. The rumors of Beltane had turned out to be true. The sounds of handfasting couples mating filled the darkness. I took a step backward, trying to get some distance between my body and his hot breath, but he again filled the space, leaving only inches between our bodies. Panic raced through me with memories of Adomnan's torture, of him touching my skin. I wanted to curl up in the fetal position and weep, but I just stood, frozen. I knew he wasn't Adomnan, but it didn't stop the fear from paralyzing me.

Suddenly Odin stepped between us. "Princess Ashling, are you alright?" Odin asked. I'd never been so happy to see Odin. His presence filled me with relief.

"She was just going to enjoy a romp with me. So bugger off and wait your turn. You can have her when I'm done," Drystan slurred.

"I'm not going to let you anywhere near her," Odin growled, pulling his knife from its sheath.

Drystan growled as he threw his mead glass against a tree, shattering it. I knew Odin would easily kill the drunk for my honor, but I didn't want anyone to get hurt.

"I'm sorry, cousin. The lady is spoken for," Brychan interrupted.

Drystan grabbed my wrist and pulled me toward him. The unexpected jolt caused me to fall into him. Grey stalked up and punched Drystan in the neck. The pressure caused Drystan to crumble to the ground with a thud, and his face scraped across the dirt.

I heard a few gasps and disgruntled whispers at Grey's rash action against Lady Rhonwen's nephew. With the amount of liquor that flowed freely tonight, the visions of a fight breaking out filled me with unease. I had disgraced Brychan's home by kissing Grey, and now Grey had knocked out Brychan's cousin. I shuddered to imagine the consequences.

"Nice shot," Brychan said. He whistled and Baran and Willem came running over.

"I can't leave any of you alone, can I?" Baran said. If it weren't for the glint in his eyes, I would have thought he was upset.

"We have a situation," Brychan said. "I suggest you get Grey to the safety of his chambers before Drystan's brothers have time to take offense. I will escort Princess Ashling to her chambers in the Kahedin suites."

"Agreed," Baran said as he kissed me on the cheek.

"Good night," I said to Grey as Brychan abruptly led me back toward the castle before Grey could respond.

"You'll have to excuse Drystan," Brychan said when we were out of earshot.

"Will I?" I asked, my voice filled with disdain.

He chuckled. "No, but know that he is harmless," he said.

"I will be the judge of that," I replied coolly. "You aren't the one he just tried to seduce . . . if you could call it that."

"You're bloody right," he said clearly disgusted by the idea of sex with his cousin. I had to laugh. "I would have done far worse to him than your Grey did."

"Umhmm . . ."

"If you were interested in handfasting, I'd be happy to try it with you," he said. The smirk on his face was ridiculous. I enjoyed his rebellious sense of humor, but I was in no mood for his charm. His warm hands covering mine just made me want to be with Grey that much more. Every moment spent with Brychan was a moment without Grey.

"I think I've had my share of fun for tonight. I just want to be alone," I said.

He nodded and led the way back into the castle in silence. I hadn't meant to be so harsh and hurt his feelings, but I was irritated with everyone, including him.

"I am sorry for Drystan. He didn't mean any harm. He doesn't know what you've been through."

I didn't dare look up at him as he spoke. The words on his lips were like poison. He knew that Adomnan had intended to rape me, to claim me. He knew. The shame of it—the torturous, illogical shame of it—disgusted me. I didn't want anyone to know what had happened and what Adomnan had planned to do to me. It was my shame, my secret, and yet they all knew.

He knew that if Adomnan had succeeded, I would have been Adomnan's wife by our laws, and that when I killed him, it would have been murder in the eyes of my kind. Self-defense against my rapist would have been murder. Thinking of it made me nauseated, and my eyes welled with tears. I didn't want to remember what had happened to me, much less talk about it with anyone. It felt shameful for him to know any of it. Even though Adomnan hadn't succeeded in raping me, I felt as though he had. The pain and guilt of it followed me everywhere, like a bad reputation. I still felt like I was in that blood-filled room with his hands on my skin.

Brychan and I stopped in front of my door and I stared at my feet, hiding my tears. His warm hand caressed the side of my face, and I finally looked up into his brown eyes.

"You will overcome this. It is nothing more than a bad memory."

I turned my face away from him, ashamed of what had happened to me and ashamed for the tears in my eyes. What did he know? How could he understand how I had felt under Adomnan's power? To have Adomnan's evil hands touching my body, to have Adomnan's repulsive mouth on mine, to be naked and exposed against my will . . . it was more than a bad memory. It was the horror I still lived with every day.

Brychan let his hand fall away. "Sweet dreams, dear Ashling."

I nodded, barely holding back the wave of tears. I pushed my door closed with my back as I slid to the floor, crying. All the emotions that I had kept bottled up came pouring out. My deep hatred of Adomnan, the unnatural resentment I harbored against myself, the filthy guilt, my father's dismissal, the overwhelming love I shared with Grey, the gut-wrenching pain of being away from Grey, and my confusing attraction to Brychan.

It was too much to carry. I hated having to harbor so much self-loathing, but I blamed myself for so much of Adomnan's attack. I knew logically it wasn't my fault, but that didn't stop the fear and guilt. I let the tides of pain wash over me, trying to accept all that had happened and brace myself for everything that was yet to come. Thankfully, the tears slowed as I drifted off to restless sleep.

7
The Wedding

I woke to Gwyn pouncing on me in bed. "Get up! It's my wedding day!" she said. She was almost too cheery in the morning for my appetite. I groaned as she giggled. "I already moved your dress into Tegan's room so we can all get dressed together! It's going to be amazing." Without warning, she almost ripped my arm out of the socket as she yanked me out the door toward Tegan's suite.

"Out, out, out!" Gwyn demanded when she spotted Mund lounging. I flopped on the white antique sofa next to him.

"Why the rush?" Mund smiled at her.

Gwyn's eyes narrowed and an almost ladylike growl came from her.

"Redmund Boru, put yourself to good use," Tegan said.

He laughed and stood. "No rest for the wicked," he said. He kissed Tegan on the cheek as she handed Nia to him. He messed up my hair on the way out of their suite.

The room was a soft blue with an elegant chandelier at the center, but it was the black wood floors that brought the stunning contrast to the space. The room embodied both Tegan's softness and Mund's strength.

Gwyn's lace dress was on a stand by the bay window. The window was illuminated with white light that glittered off the dress's embellishments.

"How is there a window down here? Where is the light coming from?" I asked.

"During the wars, we weren't able to leave our underground home," Tegan said. "I didn't smell fresh air for nearly five years. I was just a child then—barely fifteen. The wars between clans were ruthless; children and women were killed as fast as the men. It was a bloodbath. Luckily, our pack was able to join your father's, and together we were able to protect one another." Tegan smiled gently, as if something particularly nostalgic entered her mind. "That's when I first saw Mund. Father had betrothed us to secure the alliance between our packs. That's how Cadence Kingery and Bridgid Talo both came to be the wives of your brothers as well." Cadence was Felan's beautiful wife and Channing's older sister. Flin's wife, Bridgid, never seemed to like our family, but it was possible she just still yearned for home. I didn't know either of them well.

"These were dark times, and the only way for our families to ensure an alliance was through the marriage of their children," Tegan continued. "I couldn't stand the darkness of our underground home, so when Mund came to live with our pack as my husband, he built the windows for me. Those windows actually face our bedroom. They are frosted glass with a candelabra on the other side that allows it to feel like sunlight streaming through in the living room."

I'd only ever heard pieces of the war stories, but hearing Tegan talk about it made me want to cry. So much pain and suffering surrounded our history.

"Mund loves you more than life," I said. Tegan nodded and smiled.

"Don't you guys love my dress?" Gwyn interrupted.

"It's lovely Gwyn, just like you." Tegan smiled at her younger sister.

Gwyn bounced around the room like a tiny fairy. Tegan didn't seem annoyed by her sister; she just smiled and helped her. Like an older sister should, I suppose.

"Sit down so I can style your hair," Tegan said.

"I can barely sit still!" Gwyn said.

"I know, sweet one," Tegan said as she curled Gwyn's short blonde hair into 1920s-style pin curls.

Over the morning, the women of our packs slowly joined us, filling the room with soft chatter. Mother and Lady Rhonwen were first to arrive, followed by Cadence, Bridgid, and Cadence's younger sister Cara. Cara was just a tiny thing; a light breeze would likely knock the girl over. She was the youngest of the Kingery pack, barely older than me. Her blonde hair was so long it brushed just past her backside.

Tegan adorned Gwyn's head with an antique headpiece covered in diamonds, in the shape of a beautiful feather that swirled around the right side of her head. My breath caught as I watched Gwyn become a timeless goddess. She stepped into her dress and as soon as the aconite flower touched Gwyn's skin, it opened. It was a good omen.

Gwyn spun in front of the mirror, admiring Tegan's hard work. "This is perfection." She complimented her sister's design. "I couldn't be more beautiful than you have made me."

Tegan placed her hand on Gwyn's shoulder and bowed her head. Lady Rhonwen touched Gwyn's other shoulder, and Mother placed her hand on Gwyn's back. The other women did the same, creating a connecting web around Gwyn. The ritual allowed them to pour their thoughts, love, and protection into her. I gently touched Cara's back, connecting myself to all of them. I felt sudden strength that pulsed like an electric shock as the love flowed endlessly through me.

This was what I yearned for. This was all I ever wanted from my father, and what he had kept from me. I needed to run free with my pack, I needed to belong. I was whole in their presence.

"I am so honored to have you all here as one," Gwyn said as the circuit disconnected.

Tegan stood in front of me, holding my dress over her arm. "You're next," she said as she quickly forced me into my strapless, knee-length dress. Tegan was already wearing hers as she wove and spun my hair behind my neck into an asymmetrical, curly masterpiece.

"Final touch for my maids," Gwyn said as she put a large, yellow, teardrop-shaped diamond pendant around each of our necks. It hung on a simple golden chain right above my strapless dress. As I studied the gem, I saw a tiny aconite bud petrified inside.

Then Lady Rhonwen stood in front of me. There was no hint of a smile as she secured an antique diamond necklace around my neck. "As an honored guest of the Kahedin House, we present you with this."

I stared in wonder at my reflection in the mirror. The necklace hung at the base of my neck and shined in the light. It was covered in diamonds with a with a large diamond cluster pendent. The contrast of the antique necklace to the modern yellow diamond was stunning.

"Thank you, Lady Rhonwen," I said.

She nodded. "It's nice to see Brychan's necklace on your neck."

"Brychan's?" I asked.

"You are his betrothed, after all," she said. She didn't smile as she walked away. She was probably angry I had rejected the betrothal, and then my father further disgraced them by allowing other packs to declare their right to court me, even allowing a pack as lowly as the Killians to make a declaration of intent. And since I'd come, I'd mostly avoided Brychan and kissed Grey in public, though I wasn't sure who knew about our momentary lack of discretion. I had done nothing to deserve her empathy or love. I couldn't blame her for her indifference toward me.

Tegan lightly closed my gaping mouth. "As his betrothed, it's etiquette for you to wear something of his at his sister's wedding. Don't let it bother you."

I ran my fingers over the sparkling stones. Did Brychan know that something of his had been given to me? Did he still desire my hand after I'd done so much to hurt him?

"You seem to have a lot on your mind, my dear," Mother Rhea said.

I sighed. "Mother Rhea, I don't understand."

"What don't you understand, dear?"

"Whom I should love . . . is it even my choice? Why must someone claim me? I just don't understand any of it," I said.

I looked up into her beautiful face, searching for the answers I needed. I loved her curly silver hair. I had always felt safe with her, but I needed more than comfort. I needed to understand our way of life and where I fit in. I barely even understood my own family history. They had sheltered me for too long. If I was to unite them, I at least deserved to know why I had so little say in the matters related to my own life.

Her old hands covered mine in a warm cocoon as she led me to a quiet corner away from prying eyes. "A long time ago, Old Mother Earth created Uaid Dvergar, Donal Boru, Erskine Killian, and myself to lead the wolf packs and protect nature and the balance of good and evil, for there can be no light without darkness. And Old Mother is the soul of nature that gives life to the universe and takes it. Her love is poured out upon the earth, and it is she who links us to the land and the cycles of the seasons and the moon. We all are her humble servants."

"Killian?" I stared at her, dumbfounded.

"Yes, dear. They, too, are a bloodline of Elder Gods."

"But everyone treats them like commoners," I said.

"Yes, even the mighty fall, but soon they will rise again," she said. "My daughter Calista heard Old Mother's thoughts. She saw you coming, with your snow-white skin and crimson curls. She foretold of your arrival, and she foretold their rise from disgrace." Mother Rhea ran her fingers over my red hair as she studied it in the firelight. Her face looked fondly distant as she remembered something. "You have her visions. I have seen them in your eyes, but you haven't embraced them yet and harnessed their power. They are still wild inside of you and you fear them."

Did she mean my dreams? They weren't real. I couldn't see the future. Though I had seen Adomnan coming that day on the cliffs, and I had known his castle long before he held me captive there. Was it possible? If I could control the visions, could I protect everyone I loved? Could I save them all? Or was that a childish fantasy?

"How do I control them?" I asked.

"I don't know, my dear. I don't share your power," she said.

"What if I can't learn to control them?" I asked.

"Then they will remain wild, like you."

"Why is all of this happening? Why would Old Mother let this happen?"

"The balance of good and evil has been broken, and Old Mother's strength weakened; she looks to you to restore it. She cannot do it alone," Mother Rhea said.

"What caused her to lose her power?"

"The loss of faith," she said. "Faith and trust and love in each other and Old Mother. As we fought against each other, we stopped loving and protecting the humans, and they lost their way. And every step we took away from love, the humans lost more of their faith."

"That's awful. I can't even imagine; I have never questioned my faith. It lives inside of my heart and in the air I breathe," I said.

She smiled. "You are pure love and we all shimmer in your sunshine, but others will try to steal your light and corrupt it. Evil will try to dull your heart and tarnish your soul. A light as bright as yours will always attract darkness."

I shivered as her words settled on me. "Was it Uaid Dvergar who started this when he killed Calista? Or was it your daughter Vigdis?" I dared ask.

Her smile faded. "My daughter Vigdis murdered her sister Althea, and she swayed the balance of evil; Vigdis stole Althea's last breath out of hate and jealousy. When I fled Vigdis's wrath to the Boru to protect my other daughters—Calista, Faye, and your mother Nessa—she turned her attention on the Dvergars. She easily twisted Uaid's already troubled mind toward us. She manipulated his pack's strength and used it for her own will. Uaid thought Vigdis served him, but he couldn't see how he was now serving her. He thought he wanted to possess Calista's visions. He believed that with her visions he would solely rule the world. When Calista wouldn't submit to him, he killed her and Vigdis watched her die. It fractured the alliance between the packs, creating corruption in our kind. My pack was broken; two of my daughters were dead, and one was a murderer. Only Faye and Nessa remained." She shook her head in sadness. "Centuries of war continued between the Dvergars and our packs. Finally, Calista's betrothed, Ragnall Boru, stabbed Vigdis in the heart during the battle of Carrowmore, but no one found her body after the battle was won. Many speculate that her soul still walks the dark depths of the Bloodrealms."

I had tried to find a piece of humanity in Vigdis when I first studied the painting, but now I knew what she was. Her selfish hate created a world full of evil that continued long after she died.

Mother Rhea continued, "The Dvergars tainted many other packs, destroying all that resisted them, and they started hunting the humans for sport. We were created to protect humans, but the Dvergars turned wolves into feared killers. We tried to protect ourselves and our humans, but the blood continued to cover the earth. The Boru, Killian, Kingery, Kahedin, Cree, Sylla, Tabakov, and Odin's pack Pohjola attacked the Dvergars and killed Uaid on the battlefield, but evil does not die so easily. Uaid's eldest son, Crob, took his throne and began the quiet genocide of humans. Uaid's other son, Verci, took it upon himself to fulfill what his father had started and attempted to destroy the Vanir and Boru bloodlines. He and Vigdis reigned as king and queen of the Bloodrealms for centuries."

Hearing her words brought a vivid story to life inside me, and I felt her emotions as she held my hands. It was unbearable to feel the amount of pain that coursed through her. She had lost so much and so much balanced on my success. I was overwhelmed by the weight of it.

"The Dvergars killed any pack who refused to join their side. It was then, in our darkest hours, that Old Mother chose a group of humans to protect their kind. They were the wolf hunters. But human hearts are easily corrupted. When their leader drank of our blood, he stole our immortal power, and it created a physical need within them for our blood. We became the hunted, and they became the Bloodsuckers. The power that flows through our veins turned their hearts to greed."

I shuddered as I remembered how Grey's father had intended for me to die. My soul ached; there was so much death. How would any of us survive this brutal life when sadness and despair was everywhere?

"The only hope for human life and our kind is to unify the packs. We must become one. You, dear Ashling, must be claimed on your eighteenth birthday at Carrowmore, surrounded by Old Mother's stones, in order for the prophecy to come true. Calista said a wolf would stand by your side, and you would be claimed. Whoever this wolf might be, he is destined to help you lead and help you unite. If you are not claimed by him, Calista's prophecy will not come true; you would not create balance. All will be lost, and the war will never end," she said.

I stared at her hand as the weight of what she said settled on me. I knew Grey would gladly claim me, and so would Brychan. But my choice was imminent. If I chose wrongly, we'd all pay the price. I finally understood . . . though I still had no idea what I was supposed to do. According to Mother Rhea, I was pure love—yet I was completely bound and limited by how I was allowed to share my love and with whom. And somewhere in this whole mess, the only way I would ever fulfill my destiny and unite the packs was to "choose" my love correctly. If I chose wrongly, there would be war rather than unity. Everything hinged on love.

"I don't know if I am strong enough to unite the packs," I said.

"You are stronger than you think," she said.

Mother Rhea stood and walked over to Gwyn. She raised her hands above Gwyn's head and said, "Old Mother Earth, protect your child and bless her union." As she lowered her hands to each side of Gwyn, a crystal veil appeared, covering Gwyn in shimmering lace.

Cara gasped. "Isn't Gwyn lovely?"

"She already was," I said with a smile.

Mother Rhea led Gwyn out of the room first and the rest of us followed. We walked out of the underground castle to the runes above.

The ceremony was held under the rising moon. I saw Grey sitting with Baran, Willem, and Khepri at the back. I couldn't help but blush looking into Grey's eyes. Just looking at him made my pulse quicken with anticipation. I followed the other bridesmaids down the aisle and turned to watch Mother Rhea escort Gwyn down the aisle. Quinn smiled as he took Gwyn's hand in his, and their happiness radiated over us all. I stood beside Tegan, watching my brother Quinn marry the woman he loved more than life.

Quinn's friend Kaneonuskatew stood between Mund and Brychan. I knew of him though I'd never seen him before. He was of the Cree Tribe of Canada. Gwyn had told me of his striking appearance, with his black hair that was pulled back in tightly spun locks woven with black and silver feathers. He was both fearsome and intriguing. I knew that he was one of the last protectors of his people; they had named him One Who Walks on Four Claws, but Quinn always referred to him as Kane.

I hardly noticed the exquisite Spanish beauty that stood next to me. She must have been a dear friend of Gwyn's to have the honor, but I didn't even know her name.

Gwyn and Quinn recited the ancient vows and became one. When they walked back down the aisle, the wedding party began pairing up on the way out. Kane offered his arm to escort me down to the reception and I gratefully accepted.

I could feel Brychan's eyes on us as we followed the others to the great hall. I knew it pained him to see another man in such close proximity to me, but that was nothing compared to the agony I felt in Grey's heart. But it was Gwyn and Quinn's day, and there was no time for melancholy.

The great hall had been transformed into a purple palace. By every definition it was over the top, but it was Gwyn. Modern crystal chandeliers hung over every round table, and purple lights illuminated the ceiling in a bath of lavender. It was the most exquisite wedding I had ever seen. Well, it was the only wedding I had ever seen, except for the simple human ceremonies in our old home in Dumanas Bay. I used to sneak away and peer through the windows of the church as they said their vows. I smiled at the memory.

Kane led me to my seat on the dais. I was seated between Kane and Brychan. I was thankful to see that Drystan was several tables away. My skin crawled just thinking about him, I wondered if he even remembered what he had done. I looked around for Grey, but I didn't see him or Baran. My heart sank a little without them. I didn't trust Father not to do something terrible.

"Kane, have you officially met Princess Ashling?" Brychan asked in a possessive tone as he stood next to me.

Kane studied him before responding. "Lord Brychan, so nice to see you again. It's been many years." Brychan nodded as Kane continued. "I have not had the honor to be properly introduced to the lady, but I greatly thank you for the opportunity."

He turned his full attention on me, and I suddenly felt uneasy. Until Brychan had introduced us, Kane wasn't allowed to speak to me first, as it wouldn't have been proper etiquette. Brychan had just opened the door for him to speak freely with me, which I was certain wasn't his intent. Kane's eyes were intense as he took my hand in his. "It is an honor to meet the wolf with the snow-white skin and crimson curls."

"You may call me Ashling," I said nervously.

He lightly kissed my hand, and I felt my face burn bright red. Brychan didn't show any visible signs of discomfort, but I could smell his anger. Brychan stood next to me with his fist clenched and his jaw tight.

"Besides, you're Quinn's little sister, so I'm sure you're delightful," Kane said.

"It's nice to finally meet you as well, Kane. I've heard so much about you," I said.

"Oh?" he asked.

"Gwyn says such nice things," I muddled through.

"She's always too kind," Kane said. "Take a seat, Lord Brychan; you'll find it easier to relax and join the conversation." Kane's demeanor was so calm and confident. It contrasted Brychan's quick wit and hot temper. Brychan begrudgingly took his seat next to me, but remained silent.

A beautiful woman took the open seat next to Kane. Her hair was black and cut to her jaw, with feathers bound in her hair that framed one side of her face. She was petite in comparison to Kane's height and build.

"Lady Ashling, I'd like you to meet my mate, Shikoba."

A smile consumed my face as I realized Kane had just been annoying Brychan for fun. "It's lovely to meet you, Shikoba," I said smiling, I almost laughed at the ridiculousness of it all.

"I feel as though I already know you. I felt your presence in Canada last winter," she said. "I came looking for you, but they had already taken you."

"You tried to find me?" I said.

"I came to protect you," Shikoba said as she studied my face. "You have such beautiful golden eyes," Shikoba said.

"Oh . . . thank you," I said.

She practically spoke in riddles. When the food came, she didn't touch it; instead, she sat perfectly still. She and Kane didn't even touch. I suppose they were the definition of proper etiquette.

"You see much more than you know, but you should hide it from others. Your enemies will destroy you for your visions," Shikoba said.

"Shikoba, this is not the place," Kane interrupted.

Shikoba nodded. "You are right. I apologize, Lady Ashling."

"There is nothing to apologize for, Shikoba, please continue. I want to know," I said.

"It is not safe, even here," Kane replied, looking around at all those close enough to hear. "Come to us in Canada, and we will tell you all we know."

"There are many eyes and ears here tonight," Brychan agreed. "Let us toast to the wedding now," he said. Turning to face me, he said, "I will bring you to visit Kane."

I hated the way his words felt, like he was dictating my decisions, when and where I could go and with whom. There was a possessive nature to him that I was cautious of. I didn't want to drop the subject, but I knew better than to create a spectacle. Brychan continued to chat with Kane, and I let my mind wander to Grey. I still hadn't seen him in the great hall and I missed his presence, but my thoughts were interrupted as the beautiful Spanish woman from the wedding party made her way to our table. There was a stark look to her features, with her shiny black hair and blood-red lips. Her curvaceous body was undeniable even in the free-flowing lavender bridesmaid dress. She stood at least a foot taller than me, and as far as I had observed, she never smiled. She was so serious. I couldn't imagine what Gwyn liked about her.

Brychan stood and held the chair out for her. "Lady Selene, have you met Lord Kaneonuskatew and Lady Shikoba?" There was a curt tone to his voice, as though he didn't really like Selene, but I couldn't be sure.

She slowly and elegantly took her seat across from me as she gave a small, cold nod. Kane and Shikoba returned the gesture with little emotion. The tension at the table was almost visible.

"Lady Selene, I'd like to introduce you to Princess Ashling Boru, daughter of King Pørr Boru," Brychan continued.

She turned her cold black eyes on me as she studied my face and wild hair. "How interesting . . ." she said. "How interesting that you live. We were all under the impression you had perished. But clearly, you have not."

Bile filled my mouth at her words. I wanted to lash out at her and dismiss her rude behavior, but I didn't dare make a scene at the wedding, much less disgrace them by speaking ill to one of their dear friends. So I took a deep breath, clearing all the things I really wanted to say out of my mind. "Apparently you were misinformed," I said with a smirk.

"Clearly."

"It's lovely to meet such a good friend of Gwyn's," I lied.

Her expression didn't soften. "If you will excuse me." She bowed as she walked out of sight.

"What was that about?" I asked the others.

Kane replied, "She's a demon."

Brychan choked out a laugh before finally saying, "What Kane means is she is in the flesh trade. She acquires human and wolf slaves and fights them. It's a very different lifestyle," Brychan said.

"I don't understand what you mean," I said.

"She purchases human and wolf slaves from other owners in the Bloodrealms and fights them with other slaves. It is a blood sport. Most slaves never earn their freedom; they die in the fighting pits," Brychan said.

"She watches them die?" I gasped.

"It is the dark side of the Bloodrealms. Nobles and royals fight each other for sport, training, and honor, but others fight slaves for entertainment," he said. "Not all packs have evolved away from the barbaric nature of slave fighting."

"If Selene is involved in such horrific things, why is she a friend of Gwyn's?" I asked.

Brychan shook his head. "They were childhood friends long ago when they both boarded in Norway. Gwyn still sees good in Selene."

"What is her problem with me?" I asked.

This time it was Kane who laughed. "Her father was trying to betroth her to Lord Brychan here, but he was refused with no explanation. And instead Brychan was offered to you."

I was shocked; I knew my jaw hung open, but I was helpless to close it. I looked to Brychan, staring into his big eyes. I was jealous and I didn't even know why.

"You were supposed to marry Selene?" I said.

He nodded.

"Why didn't you marry her?"

"It wasn't just my choice," he said. "My family needed to select the perfect alliance; your father needed a good protector for you. A lot more goes into a betrothal than just desire. A lot of it is politics."

"Did you know who you were getting when you gave up Selene?" I asked.

"Did I know who you were?" he asked. "No, I actually had no idea whom they wanted me to marry until you walked into the room. To my knowledge, you had died."

I nodded, still confused. "In over four hundred years, you haven't found a single suitable mate?" I asked skeptically.

The smile left Brychan's face. "I was betrothed once before," he said, "but she died."

"I'm sorry. I shouldn't have asked. It was so terribly rude of me," I said.

"No, it is a fair question," he said. "Her name was Thema, and she was of the Sylla tribe of Africa."

"How did she die?" I asked.

"Verci Dvergar killed her," he said bitterly.

"Brychan . . . I'm so sorry."

"You would have liked her. She was wild like you."

A chill went over my spine, as though someone had physically touched me. I looked wildly around the people closest to me, but no one was near enough. Brychan sensed the change in my mood.

"Are you alright?" he whispered in my ear.

"She's watching you, Ashling," Shikoba said.

"Who is?" Brychan demanded.

She shook her head. "I don't know. I can't see her face; I only feel her power, but she's among us."

"I don't see anyone out of the ordinary," Brychan said.

"She doesn't want to be seen," Shikoba said. "She's hiding in plain sight."

Brychan scanned the room for anyone out of place or anyone looking in our direction, but there were too many guests in the darkened room to find the source. I was surrounded by people I was sure would protect me, and I had proven my ability to protect myself from Adomnan, but why didn't that stop my fear?

I watched my mother a few tables, away chatting with all the guests. She looked up at me with concern in her eyes—she must have felt my emotions. I forced a smile and she reluctantly turned back to the guests. Everyone received her full attention no matter his or her status. She loved everyone and didn't make exceptions, but I knew she was still watching me.

Channing walked into my line of vision. Channing looked sophisticated in his fitted suit. He always made me think of a well-dressed spy, like from the movies Baran loved; Channing even drove a ridiculously fast car. His blue eyes sparkled in the lavender lighting, but it was his overly confident smile that always made me leery of his intentions.

"Ashling, I've been waiting all my life for you," Channing said.

"Lord Channing, I'm so glad to see you here," I said. I was glad for the distraction, though I wished it was Grey rather than Channing.

"I would love to take you on an exquisite date when we meet in Maine," he said.

Etiquette plagued me. "It would be my pleasure," I said.

Channing turned his stunning smile to Brychan. "Lord Brychan, always a pleasure," he said with a tiny bit of mocking in his voice. It was obvious they were fighting for my attention. As a guest of the Kahedin Pack, I was first and foremost Brychan's guest, but Channing had an equal right to speak to me as one of my suitors.

Brychan eyed his very wealthy competition. "Channing, I've missed our little talks, but I'm afraid that I've asked Lady Ashling to dance. So we'll have to catch up another time."

A tiny smile tweaked at the corner of my lips at his lie, and he didn't use Channing's title. It was a small slight to Channing, since they weren't friends. Brychan was definitely territorial when it came to me. He nearly knocked out every man that came near me. It was a little nauseating. And I couldn't help but to think of how it all affected Grey.

"I doubt that," Channing said, blocking Brychan's path.

Brychan took my small hands in his to lead me to the dance floor, but Channing didn't move from our way. Suddenly Brychan shoved Channing, knocking over chairs. Channing snarled and stalked toward Brychan. Brychan started laughing as he pulled the sleeves of his shirt up, getting ready to fight. I felt all the eyes on us and I wanted to run away, but I forced myself to walk calmly between them. I looked disapprovingly at both of them.

"Would you both mind behaving like gentlemen? This is a wedding, and I will not be disgraced by your ill behavior," I said haughtily. I had much bigger problems than the two of them, and I didn't have time for their ridiculous fighting. "Channing, lovely to see you, and I so look forward to our date later this summer. Brychan, were we going to dance, or would you rather fight?" I felt like I was scolding a pair of naughty children.

Brychan and Channing bowed to me. Brychan gently took my hand and led me to the dance floor without another word from either of them.

"You lied," I said as soon as we were out of earshot. "We weren't about to dance."

"Oh, did I?" he asked, looking mischievous. "I must have been hoping for it so hard, I began to believe it was true."

I couldn't help myself as I laughed. "You're simply primeval, Lord Brychan."

He smiled in return as we spun around the dance floor. With his big arms wrapped around me, I felt oddly comforted. I found myself falling for his charm . . . or lack of it.

"Why do you like to fight so much? Doesn't it get terribly dull having a black eye all the time?" I asked.

"Well, I figure I'll fight until I finally stop getting punched in the face," he said.

"With all the things you say to irritate others, I doubt that day is coming anytime soon," I said.

I really couldn't figure Brychan out. Why hadn't he married Selene, or anyone for that matter? He was over four hundred years old. Was he still haunted by Thema's death? Flin and Bridgid spun next to us, interrupting my train of thought.

"Are you having a nice evening, Lord Brychan?" Flin asked.

Brychan looked down into my eyes. "Best night yet," he replied.

"Glad to hear it," Flin said; his tone was flat and uninterested. "Now if you'd be so kind to hand Ashling over to Lord Channing. You're too poor to be his competition anyway."

It was like a crushing blow on my body to hear my own brother speak so ill of Brychan.

"Ah, Prince Flin, you know how these things go. I'm required to smile at the simpleminded insults of a pompous ass."

And with that Brychan spun me to a different area of the dance floor, away from my brother. I wanted to scream at Flin, but I loved Brychan's response.

"I'm sorry for my ill behavior toward your brother," Brychan said.

"Why? He is an ass," I said. "I'm sorry he said such awful things."

"He is just an unimaginative bloke. His insults aren't even well thought out," Brychan said. "Would you care to dance more, or sit, or shall I escort you to your room?"

I looked up at him with so many emotions flowing through me, and I tried to form the words, but nothing came. It was exhausting carrying the weight of our pack around with me. My decision in a mate would affect our entire world. He crushed my small body against him in a fierce hug. I hid my face in his arms, but all I could think about was Grey.

Brychan led me to the table with my mother and Tegan. I sat next to Mother and he stood behind me with his warm hand on my shoulder, as though he was guarding me against anyone who might come near. I was thankful to have such a great friend in Brychan. He made me laugh when I was sad, held me when I needed to be held, and protected me when I needed shelter. He was a far better man than I had ever given him credit for.

I watched Odin lurking near an old mirror on the wall. He put his hand on the mirror as though he was caressing his reflection. He was the strangest man. I couldn't decide if he had personality disorders, or if he was just weird. He turned and stared right at me. I nearly jumped out of my chair. He nodded to me and abruptly stalked off.

The conversation at the table was lighthearted and friendly. Soon, I was laughing along with the jokes, and Brychan had taken a seat next to me. In the safety of Mother's presence, no one else dared bother me.

Father was conversing with Lord Kahedin and Lord Kingery, but he wasn't far away, and I knew if anyone dared bother Mother they would regret it. Father might be awful, but he would always protect us from harm . . . except for the harm he inflicted himself.

"Care to dance?" said a voice behind me.

I whipped around to see Grey standing behind me with Baran, Khepri, and Willem. He wore a gray suit with a crisp white shirt and skinny black tie and his Killian cufflinks. Everything about him screamed at me to kiss him, but I saw Mund's expression, and his warning kept me in my chair.

"You look endlessly beautiful as always," Grey said, kissing my hand.

I might not be able to show my true affection for Grey, but I could still be me. I wasn't going to let anyone stop me from being who I was. I jumped up and hugged Grey, holding him tight. He lightly kissed my neck as he caressed my lower back.

"May I have this dance?" he said.

"I've been waiting all night," I whispered as we walked onto the dance floor. I could smell Brychan's jealousy, but I didn't care. All I ever wanted was Grey.

Grey wrapped his arms around my waist, and I melted into his touch. I breathed him in deeply, letting his scent intoxicate me as I rested my head on his chest. There was something so profound about how I felt when I was with him. He was my match in every way.

"My love," he whispered, kissing my cheek. "It hurt to be away from you, but knowing that I'd be able to wrap my arms around you again made every day survivable."

"I missed you so much," I said. "I feel so strong and beautiful and desirable and powerful when I'm with you."

"The sun truly shines when you're next to me," he said. "Your love gives me strength."

"I love you, Grey," I said.

Grey lightly kissed my cheek, and as he pulled away, his lips gently rubbed across mine, and the fire lit in my soul. I desperately wanted to kiss him and feel his tongue against mine. I wanted to give all my love, laughter, friendship, lust, and all of myself to him. I wanted to be his, but I felt everyone's eyes on us, and I knew what was at stake: Grey's life.

I pulled back, letting the small space between us cool my hot blood. I wanted to make love to him so badly that it hurt to force myself to have space between us. The lust in his green eyes was almost too much to resist. I had to distract us both before we did something we'd regret.

"What did you do in Maine while I was gone?" I asked.

"Baran and Willem have been teaching me to bare-knuckle box for the Bloodrealms, but we came as soon as we received Brychan's message," he said.

I glanced at Brychan, who watched me from the table. He had chosen to invite Grey knowing Grey was one of my suitors, and that I favored Grey over the rest. He had to know Grey would monopolize my time. Was it some sort of trick to win my favor, or was he just genuinely being nice?

All I could think about was the kiss I had shared with Brychan. And I couldn't lie to myself and say I didn't enjoy it. His kiss was nothing compared to how I felt when Grey kissed me, but I couldn't deny that it happened and that I'd participated fully. I'd betrayed Grey's trust, yet here he was professing his love for me. I wanted desperately to tell him the truth, but I didn't want him to get into a fight with Brychan at the wedding either. Guilt was an evil emotion.

I rested my head on his chest and sighed.

"Are you okay?" he asked.

"I just missed your touch," I said.

He kissed my head and held me tightly until the song ended. Every moment went too quickly. We walked back to the table and Grey took a seat next to Mother. She leaned over and kissed him on the cheek.

"Grey of Killian, it's wonderful to see you again," she said.

He actually blushed, and I giggled at his expense.

"Queen Nessa." He nodded.

She laughed. "You may call me Nessa."

Grey looked so nervous in my mother's presence. Luckily, Baran filled the silence.

"Thank you, Brychan, for clearing up the invitation snafu," Baran said. "We are glad to be here to celebrate with the Kahedins and Borus."

"We all belong to Ashling," Brychan said, smiling.

I looked away from his intense eyes. He made me nervous. He made me like him. Years earlier when I first met him, I couldn't fathom thinking of him as anything but awful, but he had become my friend. It was unfortunate that he wanted more from me than I could give him.

Brychan sat down next to Grey and watched him. I wondered what Brychan saw when he looked at Grey. Did he see competition? Did he see a half-breed? Did he see a teenage boy? Did he see any of the things I did when I looked at Grey? When I looked at Grey, I saw his soul. I saw not just who he was yesterday, or who I thought he might be tomorrow, but all of him at every time before and to come. I loved him for exactly who he was.

Grey turned to Brychan and the two stared at each other for what felt like an eternity. Grey's expression was calm, but the energy that pulsed through me was pure jealousy. I was ready to leap out of my chair to stop them from fighting at any moment. The tension made my skin crawl with unease.

"Thank you for the invitation," Grey said to Brychan. "You didn't have to, and I appreciate that you did."

"I didn't really have a choice," Brychan said, smiling at me. "I did it for Ashling, of course."

Testosterone filled the air. Grey's eyes lit like absinthe and his jaw tightened. Brychan smirked as his body twisted, ready for a fight.

8

Smothered

I held my breath watching them waiting for chaos to start all around me, but Gwyn darted between us, kissing all our cheeks without a care in the world.

"It's time!" she said, giggling. "Hurry up!"

My family and the Kahedins followed her and Quinn up to the surface to say our good-byes and well wishes to them. The newly married pair drove away under the stars for their honeymoon.

A cold chill settled on me again, as though someone was watching me. I looked around, but I only saw my family and Brychan's family. Not even the Killians or Cree came up for the farewells.

Who would be watching me? I glanced to the trees. Was someone out there, hiding in the darkness? Or in plain sight, as Shikoba had said? Was someone I trusted actually my enemy? Grey no longer did that creepy lurk-in-the-trees-and-spy-on-me thing. Adomnan was dead—that I knew to be absolute. But *someone* was watching me. I instinctively grabbed Brychan's arm. I felt safer knowing I was touching him; he would fight anyone for me. I saw him smile at my small touch. I knew clinging to him was wrong, but I wanted to ward off the threat from whatever was out there. I might have proven that I could take care of myself, but it didn't hurt to have allies against whoever was stalking me.

"Are you alright?" Brychan asked.

"I think someone is watching me again," I whispered.

"Odin!" Brychan called. When he didn't appear from his guard post, Brychan called again. "Odin, son of Jarl!" Again no response came.

"House guard!" Brychan yelled.

A man appeared in moments and half bowed to us. "Lord Brychan."

"Take your men, search the trees, check the perimeter, and report back to me immediately. We may have an unwanted guest in the forest tonight,"

The man nodded and disappeared as fast as he'd come. Brychan quickly escorted me inside the safety of the underground castle as Odin ran up behind us breathlessly.

"Lord Brychan, I'm here to serve," Odin said.

Brychan gave him a cold look. "You weren't at your post."

"I'm sorry I was —"

"I don't accept excuses," Brychan said, cutting him off. "Don't let it happen again." Brychan's threat was clear. He took my arm once again and gently escorted me into the castle.

"Why are you threatening Odin? He is in my service, not yours," I said.

"He wasn't fulfilling his duty," Brychan said.

"That isn't the question I asked you," I said. "I asked why you were threatening and ordering my people around?"

He was clearly agitated, but he stopped walking and looked me in the eyes. "I am sorry if I overstepped a boundary. I did it to protect you," he said.

"As has everyone else who has dictated my life," I said. "I will not accept that behavior from you, Lord Brychan. Do not make decisions for me again."

He bowed his head. "I regret my rash actions and the pain they caused you, but I will not regret keeping you safe," he said. We continued down the winding stairs to my room.

We stopped at the door to my room. He leaned in and gently kissed my lips. I pulled back, frustrated by his constant need to touch me. I backed into my room, watching him cautiously.

"I am always yours," he said. ·

He really did care about me, that much was obvious. He probably always had; I had just been too young to see it. I knew he wanted to keep me safe, but the last thing I needed was another man protecting me by smothering me. Though I had to admit that I was more scared without him here. It was unnerving to have someone watching you. It made every shadow a terror. I wished Grey were with me. I'd snuggle into his arms and hide in his love.

Alone in my room, I slipped into a simple nightgown and snuggled into my giant bed. I sighed a bit in relief and let the day's stress release and the highlights fill my mind. I closed my eyes, trying to block out all of the what-ifs, and I drifted off to sleep.

I stood in the ruins of Castle Raglan watching the fireflies flitter about in the sky. Shadows came slithering out of the darkness toward me. I screamed and backed away, but they were all around me. They growled and snapped at me, trying to tear my flesh. I could feel a raspy, hot breath on my cheek. He was coming for me.

I woke to the sound of raspy breathing and footsteps in my silent room. My mind filled with terror as the sound crept closer to my bed. I kept my eyes closed, hoping I was still asleep. The intruder's scent was masked with frankincense. I opened my eyes, but my room was pitch black.

My haunting memories of Adomnan filled me with dread, nearly suffocating me with fear. I leaped off the bed, screaming as I blindly ran for the door, but the intruder grabbed at my hair and ripped out a clump of my curls.

I stumbled to the ground, shrieking in pain.

The intruder grabbed my neck, pressing me into the wall. His hot breath prickled my skin with moisture.

9
Poisoned

I gagged at the smell of his breath, and all I could hear was Adomnan's taunts echoing in my mind. He was everywhere. I clasped my hands over my ears and screamed, trying desperately to silence Adomnan in my head. I felt lightheaded from the lack of oxygen. My anger raged over my fear, and I kneed my attacker in the groin. He groaned, but I didn't bother to stick around. I turned and ran from my chambers, crashing into Brychan's arms at full speed outside my door. I crumbled to the floor in his arms, screaming.

The guards ran past us into my chamber as Brychan scooped me up into his arms like a babe, cradling me against his bare chest. His scent overpowered my senses, and with every beat of his erratic heart it grew stronger.

I let the fear ripple out of me. Brychan just held me tightly and began walking me away from the chaos. When I finally opened my eyes, I was in his bedchamber and he was sitting on his bed with me in his arms. The large stone fireplace burned with orange embers barely filling the space with warm light. He didn't say anything; he continued to hold me tightly, waiting for me to find my own strength. A knock at the door made me jump.

"Lord Brychan," a male voice called through the closed door.

Brychan stood and set me in the center of his large bed as he wrapped a wool blanket around my shoulders. He lightly ran his thumb over my cheek and wiped away the tears. He turned to open the chamber door. He quietly conversed with the guard only to turn back to me with a dissatisfied look on his face.

"They didn't catch the intruder; they lost his scent. He may still be in the castle, so the guards are going to stand watch outside my chamber, and I insist you stay here until morning."

I nodded. There was no way I was going back to my room alone. I looked into his big brown eyes and I shivered with fear. Fear of the intruder, fear of being alone with Brychan.

With one arm, he scooped me back up in his arms, and he flipped the blankets down as he covered me up. He sat down on top of the covers next to me. His eyes were filled with passion and concern. I was highly emotional and half-naked in his bed; he could have easily tried to take advantage of me, but he didn't.

"I won't leave you," he said reassuringly.

Grey burst into the room and rushed to my side, kneeling on the floor. "Are you okay? I felt . . ." Grey paused, looking at Brychan, "I felt sick when I overheard the guards." I knew he'd felt my fear and pain, but he couldn't admit it in front of Brychan, or our secret would destroy us. Brychan's warm scent filled the room, and Grey's body tensed with jealousy.

"I'm safe now," I said, touching his cheek.

I leaned my forehead against his and let his warmth wash over me. I needed him more than air. His love could calm the wickedest storm inside of me and start a passionate fire in its place. I breathed him in, letting his scent replace Brychan's. I lay down on the bed facing Grey as he held my hand.

I woke the next morning still in Brychan's bed with Grey still asleep, half-draped on the bed with me. When I looked around the room, I saw Brychan asleep in the chair across the room. Not one bad dream haunted me when Grey was by my side.

"Oh Ashie! I'm so sorry for your terrible night. What an awful thing," Tegan said as she rushed into the room.

Brychan and Grey woke up to her voice. She first studied Brychan's bare chest, then her eyes moved to Grey's hand, still in mine. She stared at my messed hair and me wearing only a tiny nightgown. Her tone changed. "How atrocious it must have been." The sarcasm in her words was clear as she took in the sight of us. "Brychan, Grey. You've done so much, why don't you go get cleaned up and let me care for Princess Ashling."

She used my formal title, which was rare. I knew she did it to scare them into retreating. It wasn't at all proper for me to be alone with two suitors in a bedchamber. Had any of us been thinking, we wouldn't have taken such a risk, and Brychan would have escorted me to Tegan or Mother last night. Bringing me to sleep in his bed was improper behavior; it would appall Lord and Lady Kahedin and was a disgrace to the Kahedin House. It could ruin my reputation most of all. Though Brychan and Grey should have been found guilty as well, equality wasn't something that existed in our world. Despite nothing happening, it could still endanger us all.

Tegan looked up at her brother and then back to me. Without a single word, we both knew she didn't approve. Of course, Grey and I had shared my bedroom back in Maine, but that was at Baran's house— not the formal home of another pack leader whose son was one of my suitors. Brychan bowed and quietly disappeared from the room. Grey stood and turned to whisper to me, "I'll never be too far, my love." He followed quickly behind Brychan, leaving me to face Tegan's motherly disapproval alone.

"Do you have any idea what would happen if you were caught alone with him or Grey?" She shook her head. I didn't bother to defend myself—I knew she was right. "My parents could have canceled the betrothal with Brychan, claiming your virtue had been ruined. Your parents could have put both of them to death! What were you thinking, Ashling?"

"I wasn't," I replied.

"That's obvious. You endangered Brychan and Grey. You should have come to me. I wasn't told they slept in the room with you."

"I'm sorry," I said. "But this isn't all my fault. Brychan brought me here—I had just been attacked. I wasn't in a position to be worrying about my virtue in the moment."

"Don't worry—I'll be talking to Grey and Brychan, too," Tegan said, "but it's important that you understand the potential consequences of this. First the kiss with Grey, now this?"

She paced back and forth with her hands on her hips. "Well, Mund and I are the only ones who know about last night. We'll tell everyone else that I was in here with you instead. Hurry and get cleaned up, and for goodness's sake, wash Brychan's and Grey's scent off your skin. We don't need anyone nosing around. We have to get down to breakfast."

Her tone had softened, but it was obvious she was still very worried about me. It never crossed my mind that my actions could get Brychan or Grey hurt. I never wanted anything bad to happen to either of them. She had every right to be angry with me for my part in it, but I would not take the blame for the injustice of our laws. I was the victim of Adomnan's ruthless attack and again with this new intruder. I would not harbor more displaced self-doubt. But the reality was that if Father found out, he could put Grey to death, use one of the old punishments on Brychan, and force me to marry Channing—if Channing would still take me after my "scandalous" night in another man's bedchamber. My stomach churned with stress.

I quickly dressed in something everyone would find appropriate, a simple floor-length satin dress. No leather today; I wanted to blend in with the others and not draw more unwanted attention to myself. I put Brychan's necklace on as a sign of respect to the House of Kahedin and followed Tegan to her suite, where we met up with Mund and Nia. In one glance between them, Mund knew everything I don't know how, but I could see it in his eyes.

"Ash, what have you done?" Mund said.

He looked so disappointed. I never wanted to disappoint him . . . anyone but him.

I felt my frustration raging with my fear.

"I didn't do anything wrong." My lips quivered with anger. "I was attacked. Brychan brought me to his room. Grey stayed by my side and nothing happened. I have nothing to be ashamed of."

Mund wrapped one arm around my shoulders. "I'm always on your side," he said.

He escorted Tegan, Nia, and me to breakfast. We took our seats with the rest of the family, but Brychan and Grey weren't there. Baran, Khepri, and Willem sat talking with the Kingerys. I kept looking for Grey and Brychan, but they didn't come. I watched Father for any sign that he knew what had happened during the night, but he was oblivious to my existence. Finally, Brychan and Grey walked in, and Mund signaled for them to follow him into the hall. Baran stood to follow, but Mund shook his head no.

I could feel Mund's anger, though if you didn't know him as I did, he looked as calm as if they were discussing the weather. His emotions bubbled inside me, and I knew that my family could feel it too. Tegan's posture was stiff, and Mother was smiling, but her eyes were watching Mund. Brychan just nodded and Grey's sadness collided inside me, making my stomach feel like a stormy sea.

They returned to the table. Brychan took the seat next to me, and Grey took his seat next to Baran. Brychan didn't look at me. I glanced nervously away and caught Odin staring at us. He always saw too much.

"I'm sorry," I said, barely a whisper.

"Mi' lady." Brychan nodded without looking up. Did he resent me now? I ruined everything. I looked at Grey and he winked. The tiny gesture was comforting, but not enough.

After the plates had been cleared, I sought refuge in the castle ruins in the fresh air. I stood in the shadows and watched the children play in the warm sunlight. Their innocent laughter echoed through the ruins. I missed my naïve youth. I was nearly seventeen years old, and I only had one year to grow up and fulfill the prophecy. I didn't have time to make mistakes. I had to play their games until I could crumble our archaic system. Old Mother created us as equals to love and protect, not to judge and torture each other. Women would no longer be lesser creatures in my new world, but for now I would obey their rules.

Brychan walked across the yard toward me. I tried to pretend I didn't notice his presence, but his scent was overpowering. He joined me in the shadows, leaving several feet between us as he leaned up against the stone wall.

"I'm sorry, Princess Ashling. I wasn't thinking. I endangered us all. It was my foolish actions that caused this. If you want to tell your father of my indiscretion, I will gladly face my fate."

A contorted laugh came out of my mouth. "Your indiscretions! Ha. You protected me. Thank you for that. I just didn't realize my presence there could have such bloody consequences for you."

A small smile returned to his rough face. "Oh Ashling, I am eternally sorry for the trouble I've caused, but I don't regret anything I did. If I died now, I would die a happy man."

"That's stupid, you aren't going to die." I smiled back, trying to reassure him. "I should be apologizing to you."

"You're right. I didn't stand a chance against your charms," he said. I smiled. "You're ridiculous."

"Sometimes I forget how young you really are," he said, moving closer. He lifted a hand and lightly caressed my face. "You're wise beyond your years, you know."

He was older than Mund. He was so much older than me it was nearly absurd, really. He was a mature man and I was a baby.

"What did Mund say to you in the hall?" I asked.

He shrugged. "Oh, you know, brotherly things. Like what I said to him when he married Tegan. Though I consider him my brother in life, I think he favors your choice in Grey."

I nodded. "Do you think it's more that he favors my right to my own decision, rather than favoring Grey over the others?"

"No," he said with a smile. "He made it clear he didn't like Eamon."

We laughed at that and let a pleasant silence fall over us. I felt comfortable and safe in his presence. He was everything I had been told I should want in life, but I didn't want him. I wanted endless love and passion. I wanted Grey.

Most of the wedding guests had already left, Channing included. Though he hardly had a moment alone with me, he didn't seem at all deterred. He asked me on a date when I returned to Maine; he said he'd be waiting there for me. He didn't love me . . . he loved the *idea* of me. The idea of the power I could give him over all the packs. It wasn't love. Then again, I wondered what kind of love any of them had for me, Brychan included. Grey was the only one who loved me for just me; he loved me long before he knew anything about my destiny.

I decided I would tell Grey that I had kissed Brychan once we returned back to Maine. It broke my heart to imagine telling him. He deserved so much more from me. He deserved the same loyalty he gave to me . . . instead, I betrayed him. Would he be able to forgive me for kissing Brychan? Would I ever forgive myself?

"Are you still staying until Lughnasadh?" Brychan asked.

Lughnasadh was at the end of the summer, weeks away. I didn't dare stay here. Not with someone still hiding in the castle waiting for me. And not under Lord Kahedin's roof.

"I just want to go home," I said.

"Oh . . ." he said. "Would you like me to remain behind?" he asked.

"No, I'd like you and Grey to escort me home as soon as possible, with Odin and Baran's pack of course."

"I will see it done," he said.

Brychan spoke to Mund and his parents on my behalf. He told his parents I had summer classes starting soon. He lied for me. To Mund, he told the truth—that I'd grown weary of being away from my home after the intruder. Mund agreed with my decision, but didn't agree with my preference in escorts.

As I packed my things, Mund leaned on the doorway and watched me. "You know why I'm insisting on you traveling with Kane and Shikoba, don't you?" he asked.

"Because you don't trust me?" I asked.

"No. I trust you to be young and make plenty of mistakes. But I don't trust Brychan or Grey to keep their hands off you. And I certainly don't trust my baby sister—the future leader of our kind—to be traveling with so few guardians."

"It's okay Mund, I'll be fine. What is the new plan?" I said, throwing my leather clothes in my trunk.

"You will be flying with Kane and Shikoba to their home in Quebec. You will spend a couple days there before you venture south to Maine. Channing and Cara know when to expect you. And you know I'll be home at the end of summer."

"What about Grey?" I said.

"He will still be traveling with you; just remember not to expose your love for him to the others. No one can know how you feel."

"I know." I sighed. I hated keeping Grey a secret. I loved him and I wasn't ashamed. I wanted to scream it for the world to hear, but it was a luxury I didn't have. Though my heart beat in unison with his, it had to be our secret.

I was ready to leave Castle Raglan behind, but I knew Mother was sad for us to go. She was enjoying her time with Nia; I could see the joy on Mother's face when she held her. I didn't want to leave Mother again, but it was only for a short time, and I knew she would be happy here.

"I hear Shikoba has visions to share with you. You could learn a lot from her," Mund said.

"She's weird."

"*You're* weird," Mund said with a laugh.

I rolled my eyes. "No, there is something strange about her. For one, she doesn't have a scent."

He was quiet for a long time. "Maybe you lost your sense of smell."

I threw my boots across the room at him. He barely moved as they flew past him and hit the floor with a thud.

"Don't threaten me, little princess."

I jumped on his back, trying to knock him down, but he barely noticed my weight on his back. He dropped me on the bed and walked back to the trunk. With a sigh, he grabbed my boots and placed them in the trunk next to Brychan's ring box.

"Ashling, there is one more thing I want you to know. You know I adore Grey. Everything he's done for you has earned him great honor in my eyes. I will always consider him my equal. But . . . you must know that he has nothing to offer you."

"Excuse me? What about unconditional love? Friendship? Passion?" I said. Mund was the only one on my side—he couldn't turn on me now.

"Channing could give you everything you need," Mund said.

"Stop Mund," I begged. "I thought you cared about what I want. No one else does, but I thought you did . . ."

"You have to hear this to make the best choice for your life. Channing is far wealthier than the others, and you'd be safe in Switzerland. They have a strong pack of warriors. Brychan has always been your betrothed, and he still cherishes you. He's one of my closest friends, and he is an honorable man of means. You would always be the center of Brychan's world and have a comfortable life with him," he said. "And Eamon will only bring you sadness. So if you get the chance to choose . . . choose wisely."

"I choose Grey," I said.

"Ashling, don't make choices so rashly. I want you to realize that if Grey doesn't win in the Bloodrealms and you still choose him that it will destroy the allied packs. We will all be forced to choose sides. You know I will be right behind you, but many could die for this, and you will never unify the packs if you tear them apart," he said.

I had made a horrible mess. Brychan was the man I knew everyone expected me to choose. He was of good rank and family, handsome, charming, and a fierce protector who could provide for me. Our bond would solidify the alliance between our families. He was the man I knew I should want.

Grey was the rebellious, young, half-breed of nomadic rank that had nothing more than a motorcycle and a guitar to his name. And his father was a Bloodsucker who tried to kill me. But . . . I was in love with Grey. I didn't need wealth or title or protection. I needed *love*.

Unfortunately, it was Father who would choose the winner in the Realms, not me. If Grey didn't win, it would be war and my family would fight one another. Our love could destroy all that we cared for. Mund put his arms around me, crushing me in a hug.

"Ash, I love you and I will support whomever you choose. I will always be on your side," he said.

"Thank you, Mund. I need you . . . now more than ever," I said.

Mother looked as sad as I felt when she came into the room with Nia. I was getting better at the good-byes with her. I couldn't say either of us was good at it, but better. I think we shared pieces of our soul with one another that we didn't share with anyone else. It made parting so much harder, as though I was leaving a piece of myself with her.

"I wish you were coming with me," I said.

"I have some grievances yet to address with your father," she said with a wink.

I liked how fierce she was becoming. Every day she was stronger than the day before. Father used to control her, but not anymore. Her strength and independence were inspiring to me.

"I'll miss you," I said.

"And I you."

"I love you, Mother," I said, kissing her cheek.

"*Tha gaol agam ort,*" she said.

She hugged Nia to me so tightly Nia squeaked with excitement. I rubbed my nose on the tip of Nia's as I whispered, "Take care of your grandmother. She needs you."

I paid to upgrade Odin to first class with the rest of us. I felt weird having him sit in coach. Besides, I wanted to keep my eye on him. Something was bothering him. He'd been acting stranger than usual. Shikoba sat next to Brychan and me; Kane, Grey, Baran, Willem, and Khepri sat all around us. I hated the distance between Grey and me, but every once in a while he'd peek between the seats at me, our eyes would connect, and I couldn't help but smile like a fool. I could feel him yearning to comfort me and his frustration that he could not.

We landed in Quebec, Canada. As I stepped into the fresh outdoors, the smell of the trees flooded me with memories of Adomnan. It made it hard to breathe. Everywhere I looked I thought I saw Adomnan lurking, but when I blinked it was always a stranger. It was as though Adomnan followed me around, sucking the life from my soul. His life and death were a burden on me, always waiting to consume my happiness. I tried to push it all from my mind as I followed the others, but part of him was always with me.

I looked at the land as we drove. It was nothing like I remembered it in frozen, desolate winter. It was summer and everything was green and luscious. The land was filled with hope, if I could just force myself to see it. We arrived at the Cree triballands, where Kane and Shikoba lived. They were a part of the Cree Indian Four-Claws in the forested north.

Though most lived in modern houses, the old souls still had birch-bark wigwams so they could stay in touch with Old Mother. Kane brought us into the woodlands to a small grouping of dome-shaped wigwams. They were about eight feet tall and made from wooden frames that were covered in sheets of birch bark. He and Shikoba had the largest wigwam. Each of us would stay in the surrounding smaller wigwams. Baran ushered Grey to one at the other side of the camp . . . away from me. He looked back at me, smiling wickedly. It was an open invitation to follow him. I grinned and blushed.

A little girl darted out of a wigwam and ran into Kane's arms. Kane spoke to her in his native tongue. She looked like Shikoba, but it was her startling blue eyes that caught my attention. As she turned to walk away, she smiled at me and said, *"Tansi."* I knew it to be a friendly greeting of their musical language, but it was a complicated language, and I didn't trust my knowledge of it. I smiled back and watched as she disappeared into the trees.

"That is Shikoba's niece, Tallulah. She lost both her parents to the Bloodsuckers last year," Kane said. "We care for her now."

Tallulah was just a little girl. It broke my heart to imagine her loss . . . a child shouldn't have to feel such things. At least she had Kane and Shikoba to care for her.

I walked into an open wigwam, and the smell of the earth danced through my senses. There were several caribou and moose hides in the space, but not much more. The Cree people used everything they touched. Even the bones had a purpose in their cycle of life; they didn't hold much love for material things.

Khepri poked her head inside. "Care to help me hunt?" she asked.

Excitement sparked in my veins. "I'd love to!" I said. I followed her out.

Anticipation pulsed through my veins and my nerves twitched. I was ready to hunt. Grey looked at me with such intensity that I tingled with need. The thought of truly hunting with him caught my breath.

"Shikoba, care to join?" Khepri said.

"I will stay behind and tend the fire," Shikoba said.

"Suit yourself," Khepri said.

"I'll come," Grey offered, but Willem put his hand on Grey's shoulder.

"Best not, little brother. Khepri won't like the intrusion," Willem said. "Sit this one out."

Grey looked at me longingly. I could feel his disappointment mixing with mine. I wanted us to be together as wolves again. I just wanted to be near him. I was tired of being separated from his touch. I wanted his hands all over my body, but with Brychan here, we still weren't safe to show our true affection for each other.

Khepri and I wandered out of sight, undressing before we shifted into our wolf forms, and her fierce emotions surrounded me with strength. She darted deeper into the trees and I chased after her. The thrill of my four feet connecting with the earth was ethereal.

Khepri stopped abruptly and began crawling to the edge of a hill. I crept next to her, and the strong odor of a caribou filled my nostrils. Khepri looked at me and I knew what I had to do. We lunged off the rock, startling the caribou. It bolted toward me and I charged it. Khepri leaped on its back and sunk her teeth into its neck, silencing it forever.

She gnawed at its raw flesh and my mouth watered. I stepped cautiously forward to feed and she growled. I submissively bowed to her and she let me approach. I bit into the warm flesh, tearing strips off, devouring them to feed my primal need.

She shifted back into a human and wiped the blood from her

mouth. "We better drag this back to share with the others," she said.

I shifted back reluctantly. "Thank you for letting me hunt with you," I said.

She smiled. "It was my pleasure. You're a fine hunter."

Later, we gathered for dinner around the fire that licked the flesh of the caribou as it cooked. The juices dripped into the fire, making my mouth water with anticipation. The smoke from the fire danced and swirled into the sky as the fire crackled and sputtered. Across the fire, Grey sat watching me without the slightest discretion. I knew I should look away, but the longer I stared into his eyes, the more I wanted.

Tallulah held out a plate of pemmican, a traditional Cree food made from dried meat, bringing me back to reality. *"Mahti,"* I said, which meant "please" in their language. I helped myself to a bite. I was beginning to love trying new foods. It was only a year ago that I tried pizza for the first time with Baran. I almost had to laugh at how much it had offended me at the time.

As we ate, Shikoba stood by the fire and watched the flames. There was an unspoken tension among my traveling companions and I wondered if that was what was bothering her.

"Are you a good fighter, Brychan?" Willem asked.

"Better than you, I presume," Brychan said.

Willem laughed. "You'd better hope so."

"Are you challenging me?" Brychan said as he tossed a caribou bone into the fire.

"I am merely making conversation," he said.

"Why don't you worry about yourself?" Brychan threatened.

"It's not me you need to worry yourself about," Willem said.

"Do you think that little boy can beat me?" Brychan laughed heartily at Grey's expense, and it made my blood boil.

"I'm counting on it," Willem said.

"Please . . ." I said. "Let's not fight." I was trying hard to keep my composure.

"You do have to watch that temper of yours, Lord Brychan," Willem mocked. "It lost you your last betrothed."

Brychan leaped to his feet and charged at Willem, shoving him down into the dirt. Grey grabbed Brychan, pulling him off Willem. Brychan turned and punched Grey right in the jaw. I smothered my scream of pain as I watched the chaos.

I stood up and smoothed the skirt of my cloak and took a deep breath. I shook my head as Tallulah, Shikoba, and Khepri moved to my side. Grey had Odin in a headlock, Willem and Brychan were screaming in each other's faces, and Baran and Kane were unsuccessfully attempting to break up the madness.

"STOP!" My voice rang out above their bickering.

They all turned to stare at me. Odin looked angry. Both Grey and Brychan smiled, but their handsome smiles didn't soften my annoyance with them.

"I will not ask you again," I said. "Your behavior is inexcusable. Learn to accept each other. You are my suitors, my guardians, and my pack. I will not have you fighting like dogs."

They all looked like scolded schoolboys . . . which wasn't far from how they were acting. They were naughty little boys acting on their testosterone instead of thinking. I sat back down and picked my plate back up and finished eating the delicious morsels of food.

I didn't understand why Willem was antagonizing Brychan, or what he meant by bringing up Thema's death, but frankly none of it mattered to me at the moment. I just wanted peace. One bloody day without fighting and pain. Was that too much to ask for?

I heard them mutter apologies and return to their seats, but I didn't pay them any mind. I chose to chat with Shikoba, Khepri, and Tallulah.

"Khepri, you're from Egypt?" I asked.

"I grew up near the Temple of Edfu on the West Bank of the Nile," she said.

"How did you like it compared to your home in Scotland?" I said.

"Very different climate and people, but in truth, all places are very much the same when you are surrounded by the ones you love." I looked across the fire to Grey. He wasn't watching me, but I studied his face and messy hair and his luscious lips. Khepri was right; as long as Grey was near me, I would always be home.

"And you, Shikoba, has this always been your home?"

"Mostly. We once moved around as a tribe all over these lands, but this is our home," she said.

Baran was doing his best to keep Grey and me apart. I knew he was following Mund's orders, and they were right to be worried about the others finding out about the strength of our bond. But not being able to touch Grey was making me crazy.

As night filled the sky, Shikoba stood at a distance and studied both Brychan and then Grey. She examined every inch of them, and I was quite certain she had an open view of their souls. Finally, she turned her back to us and pushed her arms toward the fire and swirled them up toward the sky. Smoke began following her every command, swirling and moving at the whims of her hands. She looked at me through the fire, and her gaze was so intense I nearly looked away. She pushed the smoke toward me, and I flinched as it surrounded me. Each tendril of smoke swirled away as though there was a barrier around me.

"Your soul is pure. The purest I've ever seen, but you carry the weight of another; he haunts your heart, letting in darkness. Even still, after death he feeds on your power, because you still have doubt," Shikoba said.

I held her gaze even though it scared me to death. I didn't want to know what she had to say, and yet I had to know. I knew she spoke of Adomnan and the torments he still inflicted on my mind. The smoke suddenly recoiled from me, filling the ground with its foggy haze and surrounding Grey, Brychan, and Baran.

"But there are those around you who are strong of heart." Her gaze flickered to Brychan and Grey, then quickly burned back into mine.

"There are three who hunt you. The woman who hides in secret leads to others, an angry warrior, and a Bloodsucker. The Bloodsucker is close now."

"Who are they?" I begged. Was she talking about the tattooed girl Æsileif, whom I had seen back in Maine? I remembered her face with her messy hair and thick black eyeliner all around her eyes. She was hard to forget. She just showed up at the dance on New Year's Eve. She didn't say anything to me or Adomnan, she just smiled and left. I didn't know if she was good or evil. Or was Eamon hunting me like his brother had?

"I can't see their faces; they won't reveal themselves to me. But the Bloodsucker wants your heart," Shikoba said. Her words startled me. She knelt down to the earth, gathering fists of it in her hands, letting it slip through her dainty fingers. Her face pointed to the sky, and her body shook with effort. "You have changed the future. Someone who cares deeply for you will die."

Her fragile body crumpled to the ground. Kane dashed to her side. He held his hands over her body as he chanted something quietly in their beautiful language. When her eyes opened, she looked directly at me as she plunged her hand into the fire.

"No!" I screamed.

Her hand came out of the fire without a single burn on it. "Old Mother asks that I give you this for protection," she said as she dropped an arrowhead necklace into the palm of my hand. "She says you will need the protection of our people."

The arrowhead pricked my palm. A tiny droplet of blood appeared and quickly absorbed into the arrowhead. The arrowhead began to glow red from the inside, like a beating heart. I clutched it in my fist, holding tightly to her magic.

"Why do they want to hurt me?" I asked. I knew it was a childish question, but it was the simplest question I could think to ask.

"Many will try to stop you in your journey for many different reasons, but you must never succumb to evil." Her statement was simple, and with it she turned her back to me as she slowly walked to her wigwam. "I am tired now," she said. And she was gone.

"It takes a lot out of her to speak to Old Mother. You'll have to excuse us," Kane said quietly. "Ashling, do you need anything?"

"I can manage," I said. "Go to her; she needs you."

I slipped the necklace around my neck. The tiny arrowhead hung at the base of my throat on a leather cord, pulsing with energy. A piece of me lived inside it now.

"I'm going to stay up until the fires burn out," Brychan said.

"I'll take first watch," Baran said.

I nodded. "Good night."

"Sleep well, Ashling," Grey said. We looked at each other knowingly—our skin hadn't touched since he held my hand in Brychan's bedchamber. I wanted to run into Grey's arms. If we were normal people living in a normal world, we would be nestled together in front of the fire, unashamed and unafraid of others seeing our lips touch, hands touch, or our arms wrapped around the other. Instead, I turned and walked to my wigwam.

I quickly shut myself alone inside. I didn't want to talk to anyone; I just wanted to be alone with my thoughts. I still needed to find a way to tell Grey the truth about kissing Brychan, but it never seemed like the right time.

"Grey, I'm sorry," I whispered to myself.

I closed my eyes and let the words Shikoba had said run back through my mind. I knew she spoke of Adomnan, but who were my three new predators? Would I find them before they found me?

A branch broke in the distance and broke the intense silence. All the animals quieted as something or someone approached. I stumbled out of my wigwam to find out what was coming.

Brychan, Kane, Grey, Odin, Willem, and Baran surrounded Shikoba, Tallulah, Khepri, and me. Fear rippled through me as we stood our ground, waiting for our visitor to approach from the darkness. Orange embers of the fire were all but faded, and only the eerie blue moon gave speckled light in the forest.

Footsteps approached from the south as a woman stepped into the light. She was beautiful, with long brown hair and olive skin. She wore a tight brown leather jacket and leather pants, with silver knives strapped to her legs. She held a silver spear in her hand.

Four men flanked her. They were all human, but I recognized the silver blades they carried, and their scent was tainted with the metallic smell of wolf blood. Bloodsuckers. My breath caught in my throat as I remembered Robert licking the blood from my palm. I looked nervously to Tallulah; she was just a child. We couldn't let these monsters hurt her.

"Bloodsuckers," Khepri gasped.

The crossbowman notched a silver-tipped arrow and pointed it right at Baran's heart. Fear ate me alive. Baran growled and the others joined in. The hideousness of the sound was enough to scare any sane creature away, but the Bloodsuckers looked eager to fight.

"You are on sacred Cree lands," Kane said.

The woman threw a small dagger at Kane; he quickly stepped aside and the silver blade cut into Willem's leg. It was barely a scratch, but enough to slice through his pants and poison his skin.

Willem dropped to his knees as the poison weaved its trickery through his mind. Khepri held him as he groaned. I could smell her fear. I knelt, trying to comfort them.

"That's her," the woman said, pointing at me. "The one with the pale skin and wild red hair. Kill them all, but I want her alive."

Grey and Brychan snarled, but when Baran touched their shoulders, they quieted and nodded. I didn't understand what happened, but they were backing up.

Shikoba leaned in close to my ear. "Run," she whispered. She threw sand into the embers of the fire, and a giant explosion filled the area with smoke and fire. I was startled, but my instincts took over, and I started running into the forest as fast as my legs could carry me.

I leaped, shifting into a wolf. As I landed, I felt Grey and Brychan had shifted too and were flanking me. We darted through the trees only moments ahead of the Bloodsuckers. My heart pounded and I tried to keep my feet under me as the soft earth tore away. Like a moth to a flame, I ran as hard as I could for Maine.

I smelled the Bloodsuckers close behind us. A Bloodsucker slammed into Brychan, and the two rolled out of sight. I could hear them fighting. I looked back and two more still pursued Grey and me. We couldn't stop, even for Brychan.

A Bloodsucker was so close behind me I could feel him breathe. I heard the sound of metal on leather as he pulled a blade. I felt the air whoosh past my side as the knife barely missed me. Grey turned and knocked the Bloodsucker down to the ground. I felt the pain as a blade cut into Grey's skin.

"Keep running," I heard his voice yell. I glanced back and he was human. The blade had made him mortal. I turned back to save him. He held the Bloodsucker's wrists, stopping the blade from taking his head clean off. "I'll follow! I promise—just run!" he pleaded.

The last Bloodsucker notched his arrow and aimed it at me. I turned back toward home and ran with my heart breaking. I weaved and darted my way through the trees, desperately trying to stay out of his shot. I heard an arrow pierce the bark of a tree as I passed. Terror flooded through me. I heard the Bloodsucker curse and start running again. My pulse beat with the rhythm of my paws on the earth.

Panic and fear ruled me. It took everything I had just to keep moving forward instead of running back to Grey's side. He was hurt—I could feel his pain and his anger. I wanted to turn around and help him, but the constant rhythm of footsteps behind me forced us farther apart.

We ran for miles and miles through the trees. Every muscle in my body screamed in agony. I heard his footsteps stop and my aching body screamed with joy. I'd won. He stopped but, didn't bother to look back. I kept running for home.

The softest whistle preceded a silver arrow slicing into my shoulder. I howled in pain as it tore through my flesh. I felt the blood seep from my shoulder, matting into my red fur. Fear and adrenaline pushed me farther. Harder. The silver began to seep into my blood. I was running as fast as I could, but every step was slower than the one before. My mind began to become a thick haze as I fell to the ground in my human form in my cloak dress Lady Faye had given me. The silver had made me temporarily mortal. I knew I had to keep running. I had to get up, but my limbs burned with fatigue, and the poison was making it difficult to think. I put my head on the ground, breathing in the moist earth. I wanted to give into the pain, but I knew Grey would want me to fight.

I began to crawl, dragging my body over the rocky ground. Sweat ran down my face, and fatigue burned through me. The gaping wound caked my arm in blood, and the rocks cut into my forearms and knees. I didn't care. I just had to crawl home and Grey would meet me there. I had to believe that.

I crawled to the edge of the lake and wanted to cry in frustration. There was no way across it—at least not in my human form. I had to go around it. The thought made me want to give up. My legs burned and my mind was messy. I tried dragging myself with my arms, but my body refused to carry me any farther. I lay on the unforgiving earth and panted for breath. I could hear the soft sounds of the water lapping nearby, and the calming rhythm made me tired.

I surely left a blood trail. It would only be a matter of time before the Bloodsuckers tracked me here; when they found me, I would be helpless. I was beginning to drift in and out of consciousness. The silver poison was debilitating. A lone wolf would always die; I needed my pack to survive. But they didn't follow me. With the silver in my blood, I couldn't even feel Grey. I didn't know if he was alive or dead.

I closed my eyes and let the sounds and smells of Old Mother calm my raging mind. I tried to convince myself that I would take just a short rest, then I would crawl home. I heard someone running toward me on the pebbled beach. I blinked hard and tried to see through the mist and my blurred vision as a figure approached, but I could only see a silhouette in the darkness. The figure was downwind, so I couldn't catch his scent. Had he come to save me or kill me? I didn't want to die facedown in the dirt. I tried to push myself up with my arms so I could stand, but I only collapsed again with my face on the cold rocks.

Was this what death looked like?

Two others ran up and the three surrounded me. My shoulder burned like fire and I screamed. I felt the blade cut through my flesh and muscle like butter.

"Old Mother, save me," I murmured.

It felt like they were tearing the flesh from my arm and devouring me alive. Panic rippled through me, and I started screaming and clawing at them. One of them licked my wound, and I scratched him in the face. I tore my fingernails into the arm that pinned me to the ground, and I felt his skin crumbling under my fingernails. They forced my arms to the ground and held me in place. I screamed.

10
Guardian

The pain in my arm began to numb. I blinked over and over again, and I saw a silver-tipped arrow and broken shaft lying on the ground in a pool of my blood. It must have been embedded in my shoulder. That was why the silver had immobilized me. I looked up at the faces and saw Grey, and I couldn't help but smile. He was safe.

He wiped the sweaty hair out of my face and held my hand. The blood still oozed out of my arm, but the werewolf saliva had numbed the pain. My mind was clearing and I started to understand what had happened.

"Grey," I whispered. "You came for me."

"I'm sorry it took so long," he said, smiling.

He scooped me up in his arms and began running with Baran and Brychan by his side. I nestled my nose into his neck and breathed in his delicious scent, letting the comfort of his arms and the protection of my pack heal my mind. The rhythm of his steps lulled me to sleep in his arms.

When I woke, I was still cradled in Grey's arms. He was asleep, leaning against the headboard of my bed in my room while Baran snored in the chair next to the bed and Brychan stood guard in the doorway. I belonged with this makeshift pack. They were mine.

Brychan saw me and winked. I smiled weakly. I needed to shift into a wolf and heal the scabby wound on my arm; it still burned with pain.

The house was quiet with Quinn, Gwyn, Mund, Tegan, and Nia all gone for the summer, but now we had new guests. I lightly ran my fingers through Grey's hair as his scent filled the air. He looked naughty even in his sleep. As I looked upon his handsome face, I felt the first pure happiness I'd felt in weeks. We were meant to live our lives together.

"You're awake," he murmured, his voice raspy from sleep.

"I love you," I whispered.

His lips curved into a crooked smile. "You are all of me," he whispered back. I lightly ran my fingers over the scars on his chest, a physical reminder of his sacrifices he had already made for me. What unseen mark would the scars of my indiscretion leave on him?

"Do you look for trouble?" Baran said, smiling. "Or does it find you?"

"Thank you for protecting each other," I said. "Is everyone else safe?"

"Our pack is safe and we killed two of the Bloodsuckers; the others fled," Baran said. "Shikoba, Kane, and Tallulah stayed in Canada; Willem and Khepri are downstairs."

I nodded.

"Eamon paid a visit while you slept. He wants to see you when you are feeling up to it," Baran said. There was a hint of resentment in his voice when he said Eamon's name.

I looked to Grey to try to understand what I had missed, but he didn't look at me. There was something he wasn't telling me. Instead,

Baran changed the subject. "You need to heal?"

"What else happened?" I asked. I looked to Grey, but he still wouldn't look at me. Something had gone very wrong. I could feel it in my bones. "I demand to know what is going on."

Baran took my hands in his. "Eamon has insisted your father give him guardianship over you until a royal member of your family comes to care for you. In Mund's absence, Eamon is arguing that you should not be left alone in a servant's care after what happened in Canada."

"And what did my father decide?" I asked with icy disdain.

"He has not ruled yet," Baran replied.

"What about Brychan?" I asked.

"Because I do not have a female family member with me, I am not considered a suitable guardian," Brychan said.

I stood up wearily and walked out of the room and down to the telephone in the kitchen. I knew Channing and his little sister Cara had come to York Harbor, and they were my best bet to stay out of Eamon's clutches.

I slowly dialed my father on the phone. "Killian, what's the update with Ashling?" Father said.

"It's me," I said. "I'm well."

"Oh," he said. "Good." There was something in the catch of his voice that gave me pause, something I'd never heard there before. Was it compassion? I forced myself to ignore it and ask what I'd called to ask.

"Have you made a decision on my guardian in Mund's absence?"

"Not as of yet," he replied. His voice was back to his usual unforgiving tone. "Anyone you'd like me to consider?"

The question was almost absurd. He'd never once taken my opinion into consideration when he made decisions about me. I nearly laughed, but knew it wouldn't help my cause. In a calm and steady voice I stated my plan.

"Father, in Mund's absence if you no longer see Baran fit to be my guardian and protector, then I would request to be put into Lord Channing's care with his sister Cara accompanying him to be my companion."

There was a long pause before he responded. "And not King Eamon?"

"I would prefer Lord Channing," I said. I held my breath as I waited for his answer. I knew he favored Channing over Brychan, but I didn't know how he felt about Eamon. Eamon was a king, which was surely appealing to Father. I was manipulating the situation, but I didn't have a choice. I would never go with Eamon. The very thought of his name made my skin crawl. Though he'd been the only one kind to me in Adomnan's abduction, I still couldn't understand how someone who participated in my abduction would even be considered at all.

"I'll see to it by nightfall." With that, he hung up the phone. No kind words, no thankfulness that Grey, Brychan, and Baran had rescued me. No acknowledgment of all they had risked for me. No expression of gratitude for my safety. No—just the lonely sound of the dial tone.

Grey stood silently in the corner of the kitchen as he watched me hang up the phone. "Is it decided? Will you be staying with Eamon?" he said.

"No, I will be staying with Channing and his sister Cara."

He nodded.

The misery on his face made me want to cry. Would our love never be easy? He was all I ever wanted, and I didn't know how to bridge the gaps between us that I had created. I sighed and walked past him back to my room to pack a few things for my stay with Channing. I threw clothes into a bag, hoping my stay would be short. I heard Baran on the phone downstairs with Channing, asking him to pick me up. I dreaded leaving Grey.

When I heard the soft purr of a sports car pull into our driveway, I knew it was time. I walked back downstairs to find Grey. His sadness crashed into my already-weary confidence.

"I'm sorry," I said quietly. "It was the only way to stay away from Eamon." I turned to leave and he lightly grabbed my hands, running his rough fingers over my delicate skin.

"I don't want to lose you," he said.

"You won't," I said. I lightly kissed his lips. The feeling of his lips on mine filled me with a familiar need. His lips crushed mine, intensifying our kiss, and his tongue massaged mine. An overwhelming surge of energy filled me, and all I wanted was to be consumed by him. He pulled me into his arms, lifting me off the ground.

"Being away from you is torture," he said.

Baran cleared his throat as he stepped into the room. Grey put me down and took a step back just as Brychan stepped into the room. There was nothing I could do to hide my pounding heart and flushed cheeks. Brychan studied us but didn't say anything.

Baran ushered me out the door, where Channing waited. I walked slowly to the shiniest sports car I had ever seen. If a man could be judged by the car he drove, it was obvious that Channing was absurdly wealthy and had a sophisticated style, driving a Lexus LFA. He was no doubt drawing attention in this little town. He was even wearing a black suit and tie. There was nothing discreet about him. He opened my door for me. I dreaded getting inside; I didn't want to spend time with him or anyone else. I only wanted Grey. I was trapped in a game that I hadn't yet mastered.

"Princess Ashling," he said with a bow.

"Please don't do that," I said.

"Do what, mi' lady?"

"That," I said. "You can't treat me like that here. The humans will think you're an alien."

He laughed and urged me inside the car, shutting the door after me. He slid in next to me and I suddenly felt trapped. I wanted to claw my way through the glass to escape into Grey's arms. I looked back at the house as Channing drove down the street. Baran was holding Grey back from chasing us down the road, and I ached to run to him. I felt like I couldn't breathe as I watched him slip away.

II

Rings

Channing talked the entire way to his house—though I wasn't sure what he talked about, nor was I sure he was even talking to me. He was just talking. I wasn't sure if it was because he liked the sound of his own voice or if he was nervous, but I couldn't focus on him. All I could think about was the look on Grey's face.

We arrived a few miles south of York Harbor in Kittery Point, where Channing was renting a home. The house was elite, fit for his status: a mix of the romantic spirit of a Mediterranean villa and clean, modern lines surrounded by a masonry wall and privacy fence. I noticed a swimming pool and endless shade gardens as well. The house was peaceful, but I didn't find it welcoming. I wanted to be where Grey and Baran were, not here.

Cara ran out of the house with her blonde hair flowing behind her. Her tiny stature was almost silly next to Channing's large presence. She wasn't quite as pretty as Cadence, but she had charm that was all her own.

"I'm so glad you've come to stay," Cara said sweetly as she jumped about like a little bird. "I've been so bored since we arrived. It will be lovely to have your company. Channing can be so dull. "

"Cara Syliva Kingery," Channing said. I could tell he was embarrassed by her playful nature. He seemed a little stuffy at times.

"Oh, calm down, you're just proving how dull you are. If you want her to like you, you need to relax," Cara said. She smiled at me.

I was baffled by how embarrassed Channing seemed. It was sort of charming in a weird way. I wasn't attracted to him, but I was finding them easier to relate to with every jab she tossed at him.

"Cara, act like a proper lady in front of the princess," he warned. "Ashling, I'm so sorry, you'll have to forgive her. She forgets proper etiquette."

"As do I," I said.

Cara giggled.

"May I take your bag, Ashling?" he asked, trying to hide his frustration. I could see that everything about his little sister drove him crazy, and she wasn't even half as wild as I was. He didn't have a clue what kind of bride he was trying to win. My behavior would certainly cause him grief.

"Sure. Thank you, Channing," I said.

Cara grabbed my hand and whisked me away into the house with Channing following behind. She reminded me a lot of Gwyn, but more innocent.

She started giving me the tour of the gigantic house. It made Baran's house look like a little shack. This house was extravagant, as was everything about the Kingerys. They had wealth, and they didn't shy away from flaunting it.

"Isn't it pretty here? I like the simplicity of this house," she said.

I almost laughed. The house wasn't simple in the least—it was simple for them maybe, but not the rest of the world. The home was exquisite, but I imagine she had never known anything but wealth. She had never seen the poverty of the Underworlds or the sadness of the humans the Dvergars killed. She didn't know real pain like I did. It made me want to protect her so her heart could always be innocent and free.

"It's lovely," I said. "What do you do for fun, Cara?"

"I like to play tennis and ski and . . ." she glanced back at Channing before rolling her eyes and continuing. "I love dance clubs." She grinned so big I had to smile.

"Cara," Channing said.

I ignored him. "I've never been to a club," I said.

"Oh, it's so freeing. I love dancing." The way she said it was so flirtatious. I thought Channing would lose his mind older-brother style, but he kept his calm.

"Cara, as your guardian on this trip, I forbid you to attend such a place," he said.

"You *forbid* me?" Cara laughed as she mocked him.

I was beginning to like her. She grabbed my arm and pulled me up the stairs, laughing, and he quickly followed behind. "He's not bad when you get past the overprotective bit," she said, as though Channing wasn't right behind us. "Our rooms are right next to each other. I can't wait to do everything with you."

I was almost certain she was going to say we were going to be life-long friends. I had to smile at her excitement—she was being far more courteous than I was; I felt like a zombie. I had just been attacked by Bloodsuckers; now, in a drastic turn of events, I was being forced to stay with people I didn't even know. If I hadn't been so exhausted, I would have been more outwardly frustrated. Instead, I just nodded and forced a smile as Channing and Cara bantered back and forth. She was pretty adorable, but I was relieved when they left me in my bedroom to get settled in. Still, it wasn't long before the giant room felt suffocating.

I paced back and forth. The room was so perfectly styled it looked like something out of a magazine. It wasn't welcoming. I was almost afraid to touch anything. I picked up one of the many blue decorative pillows off the enormous bed and studied the intricate design. I chucked it at the wall in frustration and threw myself onto the over-stuffed bed, muffling my screams into the white comforter.

I felt like a silly pawn. Every man who saw me as an asset had more power to determine my next move than I did. I wanted to be with my pack, with Grey, but because of Eamon I was trapped here with Channing. It was so frustrating. They moved me around at their whims—Father, Eamon, and even Mund in some ways. Of course, Mund was the only one who cared about my interests above his own.

A light knock came at my door. I opened it and saw Channing.

"Lady Ashling, would you care to join me in the backyard? I've started a nice bonfire," Channing said.

He actually looked rather handsome; he had removed his jacket and tie and opened up his dress shirt at the neck, exposing a little of his chest. He wore loose-fitting dark jeans and he was barefoot. It was interesting to see the more relaxed version of him; I'd only ever seen him at his most proper and refined, but even this was rather dressy.

"Yes, thank you," I said, actually grateful to get out of the confines of my room.

I followed him outside. The smell of a bonfire under the night sky was just what I needed to center my mind to Old Mother and calm my screaming heart.

"You know, you really don't have to call me Lady Ashling."

"Would you prefer Princess Ashling?" he asked politely.

"No. Just Ashling," I said. "Like I said, the people here will gossip if you behave that way. No one talks like that here."

We took our seats with a beautiful view of the ocean as the fire burned in a copper bowl and the fireflies danced around us. It was a beautiful night. It would have been romantic, but all it did was make me yearn for Grey.

"If my lady requires it," he said.

I laughed. "I do. Now stop that."

Channing got down on one knee, taking my hand in his, startling me. "Ashling, I would like to present you with this ring as a sign of my devotion to you. If you should pick me to be your champion, I would be ever yours."

Duty dictated that I allow each suitor to present a ring as a symbol of their pursuit, and when the victor beat my other suitors, I was to wear his ring. Shame filled my gut. I didn't want his ring. I didn't want his love. I wanted to be free to love Grey. I wanted to be free to choose him. Instead of having a false choice when it was Father's choice that truly mattered. Mine was just for show, until I chose Grey anyway and destroyed my family forever and any chance of unifying the packs. I sighed.

The ring he held was as showy as he was; it was a giant square canary diamond in a platinum setting with a split band filled with white diamonds. It was elegant in every definition of the word and yet entirely not me. I didn't like gaudy and showy. I was rough around the edges, outspoken, earthy, and organic. Not this.

Brychan's ring was so different, but so were the men. Brychan's ring was old and strong and a family heirloom. Channing's was rich, elegant, and extravagant. It made me wonder what Eamon's ring would bring? What symbol would he choose for our union? And how would Grey afford to buy a ring? If he couldn't present a ring, his request to court me would be terminated. Would Baran lend him the money? Or would he sell his motorcycle? I knew how much the motorcycle meant to him, but he had to offer me a ring if we had a chance to be together.

Maybe I had been setting Grey up to fail all along. He could never compete with them for status or riches. In my father's eyes, he would always be the half-breed son of a fallen house. It broke my heart to think how petty my family could be. But I would find a way to change their opinion of him. They would see what he really was and what he meant to me.

"Thank you, Channing. You honor me with your ring," I said.

"Can you imagine the power and celebrity we'd bring our people?"

He smiled at the idea.

I couldn't fathom the idea of being a celebrity among our people. I just wanted to protect them—not to be worshiped by them. Channing was different. He thrived on the attention. Having four suitors was just as stupid as having one betrothed. Why couldn't Father just let me find my match, instead of parading the sons of our allies around like fighting cocks?

"Perhaps we should try to get to know each other better before we talk of being a celebrity power couple. What do you dream of?" I asked.

"Adventure," he said and lightly kissed my hand.

"What kind of adventure?"

"I enjoy completing a challenge and finding the next one," he said.

Suddenly, Channing began to make a lot more sense to me. It was all I needed to hear. I was a challenge . . . a temporary challenge. It was all I was to him, all I would ever be to him. Once he won me, he would lose interest and move on to the next adventure. I couldn't compete with the other riches and trophies he already had. Once he had me, I would be lost among them as well.

"That's nice . . ." I said.

He didn't pursue the conversation any further; he didn't ask what I liked and I didn't offer. We sat there for hours not saying a word, watching the stars as the fire burned down to embers.

The next day, Channing drove me to the café to visit Beth and Emma. They'd found out I was in town and were hounding Baran to see me. I had claimed the humans would be suspicious if I didn't go see them, but that wasn't the real reason I wanted to go: I missed them.

We pulled up in front of the café where Ryan and Beth worked and I saw Beth and Emma in the corner booth staring, wide-eyed and openmouthed as Channing held my car door. His silver Lexus wasn't exactly your typical car in York Harbor. I missed the freedom of my own car, but I knew I wouldn't be permitted to drive until Mund returned. Channing was a stickler for etiquette. *A lady shouldn't drive.* I rolled my eyes.

"When shall I pick you up?" he asked politely as he kissed my hand.

I nervously pulled my hand away. I felt the girls' stares at my back, burning holes in my skin. "I can probably have Beth drop me off, so you don't have to wait." I held my breath waiting for him to answer.

"That doesn't sound safe. I am your guardian, after all," he said condescendingly.

"I will notify you if I have any concerns," I said.

He paused. "Do you think you'll be home for supper? I'd love to prepare a meal for you. I'm an exquisite chef," he said, flashing me an equally exquisite smile.

"Sure, that'd be nice," I said. Before he could discuss it further, I turned and opened the door to the café. As I did, a tattoo-covered man walked out the door holding Lacey's hand. She walked right by me without even looking up, like she didn't even realize I was there, but he winked at me. My skin crawled as I watched them leave. What did she see in that guy?

I darted over to the booth and sat down. Channing's presence hadn't gone unnoticed by Ryan either. He was working today. He walked over casually, leaning on the edge of the booth as he watched Channing drive away.

Ryan was cleaning off the booth next to ours. "So who's the rich guy?" he asked. The ripe stench of jealousy covered him.

I laughed. "Family friend."

Ryan used to have such a crush on me, and though he seemed to have calmed down, the jealousy was still there. I wasn't as excited to see him as I was to see Beth and Emma. Beth was such a spitfire and a true friend. I'd missed her. Beth's brown hair was tousled into a high bun, and her bright blue eyes were wildly curious.

Emma was less obvious. She hid her thoughts better than Beth.

Her black curly hair was loose and wild. I always thought she was prettiest like that. She wore a white strapless dress that contrasted so beautifully on her black skin. The two of them had stuck with me when Grey had left me for his father's lies. I loved them both deeply.

"What's Grey think of him? Does he need backup kicking this guy's ass? Because I'm so there," Ryan said.

The girls were all atwitter over Ryan's macho act, but I wasn't convinced he was much of a fighter at heart. "I don't think he needs a beating, but I could ask him for you if you like," I replied as I tried to keep from laughing.

"No thanks," Ryan said as he walked back into the kitchen.

"So what's the real story?" Beth asked, eager for the gossip.

I wanted to downplay the weirdness of the situation I found myself in, but I also thought a little bit of honesty would make their interrogation end more quickly, and frankly, it would make me feel better.

"My family in Ireland has some very old customs, and they like to set up betrothals, so their friends' sons came to see if we had a spark."

"Oh my god, that's so old!" Emma gasped. "What about Grey? What does he think?"

"A betrothal!" Beth spat the word out. "That's disgusting!"

There wasn't anything they could say that I didn't already think myself. I pretended to look at the menu. "It'll all work out; it's just a technicality."

"Hey," Emma interrupted. "You said *sons*, as in plural. How many sons are we talking?"

"Three."

"Three?" They both shouted and then whispered, "Three?"

"Channing, Eamon, and Brychan," I replied.

Ryan walked back to our table with milkshakes and a mischievous grin on his face. "What do you think you're up to?" Beth demanded.

"You'll see," he said.

He pushed in next to Beth and Emma as the rumble of Grey's motorcycle clattered the old windows of the café. My heart skipped a beat, and I turned around to see him walking into the diner. His faded black jeans were ripped and frayed. With every sexy step he took toward me, his biker boots thumped on the floor, setting my heart on fire. He slid in next to me, wrapping his arm around my shoulders as he planted a kiss on my cheek and I melted into him.

"So did you see the loser in the Lexus LFA?" Ryan asked.

Grey nodded. "I've seen him."

"What are we gonna do about him? Should we kick his ass?" Ryan asked, eager to prove his loyalty to Grey and his masculinity to us.

"Come on, guys, Channing's harmless," I said.

"Channing?" Ryan repeated. "Like that movie star?"

"Are they all that hot?" Emma asked. I kicked her under the table and she glared at me.

Ryan didn't miss a thing. "All?"

"Yeah, two other guys," Grey said. "But it's okay, because they won't steal Ashling from me."

His confidence nearly broke my heart. I'd already kissed Brychan. He just didn't know it yet. I wasn't worthy of his trust. I linked my fingers with his, absorbing his warmth. I had to tell him. Just not yet. I wasn't ready.

"Well, if you change your mind, the guys and I got your back," Ryan said as he wandered back to work.

Lunch was fantastic after that. We talked like we always did, and my suitors didn't come up again. I hated having a double life, but they didn't seem to notice much. Only Grey knew the truth about why Channing, Brychan, and Eamon were here and the real threat they posed.

Grey had his arm around my shoulders as we walked out of the café laughing, but we all stopped dead in our tracks at the sight of Eamon leaning against a black Bentley. It was the pinnacle of high-end British cars and a priceless classic. It was a car that Mund would drool over. How long had Eamon been waiting outside watching us? He was just as creepy as his brother. I could feel Grey's rage at the intrusion, and it wasn't that different from mine.

"Lady Ashling, may I have a word?" Eamon asked with his thick accent.

I walked quietly over to his car, leaving my friends to gawk. "Please just call me Ashling here," I replied. "You can't address me like that."

"I will be taking you to dinner tonight," he said.

I bristled. "I'm sorry Eamon, I already have plans," I said.

He acted like he owned me, like I was his property to command. I bit into my cheek to stop myself from lashing out at him. He was so calm—even when Adomnan had nearly killed him, he remained eerily calm. For a moment, a flicker of anger flashed across his face at my dismissal of his invitation . . . or his demand, more accurately. But the emotion was gone just as quickly as it had come.

"Tomorrow then," he said. Without another word, he got in his car and drove away, leaving me staring after him.

He made me feel small and submissive. I didn't like it.

My friends quickly surrounded me, and Grey leaned his head into mine. He knew how horrible Eamon made me feel, because he could feel my emotions. I wondered how much he had felt of my feelings about Brychan. Could he tell that I was attracted to him? By his jealousy, I was sure he could, but did he understand the guilt that went with it?

Eamon had tried to save me at Dvergar Castle, and now he acted like he owned me, like he had the right to tell me what to do. Just because he intimidated me didn't mean he could rule over me as though I was nothing but a little girl. I just had to endure it with as much grace as I could muster. Only time could free me from Eamon's unwanted attention.

"So which of the jerks was that?" Emma asked.

"Eamon," Grey answered for me.

"He's a piece of work, isn't he?" Beth said.

I nodded.

"You want a ride?" Grey asked.

"Please," I said and followed him to his motorcycle. I barely waved at my friends. I was too upset by the way Eamon had treated me.

Grey took the long scenic route by the beach to Channing's. With my arms wrapped tightly around him, I felt safe. I nestled my face into his neck, kissing him. As we got closer, he slowed the bike even more, drawing out our time together. By the time we were in front of Channing's house, the bike was crawling to a stop.

"Are you okay?" he asked.

"Just a little shaken up; it's nothing," I said, seeing Channing watching us from the window. Grey stopped the bike, putting the kickstand down.

"Don't leave," I said. I bit my lip and wanted to say so much more, but I didn't.

"I know, love," he said, kissing my forehead.

Grey took my hand, walking me all the way to the door. I didn't know what his plan was, whether he wanted to kiss me in front of Channing or something more offensive, but I didn't argue.

The door swung open. "Channing." Grey nodded.

"Grey. What can I do for you?" Channing's tone was suave yet neutral, but his posture was territorial. I still wasn't sure it was a good idea to have this many male wolves in such a small territory. They weren't of the same pack or alliances—this was a ticking time bomb of testosterone.

"I thought you should know, as Ashling's temporary guardian that Eamon is forceful and controlling, and I think he's dangerous. He tracked Ashling to the café and demanded she have dinner with him," Grey said. I knew he didn't want Channing anywhere near me, but he had to choose his enemies wisely. "I don't think that's appropriate behavior as a suitor, and thought you should be aware."

Cara gasped from around Channing's back. "Is this true?" she asked. Her protective nature came out.

"Yes," I said. "He demanded I have dinner with him tonight."

"How dare he speak to you in such a manner," Cara said, shaking her head. "Did you accept his demands?"

"No. I declined because I have plans with Channing tonight. So he claimed tomorrow night instead," I replied.

"Well, he will find out very quickly that you have a chaperone in his presence. If you don't mind me accompanying you?" she quickly added.

Grey's posture relaxed at Cara's request and Channing nodded in agreement. "I agree with Cara; I don't think you'll should be alone with him. After what he and his brothers did to you, it wouldn't be safe. What do you think, Ashling?"

It was nice to be asked what I wanted for a change, though I wasn't actually sure I got a vote. But I desperately did want her with me. "I'd appreciate if you came with me, Cara. I'd feel safer," I said.

"Grey, thank you for informing me of this situation. Not only as Ashling's guardian, but as a fellow suitor, I would never allow any harm to come to her, and I believe you wouldn't either."

Grey nodded.

"Bye, Grey," I said.

"Sleep sweetly tonight," he said.

He watched me enter the house and the door close between us. I knew he stood there after the door closed. I could feel his warmth and his resistance to leaving me behind, but eventually he did just that. I heard the rumble of his motorcycle as he drove away. My stomach knotted.

"Did he hurt you?" Cara asked.

"No," I said. "Not physically. He just intimidates me."

"What a son of a jackal," she muttered. "How dare he treat you like that?"

"Cara, calm down, I will neutralize the situation," Channing said. He was so suave and calm it was actually a little annoying.

Cara continued to ask me how I felt and if I was well. She became very worried about me. It was actually very sweet, but it made me miss Mother and Tegan. I missed a lot of things, actually.

"Ashling, I'm sorry that your father allowed Eamon to be a suitor. I don't understand his purpose in doing so, but I promise to keep you safe from him while you are here in my care," Channing said.

"Thank you, Channing," I replied. "I think I will need you all by my side." I sighed and headed toward my room. At the top of the stairs, I turned back to see Channing still watching me. "What time shall I help with dinner?"

"Dinner will be served to you, Princess Ashling, in the backyard at seven-thirty."

I spent the rest of the afternoon hiding in my room until it was time for dinner. I quickly changed into a simple summer dress and went down to the backyard. The sun had begun to set and the sky was radiant. Light classical music filled the night air and mingled with the ocean waves.

Channing had set up dinner by candlelight, but he was nowhere to be seen. I could see the amount of preparation that went into the beautiful feast—cooked hens, herbed potatoes, roasted asparagus, even pot roast. It was quite the spread.

"May I have this dance?" Channing asked from behind me.

I jumped—I hadn't heard him coming. He was dressed in a black tuxedo with a black bow tie. He had beautiful classical music lightly playing. I let him take my hands as he formally spun me around the yard. He was a smooth dancer. He really was more than handsome—he was almost pretty to look at. He didn't do anything for me, but I could admit that he was good looking.

I didn't see Cara, but I knew she was around and chaperoning even her brother. The idea made me giggle. The two of them were a little like oil and water.

"You didn't have to do all of this for me," I said. "But I appreciate it nonetheless."

"Oh, but I did, Lady Ashling. If you are to be my lady, you must know how you will be treated and honored every day," he said. He leaned forward and dipped me, flashing me his perfectly straight and white smile.

I appreciated all he had done—the elaborate dinner, the tuxedo, the dance, the gorgeous and extravagant canary diamond—but I still felt it to be a show. I was flattered that he would go to all the trouble, but if I was honest with myself, I wasn't attracted to him, no matter how handsome he was. There wasn't a spark; no part of me yearned for him. And I still didn't feel like he cared about me in an honest way, either—it was easy to put on a tuxedo and treat a girl to a fabulous dinner for one night. But I knew he had a great deal to gain beyond just my heart—in his own words, we could be the celebrities among our people. That was really where Channing's heart was. His heart was always with acquiring the next big thing—in this case, he wanted to acquire me.

It just felt like another trap, another cage. I sighed as we sat down to enjoy the decadent meal and each other's company. I decided to give him the opportunity to tell me more about himself. After all, what he had done for me this evening, regardless of the motive, was generous and lovely. And he was being far more respectful of me than Eamon had been.

"What's your house like in Switzerland?" I asked.

"I grew up in the Vufflens Castle, one of the privately owned medieval castles, but it was rebuilt due to fires in 1530. My family has kept it in pristine condition all these years. Of course, my father hasn't left out a single modern convenience, so the house is quite immaculate and modern despite its long lineage. You would be quite comfortable there."

"What do you do for fun, Channing?" I asked.

"I enjoy skiing in Verbier, spelunking, driving fast cars, and gambling."

He lived a life of privilege; there was no doubt of that. His family's wealth showed through in every story he told. I knew he wasn't trying to be showy; it was just who he was. His confidence was only matched by his courtesy.

Could two people have less in common than Channing and me? He loved wearing suits and driving shiny new sports cars and living in luxury. I wanted nothing more than to be barefoot with the wind in my face.

I couldn't blame him for pursuing me. I suppose I was the greatest trophy of all, a princess and the one who would lead, but could he really be so blind? We so clearly didn't belong together.

After we had finished dessert, he walked me back into the house to my room. "Thank you, Ashling, for spending time with me," he said as he lightly kissed the top of my hand. Always a gentleman.

"My pleasure," I said, ducking into my room.

I tried to sleep, but rest wouldn't come. My mind kept reeling, knowing that tomorrow I belonged to Eamon. I was thankful Grey had told Channing and Cara—I likely wouldn't have asked for their help. He knew me almost as well as I knew myself, and he loved me. It was pure, but not simple. Our love was never simple.

12

Burning Hate

The sun began to rise, filling my room with brilliant light. I hadn't slept. I was exhausted but too nervous to close my eyes. My stomach was upset—something that always happened when I got nervous. If I was lucky, I was coming down with malaria, and I wouldn't be obligated to join Eamon for dinner. But if my life was any indication of how lucky I was, that would definitely not happen. I would be okay—right now, I was only obligated to see him for one date. I could survive one date; it was nothing compared to what I had lived through with Adomnan.

A light knock came to my door, and Cara slipped inside the room.

"I brought you a little ginger tea to settle your stomach."

I rubbed my tired eyes. "How did you know?"

"I called Tegan and told her what was going on, and she suggested that you might need a little support with Eamon's intrusive behavior. And I love ginger tea when I'm feeling upset." Cara smiled.

She set the steaming cup of tea on my bedside table. "Rest now. I'll bring you breakfast later on. And don't worry, I'll be with you tonight."

Cara did just that. She came and checked on me throughout the day, bringing me food and beverages, but my nausea only grew worse as the day went on. I was nervous and a little scared for what the evening would bring. I didn't trust Eamon.

Only an hour was left before Eamon would arrive. I forced myself to get up, and I dressed in a conservative dress and cardigan—nothing fancy or too pretty.

Finally, I heard a honk from the street and I knew it was Eamon. I wondered if it was his arrogance or his not wanting to face Channing that kept him from ringing the doorbell. I walked into the foyer, where Channing and Cara stood. Channing's hands were balled up in fists as Eamon honked again.

"We should go," I mumbled.

"No, we shall not," Cara said. "You are a princess, and he will come to the door and ask Channing for permission to escort you out tonight. Etiquette declares he must ask your guardian for permission."

Cara brought me into the sitting room just off the foyer as we waited. We had a good view of the front door but were out of sight. A third honk screamed out into the night, followed by two quick honks. Finally, we heard his car door slam shut as he stormed toward the house. Before he could start pounding on the door, Channing swung it open, causing Eamon to lose his footing and trip forward slightly before he righted himself.

Rage filled his already-angry face. "Has she been made aware of my presence?" he asked rudely.

Channing stood his ground calmly. "A proper suitor must ask permission from a lady's guardian," Channing replied. I could hear a tiny bit of his enjoyment in his voice. He liked watching Eamon squirm.

Eamon cleared his throat. "Lord Channing, I, King Eamon of the Dvergar, request your permission to take Princess Ashling out to dinner this evening." I could see by the twitch on his face that he didn't like asking Channing for permission, but he loved using his title. The way he said "king" made my skin crawl.

"That would be proper," Channing replied coolly. "Ashling, would you mind joining us in the foyer?" His voice warmed as he said my name.

I came forward and stood behind Channing. "Eamon would like to take you to dinner . . ."

"You kept me waiting," Eamon interrupted. He seemed agitated.

"You will not speak to the princess in such a way," Channing threatened, stepping into Eamon's gaze.

Eamon's evil smile consumed his face. "As you command," he replied. "Princess Ashling, are you ready for dinner?" he asked, forcing his voice to be more accommodating.

I nodded, unsure of myself.

As I stepped forward, Channing said, "Cara, are you ready to chaperone?"

Cara stepped out and linked her arm with mine. Eamon's face contorted as the words nearly dripped from his lips: "How dare you interfere with my right to her?"

"As Ashling's guardian, I have secured Lady Cara as Ashling's chaperone on every encounter you have with her. To be proper. Don't you agree?" He wasn't asking Eamon a question—he was rubbing it in. As far as I was concerned, Eamon deserved whatever torment he got.

Cara and I followed Eamon silently to the car where he held the front passenger door open for me, but I followed Cara's lead as she held the back door and we both slid into the backseat. Eamon slammed the passenger door shut as he stormed around the car to the driver's side. He was furious, but so was I. He pretended to care about my well-being when his brother was my tormentor, but now, he was just as dominating. He clearly had just wanted me for himself the whole time.

When he put the car into drive, panic seeped through me. The car felt like a prison. I suddenly felt nauseated again as scenes from my first days with Eamon flashed through my mind. Cara reached over and held my hand.

We arrived at the beach and he held the door for us, but after I got out, he turned away as though Cara wasn't still in the car. He offered me his arm, but I refused to take it, and instead I walked next to him, Cara at my other side. I saw two waiters lingering near the dock as we started walking down it.

"It has been so long since I've seen your lovely face," he said.

I couldn't help but wonder if he was bipolar. He looked at me as though it was the first time he was actually seeing me. Like he did in Canada last winter.

"I really need you," he said.

"For what?" I asked.

"I want to take you to the Bloodrealms and win you . . . your hand," he said.

I just stared at him, dumbfounded. Was he really that crazy? Did he really think I'd ever go with him willingly?

At the end of the dock was a gazebo with a table set for two. Cara took a seat on the built-in benches a few feet away and pulled out a book to read. Eamon held out my chair and I took my seat. He sat across from me, smiling.

It was an icky feeling having him study me. He always seemed to see more of me than most people did . . . like he could see inside my mind. He looked at me with satisfaction, like he'd won some prize, but there was a hint of relief too.

He snapped his fingers and the waiters came with serving trays. They quickly opened the lids and presented the course to him. Eamon studied the raw veal, nodding in satisfaction. The smell made my stomach recoil.

"Eat," he said.

I lightly picked at the bloody meat with my fork as he talked . . . never once asking me a question.

"I am restoring Dvergar Castle. When you see it next, you will look in awe at its splendor," he said.

"That's nice . . ." I replied. The thought of returning to his castle made me actually consider retching right on my plate, but I didn't think he'd even notice.

"You'll also be pleased that I set the human captives free."

"That does please me. Humans are meant to be protected, not consumed," I said. Did he want a medal for doing something that wasn't completely evil and psychopathic?

"It was difficult to convince much of my pack that animal livestock is worth eating. I've only had to kill two of my pack for breaking my laws. I am a fair king. Eye for an eye."

I couldn't help but look over my shoulder at Cara. She looked just as disturbed as I felt. Listening to Eamon talk was baffling, to say the least he sounded just like my father.

Finally, he was done eating, and the waiters took my untouched plate away with his clean one. My stomach screamed from hunger and disgust. How could he just sit there and not even notice I was feeling sick? That I was scared in his presence? Was he that blind? Every time I looked at him, I saw Adomnan. And Eamon was more courteous to me when I was his brother's captive than now when he was my suitor.

He came around the table and stood above me, trapping me between the chair and his body. Even his body language was possessive. He thrust a ring in my face. The band was two black wolf paws with golden claws that clutched a black diamond. As I looked at the ring in his outstretched hand, a shiver ran over my spine. Even the design of the ring made it clear that he planned to own me. Not love me or care for me or even protect me, but to simply possess me.

I forced myself to reach out my shaking hand, and he dropped the ring in my hand. "Thank you for your offer," I said. It was all I could force myself to say. I hated myself for fearing him, but I couldn't help it. I was afraid of Eamon for all that had been done to me. I had the feeling that his relaxed behavior in marriage would look more like

Adomnan's than Channing's.

He took his seat once again and continued talking at me, as though he hadn't just given me his ring. A ring that was supposed to be a sacred symbol of his devotion to me was instead a leash and collar.

"After the ordeal with my brother—" He paused, I was sure for dramatic effect. "Well, I am still ashamed of his actions, taking you and hurting you as he did. I only regret I couldn't protect you from him."

He acted as though he had no part in stalking me, harassing me, kidnapping me, and holding me hostage, as though he was innocent and above guilt. Bile filled my throat, and my raw memories flooded me.

"I recall you and Bento also taking me against my will. It wasn't just Adomnan," I said. "You stalked me, kidnapped me, held me hostage, and you were going to allow Adomnan to rape me," I said. "You are present in almost every one of my most awful memories. Luckily, I was able to protect myself against Adomnan when you failed to do so."

His expression grew cold.

"I wasn't the king; I was a soldier. You will not accuse me of Adomnan's sins. I am a king now, and you will see what kind of king I can be." Anger dripped from his words, but he knew nothing of true hate. He expected me to bow to his glory, but I wouldn't answer to this little king. Watching him was like watching a toddler throw a temper tantrum.

Rage fueled my strength. I wasn't going to be scared of him anymore. I wasn't a little girl he could just intimidate. I slid my chair back and stood before him.

"A true king would not have to announce he is king, and you are not my king and I will not be spoken to in such a manner," I replied, my voice remarkably firm and unwavering. As he stared at me, I saw that he was shaking with rage. Still, I didn't stop. "I was there, Eamon. You can lie to everyone else, but I remember it all more clearly than you ever will. I still live it every moment of every day. And you are just as guilty as he is." Before he could say another word, I stood, grabbed Cara by the hand, and began walking down the dock onto the shore.

In a second, he was between us, grabbing my wrist. My skin burned at his touch; I almost screamed out at the pain, but I bit my tongue and held in my terror. The darkness in his eyes was like venom.

"You can't leave," he said indignantly. "You will be mine."

"Unhand her!" Cara screamed.

I fought back against my tormentor with all my strength, shoving him backward. He lost his footing on the small dock and fell into the shallow water.

"You will never touch me again," I said, looking down on him.

Cara and I turned back to shore, and I saw Grey, Baran, Brychan, Channing, and Odin running up the beach toward us. I was relieved to see my makeshift pack. We walked the rest of the way to them on shore. Grey ran to me.

"Are you okay?" he asked. I knew he had felt the pain on my wrist.

I hid my wrist from the others. "I actually enjoyed that," I said, looking back at a very wet and angry Eamon as he climbed out of the ocean.

Baran wrapped his arms around my shoulders and I leaned into him, absorbing his strength. Despite my ability to stand up for myself, I had been terrified. It was a mistake to turn my back on Eamon, but I didn't see any other choice than to create an enemy. I deserved to be treated like a person, not a possession.

"I didn't know you were coming," I whispered to Baran.

"There was no way Channing was going to leave either of you unprotected with such a monster," Baran said. He nodded to Channing and the others. "Sorry we were so late."

"Thank you," I said to all of them. "I don't know what would have happened to us if you hadn't all come."

Grey smiled. "I think you would have kicked his ass."

I laughed as we approached Channing's Lexus. Baran let go of me and went to shake hands with Brychan and Channing. I lightly rubbed my fingertips on Grey's as I walked by. The small, unseen touch helped calm me. Grey hugged me and whispered in my ear, "I felt your pain. It kills me that I wasn't here to help you," he said.

"You're here now," I said, holding him tighter. I knew I should let go, but I couldn't. I needed his touch. The others were distracted, so I kissed his earlobe and his breath gusted out, tickling my skin. My skin flushed with excitement, but Grey pulled away.

"Not here," he whispered. I knew he was right; I was being reckless, but it didn't make it any easier to keep my hands off him.

"Ashling, I was going to ask you to share tomorrow evening with me," Brychan said. "But I understand if you'd like to postpone after what you suffered tonight."

"Thank you, Brychan. That would be nice," I said. "I accept."

"So I will pick you up then?"

"Sure," I said as I got into Channing's car. I felt guilty spending time with Brychan. I knew it hurt Grey to see me with him. Besides, it was also selfish of me to be taking Brychan's attentions when he deserved a woman who loved him uncontrollably, like I loved Grey. I felt Grey's jealousy as we pulled away.

Back in my room at Channing's house, I started the shower and took off my cardigan. When I caught my reflection in the mirror, I gasped. My skin looked as though it had been burned and blistered by fire or chemicals where Eamon's hands had been. It didn't make sense. All I could remember was the pain when he grabbed me, but I'd thought it was just him squeezing too hard.

I couldn't show Channing; he'd immediately tell my father, who would likely make me return to the Rock—even farther away from Grey. Though I could have shifted to heal the wounds, I would have to endure them until tomorrow, when I could sneak away to have Baran look at them. He would know what to do.

I set Eamon's claw ring on the dresser. I loathed the sight of it. It sat next to Channing's canary diamond ring and Brychan's sapphire ring. I had rings from three suitors. Only one remained, the most important one. Grey had to give me a ring before they entered the Bloodrealms, or I would have to betray my family to be with him.

I hated the idea of dividing my family in two, forcing them all to choose a side. It was happening already; Mund, Tegan, Quinn, Gwyn, Baran, Mother, and even Felan seemed to have chosen me—maybe not my choice in Grey, but they had all chosen me. And my pack was growing. There was still hope.

The next morning, I awoke to my wrist burning with pain like it was breaking. I wanted to scream. The pain was so much more intense suddenly.

I called Baran and asked him to pick me up. I chose a sweatshirt to cover my arms, so Channing and Cara wouldn't see the burns in the shape of Eamon's hand.

I tried to remember if Eamon ever touched me when I was a captive, but I couldn't think of whether he had. I remembered so many details in vivid slow motion, and yet I couldn't recall with any certainty.

The familiar rumble of Baran's Harley motorcycle made me smile. I ran down the stairs to the front door past Cara.

"I'll see you later," I said.

"Enjoy the sunshine!" Cara said. I saw her notice my sweatshirt, but she didn't say anything, and I slipped out the door into the warmth of summer and ran down the sidewalk to Baran, to my salvation.

"Thank you," I said as I jumped on his bike.

"What was so important you needed me first thing in the morning?" he grumbled.

"I just missed you." I smiled and then whispered in his ear, "Not here."

He nodded to Cara and Channing, who stood in the doorway, and we drove away as I waved. We stopped a few miles down the beach at a little coffee shop. We wandered down the beach with our drinks until we were far out of earshot and sight of anyone.

"What's going on, Ashling?" Baran asked.

I looked around again and showed him my wrist. The flesh was blistered and red.

"Bloody hell," he spat. He gently turned my wrist, looking at the blistered skin in the perfect shape of fingers wrapping around my wrist. "Is he a Barghest?"

I quickly covered my arm. "A what?"

"Come on," Baran said, turning toward the parking lot. As soon as I sat on his bike, he raced toward his house. Baran handled every turn with ease and precision as I clung to his back. This was the first time I'd been on a motorcycle with him since he brought me to Maine. The memories of our first meeting flooded back to me; he raced across the Irish countryside to protect me. I remembered thinking he was going to kill me, but he turned out to be more of a father to me than my own father.

Baran drove up onto the grass in front of his house. He jumped off and I followed him inside. I looked around for Grey, but the house was empty.

"Where are Grey and Odin?" I asked.

"They ran to the store for me," he muttered as he wandered around his office, muttering to himself as he dug in the stacks until he yanked a box out from the bottom. He pulled a hide-covered book from the box and carefully set it on the desk.

I took several steps closer to the book, but something about it made the hair on my neck stand on end. The black hide almost looked wet. Baran flipped the book open, searching for something. He stopped and stared at an image, drawn with pen and ink on the parchment, of a beastly looking wolf terrorizing a small child. Across from the drawing was a handwritten list of names.

"What is that?" I asked.

"That is a Barghest," he said, almost hissing the words. "They are werewolves much like you or me in appearance, but they feed on werewolf children. They consume the children, eating their hearts. The only way to tell them from a typical werewolf is when they touch our flesh, it burns instantly."

"But how?" I asked.

"A Barghest excretes a toxic chemical from its skin. It is a byproduct of their cannibalistic diet. If they touch one of us, the toxins will burn our skin," he said.

Baran studied my burns again. "Eamon is evil."

Did Eamon realize when he grabbed my arm that my skin would burn at his touch, or did he act in haste? Was he scared that we knew what he was? Or was it all part of his plan to immobilize me with fear?

"How do we stop him?" I asked.

"We have to kill him," Baran said.

He said it so matter-of-factly. Was death the only option? Was Eamon truly evil or just rude and misguided? Did he deserve to die?

"You better shift so you can heal those wounds," Baran insisted.

I went up to my old room. I knew Grey wasn't there, but the room smelled of him. I closed my eyes, breathing in his scent as I shifted into a red wolf. The constant ache in my wrist went away almost immediately as my body healed itself. I loved being in my wolf skin. I could always feel Grey so much more clearly as a wolf. He was filled with jealousy and anger, but I didn't know why.

I returned downstairs in my human form. I found Baran in the kitchen staring at the book. "Are you okay?" I asked.

He looked up, startled. "Yeah. I was just wondering what other evil lurked in the shadows, waiting to consume us."

"Well that's not very optimistic," Grey said as he walked in.

I jumped into his arms, crushing him as I kissed him from his ear to his nose. I breathed him deep into my lungs. Bathing in his scent.

"I missed you," he said.

"Where have you been?" I asked.

He looked at Baran for a moment before answering. "Nowhere. Just hanging at the shop," he said. It wasn't where Baran had said he was. Grey was keeping something from me.

"Where's Brychan?" I asked.

He looked so hurt by my question, and I could feel jealousy churning inside of him. I didn't mean to hurt him; I just didn't understand what secrets they kept from me.

"He went to the apartment he's renting," Grey said. "What happened to you last night? I felt the pain on your wrist—I want to kill him for hurting you."

"I'm okay—I shifted and everything healed." I studied him and saw dried blood on his wrist. Now the pain that woke me up made sense; I'd thought the burn was getting worse, but I was feeling his pain. He must have broken his arm? His advanced healing as a human was remarkable, but the dried blood didn't keep his secrets. I must have been so consumed by the pain in my wrists that I couldn't tell it was his pain with mine.

"You've just been hanging out at the shop?" I said, pulling away to get a better look at him. "I suppose you beat yourself up, then?"

Grey looked down at his disheveled appearance. "I didn't even realize I was hurt," he said with a smirk.

"What are you two up to?" I asked, staring them both down with my most disapproving look.

Grey smiled. "Baran and Odin are teaching me to bare-knuckle box, so when I go into the Bloodrealms to fight, I'll win."

I shuddered to even think about the danger that lay ahead for him, Brychan, and Channing. The Bloodrealms were supposed to be a dangerous place. Just thinking of them made me uneasy. Odin walked into the kitchen with blood dripping from gashes on his face and neck. Baran took one look at him and burst into laughter.

Odin sulked. "I think he's ready."

"Grey, you should have left him a shred of confidence when you were done with him," Baran said.

"I did," Grey said. "I let him keep his life."

"Then let's finish this," Odin threatened.

Grey growled and the two faced off again. I stepped between them. "Fighting is for the ring. Not here. We have more important things to deal with." I said. "Eamon is a Barghest."

Grey stared at me like I was crazy.

"A Barghest is a werewolf that feeds on werewolf children. When they consume the heart of the child, there is a chemical reaction in the Barghest that gives them the ability to see into other people's souls, but the chemical seeps from the pores in their skin, making them toxic to us. The chemical reaction is so strong that the offspring of a Barghest can have the same power and skin," Baran said.

Eamon was a creature from a nightmare. I remembered how he looked at me and made me feel like he could see my soul. I knew there was something wrong with him.

"Dirty creatures," Odin said. "I thought we killed them; how did we miss one?"

"Eamon would have been a child then," Baran said. "He would have been easily overlooked."

"You're telling me that Eamon eats children?" Grey said, shaking his head. "That's disgusting and evil." Grey went to open the book again, and Baran shoved it out of his reach.

"Don't touch it," Baran said. "Even after thousands of years, the skin is still toxic."

"That is the hide of a Barghest?" I gasped. The book was covered in the skin of a creature that was a human, a werewolf, and a Barghest.

"One of three books like it in the world," Baran said. "The only way to prove a myth is by keeping a piece of it intact so you can always protect the future, because Barghests still exist." He lightly ran his fingers over the flesh and held his fingers up for inspection. The skin on the tips of his fingers was burning away in front of our eyes.

"In death their evil still leaks out into our world," Odin said. "We should have known Eamon was a Barghest. His grandfather Uaid was a Barghest, and so was his father Crob. It's no wonder he followed in the family practice."

"This is a list of every known Barghest in the world. The ones with dates after their names are the ones that have perished," Baran said.

I looked at the list and saw both Uaid and Crob's names and dates they died. Looking at all those names made me nauseated. It meant each one of those names had murdered at least one child, if not many, many more. It was unthinkably cruel to hurt a child. Only three of more than fifty names didn't have a date. Only three known Barghests still lived, but nowhere on the list was Eamon's name. After so many centuries, no one had realized his secret.

Baran called Channing, Cara, and Brychan over to his house to explain what we had learned and to warn them of how dangerous Eamon was. There was a long silence before someone finally spoke.

"Why didn't you tell me you were hurt?" Channing asked. He was clearly angry that I hadn't told him, my guardian, and instead ran to Baran.

I shrugged. "I didn't know if I could trust you not to tell my father . . ."

"I probably would have," Channing admitted.

"Channing, I expect you to discuss everything with me prior to taking any matters to my father," I said. "This isn't a game to earn his favor; this is my life." He nodded.

"We have to decide how we are going to protect Ashling," Baran said.

"Until Prince Redmund returns, I think it would be best if all guests came to our home to see Ashling and that she doesn't leave the premises," Channing said.

"You're just trying to monopolize her time," Brychan accused.

"Maybe I am." Channing smiled.

"Stop this," I said, rolling my eyes. "I have a date tonight with Brychan, and I plan to attend it outside of the house, Channing. Any other questions about my whereabouts can be directed to me."

Brychan smiled and Channing looked annoyed. Despite how nice Channing was, I knew he had a very traditional view of a woman's place. If he married me, I would be a constant irritation to him. That almost made me laugh.

"Ashling," Grey said. "Would you be available tomorrow?"

"Absolutely." I smiled.

"Everyone has to keep guard; we don't know what Eamon is planning. We have to protect Ashling. If you see him, don't let him touch you," Baran said.

They all nodded agreement, though the tension between them was irritating. They weren't children, but they behaved like it. The only one of my suitors who didn't behave like a teenager was Grey, and he was the only actual teenager. The others were grown men. It was infuriating.

"Would you care to start our date now?" Brychan asked.

"Sure," I said. I wanted to say no, but I was required to go on one date with him. I might as well get it over with. I just hoped he wouldn't try to kiss me again. "See you all later," I said, my eyes lingering on Grey's for a moment longer than the rest.

Grey nodded, but the sadness in his eyes broke my heart. I still owed him the truth, but every time I looked in his beautiful eyes, I couldn't imagine telling him what I had done.

13

Exposed

Brychan led me out to his military-style Humvee. I wasn't at all surprised by it. It was scratched and dented and even had bulletholes on
the side. Brychan lived an interesting life filled with danger, and he
liked it like that.

He helped me up into the doorless beast, letting his hand linger on
mine. I glanced down at him as he still held my hand and he smiled.
He walked around to his side and leaped up. I was suddenly nervous
about what his plans for the night were.

"Where are we going?" I asked.

"It's a surprise," he said.

"I hate surprises."

He laughed. "Well then it's an adventure. I know you like those."

He drove down the coast toward the carnival; it was the site of a
very early date with Grey when we first got to know each other. It was
a fond memory. It seemed like betrayal to be here now with Brychan.
It seemed like betrayal to be anywhere but with Grey.

"The carnival?" I asked.

Brychan grabbed me around the waist, lifted me out of the Humvee, and set me down in the sand. "Oh, don't look so skeptical," he said. "Live a little."

I laughed and followed him into the sea of people. It was midafternoon and the sun was beating down on us as we weaved our way into the carnival. He stopped at a game with moving targets and winked at me as he paid the carney.

"You're beautiful, you know," he said. "Looking into those golden eyes of yours is like looking into a fairy tale. I could get lost in them."

Brychan aimed the plastic rifle and proceeded to hit every target that flipped up or whizzed by. He was remarkably fast and terrifyingly accurate. Even if I didn't know there was such a thing as werewolves, I would have suspected he was one.

"Congratulations," the carney said in the dullest tone I'd ever heard. He pointed at a row of stuffed animals. "Any of those."

Brychan grabbed a fluffy wolf stuffed animal and handed it to me. "For you, mi' lady," he said.

"Thank you," I said.

We wandered around the carnival and played games. It didn't matter what game I picked; Brychan always won. I knew he was trying to show his strength as a mate in a playful way. However charming he might be on occasion, his assertion of testosterone in even the most mundane games wasn't impressive to me.

"Brychan, what do you do for fun? I mean other than fighting." I said.

He chuckled. "I haven't impressed you yet?"

I rolled my eyes.

"Well, I suppose I spend a lot of my time dealing with political matters for my family, and I chose to personally protect the humans in our lands. So I do endanger myself a lot, but typically it's for a good reason." He smiled mischievously. "But sometimes I just fight for fun."

"But who are you, Brychan? We barely know each other," I said.

He stopped walking and the smile left his face. "That's true," he said.

"You want me to choose you as my champion, but how can I do that when I know nothing about you?

He nodded thoughtfully. "Well, let me tell you a bit more. I've made a lot of mistakes in my life, chiefly letting you walk out of it, but if I want any chance of winning you now, this is my only shot." He took a deep breath and continued. "I don't much care for reading like you do, nor can I draw to save my life, but what I am good at is protecting the ones I love. And when I'm not doing that, I'm . . . well, this is going to sound strange, but I'm watching people."

"That does sound strange."

"Not in a creepy way, but I enjoy seeing the parts of them that they haven't noticed yet. Every human is a puzzle," he said. "See that woman over there? Everything about her is perfect, meticulous even, except there is a stain on her shirt. She's hiding something and it's disrupting her balance in life. And that man standing by the Ferris wheel? He's in love with the girl selling milkshakes over there, but she doesn't know it."

"And what do you see when you look at me?" I asked.

"That's the thing, Ashling. I don't know. I see you drawing and reading. I know you're a good dancer, and I know you're a rebel, but you're far more guarded than most. I think you're hiding something, too."

I blushed. "Oh. I'm not that interesting," I said. I laughed nervously.

"So you are hiding something." Brychan smiled. "I will just have to figure it out."

"I'd rather you didn't," I said.

"Are you hungry?"

"Definitely," I said, thankful for the distraction. "Corndogs?"

"Corn what?" he said.

"Have you never been to a carnival?" I asked.

"I have; I've just never eaten corn-wrapped dog."

I laughed so hard I thought my side would split. "Brychan, it isn't dog meat. Heck, I don't think it is meat at all. Just come here."

I walked up to the stand and ordered two corndogs with ketchup and mustard. I handed one to Brychan and kept one for myself. He looked at me skeptically as he bit into the breaded hotdog. At first I thought he was going to spit it out, but he gagged it down. I couldn't stop laughing watching him. He looked utterly disgusted. Sometimes I forgot he was centuries older than me.

"This isn't funny, nor is this food," he complained.

"Oh, come on, live a little," I mocked. I grabbed his hand and dragged him over to the cotton candy and bought a bag of the pink, sugary fluff. I'd always wanted to try it.

I put a pinch in my mouth and felt it melting and crystallizing, its sweetness disintegrating and exploding at the same time. It was delightful. I pinched off a piece for Brychan, who wrinkled his nose and shook his head, but I held it out until he finally opened his mouth and licked it off my finger in a seductive way as he ate the sweet treat.

I looked away awkwardly and saw Lacey stalking toward me like a lioness on the prowl. She was just as pretty as always. She wore a pink tank top, white shorts, and a pink ruffled bikini underneath with sparkly sandals. She carried a white beach dress draped over her purse, but despite all the pink, I knew all too well the fury hidden in that cute package.

"Cheating on Grey already?" Lacey sneered.

I had to bite my tongue to stop myself from saying something vicious. I had to try to see through her anger to the person inside, like Mother would. Kill with kindness. I didn't want to be rude to her. I still regretted hitting her at the dance. I should have tried harder to understand her pain.

"Lacey, it's nice to see you. This is my friend Brychan," I said.

Brychan lifted Lacey's hand and kissed it. She blushed so pink she matched her shirt. "So very nice to meet you," Brychan said. I never paid much attention to his Welsh accent, but Lacey swooned.

"Oh, thank you," she said. "I, um . . ."

"Lacey and I go to school together," I interjected. "She grew up with Grey."

"He's a nice fellow," Brychan said, smiling. "What brings you to the carnival today?"

"Well, I'm . . ." she paused as she saw the tattoo-covered guy I'd seen at the café walking toward us. He wasn't wearing a shirt, and he had more tattoos on his chest and back than what were previously visible. He was sporting a shaved head and a scraggly goatee. He had to be twice her age. He wrapped his arm around her shoulders possessively, pulling her into him as he ground his groin into her. Lacey looked embarrassed and wouldn't meet my eyes.

"This is Jimmy," she said quietly.

"Who's the fag?" Jimmy asked, pointing to Brychan with his cigarette.

"Friends from school," Lacey said.

"Friends, huh?" he said, looking me over so thoroughly I wanted to take a shower to clean his filthy gaze from my skin. "Does your little friend want to play with us?"

The urge to slap him was overwhelming. He was disgusting. Lacey, however vicious she had been in the past, deserved better than that piece of crap. I couldn't believe she was wasting her time with someone like him. She was beautiful and smart, maybe a little scary, but she could do so much better than that loser.

"No, we were just talking." She laughed uncomfortably.

"Well, I'm leaving," he said. "Let's go."

"I'll catch up," she said.

"The hell you will," he said pulling her by her tiny waist after him. Anger pulsed through me and I lunged forward, shoving him as hard as I could, and he fell to the ground with a thud. "Get your slimy hands off her. She said she doesn't want to go," I said, grabbing Lacey's hand and pulling her next to me.

Brychan stepped forward and I could see him balling up his fists, but I held my hand up, gesturing for him to wait. I didn't want this to escalate, not here. There were too many eyes watching.

"You little bitch!" Jimmy yelled as he stood before me. He was enormous compared to Lacey or me and completely intimidating as he towered over us, but I wasn't scared of his type. I'd killed one before, and this idiot was nothing compared to Adomnan's evil.

"Oh please. Go blow yourself," I said dismissively.

"Just go," Lacey whispered to me. "It's okay."

Jimmy took a step toward me, grabbing my and Lacey's wrists, pulling us toward him. He swung me around in a headlock away from Brychan, and I donkey kicked Jimmy in the balls. He fell forward, groaning. He lost his grip on me, but held so tightly to Lacey she cried out.

Brychan closed the distance and punched Jimmy right in the face, an uppercut so ferocious that I heard his jawbone crack. He flew onto his back, unconscious.

"Oh my god," Lacey said. I helped her to her feet. "What do we do? He's going to be so pissed," she said. She was nearly in tears.

"We leave him there," Brychan said. "His friends will come collect him." He pointed to a group of men headed our way.

"They'll kill us," Lacey said.

"I'll protect you," Brychan said. "This way."

We walked at a fast but still somewhat casual pace, trying not to draw attention from anyone as we fled. We could hear Jimmy's friends yelling behind us, but I kept my hand on Lacey's and we kept walking.

"There goes his little bitch," I heard one of them say.

"I have to go back," Lacey said.

"No, you don't," I said.

"It's better if I just take the blame now. If I run away, it will be worse," she said.

"I won't let them harm you," Brychan said.

We followed Brychan. He had a way of being chivalrous and commanding at the same time. I was thankful he was there—I wasn't sure she would have trusted me to keep her safe on my own, even though I was more than capable.

We heard a group of them running after us. The sounds of their footsteps thundered in my ears. We started running through the crowd to the deserted parking lot. Not a soul was there to see this gang chase us down.

"Where you going, Lacey? Got a new boyfriend?" they taunted.

"Leave me alone!" she cried.

I wanted to run faster, but I knew she wouldn't be able to keep up. "You two keep going," Brychan said. "I'll take care of it."

"No!" Lacey cried.

"It'll be okay," I said, pulling her after me. "He's good at this."

I smiled to myself. He really was a good fighter, and I was sure he enjoyed it. These humans would be easy for him to beat. He'd be behind us in no time.

I pushed Lacey into the passenger side of the doorless Humvee, and I ran around to the driver's side and jumped in. We needed to pick up Brychan before anyone saw him fighting and called the police.

Suddenly, Jimmy was at the vehicle. He grabbed Lacey's ankle and dragged her out. "Who the hell do you think you are?" he screamed at her. She screamed as her head cracked on the ground when she fell. I jumped off the vehicle onto his back and started punching him in the face. He backhanded me so hard my head swam.

Jimmy ripped Lacey's tank top and punched her in the face as she cried for help. Her wavering voice vibrated through me, and something inside me changed. I leaped at Jimmy, knocking him to the ground. It was only when I looked down at my paws and into his terrified eyes that I realized I had shifted into my wolf form.

I could smell his fear and it fueled my hate. I bit into Jimmy's leg, dragging him off to the side. His blood filled my mouth. I snarled as I tore the flesh of his thigh into shreds. He screamed in pain, but I didn't care. I wanted him to feel pain for everything he'd ever done to hurt Lacey or any other girl.

Brychan ran over to us and punched Jimmy in the face, knocking him out and silencing his girlish screams. I shifted back into a human, a very naked human. I quickly grabbed Lacey's white beach dress off the ground and covered myself as I crawled over to her.

She was in shock. She didn't scream; she didn't say anything or even blink. I'd traumatized her. She should never have seen me shift, but I couldn't let that monster hurt her.

"What do we do?" I held Lacey's hand as she stared blankly at the sky.

Brychan scooped her up and laid her in the back of the Humvee. "You get her out of here. I'll take care of this mess."

"Brychan?" I said.

"I'll be fine. I will meet you at Baran's house. Take her to him and tell him what happened," Brychan said.

"But —"

"Promise me you'll go straight there."

"I will," I said.

He kissed my cheek and hit the side of the Humvee as I drove away. Lacey started muttering to herself, but she didn't seem coherent. I'd made such a mess of things. By trying to protect her, I had hurt her. I knew better than this. We were never to expose our true selves to innocents.

I pulled up in front of Baran's house. Grey was outside before I could start honking, followed by Baran and Willem. One look at Lacey and Baran knew something bad had happened.

He scooped her up and carried her into the house with us on his heels. He laid her down on the sofa and pried her eyes open, studying her pupils. Khepri rushed in from the bathroom and laid a cold washcloth across her forehead. Lacey had a massive bruise forming where Jimmy had punched her, and her nose was still bleeding.

"Help her, please," I begged.

"What happened?" Baran asked as he checked her vitals.

"We got attacked by a gang and they were hurting her, so I . . ." I choked on the words. "I made a mistake. I shifted in front of her to protect her. Please."

Baran nodded. "Willem, get the smelling salts and yew extract from the study."

Willem rushed back with two small vials. Baran held a small vial under her nose, letting her breathe it in, and she started to blink again, but she didn't seem to wake up. I was panicked. What would she say when she did come to? Would she be okay? Would she remember what I had done? I was terrified for her and for me. Baran opened the second vial, which was filled with a red liquid.

"What's that?" I asked.

"The berries of the English yew," Baran said.

"Don't kill her!" I screamed, trying to grab the vial from his hands. "Don't give her that! It's poisonous."

Odin grabbed my arms, holding me back. I turned on him, snarling like a rabid dog. I slammed my body into his, knocking us both to the floor. The look in Odin's eyes was pure evil, and I shuddered. Did he hate me?

Grey grabbed me and pulled me off of Odin before he could react to what I'd done to him. I looked down at Odin, who looked like he could kill me any second. Grey still held Baran's wrist, keeping the vial away from Lacey's lips.

"Baby, it's going to be okay," Grey whispered to me. "What's that going to do to her, Baran?" he asked.

"Calm down," Baran said. "I am not going to hurt her."

Grey reluctantly released Baran's hand as Baran held Lacey's mouth open and put a dab of the red juice directly on her tongue.

"Then what is it going to do? Yew is poisonous," I said.

"The skin of the berries isn't poisonous, and if you extract it perfectly, it can save a life," Baran said. "It is dangerous, but if this works, it will bring her back."

"That's an old wives' tale," I said, but I watched and waited for the juices to help her. I was nauseated and anxious as I watched her eyes blink over and over again without the slightest recognition of what she saw.

Brychan walked into Baran's house. His clothes were torn and covered in blood.

"I'm so sorry," I said. "I thought I was protecting her."

"You did protect her," Brychan said, lightly touching my shoulder.

I sat down on the sofa next to Lacey, and I held her hands in mine. "Lacey, are you going to be okay?" I whispered.

A tear ran down her face and she looked right at me, but was she seeing me or seeing right through me? I wiped the tear off her cheek, and her eyes followed my hand. Hope flickered in my heart.

"Lacey, it's me, Ashling. Are you hurt?"

"I don't know," she said. She stared at me wearing her beach dress, which was spattered in dry blood. Her expression grew confused. "I think you're a werewolf." She laughed, half hysterical and half scared.

"I'm sorry, Lacey. I was trying to protect you," I said.

"You were a wolf, weren't you?"

I nodded slowly, watching her eyes fill with tears. "I don't understand," she said, crying.

I could feel the anxiety in the room. Everyone was terrified. Lacey now had the power to destroy us all. There would be nowhere we could hide if the humans believed her, but more than likely it would destroy her. She would be locked away in a mental facility because of something I'd done. I had exposed us all.

"I'm one of Old Mother Earth's guardians. I was created to protect you," I said. "I'm sorry you saw what I truly am and that it scared you, but I only wanted to keep you safe."

She stared at me, clearly shaken. Finally, she said, "Don't be sorry. I needed you."

She wrapped her arms around me, hugging me tight. The touch was surprising as she cried on my shoulder. I was relieved to have her acceptance for what I truly was. I realized I needed her as much as she had needed me. I needed the humans; their love made me feel whole. I was born to protect them.

"Thank you," I whispered.

I pulled back and smiled. We looked at each other as if seeing the other for the first time. She was just as self-conscious and scared as I was, and she just needed someone to care about her. Why didn't I see it before? Underneath her beauty, popularity, and attitude was another girl begging for a friend.

"Lacey, you can't tell anyone about me," I said. "It would endanger both our lives. Do you understand what I mean?"

She nodded. "So, like, you're here to keep me safe?"

"To protect all innocent humans from evil," I said.

She looked at Grey and sadness settled on my heart, but was it my sadness or Grey's? Did he regret leaving her? I'm sure a part of him did. In seeing her hurting, he'd blame himself for not protecting her.

"I see why you like her," Lacey said, looking at Grey.

"She is my heart," Grey said. Lacey looked down at her hands as Grey continued. "And you are my friend."

She smiled. "I'd like that."

"Shall I give you a lift home?" Baran asked Lacey.

"Sure," she said. She stood up to follow Baran out. "Wait," I said. "I know what we need: a sleepover!"

She looked at me skeptically.

"No, seriously," I said. "Let's call all the girls and have a sleepover."

"Would it be okay if it was just us this time?" she asked.

I'd never seen her this vulnerable, but she was. All this time, I saw her as an infallible, popular bully, but in truth we were the same.

"That would be lovely," I said. "I'm camping out at my family friend's on the beach tonight. Brychan, can you drive us to Lacey's house to get a bag and then to Channing's house, please?"

"I'd be honored," he said. He winked at Lacey and she giggled.

Brychan took her arm in his and led her out to Baran's Land Rover. I waited until they were out of earshot. "I'm sorry, Odin," I said, watching his face carefully. There wasn't a single sign of forgiveness or empathy. Only anger.

He nodded, but he was guarded. He didn't trust me and his dark eyes watched everything I did.

"Baran, I should have trusted you. And I'm sorry," I said.

"You fought to protect one of your humans; that is your purpose," he said. "I would expect you to kill us all if we dared to harm an innocent."

"I love you, Baran," I said.

I walked close to Grey and kissed him on the cheek. The tension in his body was frightening. I still didn't know how he felt about Lacey after tonight. Did he want to comfort her? Was he angry I had endangered her? His emotions were constantly moving; I couldn't figure it out. I turned to walk away and he grabbed my fingers, linking them.

"Take good care of her," he said, "and yourself."

"I will," I said.

We drove to Lacey's house across town. It was a simple, but truly inviting house. She ran in to get some clothes, and Brychan and I waited in the Land Rover for her to return.

"What did you do with them?" I asked.

"The only thing I could do," he said. "I called the police."

"What did you tell them?"

"I told them that I came across the drunk men and they were tormenting a dog, and it turned and bit them. They became angry and started attacking the dog, so I knocked them all out and the dog ran away."

"Thank you for protecting us in so many ways," I said.

"It is my honor," he said. "And I like you." He winked at me. I couldn't help but smile.

Lacey ran back out to the car, jumping in. A small bag hung over her shoulder, and she carried a yellow pillow. It was odd seeing her with something that wasn't pink.

Brychan dropped us off at Channing's house, and Cara welcomed Lacey in with open arms. She was ever the gracious hostess; she even ordered pizza for us. Lacey and I ran up to my room, laughing, and met Channing on the stairs.

He smiled his most charismatic smile. "A friend?" he asked.

She blushed again.

"Channing, this is my friend Lacey. Lacey, this is my family's friend Channing. He's visiting from Switzerland."

"Nice to meet you, Channing." She nearly giggled the words. I couldn't blame her. Channing was so handsome that he was nearly beautiful—though I preferred the more rugged look myself.

"And you, Lacey." He leaned in and kissed her on the cheek.

I had to pull her away before she melted. He was charming. Brychan was ruggedly handsome, but I had to hand it to Channing—he was utterly charismatic. I pulled her into my room and closed the door.

"You are surrounded by handsome men!" she exclaimed.

I laughed "I think you might be right."

"You are so lucky."

I thought about all of my pack that fought to keep me safe, and I knew she was right. I was lucky to be surrounded by so many that cared for me.

A knock at the door made Lacey jump. Cara stepped inside, handing us a pizza box and a two-liter of Coke. "Let me know if you need anything else," she said.

We flopped on the giant bed with the pizza, and our conversation flowed easily.

"Do you love Grey?" she asked.

"With ever fiber of my being," I said.

She paused for a long time. "That's how he loves you too," she said. "I can tell."

I smiled. "I feel it."

"So, if you don't mind me asking, are you a werewolf like from the storybooks?"

"I am a wolf, but not like your mythology describes us; we are the protectors of humans. We bring balance to the earth. We protect life. We don't involuntarily turn into wolves at the full moon, nor do we kill humans . . . well, most of us," I said.

Lacey shuddered. For a second, she looked like she was going to ask about the wolves that do kill humans, but then she shook her head as though it might be too much information for one sitting.

I never thought in a million years that I would tell Lacey who I was before I told Beth or Emma, or any human really. I never saw Lacey as someone who could be a friend. Her beauty always intimidated me, and I could never before see the girl hidden underneath.

"Do you live forever?" she asked.

"I can," I said, "if no one kills me."

She nodded. "What do you eat?" she asked.

I laughed, holding up the pizza. "Anything. I have grown to enjoy human food, but I still crave wild game and the thrill of the hunt." She looked away. "Does that scare you?"

"A little," she admitted.

"I won't hurt you," I said.

"I know that," she said.

"Can I ask you something?"

"Sure."

"Did you hate me?" I asked. "Because of Grey . . ."

She laughed. "Yes."

I started laughing too. I kind of liked her directness. "I'm sorry if you felt like I stole him from you. I didn't mean to fall in love with him."

"I'm glad he found you," she said. "He deserves you."

"But we hurt you along the way."

"Well, you're making up for it now, aren't you?" she said. "And I'm so sorry for all the mean things I said to you."

I smiled. "I probably would have been mean to me too."

She laughed.

"Lacey, where did you find that guy?" I asked.

"Oh, he races at the speedway. He was really nice when I first met him, but the more I spent time with him, the meaner and more controlling he got, but it was all mind games. He'd tear me down and then build me up, to the point that I started to believe I was only good enough with him, and that I had to keep him happy to make myself feel good. I know it sounds stupid, but I fell for his crap," she said.

"It's not stupid. He's a manipulator. He knew what he was doing," I said. "All you can do is learn from it and move on."

"Yeah . . ." She sighed.

"It will take time, but you have friends who care about you. I care about you."

"Thanks, Ashling," she said. "You know, I never thought we'd be friends."

"Neither did I, but I'm glad we are."

We talked into the late hours of the night before she finally fell asleep. I closed my eyes and vowed to always protect her, even if I had to protect her from herself. I had to show her what I saw when I looked at her. Those disgusting men were just using her, and she was so much better than that. She needed to surround herself with people who would support her, not destroy her. I could be that friend for her.

14
Love Spells

The next morning Channing made stuffed French toast and bacon for us. Lacey swooned over him the entire time. I thought she was going to burst when he offered to drive her home.

As I watched them drive away, my excitement began to build. Today was Grey's day. It felt like it had been an eternity since I had him to myself. I put on my favorite ripped jeans, cowboy boots, and a white tank top and tossed some cash into the pocket of my leather jacket. I was beyond ready.

A knock at the front door made my heart flutter, and I ran past Cara to answer it. I yanked open the door to see Grey standing there in his dark jeans, t-shirt, leather jacket, and aviator sunglasses. I nearly melted just looking at him.

"Lovely to see you, Grey," Cara said from behind me.

"You too, Cara," he said. "I'd love to take Ashling out for our date if that is okay."

Channing walked up the sidewalk behind Grey. "Try to get in less trouble than Brychan did." Channing laughed, slapping him on the back.

"I think I can handle that." Grey smiled.

"Bye guys. I'll see you tonight," I said as Grey and I ran down the sidewalk hand in hand to his motorcycle.

We rode off down the beach as I wrapped my arms around him and let his energy flow through me. He pulled my hand to his lips, kissing my wrist. A warm burn started in my stomach at his touch. I felt reckless and in love. Everything about him set my heart on fire.

"Where are we going?" I asked.

"My two favorite places," Grey said.

"Oh?" I was surprised to realize I wasn't sure where either of them might be.

He stopped the bike in the wet sand and turned to capture my lips with his. I devoured his love and ran my fingers through his messy hair. He pulled me around in front of him, and I straddled him on the motorcycle. I could feel his body harden against mine and I moaned. I wanted him—and not just his kisses. I wanted all of him. I wanted to feel him inside of me. He kissed up my neck, leaving a moist trail behind as he bit my earlobe ever so lightly, sending tingles down my spine.

"Grey, I need you."

"I'm yours," he said.

I heard some snickers from some onlookers down the beach and I pulled away reluctantly. I didn't want to stop; I wanted to endlessly be his.

"Why don't you drive?" Grey said.

"Me?" I looked at his motorcycle cautiously.

"Yeah, turn around."

"But I don't know how to drive, and I don't know where I'm going." I said.

"We are going to Acadia National Forest," he said. "Come on, give it a try."

He showed me the throttle, clutch, and break, but even with his reassurance I was nervous. My palms felt sweaty, and I wasn't sure I was ready to drive a motorcycle. I'd driven many different cars, but this was different. This took balance and precision. We were so exposed.

Grey started the bike and the rumbling vibrated through my core. "Don't worry," he said. "I'm right here with you."

He slid his aviator sunglasses onto my face and put his hands on the handlebars next to mine, cuddling so close to me that his face touched mine. His lips were utterly distracting, but I had to keep my eyes straight ahead. I pushed the throttle and the bike began to move forward. Grey kept his feet on the ground, dragging his boots in the sand, helping me find the balance and rhythm. There was something erotic about the way he touched me and the fierceness and freedom of the bike in my control.

The bike moved and swayed with our movement, and I began going faster and faster until Grey no longer needed to balance the bike for me; I was doing it on my own. He kissed my cheek and let his hands fall to my waist, holding me in such a simple yet intimate way.

The wind whipped by us so fast, and I felt free. It was exhilarating. The bike responded to the lightest touch and moved with my every command. It was like an extension of my body. I could see what he loved so much about it. He'd custom built it from nothing and he trusted it to me.

"Let's head over to the highway," he said. "We can drive up the coast and cross to Mount Desert Island."

The drive was exhilarating, and the vibration of the motorcycle made me tingle all over. I wanted desperately to claim his lips and his entire body as mine. We crossed the Bar Harbor road to the island and drove into the forest.

I slowed the bike to a rumbling crawl as we stared up at the majestic evergreen and deciduous forest that surrounded us. We were intruders in this peaceful place. I followed the road as it weaved deeper into the trees.

"Park over there," Grey said. When we stopped, he hopped off. "Come on, we'll go on foot from here." He grabbed my hand and flashed me a smile that made my knees weak.

"Where?" I asked.

"You'll see."

We started to hike up the terrain. The ground was dense and green and filled with the hearty smell of evergreen. I could see why he loved it here. It was intoxicating just being part of a living forest. The wind whispered through the trees and I was sure it was telling me something . . . something that filled my aching soul.

"The forest burned in 1947. What you see today is all regrowth— the forest saved itself. It didn't wait for humankind to step in; it already knew what to do," Grey said, touching the trees as we passed.

"Do you come here often?" I asked.

"After my mom died and dad rejected me, I spent a lot of time here hiking alone. I felt safe among the trees," he said. "Like they were watching out for me."

"I like that idea," I said, lightly kissing his cheek.

"This is Cadillac Mountain," Grey said. I could feel his love for this place.

We climbed up to the highest point at the very top of Cadillac, and the view took my breath away. This was some of Old Mother's finest work. I sat down and looked out across the forest to the ocean, and Grey sat down next to me, wrapping his arms around my body. I snuggled into him. This place was awe-inspiring.

"Everyone should see this," he said.

"This is beautiful, Grey."

"I knew you'd appreciate it," he said.

We cuddled at the top of the mountain without having to say a word. There was a beautiful peace when we were together and as we felt each other's emotions. I knew he felt my devotion and love for him. And I could feel his. It was perfect. It was everything love should be. I felt safe and warm with his muscular arms wrapped around me. We stayed like that for a long time, just feeling each other. It wasn't the lustful passion that still flowed in my veins. It was love.

"Come, I have something else to show you," he said.

"Whatever it is, it couldn't be better than this."

"Don't make such rash decisions just yet."

We hiked back down the mountain deep into the canopy of the trees until at last we reached his motorcycle and I slid on the bike behind him. The birds flew out of the trees when he started the engine, swirling around us in their sky dance.

"Where to now?" I asked.

"Bar Harbor," he said.

We drove out of the forest and toward the northern coast of the island. There was something about being on an island again that made me feel at home. I missed Ireland and the green grasses and the salty air. I missed the rocky cliffs and our little cottage by the sea. Someday I would show Grey my childhood home by the cliffs. I missed the simplicity of that life, and the memories Mother created with me would always make that feel like home to me.

We drove past beautiful stores, restaurants, and magnificent homes until Grey stopped in front of an old bookstore that looked partially burned on the outside, but was styled with contemporary accents. It was a juxtaposition of old and new combined perfectly. The wooden door was carved with the Celtic tree of life, a sacred symbol of our ancient people. I ran my fingers over the symbol as we entered.

Floor to ceiling, books filled the room. Some of the shelves were filled with antiques and others with new releases. It smelled of old dust and new printing. In the corner, a tall Irish man sat strumming a guitar and filling the room with his voice. He wore a black vest and a contagious Irish smile. He reminded me of home.

I loved the welcoming atmosphere; people came to read a book, hear a song, and enjoy some coffee. Over the strong scent of the coffee brewing, I could smell the faint scent of a wolf. I looked around, but didn't see anyone. It was so faint that likely they had already left. I wandered down the row of antique books. Every one was different—a different story, different paper, different author, but each one was a treasure.

"Do you ever buy books when you're here?" I asked.

He laughed. "Nah. I wouldn't know where to start. The only books I have are from my mother."

An old woman walked up to Grey, startling him. He didn't jump, but I could feel his unease. She was hunched over, with white hair and wrinkled hands, but she was unmistakably a wolf. Her eyes were white with cataracts and almost looked like miniature starry solar systems. I wasn't sure she could see us at all.

Grey studied her. There was something so sweet about her, so welcoming. She wasn't a threat to us.

"May I help you find something?" she said with an Irish accent.

"I'm looking for true love." Grey smiled at me.

She looked at him blankly for what felt like an eternity. I wasn't even sure she heard him, but then she grabbed his wrist, pulling his Bloodmark toward her. She ran her fingers over his wrist. "Killian," she said. She grabbed his other hand and felt the Bloodsuckers mark and she hissed. "What are you?" she said.

"He's a wolf," I said quietly.

She reached her hand out toward me. "May I?" she asked.

I lifted my hair and let her run her fingers over my Bloodmark. Her wrinkled fingers were soft on the back of my neck as she felt the two-headed wolf's heart, and I held my breath.

"Boru," she said. "The prophecy foretold of you. You are our Crimson Queen."

She rubbed her fingers on my hair and smelled them. "You smell of crimson and snow," she said.

I laughed nervously. What did that mean?

"Would you like to go inside?" she asked.

"Inside where?" I asked.

"Acadia, my sweet girl." She led the way past the employees-only sign to a small door. "Open it," she said to Grey.

He turned the metal doorknob and pulled the door open to reveal a brick wall on the other side. He touched it and pushed and nothing happened. The old woman laughed.

"Is this some sort of joke?" he asked.

"You aren't a pure blood," she said. "It won't open for you."

He closed the door and irritation rolled off him. I reached for the knob and turned it slowly, opening the door again, and this time a room appeared, filled with ancient books. It was a beautiful sight.

"I'm sorry, my boy," she said. "I didn't know myself if it would open for you or not. I've never seen a half wolf, half Bloodsucker before. Perhaps if you tried your other hand."

I looked down at his wrists; he had tried to open the door with his Bloodsucker-marked arm. I wondered if the Killian Bloodmark would open it for him after all. She ushered us inside.

"Enjoy yourselves," she said, closing the door behind us.

The room was small, but filled with old books. Some leather-bound, others papyrus and parchment. I ran my fingers over the spines as I walked through the room. I smiled as my fingers touched pieces of our history.

"How did you know of this place?" I asked.

He looked around, still in a bit of shock. "My mother had left the address and the symbol in a letter to me. I just thought she liked it here; I never knew this was her sanctuary," he said as he sat down on a bench with tears in his eyes. His sadness slammed into me so hard I started crying with him.

"I'm so sorry you lost your mother, Grey. I can't imagine the depth of that pain." I knelt on the floor in front of him, holding his hands in mine.

"I don't think you ever get over the pain of losing your mother," he said. His green eyes were like a violent storm as he looked down at me. "Your mother is the one person you always rely on to shelter you from the world. I miss her every day."

I stood up and crushed him in my arms. "I know you do," I said, holding him as tightly as I could, trying to let my love fill him. "I wish I could have known her."

He smiled, wiping the tears from his face and mine. "She would have loved you." He lightly kissed my cheek. He looked deep into my eyes with so much love in his that I couldn't help but smile back. "We didn't come all this way to just look at all these books."

We started walking down the aisles of books when I found a small leather-covered book that was tattered and beaten, but still visible on the spine was the tree of life burned into the leather. I delicately opened the book, and handwritten on the first page was "Love Spells." As I flipped through the book, I came across folded and torn pages; it was well loved. I handed the book to Grey.

"This one you buy," I said. I didn't know why that was the one he needed, but I could feel it. That book was meant to belong to him.

He looked at the faded title and smiled. "You already have me under your spell."

I smiled.

We walked out of the small room back to the counter to pay. The old woman smiled when Grey handed her the small book.

"You have a very special book in your hand," she said.

Grey looked at the book suspiciously. "What is so important about this book?" he asked.

"It was written by Lady Calista herself in 1092," she said. "It is the match to yours." She smiled and patted my hand.

"It couldn't be!" I gasped. How did the old woman know about my journal? I gently took the book and opened it again to study the handwriting. It matched my journal without a doubt. This was a priceless piece of our kind's history, and the secrets hidden inside were dangerous.

"Why was it just sitting on a shelf in a bookstore?" I asked.

"The safest place to hide something is right under the noses of those who seek it," she said.

"Who seeks it?" Grey asked.

"The dead woman," she said. "She's always wanted it, but we've kept it hidden until you came for it. Calista wrote it for you, you know."

"Me?" I said.

"No sweet one, for him." She pointed at Grey.

"Why me?" Grey asked.

"Are you not the soulmate of the Crimson Queen? Are you not the wolf who will stand by her side at Carrowmore?"

"I am hers," Grey said. "I belong with Ashling."

"As you should," she said, smiling. "That will be twelve dollars."

I almost laughed. It all seemed so ironic. A book that was written centuries ago by Lady Calista for Grey and was hidden here in this mundane bookstore was a priceless piece of our history, and it only cost twelve dollars.

Grey handed her exact change and we left the bookstore. We sat on the curb looking at the book. Grey clutched the book like it was his only source for life.

"Why do you suppose Calista wanted you to have this book? And wanted the journal to go to me?" I asked.

"I guess there is some lesson we both must learn." Grey kissed my cheek. "At least we know that we're really soulmates," he said, winking at me.

I looked into his eyes and put my forehead to his. "I never doubted it for a second."

"We should get back; the sun is starting to set," Grey said.

"Yeah, I suppose so," I said. I didn't want to go back—it meant letting him go again.

The twilight drive was romantic. The sounds of night surrounded us, and the sky glowed orange and pink. Grey was my best friend and the love of my life. He made me want to be a better person. If Father hadn't sent me to Maine, I somehow knew Grey would have found his way to me.

We parked in front of Channing's beach house. Grey leaned his head back on my shoulder and nuzzled into my neck, kissing me so sweetly. It was an innocent kiss to onlookers, but it was sensual to me. I burned for him. I captured his lips with mine and ran my hand inside his leather jacket, feeling his rock-hard chest. He slid his tongue into my mouth so smoothly I moaned.

"I better go before we get caught," I said as I pulled away and started walking toward the door.

"I'll dream of you," Grey said.

"I'll meet you there."

I opened the door and found Cara and Channing playing cribbage in the sitting room. They both looked up and smiled.

"Did you have a nice time?" Cara asked.

"Yes, it was a nice day. What about you guys?"

"No, not at all," Channing complained.

"Oh?"

"He's just mad I keep beating him." She laughed as she moved the peg again.

"Sore loser?" I chided him.

"You have no idea," Cara said.

"Shush," he said as he pulled her peg out of the board and tossed it into the fire.

"Don't!" she said.

"Goodnight then," I said.

I started walking up the stairs to my room when Channing came up behind me. "Goodnight, Ashling." He was so sincere.

It pained me to think I would have to hurt him too. I would choose Grey. It didn't matter how nice or charming Channing was or how much I enjoyed being around Brychan. I would always want Grey. I cupped the side of his face and forced a smile.

Channing sighed and I hid in my room. I didn't want to spend more time with him. It would just hurt more when I had to tell him he wasn't my choice.

To my surprise, I'd grown to have affection for both Channing and Brychan, and I would lose both when I was forced to choose my mate. And Father might still pick one of them, but I would destroy their bond with me when I didn't choose them and our pack would split. I couldn't even think about all the dominos that were about to fall. So much weighed on a choice that shouldn't affect anyone but Grey and me.

Did Old Mother or Lady Calista know the messy situation I'd find myself in one day? Did they know Grey would be the one I would love, or was he a complication? So many questions plagued me all the time. I wanted to call my mother and ask her what to do, but didn't dare. Flin or Father still had the power to ruin everything.

15

Imperfect

"I need to get out of this house," Channing complained the next morning. "How do you feel about basketball?"

"I'm not sure I have an opinion on the matter," I said. Frankly I had no idea what he was talking about. I knew the sport existed, but I wasn't sure what response he was looking for.

Channing laughed. "I suppose that was an odd question." He pulled out his cell phone and dialed a number. "Brychan, you in for a game at the beach courts? . . . Great . . . okay, I'll call Baran."

He hung up and dialed again. "Baran, are you guys interested in playing basketball? . . . Yep, awesome. . . . See you there." He hung up smiling. "It's on. Can you two be ready in five?"

Cara crinkled her nose. "Really?"

"You're my beautiful baby sister; you already look lovely," he said.

"You're just saying that so I'll hurry up," she said.

"Well yes, but it doesn't make it less true."

She laughed. "Oh fine." She wandered away to her room.

"Are you ready, Ashling?" he asked.

"Um," I said, looking down at my pajamas. "I might change." I laughed and ran up to my room. I put on my white bikini and white linen beach pants and a pair of flip-flops and ran back downstairs. I was excited to get out of the house and enjoy the beautiful day, and for any chance to see Grey.

"Wow," Channing said.

"Channing, be a gentleman," Cara chided.

"So sorry, Ashling." Channing bowed. "You look lovely."

I blushed and put my hands in my pockets. "Thank you."

"Shall we?" Channing said, holding the door for us.

On the drive to the beach, I grabbed Channing's cell phone and dialed Beth and Lacey. Beth was going to call everyone, and they would all meet us at the courts.

We arrived at the beach court as everyone I adored arrived, too. I saw Grey, Baran, Willem, Khepri, and Odin already on the court. Ryan, Beth, Kate, Emma, Eric, and James arrived together as Lacey pulled up behind them. Brychan opened my door and offered me his hand.

"Ashling, you look radiant." He smiled as I stepped out of the car. "Cara, you are beautiful as always." He kissed both of our hands. "Channing, you could lose a few pounds." I burst out laughing—it couldn't be further from the truth.

Brychan's wicked smile always made me laugh, but Channing looked like he might punch Brychan in the face. Instead, Channing pulled his light blue polo shirt over his head, revealing his ripped, perfectly tanned abs. There wasn't an ounce of body fat on him.

"Silly boys," Cara said, shooing her brother away to play.

We sat down in the sand at the edge of the court. Soon Khepri and the other girls joined us. I made the appropriate introductions between my wolves and my humans. Beth, Kate, Emma, and Lacey met Khepri and Cara. I could see it made my wolves nervous being so close to humans. The bond I had created with them was different than any other pack had to their humans.

Grey walked over to me and knelt in the sand. He wore navy shorts that hung low on his hips, with the tiniest bit of his underwear showing. He had removed his t-shirt, and his golden skin nearly shined in the sunlight.

He pulled off his aviator sunglasses and slipped them onto my face. The gesture was innocent to everyone watching, but his hand barely rubbed my skin, and I pulsed with anticipation.

"Good luck," I breathed.

"Don't need it," he said. "I've got you." He smiled and jogged back onto the court.

They split the teams up so that each had half humans and half wolves . . . though the humans didn't know that. The girls and I opted to sit this one out and just watch the display of attractive men fighting for our attention. Beth opened a cooler and pulled out glass-bottled Cokes for all of us.

"Thanks, Beth," I said.

"It's so good to see you," she said, laying her head on my shoulder.

"It's good to see you, too."

"What's up with Lacey being here?" she whispered. Lacey was cheering on Channing, her current favorite.

"We finally found some common ground," I said. "And we both apologized."

Beth looked at her skeptically. "So you don't need me to kick her ass?"

I laughed. "No, I think we're good."

I turned my attention back to the game. I loved watching Grey play; his muscles rippled and his body glistened in the sunshine. I couldn't take my eyes off him. Other than the occasional scuffle between the guys, my attention was devoted to Grey. The game really came down to skill, which was good, considering the drastic variance in strength among the human and wolf players. It was clear Grey and

Ryan had played together before, because they were nearly running laps around the other guys, even Channing.

I buried my toes in the warm sand as I pulled my wild hair up into a messy bun on the top of my head. It felt good to get my hair off my bare skin to let the breeze cool me off, but it wasn't the warm sun that had me hot and bothered—it was Grey.

Grey, Brychan, and Channing were all trying to show their strength and agility in the game. I knew they were all showing off. They were all pretty equally matched. Brychan was the strongest, Channing was the most agile, and Grey was lightning fast, but all of them were careful not to hurt the humans. Even if it meant they missed a shot. It made me love them all more to know that they cared for the humans, even when they were trying to show off their strength and prowess to me.

The sound of a car door slamming caught my attention. I turned as Eamon's scent drifted to me. He walked across the court straight toward me, interrupting the players without a thought. He didn't notice how rude he was being. He just didn't seem to care.

Everybody stopped and watched him. Even the humans sensed something about him that made them uneasy. Lacey sat back down next to Beth.

"It looks like you need me," he said, looking right at me. When no one responded, he added, "To even up the game." His words fell on deaf ears. There was nothing he could say that would make any of them love him. We all knew what he was. He walked over to where I sat with my friends and he smiled at me. My stomach turned.

"I saw you at the carnival," Eamon said.

"Oh no," Lacey muttered.

"Such a nice place, isn't it?" I said coolly.

"You never know what kind of bad people are hanging out there at night," he said.

I knew he knew. He must have been there watching. He knew too bloody much. I was terrified of what he might do. Eamon walked back over to the guys on the court. Baran sent James and Ryan over to us leaving only the male wolves on the court.

"Can I join the game?" Eamon asked.

"We were just about to call it quits," Brychan lied. "You missed the action."

Eamon smiled. "I'm not sure I did."

Odin and Willem backed up to where I sat and stood guard, leaving Brychan, Baran, Grey, and Channing with Eamon. They positioned themselves casually between Eamon and us. From where I sat, I knew my friends couldn't hear what was being said, but I could easily hear.

"Maybe next time," Channing said, turning his back on Eamon.

"One more thing," Eamon said. "Brychan, I know you believe you're the favored suitor, being her original betrothed, but as a fellow suitor, I find it highly improper that you kissed Lady Ashling. King Pørr should have put you to death for touching her," Eamon said. His sinister words slammed into his intended targets, and I watched Grey's expression grow cold and I felt his anger.

I was ashamed. I felt dirty. I had betrayed Grey not once, but twice. I didn't just kiss Brychan—I kept it a secret. How could I have been so ignorant?

"You kissed her?" Grey said to Brychan.

Brychan nodded and smiled. "Wouldn't you?" The question was as much an accusation as anything else. My heart sank. I could feel Grey's anger boiling inside me.

"You had no right to touch her," Grey said, shoving Brychan.

Anger rippled over Brychan, and only his age and restraint stopped him from shifting into a wolf right there on the basketball courts. "She was mine long before you, little boy," Brychan said.

"She was never yours!" Grey said. "She would never have kissed you if you hadn't stolen a kiss from her."

"Oh, but she kissed me first." Brychan smiled.

This was not how I wanted Grey to find out what I had done.

I should have told him when I had the chance; now it was so much worse. I disappointed myself over and over again.

This was exactly what Eamon wanted, to destroy us from the inside. He had successfully torn apart the delicate bond the others had made, and the tension between them was suffocating.

"Neither of you should have touched her," Channing said, shoving them apart, whether to break up the fight or join in, I didn't know. "Don't think we didn't find out about your kiss at the Beltane celebration, Grey. And how she shoved you off of her."

"What's going on?" Emma asked.

I couldn't find the words to explain the mess I had made.

"Looks like a cockfight to me," Lacey said.

I would have laughed, but I was too scared of the bloodshed that was likely to come. Grey, Brychan, and Channing shoved each other. They were territorial and forgot their audience and our true enemy. Baran, Odin, and Willem were trying to separate them, but with every move they made to end the fight, one of them would escalate it.

I could almost hear Eamon's evil whisper on the wind, feeding their hate and fueling the fight. I was desperate to stop it and repair the damage among them and between Grey and me. I could feel Grey's pain mixing with my desperation.

I rushed into the fight, begging them to stop. Someone swung and their fist connected with the side of my face. I shrieked as the pain shot through my face. I fell down onto my hands and knees, blinking back the tears. The pain throbbed through my body; dirt stung my eyes and blurred my vision. The pain was doubled inside me as Grey's pain vibrated through me.

Eamon leaned down to grab my hand to help me to my feet, but when his fingers touched my skin I screamed in pain. I punched him in the chest with all the strength in me, sending him falling backward.

"I told you never to touch me again!" I said. I felt my skin burning where he'd touched me, and it hurt worse than my face.

"How dare you attack a king? You could die for this," he warned.

"You'll die, Barghest, and I will watch you burn," I said. My skin hurt so badly it was nearly unbearable.

"Bugger off, little king," Baran said to Eamon, coming to my side. "King Pørr will not punish you lightly for your true nature you've concealed—Ashling should be the least of your concerns."

I smelled him before I saw him, and I couldn't help but smile through my tears. "King Eamon," Mund said as he walked over to us, ever my knight in shining armor. I didn't know when he arrived back in Maine, but I was so glad to see him. "Did I hear you threaten Princess Ashling's royal person?"

"No, Prince Redmund, merely an outburst from pain." He nodded as he dusted himself off. "I didn't realize you were to arrive so soon," said Eamon.

"I made a special trip just to see you," Mund said.

"You're too kind," Eamon said. "I think I shall retire. I've had enough fun for one day." Eamon gave an evil smile to Grey as he left.

I walked over to Grey to touch his hand, but he moved away. He wouldn't look at me. I was devastated; I'd ruined everything. Why had I chickened out so many times when I could have just told him the truth?

Beth and Lacey ran up to me. "Are you okay?" Lacey asked. She looked like she was about to cry. I knew she'd been hit before, and any violence would likely trigger those memories.

I hugged my friends. "It's nothing," I said, forcing a smile. "Stupid boys. I'll catch up with you guys later. Okay?"

"If you're sure you're okay?" Beth said.

"You guys have fun," I said.

As soon as all the humans were out of earshot, Mund laid into us. "What were you all thinking? You endangered all your lives behaving like wild animals in public. You will all meet me at Baran's house immediately."

Mund touched my shoulder, and I followed him to his white Jeep Rubicon. "I should have known this would happen," Mund said.

"I'm sorry, Mund."

He shook his head. "You're young. You're bound to make mistakes, but you're going to be a leader sooner rather than later. I hope you know how to fix this."

As soon as we all arrived home at Baran's, I wanted to shift, but Mund was inspecting the burns from Eamon's touch. It wasn't as bad or deep as last time. He barely touched me before I hit him, but it was nothing compared to the sadness in my heart. I hated myself for hurting Grey.

"Eamon doesn't seem concerned that we know what he is," Baran said. "It's like he believes he has nothing to lose."

"He certainly didn't see any of you as a threat," Mund said.

Tegan, Nia, Quinn, and Gwyn had all returned with Mund. There were so many werewolves in Baran's house that the smell was overwhelming. And Grey still hadn't looked at me or even gotten close to me. He just lingered on the edge of the room, away from everyone else.

There was uncomfortable tension in the room and I couldn't stand it. It was like an evil cloud looming around us. Everyone was arguing all around me and making my head spin. I slapped my hands over my ears, trying to drown out the sounds. I looked around and none of them was actually talking, but I could hear them. I could hear their anger as though it lived inside of me.

"Damn it. Don't you all see what he's doing? He's trying to tear us apart!" I screamed.

They all stared at me. Confusion, anger, and pity surrounded me, and it was too much to bear. I hated them all for making me feel so inferior. I twitched with anxiety.

"He wants you to kill each other, can't you see that?" I begged. "He wants you to save him the trouble."

"Did you kiss Brychan?" Grey asked from the darkened corner.

His mood was sour; I could taste it like acid on my tongue. I turned to face him, and his green eyes glowed from the darkness.

"I did," I admitted.

Grey walked toward me, stalking me like his prey. There was such a primal way he moved that made my pulse quicken. I felt like a twitchy rabbit before the wolf took chase. Part of me wanted to dart away to safety, and part of me craved his attention. He took my burned hand in his, studying the wounds.

"Why?" he asked.

"I don't know," I said, looking around at everyone. I was self-conscious and scared. They were all listening. I didn't want to tell him. I didn't want to let him in. If I let him in, everything I had bottled up would come pouring out. The vulnerability of it made me sick.

"Why?" he asked again.

I stared at my feet, wishing I'd never kissed Brychan. Wishing none of it was true. Wishing that they weren't all staring at me. I was desperate to escape reality.

"Say something," he said. The pain in his voice was all too real. "You can't hide yourself away."

"I don't know. I don't know." I slumped to the floor holding my head in my hands, hiding from all of them. I rocked back and forth on the floor, trying to make it all stop. They were all looking down on me. I could feel their stares. They all wanted something different from me.

Grey knelt down next to me with his cheek touching mine. "You have to talk to me, Ashling. You can't keep me out. You have to let me in," he said.

I was trying desperately to be strong, to hide the storm that was going on inside me. I didn't want to cry in front of all of them. I didn't want any of them to know the truth.

"Did you stop loving me?" he asked. His voice was raw. He asked the one question I could never ignore. The only thing Grey needed from me was the truth.

"I never stopped loving you," I said. My voice was barely a whisper as I looked up at him through tear-filled eyes. "I didn't mean to. I just felt so lost. I feel like a different person after what Adomnan did to me. Like he murdered who I was, and I just feel so alone. I'm the kind of broken you can't fix."

"You're not alone, Ashling. We are all with you. Don't you see that?" Grey said.

"You don't understand." I looked at all of them. "None of you can ever understand what it felt like to be hunted down like a dog. I was held captive and beaten for days. I watched an innocent girl die in front of me, and there was nothing I could do to protect her. Do you have any idea how that haunts me? How that feels? And when I close my eyes, I am still in that room filled with blood. I'm still his." My anger and loathing self-hate flooded out of me. "And my father is allowing his evil brother a chance at marrying me, meaning there's a very real threat that I might have to go back to that place to live for the rest of my life."

"Adomnan can't hurt you now. He's dead," Grey said. "And Eamon will never take you back there—not so long as I'm alive."

I shook my head; he didn't understand; he could never understand. "Adomnan touched me," I said. "He saw me."

Saying the words made me feel dirtier. Like admitting it was accepting what he'd done to me. Adomnan's lips touched mine; his hands caressed my body, and that disgust still haunted me. I pretended I was okay; I went through the motions of life, but I was hiding it all, even from myself. I couldn't even understand it, but I hated myself for what he'd done to me.

My heart pounded and my hands wouldn't stop shaking. I kept trying to make my hands stop, but they wouldn't. I didn't want everyone to know how weak I was.

"And you killed him for it," Grey said, taking my hands in his and gently holding them still. "Adomnan is nothing. You defeated him.

You won."

"It never felt like winning," I said.

They could all see my vulnerability, but there was nothing I could do to stop the flood of emotions. Everything I had been hiding deep inside was escaping. The dark truth of how Adomnan's vicious attack still haunted me was more than I ever wanted anyone to know. I wanted them to think I was strong, not weak.

"You protected yourself. That is winning and I am proud of you," Grey said.

I looked into his big green eyes and he smiled, kissing my tear-stained cheeks. Hearing his words gave me a small amount of peace. He was proud of me for fighting back, for surviving. Those were words I could live on for a lifetime.

He put something metal in my hand and closed my fingers over it before I could see what it was, and he lightly held my hand closed.

"Ashling, each of the others offered you an extravagant ring as their offer for a life with them, a sacred symbol of their promises. But they don't know you like I do. We fit together. You are my one true love, and my soul is endlessly yours." He kissed my hand.

When I opened my hand, I saw two thin, hand-forged, delicate gold bands that nested perfectly together. They were bumpy and uneven and gloriously beautiful. One single tiny diamond was set into the metal of one of the rings. They were so simple, just like our love. They weren't excessive like Channing's, or possessive like Eamon's, nor a piece of history like Brychan's.

They were simple and imperfect, like me.

16

A Storm of Grey & Crimson

I smiled as I held the small rings in my hand. I wiped the tears from my face and looked up at everyone around me. Brychan was shaking with anger. They all wanted to win my love, but especially Brychan. He'd been waiting for me for so long. I felt bad that no matter how I tried to explain my choice, the others would be hurt. I wanted to kiss Grey and beg his forgiveness for all my wrongs and accept him as my one true love and husband, but I didn't dare. Not right now when so many things stood in the balance. I closed my hand around the rings and held my hand to my chest and took a deep breath.

"Do any of you know what you're fighting for? Do you even know who I am?" I said.

No one spoke. I looked into each of their faces and stood. "I'm not perfect and I'm going to make mistakes, but I adore each of you and cherish your offers, your love, friendship, and protection. In that same honor, I need you all to protect each other. Eamon is the true enemy here. I know you all want to prove your love to me, so do it by protecting each other. You are all important to me. Don't let me down." I felt like I was scolding them, but they needed to understand who our enemy was—it wasn't each other, but Eamon. "I must be able to trust you all to trust each other."

Grey nodded and looked to the others. "I will honor each of you as a cherished friend of Ashling's."

"As will I," Channing said.

"And I," Brychan said.

"Thank you," I said. "Together we can form the greatest pack the world has ever seen. Together we can win."

A cheer came up from Baran and Mund, and the others joined it. I felt triumphant and unstoppable, but one glance at Grey left me feeling sad. I still had a lot of explaining to do. I owed him the rest of the truth.

I said my goodnights to the others. I kissed Channing and Cara on the cheek and thanked them for my stay; now that Mund was home, I was free to move back into Baran's. When I turned to Brychan, I couldn't help but smile as my cheeks burned red, remembering his kiss. He leaned forward and whispered in my ear.

"My love for you is strong enough to protect you," Brychan said. He bowed and took his leave.

The house quickly quieted down, leaving Grey and me alone. The silence between us was killing me. I wanted to blurt it all out and get it over with. I knew he still loved me after what I had done, but I knew we weren't done talking about it either. The look on Grey's face was pained; I'd hurt him and I owed him an explanation.

I wrapped my fingers with his. "Let's talk," I said. I was scared to completely open myself up, but he deserved all of me. He nodded and I led him upstairs to my room. He sat on my bed, but his posture was stiff. I sat down on the other end of the bed and started picking at my fingernails out of nervousness. I felt his love for me mixed with his fear. I knew we could work this out, but I didn't know where to start.

"Why did you kiss him?" he said.

"I don't really know. It wasn't a conscious decision."

"Why didn't you stop? Do you love him?"

I sighed as I took his hands in mine again. "Grey, I know you are the only one in the world who could ever truly be mine. But when I'm with Brychan, I feel love for him too. It's different. It's not a deep connection like I have with you, the soul-stirring fire I feel with you. But I cannot deny that he is part of me."

Grey didn't respond, but his breathing became uneven and I felt his panic. I didn't want to hurt him, but I refused to lie. I didn't want to hide anything from him anymore. "I probably would have been happy with him had I never met you, but I did meet you. And you changed my future—you changed everything."

I waited for him to reply. My happiness hung in the balance of his response. I'd lost him once and it nearly destroyed us both.

"I see why you like him. If I did not know all of this, I would like him, too. He's strong, wealthy, and would protect you with his life, but you do not belong with him," he said, his voice raw with emotion. "You belong with me."

"I'm sorry I kissed him," I said.

He hugged me close. "Just don't make a habit of it."

I laughed. "I'm sorry I didn't have the strength to tell you sooner. I let you down."

"Is there anything else you've been hiding?" he smiled.

It was now or never. "Yes."

His body stiffened again, and his smile faded as he waited for me to continue. I picked up my copy of *Pride and Prejudice* and flipped through until a piece of paper fell out and I handed it to him. I'd been hiding it there to protect my secrets.

Winter 1048

The Dream will be all-powerful with her love by her side. Finding this wolf is of the utmost importance. He is the key to her . . .

"What is this?" he asked.

"I found it in Calista's journal. It speaks of a wolf love of mine who must be by my side. When I found it, I didn't know you were a werewolf, so I thought I was betraying my pack by loving you. And now you are a werewolf, but you're only half-wolf. How do I know that loving you won't destroy the prophecy?" I said.

"It is unfinished. It could have said anything," he said. "But . . ."

"But what?"

"I've found something I've been keeping from you too. Not keeping from you, exactly; I just haven't been alone with you long enough to tell you. You have to see this. It might change your mind," Grey said.

Grey crossed the room and dug the leather book out of his jacket and came back to the bed. This time, he sat down right next to me. I rested my head on his shoulder and he wrapped his arm around me, holding me close. I melted into him as he flipped open Calista's book of love spells, and the first inscription took my breath away.

Spring 1048
The winds will blow you together in a storm of grey and crimson. And war will wage around you, but you will find safety in each other and dance naked under the stars as two become one.

"I saw this the other day. I think this book was a map for me to find you. Some of the entries talk of the cliffs in Ireland that you describe by your home, like she wanted me to search for you," Grey said. "I was always drawn to that store, but I never once looked at the books. I didn't know why I was there. I just felt like I was waiting for something. I think I was waiting for you."

He flipped through the book, looking for something. He stopped suddenly on another entry in 1048. He ran his fingers over the page before handing it to me.

Winter 1048

Bind rosemary and lavender with twine and repeat the words: Divine love of the grey night, my true lover is crimson light.

Grey looked deep into my eyes. In turn, I swam in his eyes and I truly saw him. I saw inside of him. His soul was beautiful and it spoke to mine, powering mine with love.

"I am your wolf," he said.

"I knew it was true," I said.

I grabbed his shirt and pulled him down to the bed next to me as I kissed his eager lips. I needed to touch him. To know this was real. He slipped his tongue inside my mouth, and passion burned through me. I climbed on top of him, straddling his waist as I bent down, intensifying our kiss, and his hands massaged my thighs. I rocked my hips on him until I felt his body respond, and I moaned with need.

I wanted him. I needed him . . . but not here. Not like this.

I pulled away, trying to catch my breath before I lost control. His green eyes shined like emeralds as he looked up at me. The doubt and anger that I saw in his face was gone, and only his love and lust remained. His hands were still on my thighs, and his body was rock hard against mine.

"I missed you," he said. He laughed and pulled me back down to the bed. He wrapped his arms around me, holding me tight. "I love you, Ashling Boru."

"*Tha gaol agam ort,*" I said, smiling at him. I snuggled in close and rested my head on his chest. "Grey, where did you get the idea for the ring you made?"

"Our love is wild and misshapen, like the trees you describe in Ireland. And when I think of you, I know we fit together perfectly." He pulled me tighter against his body, showing just how perfectly our bodies matched. His touch made me breathless. "And when I showed the two delicate misshapen bands to Baran, he said something was missing."

"Oh?"

"He gave me what was left of my grandmother's wedding ring. Only this one stone remained from what was once a diamond-encrusted ring. Baran told me he had invested the other stones already and kept this one for me . . . do you like them?"

"More than anything," I said.

We snuggled together, forgetting the past and future and losing ourselves in the present.

I awoke the next morning, shivering without Grey by my side. He must have been being careful, to not further offend Brychan and Channing. I wandered downstairs to find him sound asleep on the sofa. His chest was barely covered by the small throw blanket. I kneeled on the floor in front of him as I ran my fingers over his scarred golden skin.

"Good morning, my dream," he said, grabbing my hand and kissing it. The warmth from his lips made me yearn for more. He rolled onto his side, making room on the sofa, and I took the invitation and slid in next to him. The simplest touch from him sparked a connection that made me feel fearless. I breathed in his scent and let myself become intoxicated by it. He reached down and linked his fingers with my left hand and rubbed my ring finger, where his rings would one day belong.

It was a silent vow, but more powerful than all the words in the world.

"Ashie!" Tegan squealed as she burst into the living room. "What good news!"

"What?" I said, Grey and I sitting up quickly.

"Haven't you heard? Your mother is preparing to meet us in Norway."

"Why? What's going on?" I asked.

"I found a way we can all stay together," Mund said, following

Tegan into the room. "I was supposed to go with Brychan to train in the Realms, Channing with his guard, and Baran with Grey, leaving you here with Quinn, Gwyn, Tegan, Nia, and Odin, but I talked to Brychan and Channing. They have agreed to train as one pack. This way, we can keep you safe without having to split ourselves up, and it gives Grey the chance to train with them, and it gives you the opportunity to stay with Grey."

"So Nessa is going to be our royal matriarch while they train," Tegan said. "Because without her, none of us girls can go." Our society was filled with sexist rules to control us.

"Father will enter the Bloodrealms at Lughnasadh at the end of the summer for the final fights between your suitors," Mund said.

Kane, Shikoba, and Baran walked into the room. "My lady," Kane said as he bowed to me.

"Kane, what are you doing here?" I asked.

"I am here to be your protector," he said.

"I don't understand?" I said, looking to Mund and Baran.

"I will be Brychan's guard in the Bloodrealms," Mund said. "As Baran is Grey's. Odin and Quinn will be protecting Father during the final fights, and Flin and Felan will be protecting the Rock. So we have asked Kane to be your protector in our absence."

"Why do I need protection in the Bloodrealms?" I asked.

"While your suitors are fighting and we are guarding them, it would leave you exposed to anyone that might want to stop you from succeeding in fulfilling the prophecy," Mund said.

"Grey, you need to experience the darkness of the Bloodrealms," Baran said. "It is unlike anything you've ever seen. Nothing can prepare you for that world and all the death that surrounds it, and there is a lot you can learn from Brychan."

"When do we enter the Realms?" I asked.

"You won't be coming into the Bloodrealms, Ashling," Baran said. Did I hear him right? Was he really going to take Grey into the

Bloodrealms and leave me behind? Did they really think I would sit this out?

"Don't look at me like that, Ashling," Baran said sadly. "It's not my decision. Your father has ruled that you aren't to step foot inside the Realms. You would only be allowed in the viewing gallery. You would never be permitted to be in the fighting pits. You're a princess, and your father would have my head if I allowed it."

"I won't be left behind," I said.

"This time you must be. For your safety," Baran said. "I'm sorry, ylva."

I normally loved his pet name for me, ylva, which meant she-wolf. Today, it cut deep. Though I knew he meant it as a term of endearment, it pointed out the exact reason I couldn't go. I was a girl.

"It's time Grey used his skills in a real fight," Mund said. "There is a difference between training and actually fighting for your life. One wrong move can be your death. He can't concentrate on winning if he's worrying about you."

The idea of Grey going into that place without me was terrifying, not that I knew how I'd be able to protect him. I wanted to see the Bloodrealms. Many different creatures were said to dwell in the bowels of the Realms—not just the fighters and slaves, but mythical creatures like Garm wolves and giants. Garm were supposedly a pack of hairless wolves that consumed anything, living or dead. I had read that giants also still roamed free in the realms. I wanted to see it all with my own eyes.

"We will fly to Norway immediately. We need to get out of town before Eamon realizes we've left," Mund said. "And we will begin training as soon as we arrive."

I nodded.

It was all so surreal. We were finally going to Valhalla, and I was going to be left in some hotel. I was back to everyone making decisions about me without my input. It was infuriating. I hated not being in control—it made me anxious, but I was excited to see Mother again. Her love always made me feel invincible; maybe together she and I could take back control.

"We leave in thirty minutes, so pack fast," Baran said.

I picked up the phone and called Beth, Emma, and Lacey and told them we were going on a summer trip and would be back soon. I asked Beth and Emma to watch out for Lacey while I was gone. I hoped they'd take care of each other.

We all piled into the cars and drove to the airport, where Channing, Brychan, and Cara met up with us. The fourteen of us piled onto the airplane for the flight to Norway. It was like traveling with a village, but Willem and Khepri took a different flight back to Scotland.

On our flight, I was at least able to choose my seat—and I chose one next to Grey. When the cabin lights dimmed, I snuggled into Grey's body with his arms wrapped tightly around me.

"Grey," I said.

"Yes?"

"I'm scared," I said.

"Why?"

"The Bloodrealms were built into the blood-soaked ground of the Battle of Valhalla. It is known as the hall of the slain. There are said to be hundreds of miles of hidden levels below the fighting pits—whole towns of people and death. Some chambers are said to be filled with packs of Garm wolves—werewolves that stopped changing into human form and lost their humanity."

"I'm not afraid of packs of wolves," he said.

Brychan was walking by when he stopped and looked down at us. I shifted uncomfortably away from Grey, adding some space between us.

"You should be afraid," Brychan said.

"Are you?" Grey said.

"They aren't like us or wild wolves. They are demonic bottom dwellers that tear the rotted flesh from the corpses of the dead," he said.

"Are the Draugr real?" I asked.

"Yes," Brychan said. "They look like hollow walking corpses. They are bloodthirsty, human-like creatures with gray skin that hunt any warm-bodied creature, human or wolf, and devour them while they scream."

"Mund said the Draugr were once an army of dwarves. Supposedly, Verci Dvergar starved them to death, and then he poured wolf blood over their corpses, and it regenerated them into the Draugar," I said.

"Verci's very own army of the undead," Brychan said.

17
The Undead

"That isn't real," Grey said.

Brychan laughed. "You're real," he said. "What makes you think other mythical creatures don't lurk in the dark waiting for you?"

"I don't want you guys to go into the Realms," I said.

Brychan lightly touched my chin, "We will watch out for each other."

"Promise?" I asked.

"Promise," Brychan said. "Get some rest, both of you. The Blood-realms show mercy to no one." He walked back to his seat, but not without glancing back at us.

"You believe that crap?" Grey said, but I heard the doubt in his voice.

"Eamon was able to burn my skin with one touch, and I doubt he's the most evil creature out there," I said. "Just be careful, Grey. Please."

"I will," he said.

My heart filled with worry. Grey easily slept on the flight, but my fear kept me awake. When we landed in Norway, I wanted nothing more than to fly back home.

We filled several taxis and drove into the mountains of Norway. The sight was spectacular. Old Mother never ceased to amaze me with her splendor. The drivers left us at the Geirangerfjord, at the base of the mountain. It looked daunting. We started climbing up.

"Where are we going?" I asked.

"The Bloodrealms," Channing said.

"I thought they were underground," I said.

"Sometimes you have to climb up to climb down," Channing said.

I rolled my eyes and followed. I could see the Seven Sisters waterfall in the distance, but not much else as we hiked upward. Toward the crest of the hill, I saw a little shack with a moss-covered roof. The uninhabitable shack had the most majestic view in all of Norway. The paint peeled off the wood siding, and the grasses were knee deep, but there wasn't anything more beautiful in the world.

As we approached, I got the first whiff of wolves. I started looking around nervously to see glowing eyes crouched low in the grass all around us. We were walking into a trap.

"We're surrounded," I whispered.

My heart pounded in my ears as I sensed the wolves creeping closer to us. Mund and Baran lead our pack, and Odin, Grey, Quinn, Brychan, Channing, and Kane made a perimeter around Tegan, Nia, Gwyn, Shikoba, Cara, and me, but it didn't make me feel any safer. Tegan walked right next to me, clutching Nia to her chest. I could smell her fear.

I swallowed down my own panic and forced myself to keep walking forward as the wolves started to growl and close in on us. A large sandy wolf stalked right for Baran; the wolf growled and bared his teeth.

"Damn it, Dagny, stop scaring the ladies!" Baran said, suddenly laughing.

The beast lunged toward Baran and I screamed in horror. The wolf shifted into a man and landed in front of Baran. He didn't seem to notice he was naked. His body was thin and angular, and he had shaggy blond hair and a goatee. His brow furrowed as he studied our pack with interest.

"You looked a little fearful yourself, Lord Killian!" Dagny said as he stood proudly before us.

"I was *not* scared of the likes of you," Baran said.

"Killian, it has been almost a century," Dagny said. "To what do I owe this pleasure?"

"Dagny, I come asking for your protection," Baran said.

"And who are my honored guests?" Dagny asked with disinterest.

Baran cleared his throat. "May I introduce Prince Redmund, Princess Tegan Boru, and their daughter, Princess Nia Boru; Prince Quinn and Princess Gwyn Boru; Lord Brychan Kahedin; Lord Channing and his sister Lady Cara Kingery; Grey Donavan of the Killian pack; Kaneonuskatew and Shikoba of the Cree; Odin Pohjola; and this . . ." he looked at me, "is Princess Ashling Boru."

"The red wolf," he said, studying me. "So the rumors are true for once?"

Grey stepped between the stranger and me. Dagny turned his gaze to Grey. The tension between them was intense. "Your whelp?" he asked Baran.

"My sister Brenna's son," Baran said.

Dagny stared at Grey long and hard. "I see her in your eyes." He turned to everyone. "Well, come in," he said.

He led the way into the shack and we followed him. My heart still pounded in his presence. The smell of moss was so strong inside the shack my eyes watered. A small fire burned in the fireplace, and mismatched chairs surrounded a small shabby table. There was a tiny loft with a couple of ragged blankets above us and nothing more.

"Thank you for your hospitality, Dagny," Tegan said.

I wasn't sure what she was thanking anyone for. This tiny shack couldn't hold all of us, much less comfortably. If it weren't for the view, this shack would be worse than the trading post in Canada.

"Princess Tegan, you are far too beautiful for this meager home," Dagny said as he slid on canvas hiking pants and boots. He grabbed a wooden staff and slammed it on the floor.

The floor opened up to reveal a metal platform in front of the fire. Dagny stepped onto it. "Well, hurry up," he said to us.

Once we were all on the platform, he tapped one more time on the floor, and we began to lower into the ground. The platform stopped in the center of a large open room, and the smell of fresh blood filled my nostrils. The scent brought out the animal inside me, and I could feel my hunger raging to life. I spotted a freshly killed sheep being cut into by a small group of men playing dice at the table. My mouth watered looking at the flesh, but the scent of the sheep was mixed with the wolf pheromones of the men sitting at the table. They didn't even seem to notice our presence.

The room was a great hall; it had a large lit fireplace and a beautiful hand-carved table and chairs. The room was surrounded by doors. On one side were small barred cells only large enough for an adult male to stand, but not lie down. On the other were elaborate bunkrooms.

"Lord Killian and his guests will be staying with us," Dagny said to his men.

A few grunts and nods came from the men, but they didn't bother to look up.

"What is this place?" I asked Brychan. "Is this the Bloodrealms?"

"No, this is Asgard, one of the home bases and accommodations of wealthy wolves and barracks for their slaves that surround the realms," Brychan said. "Behind each of these doors is a bunkroom." The place looked to have a capacity for at least three hundred guests.

"What slaves?" Grey asked.

"The royal and wealthy still fight slaves in the rings as well as honored royal and noble-blood fighters," Brychan said.

"Do you have slaves?" I asked.

Brychan chuckled. "No, the Kahedins don't have slaves."

"Then who does?" Grey asked.

"Some of the old families still use the old punishments; one of the punishments is to pay off debts as fighting slaves," Mund said. "And until they pay the debt, they typically live in the Bloodrealms and can be sold until the end of their contract. And if they don't pay off their contract before they die, their children must pay the debt."

"That's disgusting," I said.

"The Boru don't have slaves for a reason," Mund said. "Say what you will about Father—he doesn't believe in slavery."

"Then why don't we stop this slavery?" I asked.

"It would take a revolution," he said.

A revolution . . . I could be that revolution. A revolution was just a well-formed rebellion, and rebellion was one thing I was good at.

"Who are the fighters?" I asked.

"I used to fight in the Realms," Brychan said. "Most male offspring of royal and noble packs train there. It's a common practice, and after your ten-year training is complete, you are no longer in the lists; your time is done. Of course you can fight for fun anytime." He smiled.

"Kingerys also do," Channing said. "Three of our cousins are fighting down there."

"You're going to love our cousins," Cara said. "We have three of the best fighters in the Bloodrealms right now."

"So they aren't slaves?" I asked.

"No," Channing said. "They are members of our pack and our family. It is an honor they choose. Sometimes they are the sons of lower families in the Kingery pack, and they fight for status, a woman's hand in marriage, or to prove their strength in battle."

"Many sons of the wealthy houses still fight for training in the Bloodrealms. It is the best fight training in the world," Mund said.

"Did you train there?" I asked.

"I did," Mund said. "As did all of our brothers, Father, and all of the men in our pack."

"Do they live there?" I asked.

"Most of the royals and nobles only go into the Realms to fight and will stay places like Asgard between battles," Baran said.

"There is also an entire community of free fighters who live inside the Realms," Channing said.

"How can they be free if they're trapped?" Grey said.

Grey knew how to really get under Channing's skin. If that was a skill, Grey had it. Channing's eyes narrowed and his beautiful face grew dark.

"They are nomadic—they belong to no one," Baran said. "Most were born in the Realms and choose to never leave."

"If they are born there, they probably don't know any better," Grey added, looking at Channing. I loved that we were aligned on the injustice of our people.

"Do the wealthy still fight to settle disputes?" I asked.

"They often have slaves who fight in their place, though sometimes they choose to not use slaves because the dispute is too personal and their anger flairs," Baran said. "Now get settled and grab some food. We begin training today."

Baran followed Dagny back up into the shack.

We were separated into two chambers—men in one, women in the other. Even Mund and Tegan were separated. One by one, all of the men disappeared back upstairs, leaving us in the safety of barracks. I rolled my eyes at the stupidity of it and climbed on the platform and raised myself to the surface once more.

I walked out into the dusk light and saw Dagny and Baran teaching Channing, Brychan, and Grey the brutal fighting style of bare-knuckle boxing. Even when they weren't connecting their blows it still looked viscious, but with the sun going down behind them, it was also beautiful. Mund, Kane, Odin, and Quinn moved like skilled warriors with them. Dagny also began training them in some sort of martial arts. The moves were like a well-choreographed dance. I envied them.

"He will train them in judo and jiujitsu and defense against multiple opponents," Tegan said. "He trained your brothers, too."

"What if they get hurt down there?" I said.

"They will all be injured," Tegan said gently. "This is war for your heart."

"What if Grey doesn't win?"

"Then you will have to decide his fate and yours," she said.

"Do you think Father will kill Grey if I disobey him?" I said.

"I don't know, Ashie," she said sadly.

"Nothing is ever easy," I said.

She laughed her whimsical laugh. "No, it isn't, but then you find out what is really worth fighting for."

She laid Nia in my arms. Nia's dark curls were moist with the summer sun, and her little lips were pursed as she dreamed. I put my finger in her tiny hand and she squeezed it. She was a reminder of life and what I was born to protect.

Tegan stood on the edge of the bank, watching Mund's skilled movements. "I love him, Ashling," she said. "We all have something to lose down there. Remember that."

I stood and touched her shoulder. "I know," I said. Mund would be Brychan's guard in the Bloodrealms; the risk to him was as great as any of the others. Both her husband and brother were risking their lives, and she was helpless. There weren't laws in the Bloodrealms—no matter what Bloodmark was on your wrist, it wouldn't protect you down there. In the Bloodrealms, all the earthly bonds that ruled us and kept Grey and I apart were meaningless. It was ironic, really, that in order for us to be together, he would be forced to fight in a place where our laws meant nothing.

The tension between Grey and Brychan wasn't as bad as when we were in Maine, as though they had both gotten better at hiding it. I could still feel Grey's jealousy anytime Brychan was near, and Brychan still clenched his fists every time Grey touched me. I knew Brychan was still hoping to win my heart.

Kane and Quinn crossed back over to us. "We are going to escort Mother up the mountain," Quinn said.

"Mother is here?" I said, excited. "I'm coming too."

I jumped up to follow and Kane shook his head, gesturing for me to stay. I scowled at him and Quinn laughed.

"Come on, Ash," Quinn said.

I smiled and ran ahead of Kane and Quinn down the mountain. I was eager to see Mother. I missed everything about her. I could feel her love with me always, but having her warmth around me was even better.

I reached the bottom of the mountain as Mother leaped out of the taxi and ran over to me with a smile on her face. "My sweet girl," she said as she embraced me. Her embrace nearly crushed me. I buried my face in her hair and let her warmth soak into me. I knew no one was perfect, but in my eyes, she was. She was a goddess. She opened her arms and Quinn joined our hug. Everything I had always been missing was finally mine. I had a pack to belong to, and that sense of belonging filled the holes in my heart. I owed so much to her.

"Kaneonuskatew, *m' eudail,* it's lovely to see you." She kissed him on the cheeks.

"My queen," he said with a bow.

"Shikoba is with you, I hope?" she said.

"You'll see her at the top."

"That's wonderful," she said. "Shall we?"

She linked her arm with mine and we walked up the mountain. She asked me questions about the last few weeks since we'd seen each other last. I told her about Eamon being a Barghest and how Brychan, Channing, and Grey had gotten into a fight. All through my story, she never interrupted and her attention never failed.

When we reached the shack, Mother watched Baran and Dagny teaching the others the style and restraint of martial arts. There was something in the way she watched, a yearning almost. She squeezed my hand, and we went inside to find the others.

The guys fought into the late evening before they finally came back to the great hall sweaty, dirty, and hungry. When Baran saw Mother, he immediately went to her side, bowing as he kissed her hand. "My queen."

"Baran," she said with a smile. "Come sit by me and tell me of your travels."

I sat alone on the floor by the fire and watched my pack. They were everything I held dear. I watched as they devoured the food set in front of them like a pack of hungry wolves. I laughed to myself. I didn't want any of them to go into the Bloodrealms, nor did I want them to fight for my hand in marriage. I'd already made my choice, and I couldn't imagine losing any of them—especially over a futile cause. My mother came and sat next to me in front of the fire.

"*M' eudail,* are you worried?" she asked.

"Always," I said with a laugh.

"Worrying is the first step toward predicting and finally protecting. It is your natural instinct telling you when it is time to act. It is how you learn to become a leader," she said. "Each person is as important as the others; even the lowest servants are yours to protect."

"Father wouldn't agree," I said.

"No, he wouldn't," she said. "But I didn't ask his opinion. Old Mother teaches us that all creatures are equal. Not even humans are above equality."

"Do you think Old Mother still watches us?"

"She watches us, she listens to us, and she feels us, because she lives inside each one of us. She gave us life," Mother said.

A couple of Dagny's guard started playing instruments and filled the chamber with music. It was cheerful but slow; the orange glow of the fire danced across Mother's face and made her hair look almost red, like mine. Baran bowed to Mother.

"May I have this dance, my queen?" he asked.

Mother blushed and nodded. She took his hand as he slowly spun her around the room. I wondered how long they'd been friends. Did she know him before his pack was destroyed? Did she know his betrothed?

"Care to dance?" Grey asked.

I jumped up and slid into his arms. Dancing was one of the only ways we could be this close to each other without the others getting suspicious . . . although I had to admit that we'd already been caught in some precarious positions. His touch ignited within me as he pressed his body into mine.

Our connection felt so much deeper every day we were together. I had told him what it was like being assaulted by Adomnan, that the pain and anger that lived inside of me. And he loved me anyway. I found my mind pondering other ways our souls could bind . . .

"Get some rest," Baran said, slapping Grey on the back. "We train tomorrow morning at dawn."

Grey reluctantly followed Baran to their bunkroom.

I went to bed too. When I curled up on my bunk, I hugged myself tightly so I could pretend it was Grey's arms wrapped around me. I closed my eyes and breathed in his scent, that had saturated my clothing, and sighed as I tried to push my anxiety what tomorrow might bring from my mind.

18
Bloodlust

"Surprise!" my pack screamed.

I jumped so high I was sure they would have to peel me off the ceiling. I stared wide-eyed at my pack, who surrounded my bed. They were all there; Mother, Baran, Grey, Mund, Tegan, Nia, Shikoba, Kane, Brychan, Channing, Cara, Quinn, Gwyn, and Odin. Had they gone crazy? I pulled my blanket up over myself a little tighter.

"Well, I'm surprised," I said groggily. "Now why am I surprised?"

"It's your birthday, *m' eudail*," Mother said, sitting next to me. "Happy seventeenth birthday."

Only one year left. I felt scared for no reason at all, but I was. Would I be ready in one year to stake my claim as leader of our people in front of them all at Carrowmore? Mother kissed my cheeks and handed me a gift wrapped in gold paper. I'd forgotten my own birthday. I gently opened it, and inside I found a beautiful crocheted veil. I ran my fingers over the intricately detailed wedding veil, feeling the exquisite design.

"I made it for you," Mother said.

My eyes filled with tears as I hugged her tightly to me. "It's beautiful," I whispered.

"Just like you."

"I love you, Mother."

"*Tha gaol agam ort,*" she said, kissing my cheek again.

Channing knelt next to the bed, and I started trying to smooth my wild hair, but it was no use. He smiled and handed me a red velvet box. Inside lay a stunning emerald-and-diamond necklace. The emerald beads were suspended from a row of diamond flowers. Like the canary diamond ring, it was extravagant and stunning.

"Thank you, Channing," I said. "You have given me too much."

"The stars aren't good enough for you," he said with a smile.

I carefully closed the box as I rubbed the velvety outside. I couldn't even imagine what he'd spent to have this made for me. It was over the top, but generally so was he. I couldn't deny the necklace's beauty or his sweet intentions, but it made me feel uncomfortable accepting it.

Brychan came forward and handed me a small brown package tied with string. The wrapping reminded me of the gifts Mund used to bring to us on the cliffs. I slowly opened the present, and inside the crisp paper was a brand-new sketchbook and pencils. He must have noticed I had almost filled mine drawing all the interesting people I'd seen at Castle Raglan. It was immensely thoughtful and far more suited to my taste than Channing's gift.

"Thank you, Brychan. I guess you watch me more than I realized," I said.

"Happy birthday," he said.

Grey knelt in front of me and took my hand in his. He looked worried, and I could feel his nervousness. He lightly rubbed his thumb over my hand as he began.

"Ashling, I tried to decide what to get you for your birthday, and many ideas came to mind, but this is the one I wanted to give you most," Grey said.

He leaned forward and kissed me. His soft lips met mine and I swooned. I felt lightheaded, and my face flushed as my body responded to his touch. I desired him, and now everyone would know it. I felt panic seep into my mind, but I still didn't stop him as his lips caressed mine.

When he finally pulled away, my face was red and my lips were raw. I couldn't seem to find the words. Everyone was quiet and tension filled the room. They couldn't start fighting now; they needed each other to survive the Bloodrealms. But what could I say that would set everyone's hearts at ease without hurting Grey at the same time?

"Wish I would have thought of that," Brychan said with a laugh.

Everyone laughed with him, and the tension began to ease. I looked up at Brychan and he winked at me. He was my savior over and over again. Without fail, he always protected Grey and me. I felt like I was using him, but it wasn't intentional.

"Thank you all for your love and gifts, but you're all my real treasures," I said. "Now get out, so I can get dressed."

I watched Brychan, Channing, and Grey train across the river with Baran, Dagny, Mund, Kane, and Quinn. I lived my whole life at a distance, always watching others live, and this felt the same. I felt separate from them. They were training to fight for my hand in marriage, and all I wanted was to be one of them.

Tegan and Mother sat in the long grass, tickling Nia's feet; her giggles filled the hills with the most glorious sound. Cara, Gwyn, and Shikoba sat talking quietly. I knew I could join them, but I was torn between the place I was given with them and the place I wanted. I wanted to learn to fight. I wanted to learn to protect myself and my people.

Oh, how I had missed Mother's laugh. I loved having her with me again. I'd missed her smile, her scent, and her strength. Every time I felt weak, all I had to do was look at her to know I was stronger than

I thought. Through so many subtle decisions she had made for me throughout my life, she had taught me who I wanted to be. Like her decision to go into hiding with me instead of having a nanny raise me. All the times she stuck up for me when Father was on one of his tirades. She made me the person I had become.

She walked over and sat quietly next to me. The wind whipped our hair around, and she turned her face to the sky, letting Old Mother surround her in the radiant sunlight.

"It's exhilarating here," she said. "It reminds me of our home on the cliffs. Sometimes I still yearn for our secret place."

I leaned my head on her shoulder and she held me close. Her long strawberry-blonde hair tickled my nose as it blew in the breeze.

"Mother, I don't like being away from you," I said quietly.

"But you never are; I'm always with you. A piece of my heart beats inside of you because I made you. And if ever you doubt my love, just close your eyes and let the wind surround you, and there I am," she said.

"Thank you for the beautiful veil you made," I said. "I've never seen anything so wonderful."

"I knew it was perfect for you," she said. "For your wedding."

"Mother?"

"What troubles you?"

"I'm not perfect enough for this journey," I said. "I'm not sure I can lead our people."

She smiled. "Not one of us is perfect or infallible. Every one of us is broken in a different way, and it is those chips in our souls that make us who we are. You don't have to be perfect; you just have to be you."

My eyes glazed with tears and I crumbled into her, holding her tight. "Thank you," I said. She played with my hair like she did when I was a child. For a brief moment, with my eyes closed, we were back on the cliffs of Ireland, and I was safe in her arms. When I opened them, I was back on the Geirangerfjord in Norway with everything at stake.

The men crossed the river and presented themselves to us. They all stood in leather armor like gladiators. Their pack marks had been burned into their armor. Grey had layers of leather armor over his right shoulder that strapped across his bare chest; his right forearm was also banded with leather to protect his right side, and he wore leather-armored pants. I wanted to devour him with my eyes . . . and my hands. He made the most handsome, rugged warrior. And he was mine. I could barely tear my eyes away from his bare chest to study the others. Baran wore a full leather chest plate of armor with the Killian seal burned into the surface; the edges were braided leather, leaving his arms bare. He wore a leather-armored kilt and leather boots. He was impressive. He knelt before my mother.

"My queen, I will lead your warriors into the Bloodrealms with your blessing," Baran said.

She touched his chin, raising his face. "My love and blessings have always belonged to you," she said.

Channing knelt before me and kissed my hand. "I will return for you."

Brychan followed suit. "I will win for you," he said.

Finally, Grey knelt before me and kissed my wrist. "I love you," he said.

I blushed and quickly turned to face all of my warriors before I couldn't resist covering his face with kisses. "Remember what you promised me: you must protect each other. Each of you is part of me. Remember who the real enemy is."

"We will," Channing said.

"May the blessed sunlight shine upon you and keep you safe in the darkness," I said. Tegan had taught me what I should say before they went into the Bloodrealms for the first night of real training.

They hooted and hollered and left with excitement flowing through them.

I watched them walk away toward the Seven Sisters waterfall to the entrance of the Bloodrealms like a warrior tribe, and I yearned to be with them. Only Kane stayed behind with us. I didn't want to be left behind to worry. I should be down there with them. I should be fighting next to them. I should be one of them.

I sat down and watched them disappear into the Bloodrealms for their first practice below. A sickening feeling settled over me as I waited for them to return to me. The sun began to set and the air felt cool. The rest of my family had gone into the shack to get ready for bed, but I stayed under the stars. I watched the sky grow dark and waited for all of the men to return.

I was thankful they would all be together. If I hadn't been able to bond them together as one pack, Grey and Baran would be alone down there; instead, they were training as one pack. They would protect each other . . . for now. Eventually, they would fight each other in front of Father at Lughnasadh for my hand in marriage, and they would become enemies for my heart.

I knew the moment that Grey was in the fighting pits. His emotions rushed over me like a tidal wave. I nearly collapsed as I let his fear and despair fill me. Evil surrounded him, and it flowed into me, and there was nothing I could do to protect him. I shivered as I experienced the Bloodrealms through him.

The night grew cold, but I couldn't go inside. I had to wait here. I had to be sure they were all safe. I put my forehead on the warm earth in a child's pose, letting Grey's emotions rage through me. It was overwhelming, but every pain and emotion I felt meant he was alive.

I smelled Grey coming long before I heard him approaching. He smelled of blood and sweat. He wrapped his arm around my shoulders as he knelt next to me.

"Grey." I smiled and buried my face in his chest.

"It's okay, my love. We have all returned safely."

I nodded, relieved. "What were the Bloodrealms like?" I asked.

"Dark, dirty, and terrible. It is like no place you've ever seen," he said.

I nodded. "And the people?"

"So many are slaves, and they are killed for sport and the illusion of honor." He shook his head. "It is so much worse than I could ever have imagined."

"Did you fight?" I asked.

"I watched the betting fights and watched men die for nothing. We didn't fight, but we trained and sparred. The purpose of going down tonight was to make our claim in the arena and let our presence be known. Tomorrow night we begin fighting," he said.

"Are you scared?" I asked.

He laughed. "I wasn't before I went into the pits, but I am after seeing the grotesque ways people died—and for nothing. There was no honoring it. Channing and Brychan sparred, and I realized how little experience I have in combat. I don't know if I can beat them."

I knew Brychan was a skilled opponent; he spent his entire life fighting wars and fighting for fun, and the idea of Grey fighting him made me sick. What if Grey couldn't beat Brychan, Channing, or Eamon? He had to beat them all, or he would never earn Father's choice. I could barely stand the idea of him fighting them, much less the chance he might lose. The chance he could die. If I chose Grey and Father chose one of the others, it could mean war. It would divide our packs for good. If Grey lost, only Mother Rhea could save us. She was the only remaining Elder God, and only she could make the final decree, but I wasn't sure she'd pick Grey either. If I defied my own grandmother and still chose Grey, I was sure we'd stand alone. Not even Mund would defy Mother Rhea.

"I wish I could be there with you," I whispered.

He wrapped his arms around my shoulders. "I hope you never have to see the darkness of the Bloodrealms, but I'd be honored to have you by my side," he said. I kissed his cheek, hoping no one was watching.

"Would you give me a favor to carry with me during the fights?"

I laughed and rolled my eyes, but when I glanced up at him, I realized he was serious. What could I possibly give him? This wasn't some ancient time when I carried a hankie with my name embroidered on it. All I had was Calista's ring, the arrowhead from Shikoba, and Baran's pin. I unclasped the pin and pinned it to his leather armor. It meant the world to me, but I wanted him to have it.

"Thank you," he said, running his fingers over the metal. "It will be good to have a piece of you with me."

"I'm always in your heart," I said. "But this will keep you safe."

He nodded as Tegan walked over to us; I knew what she wanted, but I looked away to delay the inevitable.

"Come, young ones. It has been a long night," she said.

I sighed and followed her off to bed. The last thing I needed was to anger my other suitors right before they started their fights and break the delicate balance I had created among them.

As I lay in my bunk, all I could think of was the broken people in the Bloodrealms. I needed to see them with my own eyes. I needed to understand their pain. I just couldn't fathom their agony. As a naive child, I thought my life was a cage, but I was never treated like the people in the Bloodrealms. I may have been alienated, but I still lived a life in the sunshine. The only thing I had to compare to life in the Bloodrealms was my time in Adomnan's captivity, which was the most terrifying time of my life. People in the Bloodrealms lived that every day.

I decided I would sneak into the Bloodrealms tomorrow and see it all for myself—every drop of blood, every scream, and every smell of death. I would know their pain, and I would find a way to set them free. When I became a leader, I would fight for their lives.

But whom could I convince to go in with me? There was no way Tegan or Gwyn would allow me out of their sight if they suspected what I was up to. I doubted Cara was willing to risk it. That left Mother and Shikoba.

Mother was strong and powerful, but she wasn't going to risk her baby girl in a world like that, and she would easily be recognized. Despite all the rumors about me, very few had ever seen me, so my identity was easy to conceal.

My only choice was Shikoba, but I didn't know her well enough to know if she'd help me. Or what kind of fighter she was. I knew she could talk to Old Mother, but that was very different from fighting for her life, should something go wrong. How could I ask her to do something so reckless?

I escaped my bed in the candlelit darkness and slipped on the beautiful brown cloak that Lady Faye had given me. The braided train draped down my back, and the giant hood would easily hide my face. As I was about to raise the platform to go up, Shikoba stepped on next to me. She beamed her all-knowing smile.

"We're going somewhere?" she asked.

"I want to watch the sunrise," I said.

"I meant tonight."

I stared at her, dumbfounded. "How did you know what I wanted to ask?"

"Old Mother told me you needed me at sunset," she said. "Where are we going?"

The platform began to rise toward the ceiling. "I want to see the Bloodrealms. I've come this far—I can't stop now."

"I will accompany you tonight," she said. She was so calm and peaceful, as though we were discussing the weather.

We quietly crept out of the shack into the beautiful darkness to watch the sunrise. I saw Dagny patrolling across the valley, and several of his guards. They didn't pay us any mind as we sat down. We watched the sun crest over the horizon, bathing the world in beautiful light. It symbolized the light overcoming darkness.

"I love sunrise; it is rebirth," she said.

I knew nothing could prepare me for what I might find in the

Bloodrealms, but the kiss of the sun was the best thing I had against the darkness ahead. Everything I had done and seen up to this moment in my life was nothing compared to what I was about to face. I felt anxious and scared and the strangest feeling of excitement.

As the morning sun crept higher, my pack all came outside to join us for breakfast in the grass. Having them surround me in morning's glorious light made me remember what I was here to fight for.

I stayed in the grass and watched the boys train all day across the river. Their silhouettes were like a beautiful painting in the sky. It was my duty to keep them safe, though they seemed to think it was the other way around. I wasn't a frail relic that needed protection. I was a fierce leader.

They swam across the river, and the muscles in Grey's back and arms rippled with energy. I had to force myself to look away as they walked up the bank toward me. The water dripping off Grey's bare chest made my body warm. I needed to stay focused and not get distracted by my attraction to him.

I looked at my suitors; each was so different from the others. Were they strong enough to hold true to each other? Or would their desire for me drive them apart? I couldn't see what future lay before them, and I hated the uncertainty. The fights between suitors weren't to the death, only until one yielded, but even that was too far for me. I didn't want them to get hurt for the possibility to love me. Would any of them yield before death? I knew Grey would sooner die than yield to any of them.

"Ashling, what's wrong?" Brychan asked.

"Every time you guys go down there, I fear I'll never see you again," I said. It felt good to admit my fear.

"We will come back," Grey said.

"I know." I forced a smile. I stood and walked over to each of them and lightly kissed their cheeks.

"It is time to begin your training," Baran called from behind us.

Without any more words, I watched them all walk away, and this time they knew what was at stake. I was forced to watch them leave again. I felt nauseated. Even now my father had so much control over my life. He had forced this ridiculous ritual on us. Just when I started to feel like I was truly beginning to lead my people, I realized how little control I really had. None of us asked for this torment.

I took a deep breath and sat down in the grass. I had no idea how Shikoba and I would disappear unnoticed. Surely Kane would notice our disappearance. I wasn't sure Shikoba would even keep the secret from him; they were mates, after all. Would he try to stop us?

Mother walked to my side. "*M' eudail,* are you afraid for Grey in the Realms?"

I laughed. How easily she saw through all the clutter of my heart. "What if something bad happens and I'm not there?" I asked.

"Control is a figment of your imagination. There is only hard work and loyalty," she said.

"I need to be with him," I said.

She nodded. "I knew you'd say that."

"Am I really that transparent?"

"Only to me," she said. "Which of your pack are you taking with you?"

"Shikoba," I said.

"Good choice. She is very wise." Mother said. "Will Kane be going with as well?"

"No. I'm leaving him here to guard you and the others. I need to know you're safe," I said.

"And I need you."

I hugged my mother tightly. "Thank you," I said.

"*Tha gaol agam ort.*" She kissed me on the cheek and told me she loved me. "I will take the others below to our quarters. You and Shikoba should start your journey."

As soon as the others were safely in the shack, Shikoba and I started walking to the Seven Sisters waterfall, to the entrance of the Blood-realms. My hands shook with anticipation. The rocky hole that was the entrance didn't look like anything important. It didn't even look like it was deep enough to climb into, but as we began our descent into the rocky tunnel, I soon realized the endless depths. The cold air gushed past us, making my skin prickle. The tunnel had an unnatural sweet smell to it, and it grew darker, so I had to find my footing by touch.

By the time we climbed more than one hundred rocky steps down into the darkness, my eyes had adjusted to the nothing. We reached the bottom and entered a torchlit area. I had to shade my eyes to adjust to my new surroundings. The smell had grown thicker . . . like rotten blood, and my stomach turned. We wandered several yards to the next opening in the earth. My limbs ached from the climb, and another rocky, carved ladder beckoned us deeper into the bowels of the earth. I groaned just looking at it.

Another two hundred steps down, and my body screamed with agony. We finally reached solid ground again, and my legs wobbled from strain. I pulled my hood over my wild red hair, shadowing half my face. Shikoba did the same. I didn't want to risk being recognized. We were going to get in, watch for a while, and get out. No one had to know I was ever here.

The smell burned deeper in my lungs as we entered a cavernous black room. The walls were carved out of the stone and painted in something black and sticky. I felt the goo on my fingers and knew instantly that it was the root of the repulsive smell. The walls were coated in centuries of blood. I felt sick to my stomach as I stared up at the endless walls. How many had died to paint the walls in this sickening display? I wanted to retch on the floor, but that would draw attention to us. I closed my eyes and gagged vomit back down, swallowing the nasty stomach acid. When I looked down, I saw that we were walking on metal grates above what looked like a junkyard.

"What is this?" I whispered.

"That is where the slaves live. It is known as the city of Fenrir. It runs below the arena. The owners like to watch and bet on the fights that break out within the walls of Fenrir; that is why the grates were put in. There are several other cities in the Bloodrealms, but they are deeper inside the rock," Shikoba said.

I watched two naked children run from one junkyard enclosure to another, trying not to be seen. This was the only world they knew—a world of fear and captivity. Who could look at children suffering and not bat an eye? These were innocents. They needed to be protected.

"Come," Shikoba said. "We must not linger here."

I followed her through the sea of common and wealthy wolves. Some were dressed in exquisite clothing and jewels; others were in tattered rags. Some were slaves on silver leashes, and some came to place bets on the fights to try to make money. All thrived on this evil in one way or another.

We followed the masses down the winding metal staircases, deeper into the earth to the viewing gallery of the fighting pits. We looked from the owners' balcony down onto the filthy arena. The room below had a dirt floor, with twenty small fighting rings around the edges and two medium-sized rings and one large ring at the center. There were gated tunnels leading out of the arena into darkened paths. Filthy, bloody monsters of men filled the lower level, along with trainers and wealthy fighters dressed in the finest leather armor. The contrast between them was startling. The majority of the rich stayed in the gallery, but I could see a few wandering below, getting a closer look at the fighters.

A stone ledge high up toward the ceiling surrounded the arena, with at least a hundred wolf gargoyles looking down on us. Each one was different. Some snarled, others howled, but all of them watched us. It was a terrifying masterpiece.

"Wow," I said, staring at all their stone faces.

"Those are the Wolves of Song," Shikoba whispered.

Adjacent to the gallery was a balcony, with three thrones all made of human bones. It was hideous. The bodies should have been burned and returned to Old Mother, but instead someone had desecrated them and trapped their souls. Everything I saw here made me want to scream in horror. All of it was revolting—from the blood-soaked walls, to the bone thrones, to the slaves, and finally to the wealthy owners, who mingled and chatted as though they weren't the true cause of this violence and poverty. They created this world and yet didn't take the responsibility to fix it. I loathed each and every one of them, with their perfect clothes and self-important attitudes.

Several of them had noticed us. I wanted to flee, but running would only make it worse. A Japanese couple started to approach us. She wore a corseted dress and a small feathered hat on her head, but the most intriguing part of the woman's attire was her black eye patch with crystal embellishments. The man next to her wore red-tinted glasses. He was casually closing the distance between us; luckily a horn sounded, distracting them from pursuing me any further.

The tiny blonde girl I'd seen on New Year's Eve emerged on the other balcony by the bone thrones. It was Æsileif; she wore a tiny leather dress with a short, poufy black tulle skirt and the highest black heels that I'd ever seen. But it was her arms tattooed, in the language of the Bloodmoon, that I remembered most. She paid no attention to what was going on in the viewing gallery as she studied the fighters below and took several puffs off a long black cigarette.

"May you die bloody and fight with honor," she said.

The fighters cheered and screamed obscenities at each other; their noble audience clapped softly. A different master ran each of the rings, but all were giants with shaved heads and strange markings on their scalps. I was amazed to see a giant—they were enormous. Fights suddenly began all around the pit, and the instant violence made me flinch.

I watched a man bloody another. When his opponent fell, he continued to attack him until his head was misshapen and his carcass was dragged off to a growing stack in the corner. Life was nothing here.

No one tried to stop the killing; instead they cheered, and the wealthy made bets on who would die. The sounds of fighting, blood splattering, and cheering filled the echoing arena. Life was to be cherished—this was absolute desecration.

I finally spotted my pack in a small pit below the throne balcony. I was relieved to see them together. As I watched, Odin charged Grey and they began to fight. I knew they were supposed to be practicing, but it looked far more vicious than that. I cringed with every blow.

Over and over again, Odin jabbed and punched at Grey, but Grey blocked all of the shots. Why didn't he fight back? He just kept moving and dodging. Finally, Grey started swinging back. His first punch nailed Odin right in the jaw, causing him to trip. I flinched as Odin swung at Grey again. It was nerve-racking watching someone I love be attacked.

"Enjoying the fights?" a woman asked.

I turned to see Æsileif standing right next to me. The tattoos on her arms were even eerier up close. I stared at her from inside the darkness of my hood, hoping she didn't know who I really was.

"Deciding who to bet on," I replied, trying to disguise my voice.

"Well," she said, "you could bet on Brychan; he's the best and most experienced fighter. He's been here many times before and never lost a fight. Though there is the pretty one. He has a great bloodline of fighters and high potential, but I'd hate to see him hurt his beautiful face. Or you could bet on the half-breed. I think he is likely to kill us all."

"Oh?" I said, trying to sound uninterested.

"I know who you are, Ashling Boru. Nothing can conceal you from me, but fear not, I am your friend here. You're always welcome in my gallery."

"Are these your friends?" I asked.

"As close to friends as anyone could have in the Bloodrealms, I suppose," she said with a dry laugh. "Really, they are bottom feeders."

She was frightening, and gorgeous in a creepy way, but there was something warm in her smile. She had thick black eyeliner around her eyes, and her blonde hair flowed freely and messily down her back. She took a long drag off her black cigarette and dropped its ash over the railing onto the men below. If it weren't for her enormous metal-spiked heels, she would have been just a tiny pixie of a girl. She appeared to be sixteen years old, but something in her eyes made me think she was much older.

"Don't be scared, you're safe with me," she said.

"Thank you. You're too kind." I made a point to smile at her, remembering to be courteous. "I think we will watch for a while and retire."

"You are welcome to visit as often as you like as my honored guest," Æsileif said. She nodded and wandered off to mingle with the other wealthy guests.

"Watch out for the little girl," Shikoba whispered in my ear. "She smells of secrets."

"How can someone smell of secrets?" I said.

"It surrounds her like that heavy smoke."

I didn't understand Shikoba's cryptic warnings, but I couldn't say I disagreed with her questioning Æsileif's motivations. She scared me, too, but secrets weren't always bad. I had plenty of secrets.

"Let's get a closer look at the fight," I said.

"We can't be seen by anyone else," Shikoba said. "We should linger in the shadows."

We made our way down the metal staircase into the pits and weaved our way through the half-naked men covered in blood. Most barely noticed us as we passed. A few tried to grope at us or made nasty comments to us, but none dared to actually touch us. As we got closer to my pack, cheers filled the arena, and beautiful slave women filled the pits.

They wore steampunk-style leather armor with metal rivets decorating them, and gladiator-style shoes. It was like a glimpse into the past. The fighters were every race, but all young. An elegant African beauty walked past me. She had long black hair, stunning dark skin, and plump lips. She was as fierce as Baran and lovely as Tegan.

The women filed into the largest ring and began to fight each other. The men shoved and fought to get closer to watch them. It was such a sexist spectacle of flesh. Shikoba and I had to step farther and farther back from the ring to avoid the men fighting, until our backs touched the cold, sticky wall.

I pushed myself away from the disgusting wall. I tried to move toward our pack, but the path was blocked. A fight between a slave and a wealthy fighter was happening in the ring nearest to us. As I watched the brutal force of the fight, human scent filled my nostrils. There shouldn't be humans down here. I looked around frantically as the fight continued. Suddenly, the ringmaster tossed an old human woman wearing a nightgown into the ring, and her scent flooded over me. What were they doing? What was happening? I started to move toward the ring, but the crowd was too tight. All I could do was stare in horror as the fighters shifted into wolves and started stalking toward her.

"No!" I screamed, but my voice was nothing in the crowd of bloodlust.

Every bit of strength I had wouldn't move the mountain of a man in my way. The woman screamed and cried and cowered from them, and there was nothing I could do to get to her. I shoved the man in front of me harder, and he swatted me away like a fly.

The two wolves in the pit fought each other as they started to tear her apart, fighting for pieces of her flesh. They murdered her in front of all these wolves sworn to protect humans like her. Even my pack didn't stop the injustice. Why wouldn't they save her? Her screams echoed inside my head long after she died. Panic raged through me, and the smell of human blood made some of the fighters ravenous.

"We have to get out of here," I said.

I tried to push my way toward the staircase. The giant man who had been in front of me grabbed my arm, nearly crushing my bone, and I screamed in pain. He towered over me with blackened teeth as he sniffed me. I looked around, but I couldn't see Shikoba in the crowd; I hoped she was safe.

"I found myself a new toy," he sneered.

19
Bloodrealms

"*Get your slimy* hands off me," I threatened.

His smile exposed his rotted teeth and breath. "You smell good," he said.

I fought to free myself from his grip, but he was incredibly strong. I could feel Grey's anger and fear mixing with mine. I couldn't see him, but I knew he would find me.

Æsileif shoved her way to me. Relief danced with my fear. She slapped my attacker across the face with a leather crop, cutting into his meaty flesh. His face was filled with anger, but he quieted when he saw her and moved aside as blood dripped onto his hairy chest. His dark eyes didn't leave mine.

"Out of my way, pig," Æsileif hissed.

He bowed to her and backed away into the crowd.

Æsileif gently grabbed my hand. "This can be a very dangerous place for a princess like you. These animals are hard to control."

I needed to make sure Shikoba was safe, and then we needed to leave. "We need to find Shikoba and get to my pack," I said.

"Don't worry. My guards escorted her to the viewing gallery already." Æsileif began ushering me back to the gallery. This time, the wealthy spectators didn't watch me; they almost seemed to pretend I didn't exist. She led me to a booth at the back of the gallery, where Shikoba sat waiting for me. "Please have a seat," Æsileif said. She whistled and a man appeared dressed in a full suit. He never looked at us.

I leaned in to hug Shikoba, but she held her hand up. There was something in her expression that stopped me. She didn't want my affection. Was she mad at me for dragging her down here?

"What can I get you, mi' lady?" he said with a bow.

"Bring us something dark red," she said. "Something aged to perfection."

"Oh, that isn't necessary," I said, "but thank you."

"I insist," she said.

I could feel Grey's panic; he was looking for me. I needed to be with him. I needed to be in his arms. My fear mixed with his panic and made it hard to concentrate.

The waiter returned with an old pottery jug. It was a plain jug with three lines carved around the perimeter. He poured the wine into a glass and offered it to me first. I took it graciously as he poured a second and handed toward Shikoba. She shook her head.

"No, thank you. I don't consume alcohol," Shikoba said.

Æsileif took the glass and swirled it under her nose. "Now that is a beautiful bouquet. This bottle is nearly a thousand years old." She sipped at it delicately. "It's divine."

I sipped the hearty wine. I had to admit it was rich in flavor, but it was so strong that my head was swimming and my belly felt warm. Æsileif swallowed the rest of her glass in one gulp, like it was water.

"I'd be happy to be your escort and protect you while you are in the Bloodrealms."

"Thank you," I said. "That is very kind."

She leaned forward and studied my face. "You're beautiful, you know. In a wild way."

I laughed. "Thanks."

She touched the contour of my jaw and ran her fingers through my curly red hair. Her small hands were soft. She lifted my hand in hers and studied my palm for a while, running her fingers over the lines.

"You have an interesting aura," she said. "If you found a cup in the woods, what would it be made from?"

"I don't understand," I said.

"It is only a question," she said.

"Okay. I guess it would be antique porcelain."

"And if it was broken, what would you do with it?"

What would I do with a broken antique cup that didn't exist? I didn't understand why Æsileif was asking me such strange questions, but I thought for a moment. "I would pick it up and keep it. Even though it's chipped, it is still worth saving."

"Interesting."

"What is?" I asked.

"That is how you view your loved ones."

Oddly, she was right. I did view them as treasures that I would fight to protect. It was strange she could see so much about me from looking at my palm and asking a silly question.

"I see he has come to retrieve you," she said.

I felt Grey's anxiety as I watched him run up the stairs to me. He looked at me with relief, but it was quickly replaced with passion. "Are you okay?" he asked as he hugged me tightly to his sweat-glistened bare chest. The feeling of his bare skin and raw scent was intoxicatingly sexy, even surrounded by people. I lightly ran my fingers over his scar, feeling the warmth of his skin, and it made me want more.

I blushed from his touch. "Yes, I wanted to see the Bloodrealms for myself, but we got roughed up a bit in the pits, and Æsileif helped us."

"You promise you're both alright?" he asked, looking to Shikoba. Shikoba nodded.

"Are you alright?" I asked.

He hugged me again and whispered in my ear, "I'm just thankful to have you in my arms."

"I love you," I whispered.

His lips lightly grazed mine as he pulled me to my feet, and a light moan escaped my lips. I wanted more.

"Come, I'll show you the pits," he said.

Shikoba followed closely behind us as we descended back into the fighting pits. The fighters all moved for Grey. He looked like a gladiator here. I wondered if any of them could smell the Bloodsucker in him. Did they fear him or hate him? Baran came up to us and hugged me, crushing me with his muscular arms.

"I thought you might sneak your way in," Baran said. His laugh always made me smile, but there was a tension in his expression as he looked back into the pit. "Brychan is training against a skilled killer." He pointed to the ring where Brychan was fighting a hairy Greek man. I watched as Brychan blocked blow after blow. Fighting back and forth. Moving this way then that. The man slugged Brychan right in the face, and Brychan's blood covered the sand. "See how his opponent attacks? He hits like a sledgehammer. It's incredible."

Quinn, Odin, and Channing clustered around me, and Mund stood at the edge of the pit watching Brychan. He looked casual to a bystander, but I could tell his muscles were coiled, and he was ready to leap in to protect Brychan should he need it.

"We have a guest," Baran called to Brychan. "You might want to try to win."

Channing, Odin, and Quinn laughed as Baran teased Brychan, but Mund was more serious as he watched. Brychan looked up and saw me; he looked like he had swallowed his tongue. In Brychan's momentary distraction, his opponent punched him right in the chest and sent him falling onto the dirt.

Brychan leaped up snarling as he charged at the man and knocked him to the ground. Brychan punched the man and got him in a leg lock. The man lashed around on the ground until he finally drifted into unconsciousness.

"So what did Æsileif want with you?" Mund asked.

"To be my friend, I think," I said.

"Strange . . ." Channing said.

"Tell me about it," I said.

"Let's call it a night," Mund said.

As we left the Bloodrealms, many eyes were upon us. Brychan, Quinn, Odin, and Channing were going on and on about different techniques and ribbing each other for their failures in the training session, but Grey, Mund, Shikoba and Baran just walked quietly with me. I could feel their unease. They didn't like being watched any more than I did.

When we finally escaped into the moonlight, I stopped to admire its beauty. After seeing the darkness of the Bloodrealms, it was a relief to be bathed in moonlight. The night was all but gone, and the sun would rise in a few hours. The brisk walk back to the shack was reinvigorating.

"I think I'll stay up a little longer," I said to the group.

Channing, Baran, Brychan, Quinn, and Odin headed to bed, but Mund nodded and hung out next to the shack, keeping watch over me. Or at least giving everyone the illusion he was.

"Have you seen the wildflowers?" Grey asked.

"No, where are they?" I asked.

"It would be my pleasure to show you," he said, taking my arm.

He reached out and held my hand, and the warmth of his palm took my breath away. I needed his touch. We walked down the bank in the long grass. into a thick blanket of white wildflowers. They almost glowed in the moonlight. Their scent swirled around us. We sat down in the middle of the tall blossoms, bathing in the peace.

"Tell me something interesting about yourself," Grey said, staring right at me.

"What?"

"Something you've never told anyone else."

"But you know almost everything," I said.

He stared at me, and I realized he was serious.

"I love to buy shoes and never wear them."

Grey laughed. "I've noticed." He tickled the bottom of my bare feet.

"Tell me something about you," I said.

"When I was a little boy, I wanted to be a gladiator," he said. He looked proud and determined. "I thought I could fight for honor one day, but I'd much rather fight for love."

"You are sort of a gladiator now," I said, "and you're very much fighting for love. What do you dream of?"

"Our future together and building a life with you. I want to reclaim the Killian lands and bring Baran back to his homeland as well."

I stared into his beautiful green eyes and melted into his dreams. I wanted that, too. I wanted to be his, and for him to be mine. I loved knowing he thought about our future together.

"That's a beautiful idea," I said. "I can't wait to see it."

"What do you dream of at night?" he asked.

I hesitated as I remembered Adomnan's haunting presence in my dreams. I didn't want anyone to know my vulnerability, but it was different with Grey. I wanted him to know all of me, both my struggles and my triumphs. "Adomnan haunts my dreams," I said quietly.

"He can't hurt you anymore. He's dead," Grey said.

"You're wrong, my love. He can."

"Only if you let him," he said. "If you let him linger in your mind, let the fear and hate breed inside you, then he can hurt you, but you can't live that way."

It felt good to tell him about the fear in my heart and share my burden. I knew he was right; I did have to stop torturing myself with the memories. It was easier said than done, though. Adomnan would creep up into my thoughts and destroy me. That kind of pain and suffering was hard to release.

"Grey, if we weren't here, where would you want to be?" I asked.

He thought for a while. "Maybe we'd be in Scotland at Killian Castle, and I'd be making things with my bare hands, like your rings, and singing songs I wrote for you," he said as he lay down.

"That sounds nice," I said.

"What would you do?" he asked. "If you could be anything, what would you be?"

"I'd be a teacher," I said. "I would protect all the children of the world."

I lay down with my head resting on his chest. I fit perfectly next to him, like our bodies were meant to be together. With his arms wrapped around me, I listened to his heartbeat as we watched the stars. The sexual tension between us was incredible, but I knew Mund wasn't far away. I closed my eyes and yawned as we fell asleep in each other's arms.

In the early morning, I heard the door of the shack slam and I sat up quickly. Baran and the others started to emerge from the shack. I leaned down and kissed Grey's lips, and he slipped his tongue inside my mouth, and I purred for him. I knew it had to stop as soon as it started, but the risk of being found was almost as delightful as the kiss itself.

"I'd better go," he said. "Have a good day, my love."

Grey kissed me once more and jumped up to follow the others across the river, leaving me hidden in the flowers. Mund walked past me and followed Grey; as he did, he gave me an all-knowing look. I blushed. I couldn't see the others, but I could smell them near.

I watched as the men began to train. The slow, calculated jiujitsu movements they made were mesmerizing. I wanted to learn to fight like they did. I needed to be able to protect myself and my pack. I stood up and started to mimic them. The way my arms moved made energy flow through my body. It was invigorating.

Gwyn walked over to my side; without a word, she joined me as we breathed and moved as one, but there was still a river dividing us from them.

I saw Grey and Brychan stop and watch us, but I pretended I didn't see them and concentrated on the movements. Martial arts required practice, patience, and skill in the mind and body; that much I knew. They started to spar and fight, so Gwyn and I wandered off to the long grass as we waited for them to finish. We rested from the summer sun in the shade of a tree. The breeze was light and calming, but I yearned to train with them.

I heard the men cheering as they crossed the river back to us. I knew they'd seen us earlier, and I felt nervous about what they'd say. Would they mock my attempt, or would they pretend they hadn't noticed?

The women came out to wish them well in their night of fights. We walked over to wish them well on their fights in the Realms tonight, but I didn't want to wish them well. I wanted to be one of them. I wanted to go with them. I didn't want any of them to go into the Realms, but if they had to go, I wanted to be with them.

"Nicely done, Ashling," Dagny said. "You have good form as a warrior."

I couldn't help but smile at his praise. Mother walked over to my side, smiling. I could feel her pride.

"Come with us into the Bloodrealms," Grey said.

Mund laughed. "You may as well. It's obvious we can't keep you out."

"The Bloodrealms aren't a place for a lady," Channing said.

Mund snorted as he laughed.

"Lord Channing, I appreciate your concern for my well-being, but it is my decision," I said.

"Queen Nessa?" Channing pleaded.

"Lord Channing, I think you should spend more time with my daughter; you'd soon realize she's unwilling to have decisions made for her. I'm surprised how little you know her already," she said. "Baran, she is in your trusted care."

Baran knelt before my mother and kissed her hand. She smiled and lightly touched his face before she turned to follow the others back into the shack. Baran watched her leave before he finally stood back up. There was a deep friendship between them that I didn't understand.

20

Acceptance

We entered the dark Realms at sunset, the same way as I had the night before, but this time it wasn't intimidating, and my nervousness was replaced by pride. I was proud to be invited to be with them instead of having to sneak in, and frankly, I wasn't sure Shikoba would be willing to sneak in again. I was thankful to leave her with Mother.

We walked through the viewing gallery, and I spotted Selene ducking through a doorway with the other owners. Her long, glossy black hair and olive skin were exquisite even in this lighting, but despite how beautiful she was, she was ugly to me. I remembered what Brychan and Kane had told me, how she would buy and sell wolves to fight in the ring. It disgusted me. I wanted to tell her so, but she was already gone.

Channing turned to me, smiling his most handsome smile. It was almost ridiculous how pretty he was, especially somewhere like this.

"Would you like to watch from the gallery?" he asked, hopeful.

"No, thank you," I replied. He was constantly trying to cage me. I was sure it was because he thought it was his job to protect me, but I didn't need him to save me. I needed to see the pain of our world and learn how to protect everyone. I couldn't do that while I just viewed the ugliness of the world from the viewing gallery. I needed to participate.

He sighed and offered me his arm. "I think your mother is right," Channing said. "I don't think I know you well enough yet."

"Perhaps it is time you started," I said. I needed to teach my pack once and for all what I stood for. And it wasn't just being pretty. I was a fighter.

We gathered around one of the fighting pits, and adrenaline flowed through me. The smell of sweat made my blood pulse with anticipation. I looked at Grey and caught him watching me. One look at him and my breath caught. He was so close to me, and yet I had to be careful about reaching out and touching him.

"Channing, you're going to fight first," Baran said. Channing leaped into the ring with ease as he waited for his opponent.

"SEVEN-SIX-EIGHT-THREE-FOUR!" the ringmaster yelled.

A curly-haired man stepped into the ring. He was solid muscle. Every single one of his abs was defined. His hair was so blond it was nearly white, and it was even starker over his tanned skin. He walked across the ring to Channing with a swagger of confidence.

"Lord Channing!" he said.

"Emil," Channing said. "How much longer are you planning to fight down here before you choose a wife and settle down?"

"I'll settle down when you do," Emil said, slapping Channing on the back.

"If she'll have me," Channing said to Emil as he pointed to me, "then you'll be married at Lughnasadh when I am."

Emil laughed as he swung at Channing, beginning the fight.

"Is he a Kingery?" I asked.

"I believe he's a cousin," Baran said. "They have three fighters down here. Good chaps. They room somewhere in Norddal."

Æsileif appeared next to me, smoking her cigarette. It was odd how easily she appeared and disappeared. "I'm glad you came back. It gets so dull here with so few intelligent women around," she said.

"What about them?" I asked, pointing to the gallery. I could see Selene and the Asian couple watching us. I shivered under their unwanted inspection.

"They are a bunch of snobs." She laughed. "They are too busy hiding behind their masks."

I believed that. The wealthy spectators all watched the fight with veiled interest and contempt for the fighters. They were here to show off their wealth and power and make bets on life and death, but they were shells empty of life.

"So why do you live down here then?" I asked.

"It's the only world I've ever known," she said with a contorted laugh. "Where else would I go?"

"Anywhere but here," I said. "You'd like the United States."

"I think you'd like it here," she said. "We could be the best of friends."

I didn't know how to respond. Was that an invitation or just a statement? I didn't want to live down here among the chaos and fighting. I needed light and wind. I needed freedom. The Bloodrealms were a giant cage. I knew what a cage was like—this was it.

Grey stepped up next to me as Channing jumped out of the ring with Emil following behind. Emil was bloodied up and filthy, but both men were laughing and slapping each other on the back. It was obvious that though they fought hard, they were still family. When Emil saw Æsileif, his face grew somber, and he nodded to us and retreated.

I looked at Æsileif, but she just smiled.

"Grey, you're up," Baran said.

Grey let his arm brush mine on the way by, and my skin tingled. Just that innocent touch could light my soul on fire. I yearned for the day he'd be mine. Grey jumped into the ring and waited. My nerves were raw, but excitement flowed through me.

"NINE-FIVE-TWO-ONE-ONE," the ringmaster called.

A cheer came up from the crowd as an Italian man with dark hair and tanned skin walked into the ring. He was hairy, but technically attractive, I suppose. He sauntered around the ring in a circle around Grey, taunting him in Italian. I couldn't understand him, but I assumed it wasn't very nice.

"Isn't it exhilarating to watch blood sports?" Æsileif said. "They say it's a man's sport, but really, it's for us." She watched the Italian man swagger about with lust in her eyes.

"Do you know him?" I asked.

"Not yet," she said.

I had to be very careful not to show pain when Grey got hit, especially with Æsileif so close. I didn't know how much the others knew about Grey and me, but somehow I felt she was someone who should definitely be kept in the dark. No one, including Channing and Brychan, could know that Grey and I were binding to each other. We could both die for this secret, but it was far more than likely Grey would die. Then Father would force a marriage on me, if anyone would still have me.

Watching Grey fight filled me with fear. I didn't want him to get hurt. I cringed with every move his opponent made.

"Are you lonely living down here?" I asked, trying to keep my mind busy. I didn't want to fill Grey with all my negative emotions and distract him.

She turned and looked at me, and for the first time I felt like I was really seeing her. A sad little smile crossed her face. "Lonely? With all of this?" She gestured to the arena that surrounded her. She said it so emotionlessly, I reached out and hugged her. At first her body was rigid, but she finally hugged me back.

"Thank you," she said.

The Italian man was long and lanky, but his movements weren't precise. He missed over and over as he swung at Grey. I wanted it to be over. The violence of this sport was almost too much to watch. The man was fast, but erratic. Grey easily outmaneuvered him and punched him in the ribs. The man grunted and groaned. Grey spun again and punched the man in the knee. Each blow Grey delivered sent shivers up my spine. Finally, an uppercut dropped the man to the dirt, panting and bleeding.

Grey stood over the man, and his animalistic rage flowed through me. I wanted to tear Grey's clothes off; he was sexy. There was something so primal about him that my body instantly responded to. He turned me on—the way his muscles moved, the wildness in his eyes, the glistening sweat on his bare chest, everything. Grey looked at me, and I smiled like a lovesick fool.

Two guards lumbered in past Grey, pulled the Italian man to his feet, and dragged him out of the ring. I was thankful for the distraction.

"I better see that he gets healed properly," Æsileif said as she followed the man out of the ring.

Grey walked over to my side, his body glistening with sweat and dirt. His warm, sweaty scent intensified my lust. I had to bite my lip until I drew blood to stop myself from kissing him. Grey leaned in close and whispered, "I need you."

I gasped and closed my eyes as my body warmed to the idea of his hands on my skin. The others began to rib him about the fight, but I didn't pay them any mind. I just wanted to be alone with Grey. I wanted him all to myself, without any rules or prophecies. Just two lovers lost in each other's arms.

Brychan jumped into the ring as his number was called. He was eager to fight; I could see it in his face. Grey stood right behind me, so close his body touched mine. In the tightly packed crowd, the sensual touch would go unnoticed. My stomach filled with butterflies, and I lightly let me body rub against his. His body hardened to my touch, and he groaned in my ear, sending shivers down my spine. I knew he wanted me as much as I wanted him, and I loved it. His breath on my neck invigorated every cell in my body. I wanted to turn around and wrap my arms around him and kiss his sexy lips.

Suddenly, Odin and Mund shoved between us and leaped into the arena. Grey and I rushed to the edge of the pit to see three fighters had joined their fallen friend and were attacking Brychan.

"What do we do? We have to help him!" I said.

Baran was suddenly next to me. "I need you to stay here. Brychan, Mund, and Odin can handle this."

Baran, Quinn, Grey, and Channing stayed by my side. Brychan punched one of the attackers out cold as another shifted into a mangy wolf and came snarling and snapping at him. Brychan grabbed its jaw and held it open with his bare hands, stopping the creature from tearing his face open. I could see his blood running down his arms as the sharp teeth cut into his flesh. Odin and Mund shifted and stalked forward, ready to attack.

The wolf snapped at Brychan again, nearly biting his fingers off. Brychan yelled back in the wolf's face. It was terrifying. I needed him to be safe.

"Brychan!" I screamed.

Brychan ripped the wolf's mouth open, tearing off the lower jaw. The creature fell to the ground, bleeding to death. Odin took off after the other fighter and tore out his throat and Mund stood guard by Brychan. I was horrified watching them die; even after they'd attacked my pack, any loss of life hurt.

As quickly as it had all started, it was all over, but the arena was filled with the blood of the dead. Brychan jumped over the barrier, and I ran to him. His hands were bleeding all over; I grasped them in mine and studied the torn flesh.

"You need to shift to heal these," I said.

"Not until I get you safely out," he said. "They have lost two of their own and injured more. It isn't safe for any of us to remain tonight."

"I agree," Baran said. "Let's move."

I decided not to ask questions now. We darted toward the stairs. Several fighters dared to spit at us on the way out, and every angry cuss made me flinch. I was terrified they would revolt, and our small pack would be overtaken. We quickly left the Realms, climbing higher and higher to the surface until the beautiful light of the moon fell over us. I took a breath and let myself finally relax.

Brychan finally let go of my hand. I stared in horror: it was covered in Brychan's blood. I tried to wipe it off, but the blood had dried. I just need to know he was okay. I couldn't stand the idea he was in pain.

"Please, Brychan," I said. "Shift so you can heal."

"For you," he said. His body erupted and his flesh ripped as the wolf consumed the man. He shook out his brown fur and howled at the moon. He turned and sniffed my hair, tickling me. He howled again. It was a lonely sound, yet beautiful. Mund and Odin were still wolves and joined their voices. Hearing them all howl as one overwhelmed me and filled me with emotions. Baran and Channing shifted and joined in. Soon only Grey and I remained. I smiled at him and shifted as well. I felt my body changing and Old Mother's blood pulse running through me. The power of my pack filled my veins. I howled at the moon.

Grey shifted and we were one. Our voices joined together as we filled the valley with our love song. We howled together until one by one, my pack headed back to the shack, and only Grey and I lingered back in the dark. Only Mund noticed, but he gave me a subtle wink before nudging the door closed behind him. We were alone.

I started running as a wolf through the long grass, with Grey by my side. He nipped at my ear, and we collided. We wrestled in the grass until we were panting and exhausted. We didn't have to talk tonight; we could rest together as wolves until the sun came up. We snuggled together, breathing each other in.

In the early morning, Mund walked out to us in his human form. The sun had just begun to rise. "Mother will be up soon," he said, shaking his head. I nipped at his hand and ran toward the shack. I leaped into human form, and my cloak dress magically formed around my curves. I turned to give Grey a quick smile before darting inside. It was clear he had been staring intently at that tiny glimpse of my bare skin before the dress covered me again.

"Good morning, Mother," I said as I entered. She was at the table eating breakfast.

"Good morning, *m' eudail*," she said. "Did you enjoy your evening?"

I blushed.

She laughed at my scrunched-up face. "*M' eudail*, I know you love him."

"I do," I whispered.

I joined her at the table, and we ate in silence. Shortly, Brychan and the others joined us. They chatted among themselves, and I listened to their conversations. I loved them all so deeply. Even their ridiculous banter felt like home to me.

"Baran, what do the fighters' numbers mean?" I asked.

"That is how they decide who will fight each night," he said. "When a fighter enters the Bloodrealms, the wolf's name, pack, Bloodmark, and individuality is stripped away. The wolf becomes a number."

They lost their packs, freedom, and identity. And with it, they also lost their humanity. In their loss, the wealthy gained the ability to see their deaths as nothing more than a blood sport. It was cruel.

Dagny stalked into the shack, staring at me, and the room grew silent.

"Stand up," Dagny said to me.

I stood in front of him. I was tiny compared to him, and he walked around me, studying everything about me. I didn't know if I was in trouble, or he was about to eat me. Maybe he was the big bad wolf.

"You're fierce for a tiny little thing," he said, shoving me.

I stumbled back, shocked, and Brychan and Channing jumped to their feet in my defense, but I lunged forward, shoving Dagny with all my strength. He barely moved, but a smile covered his face. I stood back. "So? What do you want from me?" I said.

"Is it true that you killed Adomnan?" he asked.

I looked around nervously. Everyone was watching, listening, my pack and a group of Dagny's men. I didn't want to have this discussion with any of them. What right did he have to ask me that?

I closed my eyes and remembered the agony Adomnan had inflicted on me, and how much more evil he had planned. Familiar rage and hate filled my veins. I opened my eyes and stared right into Dagny's.

"He dared to touch me. He thought he had a right to own me, and I took his life to protect myself from his evil," I said. My voice didn't waver. I wasn't scared anymore.

Dagny's expression didn't change as he studied me. "You have more than proven yourself as a warrior to me. Why don't you come practice with us today?" Dagny said.

I smiled from ear to ear. I couldn't hide my excitement. I was going to learn how to move energy through me. I was going to be one of them.

"Don't look so happy. When I'm done with you, your body will scream at you for the punishment I'm about to inflict," Dagny said with a smile.

When I didn't stop smiling, he half smirked and slapped me on the back with his staff. "Move out. We train now," he said.

We all finished eating and got up to train. As we exited the shack, Brychan and Channing walked next to me. "If you want me to, I can put a stop to this," Channing said.

"If she wants to learn she can," Brychan said.

"Thank you both for your endless devotion," I said, "but I am capable of making the choice by myself."

We crossed the cold water to the hill on the other side to an open grassy area. I walked past them to where Dagny stood and waited for him to start. "Today we are going to do tai chi," Dagny said.

"That's not fighting," Channing complained.

"It is internal power," Dagny said. "You could learn a lot from meditation and using your opponent's momentum against him. Now shut your mouth."

As I started to mimic Dagny's movements, I felt a focus come over me. Every cell in my body vibrated with energy. It was exhilarating.

"Tighten your core. You need to be precise," Dagny said to me.

I forced myself to slow my movements even more, to the point where my muscles twitched with strain and sweat beaded on my brow. I felt alive. Soon we started boxing, punching, and fighting; it was just light training, no actual impact, but the movements came naturally to me.

They didn't bother to question whether I would come watch them fight again. From that point on, I would go wherever they went. Slowly I was teaching them my true place in the pack. I wasn't a frail woman who couldn't protect herself; I was one of them, and we protected each other.

21
Sacrifice

"Brychan, get in there," Baran said, slapping him on the back. We gathered around the ring, this time more cautiously. We watched all the other fighters who swelled around us. We even brought three of Dagny's guards into the Realms with us for extra protection.

"NINE-NINE-FOUR-SEVEN-TWO," the ringmaster yelled.

"Yeah baby," Brychan said as he winked at me. Brychan leaped into the ring opposite a tall Korean man with scars all over his face. Even his eye had a scar through it, and the iris was discolored.

The fight was instantly brutal and bloody. I had to look away. I saw Æsileif walking on the pit wall above the crowd. She smiled when she stood before us.

"Care to watch the Amazon women fight?" she shouted down to me over the roar of the crowd. "It's always beautiful. Like watching the ballet, but with blood."

I had watched the beautiful women parade through the arena several nights before. They were goddesses with knives and spears, so fierce and uninhibited. I wanted to be like them. I wanted to be fearless. I wanted to watch them fight.

"Stay close," Baran said.

I nodded. Baran was right, but I wished I could go. "Thank you for the invite," I said.

"You're always welcome with me," Æsileif said.

"I'll join you, mi' lady," Odin said.

"What a pleasure," she said as he escorted her out of sight.

I wondered if they knew each other already, or if this was the first time they'd met. They seemed like old friends. It gave me an odd comfort to think they knew each other. Perhaps their broken souls could mend each other.

Brychan finished his fight with the Korean man. Both were bloody, but Brychan had knocked the other man unconscious. Brychan wiped the blood and dirt from the cut on his arm as he jumped into the crowd with us. They had all grown used to me being in the Bloodrealms with them. Even Channing stopped complaining about it. In the tight crowd, I secretly held Grey's hand as his opponent was drawn from the numbers.

"ONE-EIGHT-FIVE-SIX," said the pit master.

The number he called was an impossibly low number, and that could only mean Grey's opponent was about a thousand years old. How could anyone survive down here for that long? Grey squeezed my hand and let go as he entered the pit. My hand was instantly cold, and I missed his touch.

A dark-skinned Indian man leaped into the arena. His hair and beard were gray. He had three horizontal stripes painted on his forehead and one vertical red one between his eyes. The man was bare-chested except for numerous bead necklaces that rattled together as he walked toward Grey.

When the horn blew, the old man leaped in the air and landed, rolling in a ball toward Grey. He uncoiled his body and kicked Grey across the ring.

The air was knocked out of my lungs, and my back burned with pain, but Grey sprang back to his feet with barely a flinch at the pain that seethed in my bones. I had gotten better at hiding the pain by pretending to be scared.

When I watched Grey fight, I was both horrified at the barbaric nature of it and attracted to his masculine scent and glistening body. It was like my brain and my primal need were fighting inside me. But always the physical pain I endured was the strongest. Brychan and Channing sat on the edge of the arena, heckling Grey.

"Just hit him!" Channing called as Grey took another kick to the chest. The older man coiled and kicked again and again. Every blow made me want to throw up.

"Okay Grey, you let him think he was winning, now end this," Brychan said with a chuckle.

I punched him in the arm right where the blood still seeped out from his fight. Brychan only smiled as he wrapped his arm around my shoulders.

"The boy will be fine," Channing said. "We'll teach him how to be a man yet."

I rolled my eyes. The two of them were nearly as bad as my brothers. If I closed my eyes, it was like listening to Quinn and Mund squabble.

"Teach me," I said.

I couldn't believe the words actually came out of my mouth. Was I actually asking Brychan to teach me to box? Had I lost my mind?

Channing chuckled like I had made some amazing joke. He didn't even consider it or look at my face to see if I was serious. He just assumed I was a lady, and ladies didn't fight.

I dared to look at Brychan. Part of me wanted to pretend I'd made a joke so he would stop scrutinizing me, but in my heart I knew it was what I really wanted. I wanted to be able to do everything they could do, and I needed to be able to protect myself. I couldn't trust that there would always be someone by my side to protect me. Besides, it was our responsibility to protect each other.

"You want to box?" Brychan said.

This time Channing looked. His pretty face was horror-struck. "Don't be ridiculous," Channing said. "She's a princess."

"Then I command you to teach me," I said.

"Umhmm . . ." Brychan murmured.

The air gushed out of my lungs, and I grabbed the nearest arm, digging my fingernails into Baran's flesh. He almost swatted me away like a bug before he realized it was me. He saw my face as I struggled to hide the pain from Grey's injury.

Brychan looked at Grey in the arena and saw him holding his side as well. He looked back to me, and I quickly moved my hand and tried to smile through my grimace.

"Oh Ashling, I'm so sorry I stepped on your toe," Baran said.

He hadn't, but the lie was enough to get Channing and Brychan's attention diverted . . . at least I hoped it was. Brychan still stared at me suspiciously. He knelt down and took my bare foot in his hand and started lightly massaging it as his blue eyes stared up at me. He easily found ways to touch me, and I could plainly see his love for me in his eyes, but I couldn't love him the way he loved me. In another life perhaps, but in this one, he was only my beloved friend.

Cheering caused us all to look to the arena, where Grey had the older wolf in a headlock and was forcing him into unconsciousness. The man's eyes fluttered, and his leg twitched as he went limp. Grey walked back over to us as several men carried the unconscious man out of the arena. I smiled at Grey in all his bloody glory.

The pit master lumbered out of the ring, leaving us to ourselves as he watched the Amazon women fight. Suddenly Brychan shoved my leg up, flipping me into the air. I shrieked as I tightened my core and landed gracefully on my feet. He grinned.

"Not bad," Brychan said.

Baran whacked him on the back of the head, but Brychan only smiled more. "I'll teach you to fight," he said.

"Absolutely not," Channing said.

"Not your choice, Chan," Brychan said.

Grey hopped over the barrier. "What are we not doing?" he asked.

"Ashling wants to learn to box," Brychan said.

"It isn't a sport for a lady," Channing insisted. "It's bad enough we allow her to view the fights."

Mund laughed. "Ashling has never been a lady."

I smiled as sweetly as I could with all my feminine charms and said, "Bite me." I leaped at the barrier and flipped into the empty arena, landing in a cloud of dust with my skirts swirling around me. Most of the crowd had wandered off to watch the Amazons, leaving us a little bit of privacy.

"My money's on you, Ashling," Grey said.

"Don't encourage her," Channing said.

Brychan jumped the barrier into the ring with me. He circled around me like a lion circling a gazelle. The hungry look in his eyes made my skin flush.

"Fight me if you dare," he said.

"Kick his ass!" Grey shouted.

Brychan lunged at me, and I tripped on my dress and fell in the dirt. My pride and my bottom ached.

"Are you sure about this?" he whispered as he helped me to my feet.

I tied the skirt of my dress into a knot above the knee and dusted off my hands. "I've never been more sure in my life."

He smiled and swung his giant fist at my head. I leaned away, screaming as his fist barely missed my face. My heart pounded as I tried to get some distance between us, but he pursued.

"You have to be faster," he said. "Anticipate me."

He swung again, this time an uppercut that lightly grazed my cheek. I stumbled back as he closed in on me. I wasn't scared of him, but I was terrified. And angry, so angry. Every step he took made me think of Adomnan and what he'd done to me. He made me feel like a victim.

"Brychan, knock it off!" Channing yelled.

"Use your anger, Ashling. Fight me," Brychan said.

He shoved me hard from the side, and I fell to one knee. I felt the sand cutting into my skin. Adrenaline pulsed through me, and the animal inside woke. He had no idea what kind of rage lived inside of me. I stared up at Brychan, thirsting for blood. For vengeance.

I jumped into the air and swung at him. He jumped out of the way and I missed. "Good. Now hit me," he said.

I started swinging my fists at him, one and then another, just like Dagny had taught me. He blocked them all, but I was starting to feel the rhythm of the fight. He swung again, but this time I blocked his blow with my forearm. My bones vibrated from the impact, but pride filled me.

"Harder, Ashling!" Brychan said.

I heard yelling from all around us, but I didn't understand any of it. I only saw him. I was filled with the need to win. The need to prove myself.

I faked left and swung right and nailed him right in the cheek. The impact nearly broke my hand. He spat blood on the ground and charged toward me. He swung at my ribs and I blocked, but he kept coming like bull. Again he swung, this time at my chest, and I barely jumped out of the way. He swung again, and his fist struck my face and split my lip open. The metallic taste of my blood filled my mouth, and my lip burned with pain.

Grey, Channing, and Mund leaped into the arena behind him. I snarled at all of them and didn't take my eyes off Brychan. The pain fueled my strength.

"Do not interfere," I said, whipping the blood from my face with the back of my hand.

Reluctantly they stopped, and I circled Brychan. He charged forward and swung at me again. He missed my face, but nailed me in the shoulder; my eyes watered on impact. He was so close I could smell him. I swung with all my strength, and I punched him in the nose. He grunted and knelt, rubbing his nose as blood dripped out.

"Nicely done, mi' lady," he said. "I surrender to you."

I was gasping for breath as I looked down at him and nodded. He stood, wrapped his hands around my waist, and lifted me into the air as he spun me around as the victor. He set me back on my feet next to Baran and Grey.

"You fought well," Baran said. "Far better than most in their first fight. Most men just lay on the ground and get punched until they cry for mercy."

The look of approval on his face was all I needed. He patted me on the back as Channing slowly walked over to me. He looked at my bloody face, and he took a deep breath.

"You are a lot tougher than I give you credit for," Channing said.

"Thank you," I said.

Grey gently wiped the remaining blood from my lip. His touch was so erotic. With the adrenaline in my veins, I felt reckless. I licked the blood from my lip as I yearned for his touch. My blood boiled with lust. I had to look away before I devoured him in front of everyone.

"You alright?" Grey smiled.

I smiled. "Better than alright."

I felt like a warrior goddess as we left the Bloodrealms. This time Baran, Mund, and Quinn didn't leave me alone with Grey; Mund promptly escorted me inside. I watched Grey as he walked into his bunkroom with the guys, and I wanted to run to him, but Mund blocked my path.

"I see that look in your eye," Mund said with a smirk. "Go to bed, my little warrior."

Clearly, it had not gone unnoticed that Grey and I had spent the last two nights away from our bunks. I sighed and went into the bunkroom.

I flopped down on the mattress, wishing Grey's strong arms were wrapped around me. I listened to the soft sounds of Nia sleeping on the bunk next to me as she snuggled with Tegan. Someone was softly snoring in the boy's bunkroom next door, and the footsteps of the guards echoed above us in the shack. I knew I was tired, but the adrenaline rush from fighting kept me awake.

I decided I would get out Calista's notebook and my sketchbook and go out to the fire. When I got to the door, I heard the soft voices of Baran, Odin, Dagny, Shikoba, and Kane as they drank in the common area. When I peeked out, I could see Odin's face half in shadow; the firelight danced across his strong features, making him look even darker than usual.

"Odin, it is good to see you again," Kane said. "It has been far too long."

"When was the last time we saw you? Were you at the wedding of Tegan and Mund?" Shikoba asked.`

"No, I didn't attend," Odin said.

"The last time would have been the Battle of Asgard, wasn't it?" Baran said.

"Have you really been hiding in the Underworlds for that long?" Shikoba said. "That's been over five hundred years. You really should have visited."

I leaned out into the room so I could hear, but the floor creaked. Odin's eyes flashed to the door where I stood and burned into mine. I could smell his sorrow.

"My entire pack died in service to the idea that you, Lady Ashling, would come one day and save us all," Odin said to me. The others turned to see me standing behind the door. "What good did it do my father and mother? My sisters? Or my love? They all died for nothing," he said. "So many wars were waged for this idea of you—and they all died for it. I lost everything and everyone I ever loved, and we still live in fear." Odin stood up. "You can't save us. You're just a little girl."

I was suddenly livid. I walked over to him and put my face inches from his.

"You're wrong, Odin. I will save our people, but not with some imaginary paranormal power—with love. I won't rule with brutality like my father or the Dvergars, but as one pack, one people. I can see your pain; I can save you, too," I said quietly. "You lost your pack, your whole world, but we can be your pack now. I will unite us all."

He touched the side of my face as he stared down at me. I could smell the booze on his breath. "Maybe you will, maybe you won't, but all those you love will die for it, just as my pack died. Are you prepared to watch them die for you?" he said.

"No," I admitted. I couldn't fathom the idea of any of them dying. "I'm sorry for your loss, for your pack."

"I have nothing left but my hate," he said.

"Here's to the Battle of Asgard and all those we lost to save Valhalla," Kane said, raising his goblet.

Odin drank from his goblet and threw it aside. It shattered against the wall as he continued to stare at me. The alcohol had made him bolder.

"You're just a little girl," he said sadly.

Odin walked away to his bunkroom, leaving me behind. Kane, Dagny, and Baran drank down the rest of their glasses. Baran patted me on the back as they headed toward their bunks.

Shikoba smiled softly. "Let's get some sleep. It's been a long day," she said.

"It'll be there soon," I said.

The warmth of the fire was inviting, and I lay down, basking in its warmth, with Calista's journal and my sketchbook. I flipped open my sketchbook to Vigdis's face. In one of the drawings I had sketched her eyes, and it felt like she could see me through the paper.

"You couldn't have known her," Dagny said.

I thought he had returned to the bunkroom, but he was leaning against the door, watching me. From my vantage point on the floor, he was a giant—thin, but incredibly tall. He walked back and kneeled down next to me, studying my drawing of Vigdis. I glanced back at the drawing of my dead aunt.

"I believe she died long before I was born," I said. "Did you know her?"

"We all knew Vigdis," he said, shutting the notebook.

"Why did you do that?"

"She can see you."

"Through my notebook?" I said skeptically.

"She sees through paintings, drawings, and mirrors. She splintered her sight into every image of herself, and she's able to see through them all. Each one is a gateway for her to watch us."

"Isn't she dead?"

"Perhaps, but her soul exists at least. No one knows for sure whether her body also lives," Dagny said, picking up my notebook. He slipped his thumb into the page she was drawn on and quickly opened the book. "BOO!" he shouted into her sketched face. As he pulled it away, I swore my drawing flinched. He slammed the sketchbook shut. "She may be dead, she may be living, but she is definitely watching."

He handed it back. I kept it closed, too scared to look at her again. If it was true, that meant she had eyes all over our world . . . even in the Kahedins' home.

"I have to tell Brychan. They have a painting in their house," I said.

"He knows," Dagny said.

"Why don't they take it down? Or burn it?" I said.

"It is no different than having a mirror in your home," he said. "All the goddesses can see in them. Mirrors are tricks of the mind. At least a painting she can't walk through."

"Walk through?"

"You wear a cloak of Old Mother's, so you've seen it. You've seen a glimpse into the magic. Now imagine if you stepped through it. What do you suppose is on the other side?" Dagny asked.

"I don't know. Have you stepped into one?"

"No one who has done so has ever been seen again."

"Do you think Vigdis is dead?" I asked.

"The last time I saw her was at the battle of Carrowmore. I stabbed her through the heart, but she stumbled back into a mirror and slipped through. She may be dead, she may be trapped . . . either way, she's watching you."

"That's creepy," I said.

"Indeed," he said. "Do yourself a favor and draw Xs over her eyes and free yourself from her intrusions. She won't be able to see you if you do."

Baran walked back into the room and studied us for a moment. "Dagny," he said. He nodded and sipped on his beer. Dagny nodded back. There was a silent sadness between them.

"If you'll excuse me, Princess Ashling. I have to take my watch," Dagny said. He bowed and went up above into the shack, leaving me with my questions.

"I'll stay up with you if you want," Baran said.

I sighed and opened the notebook again. She didn't flinch, blink, or move. Nothing happened. Had I imagined it?

"Dagny told me . . ."

"I know what he told you," Baran said, shutting the notebook.

"Do you think she can see me through my drawing?"

"I felt her cold eyes on me the moment you opened the notebook," he said.

"Did you know her?"

"We all have a history with Vigdis, but none so much as Dagny."

"What do you mean?"

"She was his betrothed. He was being fostered at my home that summer, and my father arranged marriages for both Dagny and me. We were just children then—Dagny was twenty, and I was just fifteen." Baran shook his head. "When I saw your mother, I fell in love. We were just kids, but our connection was instant. Little did I know, I was arranged with Vigdis as the elder daughter, but my father changed the betrothal so Nessa and I could be together; Dagny was smitten with Vigdis. Unfortunately, the insult was too deep for Vigdis."

"You were in love with my mother?" I asked.

"From the moment I saw her . . . and I never stopped," he said. He had a sad smile on his face. "I lost her when I lost my lands, my humans, my title, and my home. A goddess can't marry a homeless boy."

His sorrow settled on me, weighing me down. I felt like I couldn't breathe. Baran was meant to marry my mother . . . which meant I wasn't supposed to exist. I couldn't even understand the gravity of what it could mean.

"How could you let her walk away?" I asked.

"I wasn't given the choice," he said. "When I was seventeen, Brenna and I were traveling the world on the way to Greece to escort your mother to Scotland for our wedding. That is when Verci attacked us. I swore I saw Vigdis watching my family die, but no one found her. I've told you this tale before, but I left out the part about your mother." He cleared his throat and continued. "When I lost my castle, we lost our status, and I lost your mother. But don't feel sad for us. A moment in the warmth of your mother's love is worth a lifetime of loneliness. And after all, had I married her, I would never have known you."

Mother walked into the room with her silk nightgown flowing around her. "Are you filling my daughter's head with fairytales?" she said.

"The best fairytale, Queen Nessa," he said. He stood and bowed to her.

Mother kneeled next to me. "Your sadness woke me up," she said to me with a concerned look on her face.

"You were betrothed to Baran before Father?" I asked.

"Yes. Long ago. When I was only fourteen, I was betrothed to Baran, and my older sister Vigdis was then betrothed to Dagny. She was jealous of Baran's status, and one night I woke to Vigdis cutting my hair with a silver blade. When she saw I was awake, she put the blade to my throat, piercing my skin, making me mortal, but it was what she whispered in my ear that scared me to death . . ."

"What did she say?" I asked.

"She said she'd cut out my womb, so I could never have children." Mother shuddered saying the words. And a frigid chill settled over me. "I screamed as she continued to butcher my hair from my scalp. If Baran hadn't heard me scream, I would be dead."

"Vigdis tried to kill you?" I said. The thought of it filled me with so much anger.

"She did . . . and the damage was done. I was sent home immediately under guard, and Vigdis ran away."

"What was wrong with her? Was she a monster?"

"She was my sister, but her heart was black. I heard she was living with the Dvergars, and I believe she orchestrated the attack on Baran and Brenna. Before I even knew, I had lost my right to marry Baran. Then Vigdis showed up back home and murdered our sister Althea. Mother Rhea took Calista, Faye, and me, and we fled to the Boru for protection."

"Why did you marry Father if you loved Baran?" I asked.

"When Mother Rhea, Calista, Faye, and I arrived at the Rock of Cashel, I learned my hopes with Baran were ruined, but Baran kept trying to win me and prove his worth despite losing his royal title. And he may have succeeded, but when Brenna was found to be pregnant with Verci's child, and the laws said she should die for having a child without her father's consent, Baran had no choice but to kill twenty of the Boru's finest guards to protect her. By doing so, he broke his vows to the Boru, and the laws of our people dictated that Pørr must execute both Brenna and Baran. I did the only thing I could to protect them: I gave Pørr what he wanted—me—in exchange for Baran and Brenna's lifetime of safety."

"You gave up everything to save Baran, knowing you could never be with him?" I said.

"No—I gave up a dream for the chance to save three lives," she said. "I have always loved Baran, and I always will, but that doesn't mean I don't love your father. It's just . . . a different love." She said, smiling at Baran.

"Do you regret it?" I asked.

"Saving a life is always worth the sacrifice," she said.

22

Monsters

When morning finally came, my head hurt from all the thoughts that filled it. I never went to bed, and chose to lie in front of the fireplace studying Calista's journal instead. I was trying to make sense of my future; I kept coming back to the Celtic lunar calendar she had drawn. It split the Elder Gods over the phases of the moon and year.

The Vanir were at the center of the Spring Equinox, the Boru at the center of the Summer Solstice, the Dvergar at the center of the Winter Solstice, and the Killian at the center of the Fall Equinox. Baran was a descendant of Elder Gods, which meant Grey was also. My family ostracized them when they were truly equals, even in their made-up laws.

Two Bloodmarks were drawn to each side of the Elder Gods for a total of twelve ruling packs, including Kahedin, Kingery, Cree, and Pohjola. The Tree of Life was drawn in the center. It was the same symbol I found on the love-spell book of Grey's and the door of the bookstore. I didn't know any pack in the world with that Bloodmark, but it was obviously the key to this mystery. I shook my head in frustration.

I was alone in the barracks. The men were already training and the others had gone up to enjoy the sun. They were waiting for me. The plan was to go visit Geiranger, a little tourist town not far from where we stayed that was holding a beer festival today.

"Hurry up, Ashling!" Gwyn yelled from above. Her voice carried through the floor.

She lacked for patience. I grabbed all my books and put them in my messenger bag and headed out to find my pack. I rode up into the shack and found Gwyn, Cara, Tegan, Nia, Mother, and Shikoba waiting for me. I wanted to stay and train with the guys, but I was excited to be around humans again.

"I'm so excited," Gwyn squealed with Cara right by her side.

"It's going to be so lovely to get away from this dirty shack and all that testosterone," Cara said.

Tegan laughed with them, but I was too nervous to be excited. I didn't like the idea of going into town when we were surrounded by a constant flow of free fighters and slaves traveling to and from the Bloodrealms. The concentration of wolves in this area of the world was terrifyingly high.

We arrived at Geiranger, a town nestled down among the mountains like a little secret. It was a strange little town that was built into the landscape and shaped by the lake that surrounded it. We wandered around the small festival through a sea of wolves. Some would nod at us as we passed. Others would bow, but Gwyn didn't notice any of them as she sampled the different beers. She completely let her guard down, which made me even more nervous.

She tasted one that made her groan with enjoyment. "This is lovely," she said. "Ashling, you must try it." She handed a clay beer stein toward me, sloshing it over the edge.

A few paces ahead, I saw Eamon. He turned around in the crowd and gawked at me. He wore a green velvet coat and had been bartering with a man when we approached. I hadn't seen him since we left Maine, and it was startling to be face to face with him again.

"Ashling? What are you doing here?" he said, looking around.

"I should ask you the same thing," I said.

He shoved something in his pocket to hide it. I couldn't tell what it was, but he kept fidgeting with it like he was checking to make sure it was still there. He took a step toward me, and I took a step backward. I needed there to be distance between us. I didn't want to endure his touch again, and I watched him warily.

"I wasn't expecting to see you here," he said.

"Sorry to disappoint you," I said as Tegan and Shikoba surrounded me. I felt instantly stronger with them by my side.

"No, that's not what I meant," Eamon said.

"You'll have to excuse me," I said. "I have things to attend to."

He kept looking around, like he was afraid to get caught. He was nervous, but was he nervous for himself or me? And what was in his pocket? Had he bought something, or was he selling something? I quickly turned and walked away. Whatever he was doing and whatever spooked him wasn't anything I wanted to be part of.

"What was that about?" Tegan asked.

"I don't know. He seemed genuinely confused and nervous," I said.

"Maybe he's just trying to manipulate you," Tegan said, "and get your guard down."

"Probably," I said. "But I don't feel safe here. We're too exposed."

"Let's head back before we meet any other unsightly creatures," Gwyn said.

The walk back took forever. I watched the sun setting and knew with every step we took, I was losing my chance to go into the Bloodrealms with the guys. I wanted to rush them, but when I looked at Mother, Tegan, Nia, Shikoba, Cara, and Gwyn, I knew they needed me more . . . I had the eerie feeling we were being followed.

The guys were all gone when we made it back to the shack. I'd missed them. I was angry and annoyed. I wanted so badly to be one of them.

"You coming, ylva?" I heard Baran's voice on the wind.

"I'm going with Baran!" I said to Mother. I darted around the shack and saw him in the distance, standing at the entrance to the Bloodrealms. I ran across the grassy hills as fast as I could until I caught up. Baran wrapped his arm around my shoulders, and Mund messed up my hair.

"Where are the others?" I asked.

"Already in the tunnels," Mund said. "We'll catch up in no time."

I couldn't help but smile as we climbed down into the darkened Bloodrealms. When we reached the bottom of the second ladder, I let go. Grey caught me in his arms before my feet hit the ground. He nuzzled my neck and kissed my cheek.

"You waited," I whispered.

"I'd wait forever for you," he whispered back.

He reluctantly put me back on my feet and we walked the rest of the way into the fighting pits and caught up with Odin, Quinn, Channing, and Brychan. Brychan hugged me, and Channing patted my shoulder.

"It's a good thing you're a fast runner," Brychan said.

"Thanks," I said.

"Channing, you're up first. Brychan, you're second," Baran said.

The pit master lumbered into the pit and started reading the numbers of the fighters. All the attention was on Channing and Brychan as I weaved my fingers with Grey's, pulling him a few feet deeper into the crowd, where our touching wouldn't be noticed.

Grey leaned in close and whispered in my ear, "I can't get you off my mind. I dream of you. I think of you. I yearn for you."

His breath tickled my neck, and tingles went down my spine. I bit my lip, and I pulled Grey through the crowd to some place we could be alone. I glanced back quickly to make sure no one had noticed us. We walked through many lit pathways—turning left, right, right, and another left—to a darkened and deserted tunnel just behind the gate.

He looked down at me with a look of unrestrained passion. I pulled his body into mine.

Grey devoured me with kisses and pressed himself into me. I needed his touch, and a fire burned inside of me. His tongue danced with mine and I could feel his body grow hard. He grabbed my thighs and lifted me up against the wall. I rolled my head back as I rocked against him, and I ran my hands over his bare chest. I moaned as he kissed my collarbone, leaving a trail of moisture behind. He kissed me between my breasts, where my dress exposed my skin, and I shivered desperately, wanting more. I needed him to fulfill his wordless promise, but he set me down and rested his forehead on mine. His green eyes were wild with passion as we struggled to catch our breath, but my heart pounded with need and my skin was on fire. I knew we had to get back to the others before our absence was noticed, but we stayed in the warmth of each other's arms.

I looked around and finally took in our surroundings. The tunnel walls were covered in claw marks, but I couldn't tell if they were trying to get in or out. It was an unsettling thought. A strange motorcycle lay on the ground near us. It looked older in style, possibly from the 1930s, but it was strange. It was pieced together in raw brass and nickel, and it was curved like a wolf with its hackles raised, like a steampunk god.

A horn blew and suddenly our deserted tunnel was filled with fighters running in a frenzy. They were pushing and shoving each other frantically, and Grey and I were shoved farther into the tunnel between all the men and women rushing inside.

Someone slammed into my back, knocking me to the ground, and a sharp rock cut into my palm. I gasped and panic raced through me as people tripped over my body. It was a stampede. I tried to stand up, but they were all around me. I was trapped.

Suddenly Grey yanked me to my feet and pulled me over to the wall. He made a cage out of himself around me, protecting me from the mass hysteria that surrounded us. Fear prickled over my skin as I clung to him and the mob surged past us. Not one of them seemed to notice we were there. Whatever they ran from was far more frightening than we were interesting. Finally the dark tunnel was empty, and only Grey and I remained.

Grey touched my cheek. "You okay?" he said.

"Yeah, just a little startled," I said, licking my hand to numb the cut.

The sound of heavy breathing echoed from behind us. And Grey's smile disappeared. We looked down the long dark tunnel. I couldn't see anything, but I could feel the air moving around us as the creature breathed in and out.

"What the hell is that?" Grey whispered.

I was too terrified to think. I didn't want to meet whatever it was. I closed my eyes, trying to calm my nerves. I just needed a moment to breathe.

"Ashling, we have to get out of here," Grey said.

My heart was pounding. He put his hand on the side of my face and forced me to look at him. His green eyes glowed in the darkness like a beacon to safety.

"I'm scared," I admitted.

"Me too," he said, holding my hand.

We started running toward the gate, toward safety. I heard a whip crack behind me. Searing pain shot through my ankle as leather bit into my flesh. I screamed as I was violently torn from my feet and dragged down the filthy tunnel. My body slammed and bumped into every angle of the cobblestone floor, cutting and bruising my skin. I struggled to untie my ankle, but I couldn't get a hold of it as my body was raked over the floor.

"Ashling!" Grey yelled as he started to run after me. I reached for him and he leaped for my hands, but I was yanked out of his reach, and I felt his fingers slip from my grip. The look in his eyes was paralyzing. "Damn it! No."

I heard his footsteps fading in the darkness. I was pulled from the dark tunnel into the light. I covered my eyes from the bright firelight that burned above, and I squinted up at a giant holding the other end of the whip. The blisters and sores on his face were filled with puss, and he had a lazy eye. He was enormous and ugly, twice the size of the ringmaster giants. He didn't wear leather armor like the ringmaster giants; he wore dirty rags.

"You disgusting monster—let me go!" I said.

"Mine!" the giant bellowed.

I tore at the whip, trying to uncoil it. The whip was tipped in silver ,and terror flooded through me. Was I mortal? I tried to shift, but my body just vibrated, and nausea washed over me. The silver whip had already started poisoning my blood.

"Grey!" I screamed. "The whip was tipped in silver—I can't shift!" I screamed. Where had he gone? Had something captured him? Was he hurt? I hated that the silver poison blocked me from feeling Grey. It was terrifying not knowing where he was.

The giant came lumbering at me with his enormous meaty hands outstretched. I screamed and scrambled backward, but the whip chained me to him. I had nowhere to go. I shook with fear as I realized I was alone.

23
Fenrir

Grey rode into the light on the steampunk motorcycle and skidded the bike between the giant and me. He whipped the back tire of the bike around, knocking the giant to the ground. Barely stopping, he reached his arm out to me and pulled me onto the bare metal seat behind him.

"I've got you," he said.

I wrapped my arms so tightly around his chest I could feel his blood rage through his veins. I buried my face against his back and tried to stop shaking, but it was no use. I was terrified. We drove back down the tunnel toward the arena, but the gate was closed. We skidded to a stop and Grey leaped off trying to force the gate open. It didn't budge.

"Baran!" he yelled, but no one was coming to save us. He kicked the gate and the dried blood shattered off, revealing that the gate was made of silver. I should have known—how else would they hold an entire population of wolves captive? The dried blood actually protected Grey from the silver.

The giant bellowed, and his feet thundered and echoed off the rounded walls as he lumbered toward us. "Come here, little dolly. I want to hold you!" the giant hollered. He sounded almost childlike.

"Mund . . . Brychan! Please!" I screamed. "Grey, what do we do? I'm mortal."

He jumped back on the bike, pulling me with him. We sped down the dark tunnel, right at the giant. Horror was the only thing waiting for us. I stared up at the monster as he swung his whip. I buried my face behind Grey's back. The air whooshed by my head as the whip missed us by only inches. Grey popped a wheelie, and the giant moaned and stumbled backward. We raced under the giant's legs as a blob of his drool dripped on my arm. I cringed as the warm ooze ran down my skin. Grey drove us across a thin stone bridge deep inside the Bloodrealms. Dread settled on me—we were going the wrong way. I had no idea whether there would be another way out.

Ten minutes later, we entered the junkyard city of Fenrir. I recognized it from what I'd seen through the grates in the floor, but from down here, I could see it was so much bigger. It went on for miles. People had stacked old rusted cars together and welded them into little shacks. There were even cars welded on top of stands high in the air, like watchtowers. At first glance, the city looked deserted, but when I looked carefully, I could see faces peering out of the cracked windows.

"How are we going to get out?" I said.

"I don't know yet," Grey said. "But we will think of something. We just have to find somewhere to hide."

We drove through the endless, desolate junkyard city. The few people who peeked out at us quickly hid again. None of them dared interact with strangers here. They didn't know if we were friend or foe, and they certainly weren't going to risk their lives to help us.

The giant came clumsily stomping into the city as we reached the far side. Before he noticed us, we ducked behind an empty car. The giant swung his whip and tore the roof off a car. I heard a woman scream. Warriors jumped out of hiding and attacked him, forcing him back the way he'd come—they looked like steampunk gladiators. The city was heavily guarded, despite us not seeing anyone out in the open. I was thankful there was someone there to protect these people from the evil we led right into their city.

"My dolly!" he bellowed as he was forced back the way he came.

"We'll have to find another way out of here," Grey whispered.

Hidden in shadows across the town, I spotted a significantly smaller tunnel in the stone. It wasn't close, and it looked less than ideal, but it appeared to be the only way out of Fenrir. "What about there?" I said.

"It's worth a shot," he said.

Fear prickled over my skin as we rode into another tunnel with only our dull headlight to show us the way. We drove in the darkness with the only sound coming from the motorcycle. The noise was deafening. Just because we couldn't hear anyone didn't mean they didn't hear us. I shivered at the thought.

The silver poison was starting to wear off already. The tips had barely touched my skin, so the effects were short lasting. I was thankful for that. I was thankful for a lot of things, most of all not having to do this alone. I would be terrified if Grey wasn't here with me, but he shouldn't be here at all. It was entirely my fault; I shouldn't have pulled Grey away from the others to kiss him, but there was no point in dwelling on it now. Regret didn't help us survive. It only got in the way.

We drove for an hour without stopping or seeing another living creature. I had no idea the Bloodrealms went as far or as deep as they did, and after an hour, I had a feeling we had just started our descent. I was exhausted and hungry. I felt like I might fall from the motorcycle from fatigue, but we didn't dare stop. The stone walls were blackish green and crudely chiseled, but it was the endless claw marks in the stone that struck fear into my heart. Everywhere I looked were the claw marks of forgotten souls trying desperately to survive. Occasionally we'd pass cracks in the stone just wide enough for someone to hide, and when I had the strength, I would glance in them as we passed and see glowing eyes. I had to stop looking. I didn't want to know how many watched us flee or how many would pursue us.

We entered an old throne room, but everything was broken or missing. The enormous ceiling was black carved stone that sparkled in the dim light of the motorcycle. The size of this room made the throne room at the Rock seem dwarfed.

Grey slowed the bike as we neared the head of the room. The floor was covered in black stones that glittered in the light. I stepped off the bike and picked them up in my hands, studying the surface. I'd never seen anything like it. They were black but glittered red in the light. I smelled the stones, and I quickly threw it aside.

"What is it?" Grey asked.

"Blood," I said.

"It looks like glass?"

"This must be the Throne of Blood. It's a myth. No one knew where it was, but it is said that Verci Dvergar had a secret castle where he tortured his enemies. I read in one of Baran's old books that Verci would tie up his enemies, cut off their feet, let the blood drip out into a bowl, and boil it until it thickened. When the blood was poured into a silver mold, it turned to stone."

"That's messed up," Grey said. "Are the Dvergars all crazy as hell?"

"I don't think we should stay here." I felt like there were eyes all around us, but I didn't see anyone.

"Yeah, let's get out of here," he said.

We rode out of the throne room through a doorway into a mine filled with raw gold and uncut diamonds.

"What is this place?" Grey said.

"This must be King Uaid's missing treasure." It was covered in years of dust and cobwebs. Completely untouched, but not unknown. A path continued down into the mine; there were many footprints in the dust and dirt. It was obviously still a common road here.

"Why don't they use their wealth?" Grey said.

"Maybe Eamon doesn't know it's here. Or maybe there is a reason no one touches it," I said. "People travel through here all the time, and yet no one touches it . . . and I don't think we want to know why."

We rode onto an overlook that looked deep into a mineshaft. An ornate mirror hung on the chiseled wall near a table and two chairs that were covered in filth. The chandelier barely hung above the table, and all the candlesticks were broken or missing. When we walked toward the table, I noticed the mirror didn't show our reflections. Instead, it showed the chandelier lit in all its glory, and the table and chairs were pristine. Was it a painting of the past?

I grabbed the edge of the mirror, turning, it and it reflected the mine in full working order. It was filled with slaves harvesting gold. They just kept working like we weren't there. Was it an eerie glimpse into the past? No matter how I turned it, the room came alive, but it never showed us.

"What kind of magic does that?" Grey asked.

"I saw Lady Faye put her arm through a mirror once. The way the glass pooled around her skin when she dipped her arm inside it . . . it was amazing. She retrieved my cloak from the other side," I said. "Like the magic of balefires, mirrors hold unthinkable powers."

Grey reached for the mirror like he was going to try to reach inside it. I held my breath. Out of nowhere, a silver dagger flew past my head, barely missing Grey's hand and slammed into the mirror, shattering it. As the glass began to fall to the ground, I saw a reflection of a woman in the broken shards. She had a black lace veil over her face, and she was standing right behind me. I didn't know if she was really standing behind me or who she was, but I turned around and swung as hard as I could, slamming my fist into her face. She screamed as she stumbled back. My fist pulsed with pain.

"Get away from us!" I yelled at her.

She stood, and as I stared at her veil-covered face, I saw the bloodmoon lettering. I was staring at the dead . . . Vigdis.

"Vigdis?" I gasped.

"Garm," she hissed, "consume them."

I grabbed Grey's hand and yanked him back to the bike. The rocks flew up in a cloud behind us, and we raced down into the mineshaft. He kicked the wall to stop the bike from skidding into it, and an avalanche of stone and gold rained down on us as we drove deeper into the earth. Every few yards, another tunnel appeared. There were hundreds of different paths to take and no way to know which one was the right one, or even how to follow our paths back out.

Barking and snarling echoed in the mine behind us. I looked back to see how close they were; I couldn't see them clearly from afar, but they didn't look like normal wolves. As they gained on us, I could see a pack of giant hairless wolves with bloodstained skin tearing after us. I desperately tried to find my strength, but my fear was winning.

"Grey, they're getting closer. I don't know what to do!" I shouted in his ear. Grey's hands were clenched tightly on the handlebars, and I could tell he was shaking, but he reached back and put one hand on my cheek. I knew we would either live or die together.

As the Garm wolves closed in on us, Grey maneuvered through the thin tunnels, weaving us deeper and deeper into the earth. With every turn, fear settled deeper in my mind. Would we ever find a way back out? The Garm were so close I could feel their breath on my skin. One snapped and sank its teeth into my dress, pulling me from the bike. As I fell to the ground, I shifted into a wolf and let Old Mother's strength flow through me. The rest of the wolves continued to follow the bike, but the one who tore me from the bike stayed on me. I snarled and bit into the skin of the hairless beast, tearing away his rotting flesh. I gagged at the taste on my tongue, but I kept fighting.

I heard the bike crash to the ground and skid. Some of the others circled back and surrounded me, pacing forward to make their kill. Grey's hideous growl filled the room. He was a dire wolf—equal in size to the Garm. He leaped onto the back of one of the beasts and tore it apart.

Another lunged at me. I bit into its throat, silencing his snarl. Grey fought through them to my side. Killing one after another. Together we protected each another, and we killed them all.

Grey howled, and we raced back down the path toward the motorcycle. He shifted into human form midstride with his back to me. He quickly picked up his leather armor and put it on his body. I shifted back, and my cloak formed around me. His naked skin was a delightful distraction from our near-death experience. Even here, in the evilest place on earth, I wanted nothing more than to be comforted in his arms.

Grey and I jumped on the bike, and we raced down the tunnel. When we turned a corner, the path ended.

"We're trapped," I said. There was nowhere else to go. Grey leaped off the bike and looked down into a tiny shaft in the ground

"There are some steps down; this is our only way out," he said.

The hole was barely larger than my body. I wasn't even sure Grey would fit down it. I looked at the rotted wooden steps cautiously.

"Hurry," Grey said. "Get in."

I climbed on the first step and it broke. I fell deep into the dark shaft, as step after step shattered under my weight. A splinter gouged into my hand as I finally caught my grip.

"Bloody hell," I moaned.

Grey jumped inside the shaft and slid down the rough wood until he was right above me. "You okay, love?"

"Yeah, just a little cut," I lied. It hurt like hell as I pulled the splinter out with my teeth. He probably knew that—he could feel my pain as I could feel his—but I still pretended it didn't.

"I hope that witch burns," Grey said. "She and her demon pets."

"Why could we see her and not us in the mirror? It doesn't make any sense. She was real. I hit her," I said.

"Yeah, you did," Grey chuckled. "Looks like you have a mean right hook."

As we climbed farther into the shaft, I couldn't help but wonder where he would be—were I would be—if I hadn't ever met him. Would I be marrying Brychan soon? Would Grey be with Lacey or someone else? "Grey, do you ever regret giving me that ride in the woods when we first met?" I asked.

"And what—miss out on all this?" he said with a laugh. "Ashling, someday you are going to have to accept that we are meant to be together."

"I suppose I will," I said.

The passage went on forever, and my limbs ached when we came to a carved-out shelf. I climbed on it, shaking, and lay down, thankful for the break.

"Let's rest. Just for a minute. Okay?" I said.

Grey crawled next to me and wrapped his strong arms around me, spooning me tightly to him. We cuddled and I closed my eyes, letting my exhaustion consume me.

I woke up with Grey still snuggled close. I leaned my cheek against his and breathed him in. Even on this tiny shelf in the middle of the earth, I was still the happiest girl in the world to have him with me. In the middle of this ancient war, we still had each other. I kissed his cheek and he murmured.

"Good morning, my love," I said.

He yawned and stretched. "Should we keep going?" he asked.

"No time like the present," I said.

"You're my present," he said, kissing my neck. I giggled and wiggled away from the tickling sensation that vibrated down my body. It was innocent and sensual at the same time. He cupped my face and slid his tongue into my mouth, and I gave in to my passion. He moaned as he ran his fingernails over my body. I licked the edge of his ear, nibbling and sucking on his earlobe. The shelf wasn't big enough for us to move around, but I wanted his touch.

"I'm glad you're mine," he said.

"And you belong to me."

"Where do I sign up?" he said, smiling so deviously.

I kissed him again, gentler and sweeter this time. "We should keep moving," I said, but I didn't want to. I wanted to stay in his arms.

We climbed down another fifty feet when I found another passage. The air was cool, but I didn't smell blood. Our only options were to continue down or try this path. Neither was a sure bet.

"Should we try it?" Grey asked, jumping onto the rock ledge.

"I don't know," I said, leery.

"Well, no way to find out unless we explore it," he said. "Come on, we'll do it together." I jumped onto the rock after him. He held my hand as we walked down the long passage in the near darkness. I would have been afraid, but I was content with him by my side. Still, the endless darkness filled me with dread.

"Grey, what if we don't survive?"

"We'll get out of this; it just seems bad right now," he said.

"We've probably been here for more than a day. We haven't eaten. We may never get out of here alive," I said. "What if whatever is on the other end of this passage is waiting to kill us?"

"Then I guess we fight until we either win or die," he said. "We don't have any other choice than that. What are you really afraid of?"

"I'm afraid that I'll never get to see my mother again, or Mund, or Nia. I'm afraid you'll die and I'll never get to feel your lips on mine again," I said. Saying the words nearly took my breath away. My greatest fear was living in a world without him. "I don't want our journey together to end—we've only just started our story. These may be the last days we have on earth."

Grey smiled and got down on one knee, holding my hand. "Ashling, I will love you every day of my life, and beyond. Even death is just the beginning of where my love for you will go."

"You are the blood in my veins and the beat of my heart," I said.

"Ashling Boru, will you marry me?"

My breath caught in the cold air. I looked into his green eyes and knew without a doubt he was made for me, and I was made for him. It was no coincidence that we found each other; he had to be the wolf by my side at Carrowmore. There was no one else it could be. I loved him with every piece of me, and I wanted to spend the rest of my life with him by my side. I had no doubts or reservations. Grey was mine . . . and I was his. "I will."

"When?"

"Now. We may not have tomorrow," I said. "Marry me now, Grey, for Old Mother to see."

"What do we have to do?"

"Say our vows," I said. "She'll hear them. She can always hear us."

Grey smiled and his eyes glinted and glowed in the dark tunnel. "Ashling Boru, I never truly lived until I met you. I was frozen and broken, but you brought me to life. You are my beginning, and together we will never end. Our love is endless," Grey said.

My eyes welled up with tears as I looked into his eyes. His love for me was more than I ever dared to dream. He loved me for exactly who I was.

"Grey, I love you with every fiber of my being. You are in my every thought and every dream. In front of Old Mother, I give you all of me, from now until forever," I said. "We are one soul with two hearts, so we must bind our soul back together. Repeat after me: *We join our bodies so two may be one, until our lives are done. We join our spirits in eternal forever that no evil can ever sever,*" I said.

"*We join our bodies so two may be one, until our lives are done. We join our spirits in eternal forever that no evil can ever sever.* I'm yours, Ashling," Grey said as he kissed me.

"And I'm yours," I said barely holding back my tears.

I'd always dreamed of marrying Grey, but I never thought it would be in the dark levels of the Bloodrealms, but nothing could stop my happiness today. Grey kissed me again, and his tongue slid into my mouth, filling me with need. As quickly as he started, he stopped again, leaving me wanting.

"I will marry you again in front of our families when we get out of here, and I will slide my ring on your finger," Grey said. "And claim you as my love for all the world to see."

"I love you, Grey."

"And I love you," he said.

Grey weaved his fingers with mine, and we continued together down the passage to the unknown.

24
Wonderland

We walked for half an hour before we finally reached the end. There was a two-way parting in the passage; it went fifteen feet to the right and about forty-five to the left, but both were dead ends. We had spent half a day walking for nothing. I was so frustrated that I screamed and sat down on the rough stone.

"We are never getting out of here," I complained.

Grey sat down next to me and smiled as he nipped at my earlobe. I captured his lips with mine and kissed him so passionately he couldn't pull away. His heart thundered in my ears. I was out of breath, but I kissed him again. He guided me down to the cold stone, kneeling above me as he kissed my neck and shoulders. I loved the weight of his body over mine. He was so sweet and so masculine at the same time.

"At least we have something to pass the time," he said. The wicked grin on his face made me laugh.

I kissed his bare chest and ran my fingers gently over his hips. I wanted to devour him. My soft touch made his pulse quicken. I lightly nipped at his chest, marking his skin with my teeth. His breath rushed out and he panted. His primal need burned through my veins, igniting me even more. He slid his hand up my leg and massaged my thigh. I arched into him, craving more. I reached around, trying to unfasten his armor, and he sat up out of reach, but I could see the lust in his eyes as he looked at me. He wanted me as much as I did him, and it wouldn't take much to push him past the point of no return, but we both knew this dark, lonely passage wasn't the right place. He helped me to my feet, and we walked back the way we came.

By the time we got back to the ladder, we were both exhausted. We curled up in the darkness on the cold stone and spooned for warmth and love.

I woke up to Grey playing with my wild hair, twirling it on his finger. "Good morning," he said, flashing me a mischievous smile.

My stomach growled and he frowned.

"We better keep moving," he said.

"Or I might get hangry," I said.

"Hangry?"

"Yep. Hungry-angry." I smiled.

"Well, we wouldn't want that to happen," he said with a laugh.

We resumed our climb down the ladder's steps. It seemed endless at first, but eventually I could see the dimmest light from below. I stepped down again and again, trying to reach the light, but this time there weren't any more steps, and I had to cling to the ladder to keep from falling. The shaft ended and the ground was about fifteen feet below.

"Shh," I said. "I'm going to see if it's safe."

I let go and let myself drop to the bottom rung, grabbing it and holding on. I hung down into the room. It was another mine that looked like it hadn't been touched in over a century. A small waterfall washed over the cold stone, and perfect snowflakes formed from the overspray of the warm water in the cool air. The pool of water at the bottom was clear and steaming. The mix of the hot spring and the frigid stone created a winter wonderland.

"It's beautiful down here," I said. I dropped down into the snow.

Small holes in the ceiling allowed little particles of light inside that shined like stars. Where were we? I had thought we were so deep in the earth, but somehow we seemed to be getting closer to the outside. The stone right around the pool was glistening with the melted snow, and the soft, rhythmic sounds of the water were serene. Grey dropped down next to me and studied the space. There were no doorways or tunnels out; it was yet another dead end.

"It looks like the only way out is to climb the waterfall and follow the stream out," Grey said. "If the water can get in, we can get out."

"We should be safe here for a night," I said. "The Garm shouldn't be able to reach us. It will be like sleeping under the stars."

I walked over to the edge of the water and dipped my bare foot inside. It was warm and welcoming. I sat down and hiked my dress up so I could dangle my legs into the hot water. The healing energy of water was incredible. I sighed and let it ease my aching muscles.

"After the prophecy is fulfilled, do you think this evil will die?" Grey asked.

"I think evil will always exist, but we will never stop fighting against it and trying to make a better world," I said.

"For our children someday," Grey said.

I'd never heard him talk about our future with children in it. He just always talked about wanting to be with me. My heart swelled with love at the thought of our children and what they might be like, and seeing him as a father.

"If they're anything like us, we'll have our hands full. We sure seem to attract danger," I said.

"We?" he smiled.

I splashed the water at him, soaking his feet. I laughed. He leaned up against the stone wall with his muscular arms crossed over his chest.

He didn't look like the boy I'd fallen in love with only a year ago—he looked like a warrior. My skin tingled just watching him. Even just the way he moved turned me on.

"Do you think you'll write a song about this adventure?" I asked.

He hummed an eerie tune that filled the cave with beautiful echoes. It was melodic and sad, but it had undertones of hope. His voice was thick and arousing. I bit my lower lip as I watched him walk around the perimeter of the small cave.

He ran his hand over the rough walls as he walked, and stones fell from his touch. He knelt to pick up one of the largest. He held it in his palm and seemed to be weighing it. He smiled and handed it to me. It was a drab and boring rock, but far lighter than it should have been. I wacked it hard against the ground, and it cracked open. Inside was a sparkling amethyst.

"I love rocks," I said. "They are pieces of the earth that hide memories inside." I handed it back for him to see.

"What memories do you suppose this one holds?" he said, looking inside.

"Ours."

I pulled my dress off over my head in one smooth movement as I slipped into the warm water in only my underwear. I floated in the hot water topless; the water covered me from his view, but I wanted him to see. I was done waiting.

Grey smiled and his green eyes twinkled with excitement as the light snow fell around us. The cold snowflakes were exhilarating as they landed on my bare skin only to melt moments later. It was like a dream. I was nervous, and I bit my lip to stop it from quivering. The warm water swayed around me and aroused every cell in my body. I waded in the water, hoping he'd join me. Praying he'd be mine. He unfastened the leather armor from around his arm and removed his shoes, tossing them aside.

I swallowed hard as he jumped in. The water splashed and lapped over the rocks. He stared deep into my eyes with longing as he pulled his leather pants out of the water and threw them onto the rock. I knew he was naked and only the water separated us. Anticipation filled me with need. I swam closer to him and kissed his lips as I wrapped my legs around his waist and pulled myself against his hard body. My bare breasts rubbed against his chest, and my skin tingled.

He groaned as I rocked my pelvis into him. He bit at my neck as he layered kisses over my skin. I moaned and my skin ignited with his touch. I needed all of him. We belonged to each other.

"We should stop," he said.

"No, we shouldn't," I breathed. "We may only have tonight."

"What about the prophecy?" he said.

I smiled as I threw my underwear onto the rocks. "I've chosen you."

Need filled his eyes, and he pulled my naked body onto his. He kissed my breast and his warmth filled me. Our bodies were one as they were always meant to be. I moved in rhythm with the water as we made love with the cold snow melting on our glistening skin. Every nerve in my body was alive, craving more. His fingers dug into my thighs, and every thrust made me lose control a little more, craving release.

We collapsed into each other's arms and floated in the water. Our bodies glistened with sweat and steam, pulsing with raw energy. He held me tight as he moved my wet hair from my neck to kiss me.

"I want to do that again," Grey said.

"For the rest of ever," I said. I laughed as I nibbled at his earlobe.

I finally understood what it meant to fully bind with Grey. Mating was the final euphoric connection. When our bodies were one, I could feel all of his memories, and he could feel mine. We shared every emotion, hope, and fear in those enlightened moments. I finally understood that binding didn't mean that we couldn't survive without each other; it meant that we would always yearn for the pieces we'd given to the other, and forever cherish what we received. It was better than I imagined. It was pure love, trust, and primal lust. Many species mated for life, and werewolves were no different. It was how we were made, to love and protect one another. Wolves couldn't survive alone, but we thrived as a pack.

"Ashling," Grey said. "Whatever happens, I will always be with you."

Did he sense the fear in the back of my heart? "Grey, we have to protect our secret when we get out. We can't let them know."

"I know," he said sadly. "I know."

I was afraid that our secret vows and mating would be hard to hide from the others. We were completely bound to each other now, but if I had to die here, I was thankful it was with him by my side as my husband.

"Make love to me?" I said with a smile. He slid into me, and we lost ourselves again.

Eventually, we climbed out of the water and dressed. His back was covered in scratches, but I knew they weren't from the fight with the Garm—they were from me. And his teeth marked my breasts. I lightly kissed his back where my fingernails had damaged his perfect skin, and we curled up on the warm stones with Grey's strong arms around me, and I felt whole. We held each other under the faux stars and fell asleep.

I rolled over and kissed Grey's lips until he woke and kissed me back. Every kiss made me want to have him inside me again, but we couldn't stay in this place, forever lost in ourselves. We had to find a way out and protect our pack.

"Good morning again, my love," he said.

"I think it's a good day to escape this place," I said.

"Good, because I'm getting hangry."

He yawned and stretched as he put the rest of his leather armor back on. He kissed my cheek and started to scale the rock face toward the top of the waterfall as I admired the muscles rippling in his back with every move he made. He looked down at me still on the ground.

"You coming?" he said.

"Sorry, just admiring the view."

He laughed. "Well, don't let me stop you."

He let go of the rock, dropped to the ground next to me, and picked me up, wrapping my legs around him. He crushed my lips with his, and I burned for him. Twice was not enough.

"When we get out of here, I'm going to make love to you every day for the rest of our lives."

I moaned. "Yes, please."

He lightly kissed my forehead and set me back on my feet.

We started climbing up the face of the slippery rock, but the stone was frigid to the touch. Grey didn't seem to notice how treacherous and cold it was. He nearly flew up the rock. I struggled a little more with it, but my mind was preoccupied. Grey disappeared over the top into the water. I heard a splashing and then nothing.

When I finally reached the top, Grey gave me a hand, pulling me into the flowing water. He was soaking wet, and it reminded me of the night before. We stood in the warm water high above the pool where we'd made love. The memories made me excited again, but the air was uncomfortably crisp.

The water flowed through a small crack, but there wasn't a tunnel or even a crawl space we could escape through.

"There's no way out," I said, panicking.

"Trust me," he said, pulling me into the water up to my neck.

"Are you crazy? What are you doing?"

He smiled and pulled me underwater. I was frightened at first, but I trusted him. We swam through a tiny passage in the rock. My lungs began to burn from lack of oxygen as we surfaced in a still pond on the other side. I gasped for air as I looked around. The water grew dark and seemed to drop off toward the center of the pond. A thin stone bridge was suspended from the ceiling on a pulley.

On one side of the bridge was a tiny rock shelf with human remains and on the other was a tunnel leading out to the light. When the bridge was raised, whoever was on the rock ledge would either drown or starve to death.

"It's an oubliette," I said.

"A what?" he said.

"A place for the forgotten."

I swam over to the bridge, and the closer I got, the stronger the current flowed. I struggled to reach the ledge, but Grey pushed me forward. I grabbed on and pulled myself up onto the bridge. There was no way I could have swum that if the bridge hadn't been down; the current was too strong.

We were soaking wet, and I shivered in the cold air. I crawled over to the bones. I could feel his loneliness. He'd been here for centuries, waiting to return to Old Mother's arms. His despair was debilitating. I began striking rocks together, trying to create a spark. If I accomplished nothing else, I could set this one soul free.

"They'll see the fire. They'll find us," Grey said.

"Can't you feel his sadness?" I said. My eyes filled with the dead man's sadness.

"Let's burn this place to the ground," Grey said.

Grey took the rocks from my shaking hands and sparked a fire in the rags left from the man's decomposing clothing. The warmth of the flames wrapped around the bones. His peace settled over me, easing my emotions. He'd be home soon.

We crept down the tunnel into the darkness. Small rodent bones cracked under my bare feet, and the air was damp. The tunnel split and it seemed hopeless, just looking at our choices. We'd come so far, and yet we were no closer to escaping.

Grey turned left. "We just have to keep moving. We'll be out of here by nightfall," he said.

"Is it even daytime?" I asked. "I've lost all sense of time. I don't even know how long we've been down here."

"Well, we'll just walk until you get tired, and then I'll carry you the rest of the way," Grey said rubbing his fingers over my ring finger.

I smiled in the darkness. I found comfort knowing we could overcome anything together. He gave me strength when I lost mine.

Grey pulled me to him. "I want to kiss you," he said.

My stomach filled with butterflies, and my body yearned to be touched. I gently kissed his lips as his hand caressed my body, over my breasts and waist before finally grabbing my thighs and lifting me up and grinding into me. Passion fueled my soul, and I kissed his neck, breathing him deep into my lungs.

"You make me crazy," he whispered breathlessly.

The sound of footsteps surrounded us, and hushed whispers crept through the walls in a language I didn't speak. I looked at Grey in pure panic. They'd never stop hunting us.

"Run," Grey said.

25

Passage Grave

Grey grabbed my hand and we ran as fast as we could, but the footsteps weren't far behind. I looked back to see a gang of men chasing us. They didn't look like the pit masters or the simpleminded giant. They looked ruthless and they hunted us. They were so close I could smell their rancid breaths, and they smelled of old blood and soured alcohol.

We darted down a dark tunnel, but it was a dead end. We were trapped, and it was only a matter of time before the trackers found us.

"Wait here until they follow me. I'll lure them away," Grey said.

"No, Grey. I won't leave you."

"It's the only way," he said. "I'll be fine. I'll catch up with you. I promise."

He looked so confident. Like he was just going out for coffee, not running toward our enemies. The likelihood I would ever see him again was impossible to imagine. Didn't he realize what he was giving up? He was giving up everything.

"Grey, NO," I said.

I lightly touched his arm, and he turned back to me. A flicker of uncertainty crossed his face. He half smiled that mischievous grin I loved so much.

"I know," he said. "If I die, I will find you again."

He crushed my lips with his and ran out of the tunnel. I hid around a corner and listened. I heard them run after him, but I knew how fast Grey could run. He'd easily outrun them. Still, I was terrified.

I waited until I couldn't hear their footsteps anymore and I crept back to the open, smelling the foul air. There wasn't any sight of them. I began walking in the other direction when a heavy net fell over me.

I struggled and screamed as I tore at the ropes, but I couldn't get free. I shifted into a wolf and I ripped at the net with my teeth. The twine tore away and I bit into silver threads, cutting my lips. The silver poisoned my blood, and my mind thickened. I tore at the silver threads, desperately trying to break free. I howled in mournful rage as I involuntarily shifted back into a human; I was their captive.

"Grey!" I screamed, but he didn't come back. He was already gone or captured or worse. I couldn't feel him with the silver in my veins.

The men were walking back to me, speaking animatedly in their language. Had Vidgis sent them after us? Did they work for Eamon? What were they going to do with me?

They started carrying my net suspended from long staffs balanced on their muscular shoulders. The net swayed with every step they took, and it made me feel nauseated. I tried to memorize the tunnels we traveled through so I would know how to escape, but they all looked the same. The same old bloody smells and rot and the occasional dead body or skeleton. There was nothing distinguishing about them.

They suddenly stopped and listened to the tiniest echo coming from a doorway we passed. It was pitch black inside, but I heard it too: the faintest sound of a baby crying.

The men dropped the net, and I groaned as my body slammed into the cold ground and the bars hit me in the head. Only one of them stayed near me. They split up, one going to each possible exit and one went into the doorway.

"Hide! Whoever you are, hide!" I screamed.

The man kicked me hard in the ribs as he cussed at me in some other language. "Run!" I screamed again. He kicked me over and over again until I couldn't breathe. I held my side and gasped for breath.

The screams of women and children chilled my bones. They came running toward us, holding children in their arms. I could smell their fear as the chaos began and they were trapped between these skilled hunters.

"Stop! Stop this!" I screamed. "Leave them alone, you bastards!"

I watched in horror as the men threw nets on them. One mother was captured in a net, but as she fell to the ground, she thrust her child into the arms of another, who ran through an unguarded doorway with several others behind her. I felt full of envy and pride as I watched them flee.

Two men pursued a woman, taunting her as she backed into the wall. Tears streamed down her face as she clutched a baby boy in her arms. Her scent hit me, and I wanted to cry. She was human. She tried to run past them, but they grabbed her hair and nearly ripped it from her skull. When she fell to the ground, they ripped the baby from her arms. She wailed so painfully and tore at them to save her baby, but one of them began punching her in the face.

"Please stop! You're killing her!" I cried.

One of the men looked at me before stopping the other man. He looked at me again and I nodded. He put the baby in a separate net from the mother as they both screamed for each other. I was overwhelmed with their grief. It filled my soul with agony. What was a human mother doing down here?

They tied the baby's net next to mine and picked us up. The baby was crying, and it broke what little confidence I had left.

I reached my arm into the baby's net and held his hand as I cradled him to me. He had the loveliest blue eyes, glistening with tears. He looked so familiar. The baby soon quieted, and his mother gave me a mournful smile. His blond hair was curly and bouncy as he burrowed into my arms. They had hunted down and captured six women and five children like animals. It was horrific and senseless. What were they going to do with us? What was the point of this suffering?

They walked through tunnels for what felt like forever. It was an endless droning march. I closed my eyes from it all and just held the baby boy with all my love, trying desperately to comfort him.

We entered a half-circular room that opened to at least a hundred-foot drop into the darkness of a waterfall. Through a glass floor below us, the waterfall raged over the edge. The sound was deafening. There was a balcony overlooking us filled with the faces I'd seen in the gallery of the arena. We were nothing more than merchandise to be auctioned off. Terror ripped through me.

"Help us!" I screamed.

Not one of them looked at us. They just continued chatting amongst themselves. I was disgusted by everything they stood for. They had no humanity left in them—they preyed on the weak and stole their souls. I tried to shift, but the silver poison still seeped through my veins, and I was nothing more than a little girl.

They started separating the women from the children, and the sadness in the room was deadly. I heaved under the weight of their desperation. I felt like I couldn't breathe from all the heavy emotions that crushed my chest. One mother wouldn't let go of her child. She sheltered the babe, but the man slit her throat to silence her cries. I screamed at the horror that surrounded me. The tracker who had stopped the beating came over to me and wiped the tears from my dirty face as he pulled the little boy from my arms.

"No, no, please!" I begged, but he pried him from my mortal fingers. He gently placed the boy in a small cage with the others, and they were carried out of the room. The women screamed and cried for their children as they were released from their nets.

They tried to rush after the children, but they were beaten back so brutally I had to look away. My hands shook with anger.

"Stop!" I screamed. "Stop hurting them! You're monsters!"

Only one of the gallery viewers even looked at me. He was the Asian man with the red-tinted glasses who had noticed me with Shikoba when we first entered the Realms. He smiled at me. My stomach knotted, and I realized no one was going to save us. All the doors were guarded—there was no way out. A tracker kicked me as he released me from my net.

The mothers were herded into a cage, and I tried to follow, but the tracker slammed his fist into my stomach. I dropped to the ground, gagging. When I blinked away the tears, I was alone with the trackers. There was nothing I could do to save any of them right now. I couldn't shift to a wolf. I was nothing more than a human girl. I saw Selene in the gallery, and I foamed with rage. She was Gwyn's friend—how could she be so cruel? She looked right at me and didn't do a thing to protect me.

"I will kill you all," I hissed.

The man charged toward me to silence me, but the nice one blocked his path.

"To hell with you all," I sneered. I ran toward the waterfall and I leaped with every bit of strength and plummeted down. I watched in horror as the room above became nothing more than a dim light. My body plunged into the icy black water.

The water rushed fast and deep into the earth, churning and threating to drown me. My skirts twisted violently around me as I broke the surface. I struggled and clawed to stay above as the water twisted my body around. It felt like cold hands trying to wring me and drag me down. I desperately grabbed onto something floating in the water. As I pulled myself onto it, I looked into the dull eyes of a dead body snagged on the jagged rocks. The smell of the bloated flesh made me gag. I heaved myself onto the ledge to the safety of the stone with my legs still dangling in the dangerous water.

"Old Mother, thank you for sparing my life," I whispered.

I lay on the cold stone that was my salvation. I ran my fingers over it in each of the Neolithic spirals, thanking Old Mother for my life.

I closed my eyes and thought of Grey and his warm arms around my body. His lips urgently seeking mine. His hard body pressed into me. I wanted to seek refuge in his love. I could almost see his face and his beautiful green eyes as though he was right in front of me, but when I opened mine, I was still alone and afraid in the darkness.

I wiped my wet hair from my face and wrung out my dress as I looked up to where I'd jumped from. I could barely see the light of the room. It was a miracle I survived. The vicious water could have taken me under, or the jagged rocks could have claimed me. I was alive and alone in the bowels of the earth.

I couldn't see any exits from where I sat, so I started walking toward nothing, searching in the dark for a way out. I ran my hands over the stone in the darkness so I wouldn't lose my way, and the sound of the river guided me.

It was unnerving having my eyes taken from me in the darkness. I had to rely on touch, smell, and sound. I was too scared to pretend to be strong. I wanted to go home. I wanted to shift. My body ached with hunger and fatigue, but I forced myself forward. As I moved, my steps became more of a shuffle, and just moving took more energy than I had.

Small beams of light from high above lit my path every few feet. I was thankful for even the tiniest bits of light—they made me feel less alone. I looked around desperately for somewhere to hide for the night, but there wasn't anywhere safe. Finally, I just sat down with my back against the wall in the darkness. I was halfway between lights on each side; I hoped it would give me the upper hand if something came lurking in the night.

I leaned my head back against the wall and curled my knees to my chest and took several slow breaths, trying to calm my fear. I thought of Grey lost in the Realms, of Mother worrying, and of all my pack. I knew I was a symbol of hope for them. I was more than a daughter, a lover, or a friend. I was their beacon of change, and without me they would lose sight of hope. I didn't have a choice—I had to survive.

I woke later, unsure how much time had passed, but the soft sounds of something scurrying brought my hunger to life. A heavy rat scampered into the light, headed right toward me. All I had to do was wait until it was close enough and shift, and he'd be mine. My mouth watered at the thought of eating.

I lost sight of the rat as he entered the darkness with me. I listened to his steps and knew exactly where he was. Ten feet. Eight feet. Six feet. I leaped up to pounce on him, but instead of shifting, my human body slammed into the ground. I gasped and gagged for air as I clutched my side, and the rat scurried away.

"Damn it!" I cried in frustration. I couldn't even catch a fat rat.

The silver was still poisoning my body, and I'd just lost my only chance to eat. I wanted to cry, but it would take too much damn energy. I pulled myself to my feet and started walking again. To where I didn't know, but if I sat down again, I was afraid I wouldn't get back up.

I passed another dead body, and the stench was nauseating. I had to gag down stomach acid as I forced myself forward. I was surprised there was ever another soul down here, even if it was a dead one. Had it been a woman who had leaped from that balcony? Or was it a guard who fell to his death?

The sound of snarling wolves vibrated on the stone and echoed behind me. I started to run away from the sound as fast as my feet could carry me. I tried to shift again, but it was no use. I was human. A pack of Garm wolves tore after me.

"Old Mother, save me!" I gasped as I ran.

The Garm started tearing the dead body apart as I ran for my life.

I didn't know where I was going, but I didn't have time to care. Three of the Garm started chasing after me. My heart pounded so hard in my chest I thought it might explode. The sheer size of the hairless, wrinkled beasts behind me was terrifying. I could barely kill them as a werewolf. What chance did I have as a human?

The idea of being torn to death made me shake with fear. I just had to outrun them. In the back of my mind, I knew that I wouldn't last for long in my mortal condition. I would tire quickly. My only option was to run for as long as I could and at the last second jump in the water and take my chances with the raging river. My feet pounded against the cold and unforgiving stone. I looked to the water . . . was it time to drown?

A small ledge in the rock about ten feet aboveground caught my eye and I ran toward it. As an immortal, I could easily jump that, but with the silver poisoning me, I wasn't sure I could make it. Risking it and falling would be the end of me. I could smell their foul breath behind me. I had to choose; there wasn't time to think: water or earth? I jumped up and my fingers scraped for life. I felt my fingernails tear away and blood pool around them, making the stone slippery. The pain pulsed in my aching hands, and my adrenaline flowed freely. I swung my legs up and rolled my body onto the ledge as the pack started jumping at me. They could nearly jump as high as the ledge, and their enormous jaws snapped at me. They weren't agile like werewolves, but they were fierce. They kept jumping and howling and tearing at the rock. Their desire for my flesh was unending.

I crept backward on my butt, trying to push myself into the wall so they wouldn't be able to reach me. I felt a small opening in the rock just big enough for me to fit through. I crawled inside and felt my way into the passage to a large open room of stacked stone with a corbelled ceiling. A small opening at the top went all the way through the stone to the surface of the earth, and the light shown in, illuminating the darkness with hope. It was the first sign I might survive since I lost sight of Grey.

Several rocks were shaped into bowls, and inside each one was a pile of tiny burned bone remains. The spiral symbols of each of the bowls were exquisite. This place belonged to the dead—it was a Passage Grave. A Passage Grave was a place of honor among the dead; the bodies were to be burned and placed in a Passage Grave under the stars. Only important priestesses were cremated in this way.

I could almost feel death here—like a cold wind of many souls talking at once. It was eerie, but I felt safe surrounded by Old Mother's priestesses.

I picked a mace off the floor, and I wiped a thick layer of dust off with my dress. It was made of solid flint in shades of cream and umber, with a face carved into it. The handle went through its mouth. It was a piece of our history.

The weight and balance of it felt good in my hand, and I clutched it to my chest as I lay down in the dirt and listened to the angry, snarling creatures that lurked outside. I closed my eyes and thought of Grey. I hoped he was safe. I desperately wished I could feel him. Even his pain meant he was alive. Even in his pain I could feel solace.

I woke to the sound of complete silence. The light had changed; it was a mysterious blue now—the moon. I didn't know what time it was, or how many days had gone by since Grey and I first got lost, but the moonlight shined brilliantly down on me. I closed my eyes and lightly rubbed my thumb over the carved mace head.

"Protect me, Old Mother," I whispered. "I need your strength, for I have a long way to go."

My stomach growled and my body ached. I was desperate for food and water. And sleeping on the ground in the cold made every muscle in my body scream, but I forced myself to leave the safety of the dead.

I crawled out of the passage onto the ledge that was now covered in teeth and claw marks. If this grave hadn't been here, they certainly would have pulled me down and eaten me alive. As I peered over, I saw that the Garm had killed one of their own. Most of it had been eaten, and the bits left were covered in maggots. I cringed at the sight.

I shimmied my way down to the ground and started walking into the darkness once again. I hated the darkness. It surrounded me and made me feel desperate. I missed the light, the warmth of the sun. I wasn't sure Old Mother could even find me all the way down here in these layers of darkness and hell. Could she hear my cries and prayers? Did she even know I was here?

The roar of an engine in the distance began to fill the cave, and my heart leaped with excitement. Finally someone was coming; another person was going to save me, and I wouldn't have to be alone anymore.

I hid in a crack in the stone, watching and waiting for the car to approach. It crept closer and the sound thundered around me. As the bare metal car came into view, I started to creep out to beg for help when a small hand grabbed mine. I nearly jumped out of my own skin. Before I could scream, a large, strong hand clamped over my mouth and held me in place.

"Shhhh!" was all I heard.

I struggled to see the car as it began to drive slowly past. I was desperate to get to it. It was my salvation. It was my only way home, but the harder I struggled, the firmer the grip on my face was. I couldn't see who was behind me, but I glanced down at the small hand holding mine and barely made out the silhouette of a child.

As the car rolled past me, I looked back up and saw the driver. My heart sank. It was Eamon. He was hunting for me. I'd almost run out to him for help. If it weren't for the tiny hands clutching me in the dark, who knows what he might do.

When the sounds of the car died away, the hand finally let go of my face, but the child held onto my fingers. I turned to see the face behind me, but it was too dark. I couldn't tell how far the crack went into the stone, but there were surely more than three of us hiding in here.

"Thank you," I said, "for saving my life."

No one responded. The adult tried to pull the child farther back into the darkness, but the child didn't let go of my hand.

"Who are you?" I asked, kneeling down to the child.

"Jutta," she said.

"I'm Ashling," I said.

"That was a bad man," Jutta said.

"I think you're right."

She pulled me to the dim light outside the crack, and I saw her little face was covered in scars. It looked like she'd been whipped, and my heart burned with sadness. I touched her cheek, running my fingers over her damaged skin.

"You're beautiful, Jutta," I said.

I wanted to hide with them, or have them show me the way out, but I knew that my presence with them would only get them killed. Even though every part of me wanted to hide with them, I knew I had to leave.

A man stepped out from the crack. He had Jutta's dark eyes, and similar scars covered his entire body. He wore only a tattered loincloth.

"Come Jutta, we must go," he said.

She reached her tiny hand back out for me, but I knew I couldn't go with her no matter how much I wanted to. I took off my arrowhead necklace that Shikoba had given to me, and I put it around her neck.

"This will protect you," I said. "I will find you again someday, Jutta."

She smiled and kissed my cheek. She ran after her father back into the crack. If it was a way out, I didn't know, but I left them, to save them.

I started walking along the river again. In the light across the raging water, I swore I saw something move. I crouched down to the ground, trying to be as small as I could as I waited for it to move again. I watched for a long time, but nothing moved again. Had I imagined it?

I crept back to my feet and continued. I walked as long as my legs would carry me from light to darkness. I had been in the darkness so long that I almost welcomed it. My legs wobbled with fatigue. I couldn't even remember the last meal I ate or what it tasted like. After a while, I sat down and curled into a ball in the dark and closed my eyes.

I pictured Grey with his lips on mine, and I yearned for his touch. He was my soulmate. It didn't matter that Eamon could give me power, or Channing could give me unending wealth, or even that Brychan could offer me protection and friendship. I loved Grey. Love knew no bounds, nor did it give me an option. Love was pure and absolute. No matter what the others could have offered me, I knew Grey was the right choice. I was bound to him. His energy calmed mine. My energy activated his. It wasn't just lust or even love; it was the perfect balance and partnership. We were one soul in two bodies, and it didn't matter what anyone said; he was my love. He was my dire wolf.

The silver was wearing off. I could feel Grey's rage telling me he was alive, but I didn't know if he was safe. I prayed to Old Mother to protect him. If I ever got out of here, I was never going to let him go again.

I stood and continued my walk along the river. I saw a fire burning in the distance. Part of me wanted to rush to it, but I had to force myself to be cautious. I slid the mace into the braided belt of my dress and silently walked toward the light. The sound of the gurgling water drowned out what little sound my bare feet made on the stone. As I grew closer, I crouched down to watch a hooded figure hunched over the modest fire. I yearned to crawl closer to the warmth. I watched for a while as the figure began cooking a large rat. The smell of the dripping grease made my stomach roil with hunger.

The figure's head spun around and stared right in my direction. I was frozen with fear. I wrapped my fingers around the handle of the mace and waited. I waited for them to attack me, but the person reached out a dainty wrinkled hand.

"Come child, warm yourself," she said.

I forced myself forward, watching her every move. She patted the ground next to her and pulled the hood down to reveal her weathered face. Every wrinkle told a story. Her eyes didn't glow like a wolf, nor did she smell like one. She smelled human.

I stood and slowly walked over to her. When she touched my hand, I nearly jolted with the energy that pulsed through her. She wasn't a mere human, but I didn't know what she was. She handed me part of the rat. I didn't wait to be polite or dance on courtesies. I was starving, and I devoured the greasy meat, nibbling every morsel from the tiny bones. It tasted better than anything I could remember eating.

"Thank you," I said, licking the grease from my dry lips. "What is your name?"

"I don't have a name. We are all one."

"Who are?" I asked.

She just smiled.

She was old and frail. Her back was hunched and she was tiny. She picked up her short staff and used it like a cane to bring herself to her feet. The head of the staff had a flint mace, with carvings similar to the one I now carried. She saw me looking at it.

"Do you live down here?" I asked.

"This is where I belong," she said. "To shepherd the dead home."

"Are you a priestess?"

"No more questions, my dear. Eat up." She handed me the rest of the rat.

"But—"

She shook her head and started to leave. Her curved body slumped over her mace as she hobbled away. She turned and smiled at me.

"Aren't you afraid?" I asked.

"Fear is the enemy of love. And I only hold love in my heart."

She waddled off into the darkness, leaving me alone at her fire to eat her food. I felt greedy but thankful. Just seeing someone alive down here made me feel like I would survive. I regretted not asking her which way to go, but she left me hope.

I curled up next to the fire and rested. The warmth and food in my stomach made sleep feel so much more inviting. I didn't even mind lying on the cold stone.

I stood in the green grass on the Carrowmore in Ireland, waiting for Old Mother to approve me as her queen. I stood in the center circle with my pack surrounding me, every one of them kneeling before me. Grey had claimed me, and now I only needed Old Mother to give me a blessing and I could save my people. I could save the earth.

Vigdis walked into the center of the other adjoining circle. The tattoos on her face moved and changed with her thoughts.

"I will rule here," she said.

"This is my island," I said. "And these are my people."

"You will have nothing left to love," she said.

My pack began screaming and clutching and clawing at their throats as they fell to the ground, writhing in pain. They were dying. I ran to my mother and grabbed her hand, holding it to my face, but she was already dead. Her beautiful eyes were dull and didn't see me—she didn't see anything. I sobbed and held her in my arms, rocking back and forth, letting my agony rip through me as I wished and prayed for just one more day with her by my side.

"Please don't leave me. I need you. Old Mother, please give her back to me," I pleaded. "Please."

"Old Mother won't save you now. The wrong wolf claimed you, and now you're mine," Vigdis hissed.

I woke shaking and crying. I couldn't breathe. I clutched the mace and closed my eyes, waiting for the anguish to stop raking through my soul. The light and warmth of the fire had burned out. I was surrounded by darkness again. I was tired of the darkness.

I sat in the dark trying to understand the dream. What did Vigdis mean? Would everyone I love die if Grey claimed me? Was he the wrong wolf? If it wasn't him, who was supposed to claim me? Was it Brychan or Channing or even Eamon? What could it mean? I had to get out of here before any of that would matter, but it plagued me.

I started down the river's edge once again, hoping it would lead me somewhere safe, or just somewhere at all. The unending darkness and shadows were daunting. With every step I took, I felt like the shadows moved with me, lurking and waiting for me to fail. Were they the shadows of the dead? Or just shadows?

As I walked along, I started to see a strange structure rising out of the ground like a stalagmite. It twisted and turned from the ground over the water.

As I got closer, I realized it was a stone staircase high up above the water like a bridge. The steps were carved out of stalagmites. It looked like the stairs from hell, but would they be my escape or my doom? There wasn't a railing or anything to hang on to, just these tiny carved stairs. Would every step I took be a step closer to freedom? I had to find out. I had nothing left to lose.

I slowly started my ascent; every step was uneven and treacherous, but I forced myself to continue. The river raged below me, inviting me to fall. I forced myself to look up, and I could see a door at the top of the stairs carved into the rock. I was almost there. I just had to keep going.

My hands shook as I opened the door and entered an ornate room. Every detail of the architecture and lighting was exquisite black dragon glass, but I was drawn to the fireplace. The warmth of the flames licked out toward me, beckoning me closer. I sat on the floor in front of it, letting the heat soak into my cold skin, warming my aching bones.

"Are you okay?" a woman said. I turned around to see Æsileif. "I have been searching for you for days. How did you get here?"

26

Warrior Queen

Relief washed over me—she would help me find Grey and get us out of here. I wanted to go home. I wanted out of this dark place. This was hell itself.

"I will get you something to eat and drink," she said reassuringly.

Eamon walked into the room, and when he saw me, his smile faded. He just stared at me. His expression filled me with unease.

"You did this, didn't you?" I said, pointing at him. "You're behind it all, just like your brother Adomnan!"

"How did you get here?" he asked, looking around frantically.

"I could have been killed in your little game," I said. Anger and fear raged through me, and I couldn't stop my hands from shaking.

"You shouldn't be here," he said.

"I demand you let me go home immediately. I don't want to play your little games anymore, Eamon. I want to go home." My voice wavered, but I swallowed back my tears.

He reached out for my hand and I leaped backward, avoiding his dangerous touch.

Æsileif walked back into the room and I rushed over to her. "Æsileif, he's evil. We have to get away from him," I begged.

"Eamon, is this true? Are you evil, Eamon?" She asked. He didn't answer. "Oh Ashling, my precious one. I can protect you."

She started curling and twisting my hair in her fingers, like she was playing with a doll. Fear settled over me as I looked into her dark eyes. She pulled on black lace gloves as she stared at me, smiling.

"Æsileif, help me. Please," I said.

"I am, my dear."

She held a thin silver chain in her gloved hand, a dainty piece of pure evil. It was absurd to fear a little decorative chain, but it would destroy me. I backed away from her.

"Don't run," she said. "You'll be my pet."

"Never."

"Oh, you will," she said as she whipped the silver chain at me. I covered my face with my hands and it sliced into my palm. The poison leached into my blood. I gasped and stumbled backward. Why was she doing this? I thought she was my friend. Was there no one I could trust?

Eamon grabbed my arm and pulled me back to my feet. He lightly traced his fingertip over my wrist. With every twist and flourish of his finger, my skin burned and ached. I tried to pull away from him, but he just tightened his grip and finished.

"I think she needs more time in the Realms before she will learn to obey," he said.

Æsileif's laugh was beautifully vicious.

"Do it!" she taunted. "Do it!"

"With pleasure," he said.

He opened a trapdoor and shoved me into it and closed the door. The darkness surrounded me once again. I plummeted down a slide in pitch black. I was scared of the dark and what lurked there. I slammed into the slide and screamed in pain, but covered my mouth to stifle the sound. I didn't want the Garm to hear me. I was terrified, and the silver made it hard to think. The slide opened up and I fell in a heap, gasping for breath.

I was lying on a pile of corpses, and they were still warm. I cringed away from their open eyes, but everywhere I looked they were around me. It was like they were watching me, accusing me, and they had every right. I was meant to save them, and I had failed them all.

Blood dripped on me from above. It was thick and coagulated. I tried to wipe it from my skin, but it smeared. I scrambled away from the pile of bodies on my hands and knees. I was defeated; I didn't even know where to begin to escape.

The familiar sound of the Garm wolves filled the room. The little strength I had left evaporated with their snarls. I had nothing left. I froze in horror as a pack of the hairless creatures came running toward me and the pile of fresh flesh. I was sitting in their dinner like a cherry on top.

The Garm started feasting on the bodies. The popping and cracking sounds made me shiver. I hid behind the pile. My heart was pounding so loudly that it vibrated in my ears. I didn't know where to hide. There were ten tunnels out, and I had to pick one and hope it would lead me to safety. I slowly backed away from the beasts, one step at a time. I froze as one Garm wolf fixed his hideous red eye on me and started stalking forward.

"Not today, devil dog!" I pulled my mace from my hip, readying for battle.

It leaped toward me, and I screamed as I slammed the mace into its face, tearing open its rotted flesh. It shook loose the hanging skin and charged. It was nearly on top of me when a six-foot-long spear ripped through its body. It collapsed to the floor with blood seeping around its carcass, covering my bare feet.

I jumped to my feet, adrenaline rushing through me. A beautiful African goddess pulled the spear from the creature's side, twisting it as she yanked out the heart on the end of her spear. I remembered her steampunk-gladiator leather armor from the arena. Her skin was as black as midnight and as beautiful. She moved with the instinctiveness of an animal and the agility of a dancer. She stared at me for a moment before grabbing my wrist and pulling me after her into a hole in the rock.

"Hurry," she whispered. I didn't know who she was, but in that moment, I would have followed her anywhere. We began to shimmy through sideways.

I could hear the Garm clawing at the stone; their nails sounded like metal spikes scraping on a chalkboard. The hideous sound mingled with the sound of tearing flesh. I was surprised when hot tears filled my eyes, believing there was nothing left. I blinked them back; I didn't have time for weakness. My fear almost cost me my life. A moment's pause here was almost certain death.

We came into a darker, wider cavity. I raced after her through the gloom, trusting my ears and my nose to lead the way through the tunnels. The darkness abruptly ended as we entered a firelit cave. I pulled my hood over my face to shade my eyes as I adjusted to the light. Fires were lit all around the space, and three men stood waiting for us.

"Dilara, you risked your life for this pup?" one man asked. He stood much taller than the others. He had golden hair and golden skin and bright blue eyes, and every inch of him was rock-hard muscle. He wore leather armor that was marked with the Kingery Bloodmark. Was he safe? Was he my ally? Was she? Or was this another trap? "You know we have orders."

"What is she to us?" another asked.

The woman looked at me and smiled. "She is everything," she said.

I was covered in blood and filth. I felt self-conscious under their scrutiny. The woman was even lovelier than I had first thought. Her features were extraordinary, and her black skin was flawless, except for a scar on her shoulder. Her dark eyes were luminous in the lighting, like beautiful pools of chocolate. Her gaze was intense.

"Who is she?" the golden man asked.

"Princess Ashling," she said.

She knew my name. I had no choice to hide as a common wolf now. Now I was worthy of a price on my head. He laughed as he knocked my hood off to reveal my face.

"So you're the one they all want," he said, studying my face.

"Who wants me?" I asked.

"Everyone, from the way I hear it," he said.

From the smirk on his face, I imagined he was referencing my many suitors, but I didn't engage. I just stared at him, waiting for him to answer the question.

"Æsileif put a price on your head," he said.

I remembered Vigdis attacking Grey and me in the mine and Æsileif and Eamon's treachery. Could I even trust these new people?

"You know who I am, so who are you?" I demanded.

"My lady," he bowed extravagantly. "I am Marcius of the House Kingery, and glad to finally make your acquaintance."

I didn't know if I should hug him or try to run. Was everyone a traitor? Had Channing and Cara been part of this plan with Eamon and Æsileif? Or had these people truly come to save me?

"Don't be afraid," he said. "We are sworn to protect you. You are as much our princess as Lord Channing is our lord. These are my brothers in combat, Dominic and Emil."

Emil stepped forward and smiled. I recognized him immediately from the fighting pits. I wanted desperately to feel safe with them. I chewed my lip, trying to decide if I even had an option.

"Channing sent us to search for you," Emil said. "Marcius just hadn't had the honor of seeing your beautiful face yet."

"Is my pack safe?" I asked.

"For now," Emil said.

"Did Grey get out?" I asked, holding my breath.

"He did, and they had to stop him from coming back for you,"

Emil said. "It was safest if they thought you both escaped, to give us time to find you."

Marcius continued, "And this is our guide, the Lady—"

"Dilara," she interrupted. "I am no lady."

"That much is true," he said with a laugh.

"Are you planning to sell me to Æsileif and Eamon?" I asked.

"I was planning to help you escape, but we all make our own futures. If you prefer to surrender, that is your choice," Dilara said. "But you can come with us if you would like our protection."

If she was trying to be funny, I couldn't tell. I just didn't want to be alone anymore.

"I would like to stay with you," I said.

"Good," Dilara said.

"I would have carried you out kicking and screaming regardless," Marcius said. "I have orders from my Lord Channing to return you to him on Prince Redmund's command."

I liked his direct nature. He was rough, and not particularly friendly, but at least I was safe for now . . . as far as I could tell.

"Do you live down here?" I asked.

"No, ma'am," Marcius said. "My brothers and I chose to fight for honor among the Kingery pack. It is in our blood, as it was in the blood of our fathers before us, but while we are here, we protect the people."

"I, on the other hand, made a bad deal," Dilara said. "You can't trust everyone now, can you?"

"I don't understand . . ." I said, backing away from her. Was she threatening me?

"I bet I'd win a fight and I lost. My punishment was for all of my pack to die, but instead I waged a second bargain with Lord Verci. My people were set free, and I am trapped here . . . for now."

"So Verci owns you?" I asked.

"No one owns anyone," she said. "We are all free."

I didn't understand what she meant; if we were free, why were we all here trapped in the Bloodrealms? Sure, she chose to be trapped to save her people, but didn't that still make her a victim?

"What are we going to do with her?" Marcius asked. "We can't march her out the gate?"

"Only Conrad knows the way out of here undetected," Dilara said.

"Let's get going before someone picks up her scent," Emil said.

"Oh, they won't." Dilara held up the heart of the Garm; it was torn and nearly dried out.

"Clever," he said.

"What's clever?" I asked.

"The blood of a Garm smells so strong of every carcass they consume, no one will ever be able to track our scents through it," she said. She was brilliant and resourceful.

I followed them through a labyrinth of tunnels and corners. It was a maze to me, but she seemed to know the way easily. It reminded me in a small way of navigating the Rock, but this was something so much bigger and so much more dangerous. Even with these four fighters by my side, I couldn't stop my hands from shaking.

Marcius stopped suddenly and signaled with his fist in the air. We all stopped behind him and clung to the shadows. I could smell someone on the other side of the stone wall; they smelled of incense. We waited as still as stone until their footsteps and scents faded.

"Where are we?" I asked.

"We are entering Stonearch," Dilara said. "This is the city of the living."

"Stay close to us," Marcius said. "Many here would sell you for something to eat."

"Though selling you wouldn't earn them any favor from Æsileif," Emil said.

I shuddered to think what bargains these people might make with evil for the illusion of safety for their families. I was nothing to these people. Nothing more than a meal ticket. I put my hood up over my face to hide from their curious stares.

We entered an entire city of moveable homes. Some were jumbled-together vehicles. Some were nicer cars. Others were tents on wheels. Two men walked by us carrying a small home strapped to their backs, and a little girl smiled at me from the window. This was both Victorian elegance and the industrial age in one. Everything about these people showed their resilience.

"Guard the exits," Dilara said. "We are going to find Conrad. Blow your horn if trouble is coming."

"Bye," I whispered to them. I wanted them to come with us. I was scared watching them leave us, but I followed her through the endless streets of interesting people. They all moved from her path. It was clear she was respected here, but not because they feared her. She protected these people, and they clearly loved her.

"Are you really a Lady?" I asked.

The city was filled with old and young, men and women. These people lived, breathed, bred, and fought here as a forgotten society. Some were the slaves I had seen in the fighting pits, and some were likely born here and kept hidden.

She glanced at me. "Yes, I suppose I am," she said. "I am also a warrior."

"What pack are you from?"

"I am the queen of the Tabakov pack," she said.

"You gave up your royalty for this?"

"No, I gave up a little bit of wealth to protect my pack," she said. "And they are protecting each other and my throne in my absence. This is just a small piece of my story."

"But what if you die here?" I asked.

"We all must die sometime." She smiled. "Even the immortal. If our deaths serve a greater purpose than our lives, then must we not give it for the greater good of our people?"

Her words hit me like an avalanche. She was everything I hoped I would one day be as a leader, but I found her words terrifying. She spoke of her sacrifice as though it was nothing more than a decision, but it scared me. I had so much to live for. I wanted a long, beautiful life with Grey. I wanted to see my mother holding my babies. I wanted to lead my people to safety. Death was final—there was no coming back from death.

She put her hand on my shoulder. "Neither of us is dying today."

I hoped she was right, but I didn't feel as confident. Everywhere I looked, people stared at me, trying to see my face hidden in the shadow of my hood. It took everything I had not to run.

We found our way to the strangest house I'd ever seen. It was a tiny split-level home in three stories. The architecture was Victorian to be sure, but it was seamed together with thick metal plates. It was all built on old wagon wheels and had an engine and steering wheel at the front of the house. It was incredible. There was a bay window and even a tiny balcony. An older man with a straggly beard and a bowler hat sat on the steps. He wore a white linen shirt with a green vest. He was stocky and hairy and covered in weapons, but the most intriguing part was the odd multilensed goggles on his hat. I'd never seen anything like them. This entire place was surreal.

"Conrad, we need to talk," Dilara said.

"And what trouble follows you this time, Queen Dilara?" he asked, watching me.

She rolled her eyes. "Shall we step inside?"

"By all means," he said, waving us past.

Inside it was homey but dusty, and every bit as mismatched as the outside. When Conrad closed the door, Dilara continued, "I need you to tell me the way out of the Realms."

"There is no way out without Æsileif's approval or beating Lord Verci in a fight to the death," he said. "You know that."

"Don't toy with me, Conrad," she said angrily. "I know you got out once; tell me how." If that was true, I couldn't fathom why he ever returned, but there was always more to a story.

He looked at me again. "No matter what this child told you, your life is worth more than this. The Bloodrealms are no place to be a savior. The strong survive, not the weak or stupid."

"Look at her Conrad—what do you see?"

"I see a little waif of a girl who isn't worth saving," he said.

"Look at her," Dilara said.

He sighed and put his goggles on and turned them in focus as he studied me. He began flipping the lenses up one at a time until only the final remained over his eyes. "It can't be," he said, looking again. "In this sea of darkness and evil, you found the one pure light that can set us all free?"

What did he mean? Did he mean the prophecy to unite all the packs? Or was he speaking of something else?

"It's her, Conrad, and if we don't get her out, they will find her. It is only a matter of time," Dilara said. "This has nothing to do with your life or mine; it is all of our lives at stake. She is the one."

He slowly took off his goggles and touched my hand. He shook his head, smiling. "I never thought I'd live to see you," he said. "Well, you better win."

He pulled his shirt up to reveal his back full of scars and moles, but when I looked closer, I realized it was a highly detailed map.

"You'll have to cut the skin off," he said.

"No," Dilara said.

"There isn't time," he said. "I will bind the flesh after you've gone; it will heal."

"You'll bleed to death," she said.

"Can't you come with us?" I asked.

"If I move, the camp moves, and Æsileif will know. And in truth, I'm not strong enough." He smiled, pulling a knife from his belt. "Cut smoothly." He handed the blade to Dilara.

"Conrad . . ." she said. Her voice was sad.

"It is the only way, child. Save her," he said, holding her hand. I didn't know how they knew each other, but I could feel their sadness. I wondered if he was her version of my Baran.

Conrad put a wooden spoon in his teeth and she flayed him, cutting the skin with precision. Conrad grunted and breathed heavily as she peeled the skin away from his body. The wound bled awfully, and the muscle underneath was pink and angry. The smell of fresh werewolf blood turned my stomach, and the sight of it made me want to vomit.

I tore a strip off the train of my cloak and wrapped it around his back and torso and tied it in a knot, securing it to his body. To my amazement, the bleeding stopped as soon as the cloak touched his wounds. There was more power in the dress Lady Faye had made for me than I had originally thought. It might be powerful enough to save his life.

A horn blasted, and Dilara quickly rolled the bloody skin up and tucked it in her belt. The sight of it was disgusting. Though it was my salvation and Conrad's sacrifice, it made me sick.

"Thank you, Conrad," she said, kissing him on the cheek. "I'll come back for you."

"I'd hope so," Conrad said with a wink. "Head north to the upper shelf and follow the map from there."

27
Bloodmark

Dilara and I ran out the door and through the sea of people toward the north tunnel. I didn't even know what we were running from, but I ran as fast as I could to keep up with her. Out of the corner of my eye, I swore I saw a man with a top hat; when I looked again, there was no one there. I'd really started to lose my mind. I turned the corner and ran right into Marcius's chest. He steadied me from falling.

"Where are Dominic and Emil?" Dilara asked.

"It's the Garm. We have to stay to protect the people," he said. "We'll catch up if we can. Otherwise, we'll meet you on the outside."

She nodded, and we fled to the sounds of the Garm pack attacking the city. The screams were chilling. Were the Garm hunting me? Was it my fault they were killing people needlessly?

Dilara ran through a doorway with me just a heartbeat behind her. We ran into a huge room with industrial piping running through the ceiling. She ran to the center of the room and leaped up to a ladder twelve feet above our heads and started climbing up. She made it look so easy.

"Jump!" she screamed.

I did as she commanded. I jumped as high as I could and my fingers barely reached the ladder, but I couldn't get a grip. I was mortal. I fell back to the ground and slammed my knee into the floor. I grunted in pain and took several steps back and leaped up again. This time, I wrapped my arm around the bar and fought and wriggled to pull myself up. My body felt like dead weight, but I struggled after her, far up into the ceiling. We crawled onto a little shelf in the rocky ceiling that hid us out of sight. The space wasn't tall enough to stand. A small metal grate closed us off from the level above us; I couldn't see enough to know what room we were below or how close we were to escaping, but I knew it couldn't be that easy.

In the corner of the shelf were a few little treasures. I picked up an oval music box, ornate and old. It fit in the palm of my hand. I opened the lid and a tiny dancer started to spin to the music of Tchaikovsky.

"That was given to me by a human I saved in my kingdom," Dilara said.

"Why is it hidden here?" I asked.

"This is the only place I dare call my own. Æsileif makes a point to steal away any happiness I find. She destroyed any home I dared to make down here. So I stopped having a home, and I just move around. This is a collection of my little treasures."

"Oh . . ." I muttered. "Does Vigdis bother you, too?"

"Vigdis is dead. No one has seen her in over a century," she said.

"But I saw her," I said. "She attacked me."

"Are you certain it was Vigdis?"

"She had the Bloodmoon markings on her face," I said. "It was her."

"Then we have more to fear than we realized," she said, changing the subject. "So, what's your story, Ashling?"

"I refused my betrothed at fourteen, got sent away at sixteen, and fell in love with a human who turned out to be half wolf and half

Bloodsucker," I said with a laugh. "My father put me up for declarations and now I have four suitors who have to fight in the Realms for my love."

Dilara raised her eyebrows as she waited for me to continue.

I closed the music box and carefully set it back with the other trinkets. "Well, I am the daughter of King Pørr and Queen Nessa Boru of Ireland."

"Yes, but who are you?" she asked.

"I don't understand. I am Ashling Boru."

"And?"

"I like to read and draw. I like vintage cars and rocks."

She smiled. "You are more than that. You are pieces of all those who love you and so much more. What do they see in you?"

I thought for a while what Mund, Baran, Father, Mother, Grey, and Tegan might say about me, and I knew the answer. "Some would say I'm opinionated. Others would say that I'm undisciplined and emotional. But my true pack would say I am the feisty little girl who will save our people," I said.

"You are a leader," Dilara said, smiling.

"I suppose I am, but who are you then?" I asked.

"Someone who made the best mistakes of her life." She laughed. "Rest now. We will be on the move soon."

She handed me dried meat from a leather pouch at her hip. She took out the skin map and unrolled it on the ground to study it. None of the markings meant anything to me. I had no sense of time or direction down here. She ran her fingers over the scars like they were a braille story, like it was telling her something.

I envied her strength to survive down here. If I'd lost everything like she had, I wasn't sure I would be able to still find the will to carry on. I closed my eyes, but sleep didn't come. I heard every sound from below us. Mice scurrying, whispers as people hid in the shadows, never knowing we were high above them, even a pack of Garm traveling through.

My mind wandered to Grey and all we had seen together and all we had done. I blushed at the thought. I yearned to be wrapped in his arms. I dozed in and out for a long time before I gave up on trying to rest.

"When do we leave?" I asked.

Dilara slapped her hand over my mouth and pointed to a man and woman standing in the room above. We could see them through the grate in the floor. I instantly recognized Vigdis with her black lace veil pulled back revealing the Bloodmoon tattoos on her face. She was just as sinister looking as when she'd attacked Grey and me. Her skin was chalk white and her lips black, and her body was covered in black lace, even her fingertips. A black stone amulet hung from the center of her forehead, and her black hair was smooth and as stick straight as her posture. The stone looked like blood glass, and I shuddered wondering whose blood it was.

The man next to her had a shaved head and cold eyes. He wore a leather armored kilt and leather sandals. His enormous muscled chest was bare, and a necklace of dried eyeballs hung around his neck. Most had turned black, but others were still juicy. I wanted to scream, but Dilara's grip over my mouth and chest held me silent in her arms.

"We pushed her into the Realms to teach her a lesson," Æsileif said as she walked into view; rage flooded my veins. I hated her.

The man opened his mouth and screamed as black flies flew out. I was mortified. Evil flowed out of his mouth and swarmed around them like a black fog.

"I'm sorry, Father!" she said, bowing to his anger.

Æsileif was his daughter? Was Vigdis her mother? Making Æsileif my cousin? Was I really related to all of these monsters? My own family wanted me destroyed. The realization was numbing, but I still couldn't fathom what they wanted from me.

"We will find her, Verci," Vigdis said.

The man was Verci Dvergar—infamous murderer, supposedly dead, and Eamon's uncle. How had both Vigdis and Verci lived down here without anyone seeing them for so long?

"What if she escapes?" Æsileif asked.

"No one escapes the Bloodrealms," Vigdis said. I shuddered.

"It is not her I want," Verci hissed.

If Verci wasn't after me, who was he after? Was it Grey? Or did it stem back to his fight with Baran when Verci raped Brenna? Were they after my mother? There were so many horrible possibilities.

Vigdis walked over to him and lightly ran her fingers over his lips before kissing him. "Vercingetorix, we will have our revenge, and you'll kill them all." She smiled. "You will reclaim your son. That is my gift to you."

Did he mean Willem, Brenna's first son?

"He is mine," Verci said.

"Yes, my love, he has always been yours," Vigdis said quietly.

Verci was frightening, but she was the one I was afraid of. She ruled over him in a quiet way. She was secretly in charge, and he didn't realize that he was merely a pawn. Verci and Vigdis wandered off with Æsileif and Eamon trailing behind. When they were long gone, Dilara finally released me, and my face ached where her fingers had dug into my flesh.

"They're alive," she whispered.

"I think I know who they're after. I think he wants Willem Killian," I said. "We have to warn Baran."

"I don't think he is all they want, and we have to get out of here first. We better keep moving. You may be bait in their game, or you may still be Vigdis's prize," she said. "The longer you are here, the more likely your pack will come looking for you when they realize we were separated from the Kingerys. This is not a good omen for us. It is a thick web of lies they weave over generations of war. You were always in their plan and ours. They want to destroy you, and to us, you are our savior. Only you can decide how this turns out."

"But how can I control fate?"

"Control is a figment of your imagination," she said.

"I don't understand."

"Stop waiting to understand and start fighting."

She carefully pushed the grate open and slipped through, and she held it as I followed. She smelled the air and I did the same, but it only smelled of death to me. I didn't smell any subtle differences, but she began running down the hall in the opposite direction of Verci, and I followed.

We crept in the shadows toward another stone passage. A sleeping wolf blocked our path. He was large, with brown, matted fur. My heart pounded with every step we took as we tried to sneak past the beast. Dilara stepped over him to safety, but as I stepped over him the wolf's eyes opened, and he stared up at me. His lip curled, baring his teeth. Dilara held her spear over him, waiting to plunge it into his heart if he so much as moved. He slowly lifted his head, and we saw the chains that bound his neck and feet. He was a captive, like us.

I knew what that felt like, and my heart ached for him. Whoever he was.

He turned away from us, laying his head back down on the cold stone ground. It was a small gesture, but I knew he'd saved our lives. He could have attacked, he could have alerted our enemies, and Dilara could have taken his life, but he chose to let us continue on our journey. We ran down the passage, and Dilara pulled me into a doorway out of the firelight as she studied the map.

I had no idea where we were going or which way would lead back to Stonearch. Without Dilara, I would be lost forever in this dark hell.

"Head to the staircase," she whispered. "Be as quiet as you can; we don't want to wake them up."

"Wake who?"

She pointed to the ceiling, which was covered in gray-skinned humanlike creatures. They were the Draugr, bloodthirsty creatures that ate any warm-bodied prey, like us. Brychan had said they ate only living bodies, and once the heart stopped beating, they left the corpse for the Garm to finish off. They only wanted the flesh with blood still pumping through it, and then the rest was left to waste. How long did it take a heart to stop beating? How long would I feel them eating my flesh before I died?

Fear ripped through me, and I wanted to sob in terror. There were hundreds of the undead creatures sleeping on the ceiling, like bats. Only one had to wake and we'd be dead.

I nodded as I swallowed my fear and started running with my skirt in my hands. My bare feet met the cold ground in silence as I screamed inside. I didn't dare look up, or I'd lose my strength.

We slipped unnoticed down the stairs into a room filled with tiny cages, no more than four by two feet, and they were stacked on top of each other six high with a bathtub at the center. The room was poorly lit, but I could see and smell the small lifeless bodies in many of the cages. I stepped over a child's doll that was soaked in blood, and my heart sank. I crept toward the cages, but Dilara swung her spear in front of me, blocking my path, and she shook her head.

I started to follow her out when I heard the smallest cry, just a whimper. I searched the cages and saw a tiny outstretched arm of a baby. I ran toward the cage and Dilara reached for my arm, but I wrenched my body past her.

As I got closer, I realized the cages were made of human bones. I shuddered as the little boy reached through them for me. I looked into his tear-filled eyes and recognized him. He was the baby I had tried to comfort in the nets when I had been captured. His blond hair was matted to his round face, and he was naked and covered in filth, but he was alive.

Many of the cages had been filled with babies, all in varying decay. Now only one lived, this one innocent child. They preyed on the lives of children. They must harvest the children for the Dvergar Barghest diet. I was disgusted by it all. I wanted to tear the cages apart with my bare hands. The horror that surrounded me was overwhelming, but all I could see was the fear in that child's eyes and the hope he saw in me.

"We don't have time," Dilara said.

"But we are all he has left," I said. "If we leave him, what will happen to him? Will the Dvergars consume him? Eamon is a Barghest."

Dilara shuddered. "They used to eat the children and bathe in their innocent blood, but that was long ago."

"Clearly they are still doing it," I said, pointing at the dead children that surrounded us and the bathtub of cold, coagulated blood. I was so angry my hands shook.

I started to unhook the cage, and Dilara gently covered my hand. "I know you want to save this child, but you'll wake the Draugr."

"If I don't do something, I'm just as guilty as they are."

"We will die," she said. "I can't fight them all, Ashling."

Something in my expression made her smile. She tucked the map in the braided waist of my dress with my mace. "I will hold them off as long as I can. Run until you smell brimstone and follow the map out from there," she said.

"But I don't understand the map."

"You will," she said. "You have to."

I nodded and opened the cage. The soft clink of the latch barely made a sound, but the sound of the creatures falling from the ceiling and clawing their way toward us filled my heart with dread. Had I made the wrong choice? I tore what was left of my train off my dress and I quickly wrapped the baby in it like a blanket, and he smiled at me. He was worth saving. He was worth dying for.

Tears ran down my face as I held him close to my body and we ran for the exit. Adrenaline pounded in my ears, but it didn't drown out the hideous sound of the Draugr dragging themselves into the room. We almost reached the doorway, but more Draugr came flooding in, and we were surrounded.

They were hunched and emaciated, and the smell that emanated from them made me gag. Their jaws nearly unhinged when they hissed, showing their sharp black teeth. I could hardly look at the ghastly creatures.

"I'm sorry, Dilara. I couldn't leave him!" I said.

"It was the right choice," she said.

We backed slowly toward the wall, and they followed, filling the room with their stench. The baby cried in my arms, and I held him tighter. Dilara didn't say I told you so or curse me for my choice; she just stood her ground next to me with a spear in hand. One of the creatures came at her from the side, and she started slashing and fighting for her life as my back bumped into the cages, knocking them down. The bones broke and shattered all around us.

A Draugr came so close to my face, I swore I could taste its rotting flesh. It screeched, unhinging its jaw. Spit flew out onto my face. I sheltered the baby to the side of my body away from them and covered my face in my free arm.

The creature hissed and leaped back.

I held my arm out and the creature screamed and ran back, cowering with the others. I looked at my wrist and saw the Bloodmark of House Dvergar's three circling wolves that Eamon must have burned into my skin. I hadn't noticed what he'd burned into my flesh. It was fading, but still clear.

I held my wrist up again, and the Draugr scampered away from us, hiding their faces as they hissed and bowed, backing away. Eamon's Bloodmark was protecting us from these evil creatures. I didn't have time to think about it. I just held the baby to my side and walked over to Dilara, keeping my wrist between us and the creatures as we made our way to the exit.

Every step took an eternity, and my heart pounded louder than the hissing monsters. I didn't understand what magic was protecting us, but I was thankful for the protection—even if it was Eamon's.

"How are you doing that?" she whispered.

"Eamon burned his Bloodmark into my skin; they seem to be afraid of it. I don't know. Just keep going," I said.

We slammed a stone door shut and started running as fast as we could. Adrenaline and fear fueled us on. We ran for our lives with the baby nestled in my arms. I ran to forget all the death and fear. I ran for him, for me, for everyone I loved. This evil place would not consume us.

I would destroy it.

Dilara matched my pace easily. There wasn't any part of her that wasn't feminine, and yet every part of her was as fierce as any man. She had chosen to die for me if she had to, and for the child I carried in my arms. That was how much she believed in me without truly knowing me. That was a leap of faith I couldn't even fathom.

We ran upstairs for what seemed like an eternity, and then the stairway would turn and go down, like an endless maze. I was tired and frustrated, but as we ran farther I started to smell brimstone—this had to be the way out of the Bloodrealms. This would be our salvation. The tunnel led us to another oubliette, but in this one the grates were open, and only the thin bridge remained. As we started running across it swayed, and I stumbled. I fell to my knees with the baby in one arm and clinging to the bridge with the other.

"Hang on!" Dilara yelled, but my fingers slipped and I fell to the floor below. She dropped down beside me in the dark tunnel. "Come on, we can still get out here."

We started running down the tunnel as a horn sounded.

"The warriors," Dilara said as she pushed me up to the wall, protecting the baby between our bodies. "The fights are about to begin."

Fighters filled the oubliette from all the doorways, squeezing into the tunnel and nearly crushing us as they waited for the gates to the main arena to open. They came to fight for blood, but could I ever get them to fight for their own freedom?

"Are they going to try to hurt us?" I asked, watching them surge past us.

"No. They don't concern themselves with the lives of others," she said. "Maybe this is better. We can hide among them while we escape."

I spotted Marcius across the tunnel, and he forced his way through the fighters to us. I was relieved to see him.

"Old Mother be praised, you're both safe," he said. He looked to me and saw the baby in my arms, and a sadness swept over him.

"Is he yours?" I asked.

"That is Grete's son, Fridrik," Marcius said. "We were trying to protect them. Æsileif was holding Grete and Fridrik captive in the Realms. We hid them with a clan of mothers, but the harvesters must have captured them."

I remembered her face and the heart-wrenching sound of her crying. I regretted that I couldn't save her. I wished I'd saved them all. I hated myself for being weak when they needed my strength.

"Ashling saved him from the bone cages," Dilara said.

"How did you escape the Draugr?" he asked.

"Eamon," I said, showing him the faded Dvergar Bloodmark on my wrist. It was all but gone now. He just stared at me. I didn't understand it myself. Had Eamon done it to protect me or own me? I didn't know his motivation, I never knew what he wanted from me. I'd thought he was my friend when Adomnan had tortured me, but now I didn't understand what part he played. Was he Æsileif's lover, or was he my secret guardian?

"Let's finish this," Marcius said. There was a renewed anger in him that I didn't understand.

The gates opened, and we walked among the other fighters into the main arena. Walking in from the blood-filled tunnels gave the fighting pits an even more dooming feeling. We walked among the fighters, hiding from plain sight in the masses. I covered my face with my hood, hoping no one in the gallery would notice me. Æsileif walked out onto the balcony with her arms raised over the crowd. They screamed and banged their chests, and she smiled beautifully for them.

"Bow to your king and queen," she said as Verci escorted Vigdis to the bone-built thrones. The entire arena was deafeningly silent as they looked upon them, their dead rulers standing before them in the flesh. Not the fighters or the gallery made a sound.

I looked to the gallery and saw my mother. She sat still as stone, and her porcelain skin looked even paler. Her fear vibrated through me. Seeing her sister seemed to make her almost catatonic. Father sat by her side with Kane and Quinn guarding them, but none of them seemed to have seen me. All eyes were on Verci and Vigdis.

It was the first time I'd seen Father since Gwyn and Quinn's wedding, and my throat caught. He'd finally come to watch my suitors fight. I had lost all track of time in the Bloodrealms, but Lughnasadh had come, and with it came Father's final rule over me. It was here that my Father would make his choice . . . and so would I.

28
Betrayal

Vigdis sat in the throne, basking in the fear in the room. It almost seemed to fuel her. Her eyes were fixed on my mother, and it terrified me.

"My servants, we have returned," Verci yelled. "Bow to us."

All the fighters in the crowded fighting pits bowed to them, and we did, too. We couldn't draw attention to ourselves, but it made me sick to bow to their evil reign. I peeked at the gallery and saw all the rich wolves bowing to them, except Father, Mother, Quinn, and Kane. They stood proudly. I looked around the fighting pits for my pack, but I couldn't see them through the crowd.

Verci laughed. "King Pørr, you look like you've seen a ghost," he said. "Shall we let the fights begin?"

Father nodded, reluctantly. Verci put his hand in a large urn and pulled out a number. "TWO-ONE-SIX-FIVE-FOUR!"

A dangerous-looking man stepped forward, beating on his chest. He was missing one eye, and only a scarred cavity remained. The sight of it was gruesome. He had scars all over his body, but none as vulgar as his missing eye.

"EIGHT-SEVEN-ZERO-ZERO-TWO!"

Another man stepped forward. He was fat and hairy and at least three feet taller than all the other men; he was a giant. His neck was the size of my waist.

"SIX-ZERO-TWO-FIVE-FIVE."

I watched in horror as each fighter came forward. I knew they were going to fight my suitors. One of these deadly killers would fight Grey.

The third man was small and of Asian decent. He looked like a child next to the giant, but I couldn't deny his still-frightening appearance.

"NINE-ONE-FIVE-NINE-ONE!" Dilara gasped, and Marcius stepped quickly away from us to draw the attention away from where I stood. His number had been drawn. I wanted to go to him, but Dilara held my arm.

Verci and Vigdis wanted us to watch these people die? Even my own precious father sat in the gallery observing the fights as though these weren't people, these weren't souls being lost—to everyone around me, they were only numbers. I was disgusted and angry. What right did those in power have to steal freedom from the weak? Even my own father was guilty; he had chosen to fight my suitors here. Our entire history was filled with the evils of discrimination and hate. I was appalled by it all.

At the railing of the gallery, I saw the Asian couple again, but this time they had Fridrik's mother on a leash as their pet. Her eyes were wet with tears, and her face swollen from being beaten. She was a human; she was ours to protect. Rage flared inside me. When I looked at her beaten face, I saw myself. I saw Adomnan, and I was filled with hate. I had to let her know her son lived, and I needed to give her something to fight for until I could save her.

"We have to get up to the gallery," I said.

The horn blew again, signifying the fights were to begin, and the crowd pushed their way to the center arena, blocking our path. They were to fight in the giant arena, all four of my suitors in the largest pit at the same time. We were forced tightly around the blood-covered arena as the four fighters stood in each corner. I saw a wolf jaw protruding from the dirt, and I mourned for his forgotten life. The entire world of the Bloodrealms needed to be burned to set all the lost souls free.

A pit master walked into the arena. "Grey Donavan of House Killian!" The master pointed his wart-covered finger at the giant, and my heart dropped into my stomach. Grey shoved into the arena dressed in his leather armor. He was as handsome as the first day I'd met him in Baran's garage, but today he was my warrior. Fear prickled over my skin as I did nothing more than watch. He flinched, and I know he felt my fear. He turned and his eyes instantly found mine in the crowd. It was like he could even sense my physical location now that we were fully bound to each other. When he saw me, he mouthed, "Run."

I shook my head to say no. Not this time. This time I would protect him. He smiled like he expected, that and I smiled because he was mine.

"Channing of House Kingery."

Channing wore all-golden armor; he looked like sunlight. He walked over to the one-eyed man. Channing looked out of place here. He was too pretty to live in a world such as this.

"Brychan of House Kahedin."

Brychan wore his leather armor that was covered in claw marks. Every disk of leather was burned with the Kahedin Bloodmark, a knotted stag. He looked fierce; I'd never seen this side of him—he was a war god. He stood across from Marcius.

"Eamon of House Dvergar."

Eamon walked into the arena with a steel-black half helmet and armor. Everything about his armor was dangerous. The edges of every piece were sharp and sinister. He stood before the Asian man, barely noticing his opponent. He waved at the crowd, and they cheered the

Dvergar name.

My blood boiled with anger as I watched this display of ignorance. Why could no one see what evil lurked here? It surrounded us, consumed us. Not one person in the crowd stood against this wrong. I vowed that none of this pain and death would be in vain.

Verci and Vigdis sat in their thrones and watched the spectacle from high above us. I didn't think they were all that concerned with seeing who would earn my hand in marriage, as all of this was a trap. Æsileif walked into the arena in her spiked heels and smoking her black cigarette. I hid my face in the crowd, trying not to be seen.

"You will fight for blood and honor!" she yelled to her fighters. "You fight until you die, or your opponent cries for your mercy!"

The fighters screamed and roared and pounded on their chests as they stared hungrily at their opponents, my friends. The warriors didn't see souls—they saw their ticket to survival. They either won or died trying.

"What do we do?" I said. "How do we stop this madness?"

"You can't stop a fight, it would destroy their honor," Dilara said.

"There is no honor in dying like this," I said.

I looked around the arena, panicking for a solution. Baran stepped up on the edge of the ring behind Grey to stand as Grey's guard. Baran wore his leather chest plate of armor and leather kilt. Mund climbed up behind Brychan wearing light leather that looked like white metal. He always looked like a knight in shining armor to me. I wanted to run to him, to his protection, to his unending love, but the crowd was so tight, I was nearly pinned in place. Behind Channing stood Emil. He stood guard over Channing and prepared to watch his own brother, Marcius, fight Brychan. Bento stepped up behind Eamon, as awkward and quiet as I remembered him. Seeing Bento was a slap in the face. I hated them all. He was as guilty as Eamon. Every last Dvergar was my enemy.

The horn blasted again, and the fight began, and agony filled my soul. It was more than I could watch. The room was deafening with all of the screams and cusses blurring together into one thunderous sound. I started pushing my way through the crowd as they surged around us.

"We have to get to Baran," I said. "We have to tell him about Willem, and he can stop the fight."

She looked at me with an expression that nearly made me cry. I knew she thought it was useless, that I was better off just watching the bloody fight than trying to stop it, but I had to do something. I couldn't just stand by and watch my pack be destroyed.

I heard the sounds of the fighters, and I glanced at them to see blood everywhere. They fought for me. They fought as men, not as wolves. Even in this arena, they were being *civilized*. The disgusting irony twisted my guts in knots.

I clawed my way through the mass, protecting Fridrik with every move I made. The closer I got to Baran the harder my heart pounded. I reached up to touch his leg and get his attention when someone grabbed my arm so hard tears filled my eyes. I turned to see Odin holding me back and Dilara's spear at his throat, the tip just barely cutting into his flesh. Odin wore his dirty top hat, and he still wore that wolf carcass on his back. I hated that he did that.

"Odin," I said. "I'd like you to meet Dilara."

He smiled his sly smile. "My queen." He mock bowed.

"The failed guard," she said.

He snarled at her.

"Stop this at once. I don't have time for your old feuds. Kill each other on your own time. Right now you are both in service to me," I said.

"I'm sorry," Dilara said, lowering her spear.

Shikoba appeared next to Odin. "Thank goodness, child."

My shoulder seethed with pain, but it wasn't mine. Grey, my sweet love. I closed my eyes, trying to ignore the pain. I had to be strong. We, Grey and I, needed to win.

"Your father wanted to cancel the fight, but Baran convinced him it was the best way to get us all into the Realms without suspicion," Shikoba said. "We've been searching for you." Odin smiled again, that weird smile of his.

I nodded. "Good, you've found me. Now help me stop this bull-shit."

"We are far outnumbered here, Ashling; they need to fight so we can escape," Shikoba said. "That's the plan."

"We aren't leaving without all of my pack," I said.

"Vigdis and Verci both know Ashling was in the Realms. It was Æsileif and Eamon who trapped her in here," Dilara told Shikoba and Odin.

"All the more reason to leave while we can," Shikoba said.

"Not without my family. Stop the fight!" I demanded.

Dilara put her hand on my arm. "If you stop the fight, the fighters will all be put to death for not finishing. Marcius will die," she said. "They will all die."

I looked at my pack fighting in the ring, and every blow made me cringe. They were all bleeding for my love. The ruthlessness was unbearable to watch. Grey's armor was half torn off, and his shoulder seeped blood. The giant man made Grey look like a toy, and his meaty fist swung at Grey over and over again, but Grey was faster. Blood ran down Brychan's mouth and chest, but Marcius looked equally injured. They were both skilled fighters. The smile on Brychan's face almost made me laugh despite everything. He loved to fight—it was part of him. I'd never change him. Eamon was unharmed except for a tiny cut on his arm, but the Asian man was cut badly from all the sharp points on Eamon's armor. Eamon easily maneuvered around him, punching the man in the back over and over again. Watching Eamon fight made me truly scared for Grey. I couldn't imagine them fighting each other in the next round. Channing looked badly beaten by the one-eyed man. His perfect golden face was red and bruised, and a nasty cut leaked from his side. I cringed to see him so injured, and for what? For my choice in him? My father's choice in him? It was so stupid. If I had just spoken up about my choice, maybe none of us would ever have had to set foot in this unholy place.

I stumbled to my knees and held my face in my hands—Grey had been hit hard. His pain flowed through me, making my dizzy. I struggled to my feet to look for Grey. He was lying on his back in the blood-soaked dirt, and he wasn't moving. I gagged with pain and fear, and I started climbing the barricade into the ring to protect Grey. But Dilara pulled me back.

"You can't go in there. They will tear you apart," Dilara said.

"Let go of me," I demanded.

"You can't save him," Odin said.

"Get up, Grey. Please," I begged.

I knew he couldn't hear me, but I knew he could feel me, and I sent all my love to him. The giant towered over him and swung again at his lifeless body, but Grey punched the Giant's fist. The giant fell back on his knees, screaming in pain and cradling his mangled wrist. Grey's face was swollen, and his lip was dripping a river of blood. I'd never seen him injured like that before, and it was terrifying. Grey always healed almost instantly.

I wanted all of this stupidity to stop. I couldn't lose him. I wouldn't lose any of them. I desperately wanted to escape this horrible place with every pure soul, and leave the monsters to destroy themselves in the hell they created.

"Do you yield?" Grey yelled.

"Never!" the giant bellowed. He hit Grey in the leg, knocking him to the ground. The pain burned in my leg. I tried to hide the pain from the others, but I knew they saw. They knew the truth. There was nothing I could do to hide it anymore.

I belonged with Grey, and it was time they all knew.

Grey jumped and came crashing down on the giant's chest, knocking the giant unconscious. Baran leaped into the ring and grabbed Grey's hand, raising it up for the crowd to see he was victorious. His Killian Bloodmark was held high for all to see, but the pain on his face was clear. Grey's injuries weren't healing. Something was wrong. But he'd won—he was safe for now.

Channing gouged out his opponent's good eye. The man screamed, grasping at his eye socket as he blindly ran out of the arena, breaking the barricade on his way out. Channing was victorious. Emil jumped in the ring next to Channing, protecting him from the angry spectators.

"Eamon, finish him!" Verci called from his throne.

Eamon's opponent was bleeding profusely, but still the man didn't quit. He kept charging at Eamon, but it was clear he was beaten. Even I could see his time was limited. Eamon backhanded his opponent so hard that the man spun around before hitting the ground. The blood ran freely from the man's mouth, coating the sand in death. I closed my eyes to the senseless violence. Bento handed Eamon a black cloth; Eamon wiped the blood off his armor and tossed the rag aside—the blood of a person was nothing to these monsters.

The fight still raged between Brychan and Marcius. They were so evenly matched each seemed to know the other's move before they made it. I wondered if they had ever fought together before. It was like a choreographed dance.

"We have to stop this," I said. "They are both our friends."

Odin shook his head. "It isn't your place. This is House Dvergar, and you dare not break Verci and Vigdis's rules."

I fumed at him. Men were so stupid. Fighting like this didn't solve problems, it just stole lives. "No war was ever truly won with violence, because you can't kill an idea, Odin. You can't end all good or all evil, because they live inside each of us. That is humanity. The only true test of humanity is what you will sacrifice for another to live," I spat.

Channing watched Marcius fight with concern plainly on his face.

Blow after blow, neither Brychan nor Marcius landed a shot. The frustration between the men and the onlookers was clear. The crowd wanted blood, and I needed both men to win.

Brychan started running away from Marcius. I couldn't believe it. He was fleeing. The crowd was going crazy as Brychan suddenly turned and punched so hard Marcius fell to the ground with a thud, but he breathed. I could see his chest rising and falling. It was the only way he could survive the fight. Brychan saved his life and was named the victor.

All of my suitors had won their matches. Which meant they would all fight again, but this time against each other. This was my dark destiny predicted in the dream with Vigdis. I bowed my head as the horn blew, and dread filled my stomach with acid. For all the pain I suffered at Adomnan's hands and the evil I survived in the Realms, I'd take it all over again just to save them.

"Channing of House Kingery shall fight Eamon of House Dvergar," Verci said. "Grey of House Killian shall fight Brychan of House Kahedin."

I couldn't look up. I didn't want to watch. This was my torture. I heard them fighting, the crowd cheering. I could smell their blood, and Grey's pain pulsed through my heart as Brychan attacked him. All my love was turning to dust. Every hit, every blow, was mine to endure. Tears seeped from my closed eyes and ran down my cheeks as I prayed for it all to be over. Dilara gasped and Odin laughed, but I didn't want to see.

"Oh no," Dilara said.

I forced myself to look, and Channing was nearly beaten. His face was swollen, and his golden body dripped blood onto the ground. He stumbled as Eamon punched him in the ribs. Eamon attacked like a viper. Channing fell to his knees, gasping for breath.

"I yield!" Channing gagged.

Emil leaped into the ring and stood between Eamon and Channing. He snarled at Eamon. Eamon slowly backed away as the crowd chanted his name. Channing stood and leaned on Emil as he waited for the other fights to end. By losing, he lost his right to continue fighting and lost my father's choice.

Brychan and Grey were circling each other, fighting, but I could see their lips moving. I couldn't hear them over the crowd, but Brychan nodded and kneeled in front of Grey.

"I yield!" Brychan called out. "This match cannot be won in a thousand years."

I couldn't believe my ears. Brychan had willingly given me up. He knew what losing meant, and yet he stopped fighting. He let me go. He loved me enough to let me go. I didn't know who would have won between them if they truly fought, but I was thankful I didn't have to know.

Baran grabbed Grey's hand again, holding him up as the winner. The crowd pulsed with energy. They thrived on the metallic smell of wolf blood that filled the arena. The crowd booed as Brychan and Mund shook Grey's hand before joining Channing, Emil, and Marcius. Marcius whispered something in Mund's ear. Mund nodded slowly and didn't look up. But the funny little crease between his eyes relaxed, and I knew Marcius had told him I was safe. Mund didn't search the crowd for me; he was too discreet for that. They all joined Grey and Baran as one pack . . . my pack. It was finally happening; I was uniting the packs, as Calista's prophecy had always said.

Verci whistled and the entire room quieted. "Some victors, some losers, but a bloody fight is a celebration for the gods!" he said. "King Boru?"

I looked to my father in the gallery. He was angry, and the blood vein in his forehead bulged out of his red face. He looked at Grey and Eamon, the winners. He then looked to Channing and Brychan, who had both yielded, one from pain and one by choice. I knew he was pondering whom he would choose for me—Grey without a title or

Eamon, who was a king. His two top choices had been defeated.

"Grey of Killian and Eamon of Dvergar," Father said.

"To the death!" Verci said.

"Until one yields!" Father said.

Vigdis put her hand on Verci's and whispered something to him.

"We all must die, King Boru," Verci said. "It is our destiny."

"This is a fight of honor, not a death sentence," Father said.

"It is an honor to die in the Bloodrealms," Verci said with a smile.

"This fight is under my decree," Father said.

"But you're in my house, and this is my rule," Verci sneered.

I didn't know if Eamon's skin would hurt Grey or not. Being half hunter, maybe Grey was immune, but what if he wasn't? I knew how badly it burned and festered the skin. The simplest touch could destroy Grey's concentration. Eamon would have to kill Grey; I knew Grey would never yield. He'd never give me up. Everything was at stake for us.

"And I think you'll see it my way when you see what I have that belongs to you."

A silver blade came within an inch of my neck, and I gasped, backing into Æsileif. The blade didn't touch my skin, but the threat was enough to get everyone's attention. She could make me mortal, or she could easily take my life. It was all her choice.

"I saved you a seat," she said, smiling sweetly as she touched my face.

29
Barghest

I looked frantically to Dilara, Odin, and Shikoba; they, too, were held at knifepoint by guards. My father looked down on me with disapproval, anger rippling over his flesh. I felt like a child again under his disapproving eye. Even in the midst of this, I still just wanted him to love me.

Mother was distraught and crying as she watched. I felt her fear, but the look on her face scared me to death. It made me feel like I might not survive this. She was truly scared. Grey's panic tore through me. If we didn't survive this, he would have fought for nothing.

"Stop," Father's voice boomed.

"You dare threaten me in my house?" Verci yelled as he stood.

I watched in horror as a guard slammed Quinn to the ground and put a silver knife to Mother's throat. She didn't flinch, and her expression didn't change.

"Do you see it my way yet, Pørr? Or do you need me to prove my power?" Verci said.

Father nodded.

Æsileif escorted Fridrik and me up to the balcony, and her guard followed with Dilara, Shikoba, and Odin. I stood face to face with Verci and Vigdis. Terror stole my voice, and all I could do was stare. Vigdis reached for Fridrik and I snarled. Her expression didn't change, but she gestured to the seat next to her. When I didn't sit in the human-bone throne, Verci punched me in the back of the head. I cried out from the pain, but didn't let the tears fall. I had to pick my fights, and sitting wasn't the one I needed to win. I ground my teeth, trying to absorb the pain so it wouldn't drown Grey.

I sat in the disgusting chair, trying not to touch it. I could hear the dead cry. It was stifling. I kissed Fridrik's head and tried to soothe him. He buried his face in my hair. I looked down at my pack, and I wanted to cry for them all. They looked as scared as I felt. Vigdis had been right—they would all die for me. I felt so defeated.

Æsileif stood next to me, smoking her cigarette in her sultry way. I hated her. I hated them all. I'd seen so much evil in my short life, and I had survived it all, but this would destroy me. I couldn't watch my pack die.

Odin leaned against the railing of the balcony so casually it was frightening. Like he almost belonged here, and they barely gave him a second look. Was it because they didn't see him as a threat, or because he was a traitor?

"Kneel," Æsileif said to Dilara.

When Dilara hesitated, Æsileif put her cigarette out on Dilara's arm. I could smell her flesh burning, and the cooked flesh mingled unnaturally with the sweet smell of the cigarette smoke. My stomach recoiled from the stench. Dilara cursed, but she bent her knees and stared at Æsileif.

"How dare you look upon my face? You are nothing but a common slave." Æsileif tried to strike her, but Vigdis's soft voice cut in.

"Don't waste your energy on such filth. We have a guest of honor with us," Vigdis said. "We don't want her to lack for attentions."

Æsileif turned away from Dilara. She smoothed her clothing in a methodical way as she turned to face me once again. "My apologies, Princess Ashling. Sometimes I let my temper get the best of my manners."

The way they spoke in the midst of such a horrific injustice was enraging. They didn't seem to notice that they were the roots of evil. The way they chose to treat other living creatures showed the measure of their souls and the lack of humanity left inside them.

"Aren't you excited for the fight?" Æsileif said. "They are fighting for your hand in marriage. Oh, to be loved by so many," she cooed.

"This is an atrocity," I said. "End the fights. Stop this madness before it goes too far."

"Don't they look heroic?" she said.

She couldn't even hear me. She was possessed by the idea of the chivalry. She couldn't even see the sad, broken people who surrounded her. They needed her love and protection, and all she saw were pawns to die in her game for her entertainment.

Shikoba shook her head, and I knew she wanted me to stop arguing with them. She was scared for me. I could feel Grey's fear, and Mother's. I didn't dare look at Mother; I might cry.

She smiled her odd smile again. She leaned in so close to me that I could feel her hair as it tickled my arms, and I tried to lean away, but there was nowhere to go. Her lips were barely touching my ear as she whispered, "They will die for loving you. Every one of them will die, and you'll watch them die from the best seats in the house."

The horn sounded, and Verci stepped forward. "Let it begin."

Baran, Mund, Brychan, Channing, Marcius, and Emil stood together, guarding Grey as the fighters surged around the arena. I was terrified they'd break the wall and attack my pack . . . for no other reason than their desire for blood.

Æsileif wrapped her fingers with mine, holding my hand. Grey and Eamon began circling each other. I tried to pull my hand away, and her dark eyes fixed on mine.

"No, my pet," she said as she turned her attention back to the fight.

I felt so trapped and out of control. Anxiety ravaged me, and I couldn't catch my breath. The sounds of the cheering below washed over me like waves of sadness. I was terrified for Grey. Even if he won, it didn't mean they would let any of us live. And every injury he suffered, I would endure as my punishment for loving him.

I lowered my eyes and let my fear and tears seep from my eyes. I was scared to watch and scared to look away. In the blink of an eye, my entire future could die before me. Everything I ever dared to dream about was so close to slipping away from me that I forced myself to watch the fight.

Grey swung at Eamon, but Eamon dodged his blow easily and took a smooth step backward. Eamon's movements were smooth and calculated. Grey was unpredictable; he was a predator. The way Grey moved made me think he was testing Eamon. Even though none of his blows connected, there was something in the way Grey watched him that made the hair on my arms stand on end. Grey swung with his left hand, and as Eamon moved out of the way, Grey cracked him in the face with his right hand, sending Eamon stumbling back. The roar from the crowd was ear piercing; they wanted Eamon to win.

About fifteen of the fighters in the crowd began to push over the barrier into the fighting pit, closing in around my pack as they tried to protect Grey while he fought. Eamon lurched at Grey, and Grey jumped out of the way, but the crowd shoved him back toward Eamon, and fights erupted in the crowd.

"You don't deserve her anyway," Eamon shouted, taunting him.

Grey smiled. Though his exterior was vicious, I could feel Grey's fear. He wasn't infallible, and he was as scared as I was. His winning or losing likely wouldn't save either of us, and he must have known. Either way, we would both likely die here.

"She is the embodiment of perfection," Eamon said. "What makes you think you are worthy of her?"

Grey punched Eamon right between the eyes. "Because she loves me," he said as he punched him again.

Eamon blindly punched at Grey and struck his shoulder. The pain nearly took my breath away, but I was able to keep from toppling over. Æsileif looked at me curiously as she petted my face and hair.

"Shh, my pet," she cooed. "Don't be scared."

I tried to ignore her. Grey knelt on the ground, and the crowd nearly consumed them. He leaped to his feet, and Eamon was struggling to keep his balance. Eamon stumbled forward and punched Grey in the kidney. I gasped as the pain vibrated through my organs. I felt my face flush with sweat from the pain. Æsileif lifted my hand to hers and kissed it. Everything she did creeped me out. I just wanted to rip my hand away from her and scream until it all disappeared.

Grey lay on the ground, and Eamon kicked him in the ribs, over and over and over again. I could taste blood in my mouth with every blow. I squeezed my eyes shut, trying to close off the pain, but the pain meant he was still alive, and that was all we had left.

Eamon punched Grey in the side, and my ribs ached, and my breath caught. Could Eamon kill me without ever laying a hand on me? The crowd was so tight around them; I almost couldn't see them anymore. Grey was on the ground, covered in blood and dirt. He struggled to stand, but the crowd held him down, and my pack was fighting to save him, but there were too many. They had no right to interfere with the fight, but they were going to kill him.

"Grey!" I screamed.

He couldn't die. I needed him. I tore my hand away from Æsileif and jumped over the edge of the balcony down into the arena, screaming, with Fridrik still in my arms. I landed in a crouch and snarled at the onlookers who thirsted for death. My fear and hate mixed in my blood like napalm, sending a fire of rage through my body.

I walked slowly and the crowd parted, and the arena was silent. Eamon stood over Grey, but he had stopped hitting him. Grey's chest rose and fell with each labored breath. I knelt and touched his cheek. His eyes opened, his beautiful green eyes. I could feel his pain and worry as I wiped the blood from the open cut on his lip with my dress. I turned on Eamon with my cold hate.

"This ends here," I said. "You will not touch him again."

"He's not worthy of you," Eamon said.

"No, Eamon, *you* are not worthy of me," I said. "And it is not your choice. It is mine." I looked up at my father, who was gripping the railing so tightly his knuckles were white, and his face was red with anger. "This is my choice!" I repeated for all to hear.

I helped Grey to his feet, and he stood next to me. I held Fridrik tightly as Baran, Mund, Quinn, Brychan, Channing, Marcius, and Emil fought their way to my side. I felt calm in their presence.

I looked for Dilara, Shikoba, and Odin on the balcony. Shikoba stood between Dilara and Æsileif, protecting Dilara. Shikoba held her hands up in quiet submission, but Æsileif swung a two-headed silver ax at Shikoba's head. I screamed as it sliced through her neck like air. I shook with terror and tears ran down my cheeks, and I gagged and I screamed.

The blade cut clean through her, but not a drop of blood spilled.

"You can not kill me, little girl. I'm already dead," Shikoba said.

Æsileif screeched like a banshee.

Every moment with Shikoba flashed back through my mind. She never touched anything or anyone, she never changed clothes, and she never ate. She was a spirit bound to the earth with no earthly body left to carry her.

Shikoba threw something in the balcony. Smoked coiled and filled the balcony with fog. Dilara shifted into a wolf and leaped down to the arena, padding toward me. She was a tall, thin wolf with black fur tipped with brown; her beautiful dark eyes were the same. She looked as regal in wolf form as she did in her human form.

Shikoba appeared next to Father as Kane slammed his tomahawk into the guard who held Mother, slicing the man in two. Mother rushed to the railing and stared down on me in horror. Quinn and Kane stood guard over her. The gallery was full of screaming onlookers who were fleeing the Realms; they weren't loyal enough to the Dvergar to risk their lives witnessing my family's mass murder. The arena was still packed with vicious fighters out for blood.

Æsileif stared down on me with an odd look on her face. She leaped down, landing in the sand with her spike heels gouging into the earth. Her hair was wild as a snowstorm.

"Fight me or join me, little princess," she hissed.

"I don't want to fight you, Æsileif," I said.

"You will be mine, or you will die."

"No," I said. "I won't."

Eamon took a step between us. I wasn't sure if he was going to fight me himself, but she snarled at him, and he looked down and stepped away. Brychan and Mund moved forward to Grey and me. Brychan, Baran, Marcius, and Emil kept a larger perimeter around us.

Æsileif smiled and blinked her beautiful long lashes at me. "Either you fight me, or I will have your little pack killed, and then I'll kill you anyway."

I looked at my family, my friends, my loved ones, and I couldn't bear the idea of them dying for me. Not when I could stop it. I kissed Fridrik on the forehead and handed him to Mund. The long train of my dress had been ripped off to protect so many lives that I knew it wouldn't interfere with me while I fought this strange little girl. Grey touched my shoulder and I smiled. Just looking at him I felt like I was home.

I stepped free of my pack. I could feel their unease, but not one questioned my decision. Had I finally earned my place in my pack, or were they too scared to interfere? The crowd backed up as Æsileif tossed her silver weapons onto the ground.

"Will you be my pet?" she asked. "Or do you choose death?"

I smiled watching her. She was agile like a cat, but far too overconfident. Every step she took circling me, I watched her heels sink into the sand.

"I choose freedom," I said.

"Then you will die," she said, and just like a cat she coiled and pounced at me. I blocked with my arms, but the impact knocked me to the ground. I groaned as the sand embedded into my flesh.

She laughed as she twisted her head to the side like a psychotic animal. I don't know why I didn't see it before. She was a sociopath. She was a chameleon; she turned into whatever personality suited her needs. I wasn't even sure which personality was the real one. I crouched down, waiting for her muscles to move, waiting for the right moment.

She pounced into the air and so did I. We collided in midair. I punched her in the face as we fell down to the earth, using the impact of our fall to bash her head into the ground. We rolled until she held me down, my arms and legs pinned beneath her. My heart pounded, and Grey's fear flooded me, but I knew my place.

"Æsileif?" I whispered.

She leaned in close, smiling. "Yes, my pet?"

I smiled and her face came closer to mine and I head-butted her so hard my head swam with confusion. I just kept coming like Brychan taught me. I punched her over and over again in the face, busting open her lip and boxing her ears. She moaned with pain, but I didn't let up. She stumbled backward—she was afraid. I could smell it on her. I walked toward her as she crawled backward away from me.

"You dare threaten my people? You dare hurt your own people? What the hell is wrong with you?" I said.

She looked like a little scared crab crawling away from me. It was almost comical watching her, but part of me felt bad for her. She was a product of an insane family—did she ever stand a chance?

"Fight me, Æsileif. Fight me," I threatened her.

I was ready to end all of this. No matter what it took, I was done with her little games. I was done with all of it.

She flung a handful of sand at me and it stung my eyes, making it hard to see. I rubbed at it as she slammed into me. The wind gusted out of my lungs and my eyes burned. I looked up into her rotten face.

"I want to keep you."

"Never," I said kicking her off.

She skidded into the sand, cutting up her pretty face. I pulled my mace from my belt and held it, ready to finish her. She stood to face me, but her eyes were wild. She looked from me to my pack and back again.

"I will drink your blood while I watch your family die," she said.

"The hell you will," I said.

She charged at me, and for a moment I was scared of her, but the emotions from each of my pack members flooded into me; I felt their strength and their belief in me. I slammed the mace into her face as hard as I could. I heard the cracking of her bones as she screamed and crumbled on ground, dying. Half of her face was missing, and her teeth were shattered all over the ground and the sound of Vigdis screaming echoed in my ears.

Verci leaped from the balcony like a golden god from hell. He landed on top of one of his own guards, crushing him. Blood splattered out of his eyes and mouth all around us. He rushed to Æsileif, but she was already dead. I hated that I'd taken her life, that I destroyed another of Old Mother's creatures, but Æsileif had left me no choice. I had to protect myself and protect my people.

Grey grabbed my hand and stood in front of me. It was an obvious sign to everyone that he was claiming me as his and protecting me, but I didn't like the idea of him fighting Verci. Dilara padded forward with her hackles raised. A pit master picked up Æsileif and carried her away from the arena while Verci snarled at us. Desperation and rage were clear on his face.

I stepped back toward my pack, pulling Grey with me. Mund handed Fridrik to me so he could fight. Baran, Brychan, Channing, Emil, and Marcius closed in around Grey and me, but even with their presence I didn't feel safe. Eamon was closer to us than Verci, but I was far less scared of him.

"You can't hide behind the half-breed," Verci said.

"You'll have to go through me to get to her," Grey said.

"With pleasure," he hissed.

"Da . . . da da!" Fridrik said. Startled, I looked around to see Fridrik reaching for Eamon. Eamon looked at him with so much love.

"Eamon?" I gasped.

"That's my son," he said.

"He's your son?"

"Verci found out about Grete and Fridrik and used them against me. I'm sorry," he said. "I didn't have a choice. I never meant to hurt you."

I thought of Grete on that leash, beaten and hurt, and Fridrik in the bone cages, scared and alone. I couldn't imagine the pain and fear that Eamon had to endure not knowing whether his son was even alive.

"Promise you'll protect him," Eamon said.

"What?"

"Promise me," he said.

"I will," I said.

"And his human mother Grete, if you can."

It made sense. It all made sense. He had to love a human, because there wasn't a wolf in the world he could touch without hurting them.

"I will try," I said.

"Stop this, Uncle!" Eamon said. "This doesn't have to go any further. You already lost your daughter; don't shed any more blood."

Verci snarled, his face only inches from Eamon's. I was terrified for him not even Bento stood by his side. I heard Vigdis wailing from the balcony. Verci drew a silver khopesh, an Egyptian-style sickle sword with green-gold inlays, from a leather sheath on his back. The khopesh glimmered in the firelight that surrounded the arena. Verci held it at his nephew's throat, forcing him to kneel. The blade lightly grazed Eamon's throat, and a thin line of blood trickled down his neck, but Eamon didn't cry out or beg.

That one little knick made him mortal, a tiny cut that meant he'd die. Fridrik cried in my arms, reaching for Eamon, and all I could do was hold him back to protect him. I felt like I was absorbing his and Eamon's sadness; I was drowning in it. Fridrik wailed and wriggled, trying to get to his father.

"You take the half-breed's life, or I will take yours," Verci threatened.

"No," Eamon said.

"Kill him, Eamon," Verci hissed.

Eamon looked at Fridrik and then me. "No," he said.

Verci screamed, and his mouth looked as though it might unhinge and consume us all. He panted, and rage rippled over his flesh. He looked around the arena at all of us. He stared at me for a long time, until his breathing finally calmed, and he focused on Eamon again.

"You have already served your purpose," Verci said. With a flick of his wrist, he sliced deep into Eamon's throat.

Eamon crumbled to the ground and gasped for air. Blood leaked from his neck and bubbled with each breath he took. I ran to him, and my pack closed in around us. I knelt with him and wrapped my hands over the bloody wound. I couldn't help but remember Svana, the human girl Adomnan tried to force me to murder, and ached for both of them. I'd lost her—I couldn't let him die, too. Fridrik crawled on Eamon's chest, and the smile on Eamon's face broke my heart.

I tore a piece off my cloak dress and wrapped it around his throat. Tears streamed down my cheeks as I tried desperately to stop the bleeding.

"Why did you do that?" I asked Eamon.

"Because I couldn't kill the one person you love most in this world," Eamon sputtered. His breaths were slowing down, but the blood was still pouring out of his neck.

"I don't understand," I said.

He touched my cheek with his bloody hand, caressing it lightly; his hands were caked in sand, which protected my skin from being burned. "I never meant to hurt you, but I couldn't watch Grete and Fridrik die. I'm sorry I was so weak. And you were so strong—you risked everything to save my son. I failed you."

"Eamon, what are you?" I couldn't understand. I'd thought he was evil. I thought he was a Barghest. I thought he ate children.

He smiled weakly. "I am a Barghest, but not because I eat children. The recessive mutation passed from my father to me. I'm not the monster you think I am," he said.

"I was so wrong, Eamon. I'm so sorry," I said.

"Surrender the girl, or you will all die," Verci said to my father. I barely heard any of the shouts around me. I was too stunned. "She belongs to me now. An eye for an eye."

"No, she doesn't," Grey said. "We are her pack, and we all stand between you and her."

Verci laughed. "You're nothing."

"Then fight me," Grey said.

Verci swung his khopesh and sliced the air between him and Grey.

"Fight me without your tricks. Drop your sickle sword," Grey said. "Fight me as a man. Fight me with your so-called honor, as you've witnessed countless others do in the past—die as you've watched countless others die."

Verci swung the sword out of the arena. The blade slammed into the chest of a fighter, killing him. Life meant nothing to Verci, not even the lives of his own people. Verci stalked toward Grey like a golden devil.

"Old Mother, please, no!" I cried.

Verci circled around Grey. He punched Grey in the ribs. The sheer force of the blow made me gag, and I clutched at my side. I watched in horror as Verci slammed his fists into Grey's ear. My ears were ringing from the impact, disorientating me. I forced myself to take slow breaths to block out the pain and fear that ate at me. Channing, Marcius, and Emil shifted one by one, joining Dilara as they started ripping apart the guards surrounding us. Mund and Brychan fought in human form. Baran stayed by my side as I cared for Eamon and Fridrik. It was a bloodbath all around us.

The majority of the fighters fled back into the tunnels; they didn't want to die today, not for a false allegiance to the Dvergars. Those remaining attacked, still outnumbering us.

Eamon lightly touched my wrist where he had drawn his Bloodmark. He'd given me the one thing he knew would protect me here, the Dvergar Bloodmark. His Bloodmark. It had faded, and I felt like I lost more than his protection. I was losing him. I stayed by his side. I wouldn't leave him to die alone.

Baran yelled. There was a silver blade stuck in his back. Two guards grabbed him, but Baran knocked them both out. Even as a mortal he was fierce, but three more just replaced them. They overpowered Baran and dragged his mortal body away from me. They held him, beating him bloody.

Everything was unraveling. He was the only father figure I'd never known. He was my friend. I didn't know what to do. He was already so far out of reach. I looked to Grey as Verci punched him in the chest with both hands, sending him flying backward. His body slammed into the ground, and I shook with pain. Verci jumped onto Grey's chest, hissing like a demon and holding him down. Even as a human, Verci was maliciously primal. Verci tried to bite Grey in the face. Over and over again, twisting and reaching as Grey barely held him back from tearing his flesh. Grey head-butted Verci and knocked him to the ground. Every blow made me wince with pain, and I could barely tell who was hitting whom. They rolled so close to me that I could touch them. All I had to do was kill Verci.

I slammed my mace into the back of Verci's skull. The bone crushed in, but it didn't stop him. Adrenaline must have been the only thing keeping him alive. Verci fought even harder as blood leaked out of his skull. He lunged at Grey, tackling him as he punched Grey in the ribs over and over again.

I looked to my father, hoping he'd intervene and protect Grey, but he held Mother back to stop her from getting to me. He wasn't going to help me or Mund or any of us. He was just going to watch his own children die.

Grey shifted into a wolf and tore at Verci's neck, breaking his necklace of eyes and scattering them everywhere. Verci's neck was in shreds of muscles and tissue, and his head hung slightly off center. Verci laughed, taunting Grey. It was like he couldn't be killed.

I held Fridrik in Eamon's arms as I watched Mund, Channing, Marcius, Brychan, Dilara, and Emil fighting off men all around us. There was blood everywhere, and with every passing moment the fighting grew closer and closer to where I sat with Eamon. I could still see Baran fighting, but they were forcing him farther and farther from me. Through it all, I couldn't see Odin—had the Dvergar killed him or taken him captive?

Grey turned and tore a bite out of Verci's arm like a vicious predator tearing his prey piece by piece. Grey closed the distance between them, but Verci's guard surrounded him as Verci ran away into the tunnels. Grey howled and chased after him, ripping the life from every creature that crossed his path, but no matter how many he killed more guards appeared and slowed him down. Finally, Verci escaped.

Grey turned and ran after Baran as the guard shifted and tore after him. He was going to save Baran. Relief filled me. I wanted Baran to live far more than I wanted Verci to die.

Several guards closed in on Fridrik and me, and panic flooded me. I couldn't shift, or I'd have to put Fridrik down and leave Eamon. They'd be unprotected. I held my mace in my hand and waited as a huge wolf came barreling toward us. Dilara lunged in, tearing his face off before devouring another.

"I command you to stop," Eamon said, holding his wrist up with the Dvergar Bloodmark. The guard just sliced his wrist with his sword, destroying Eamon's Bloodmark.

I screamed as another wolf jumped toward me and tried to snatch Fridrik from my arms. I hit him with the mace, shattering his eye socket, and Dilara finished him.

"Stay with Ashling!" Baran yelled to Grey.

I watched in horror as Baran was pulled into a tunnel, into the darkness of the Bloodrealms . . . into an evil world I now understood all too well. I could feel Grey's anger and indecision. I knew he needed us both, but he turned running back toward me, leaping over several guards.

Five men surrounded me, cutting me off from Dilara and Grey. A pit master with boils on his face was among them, and he uncoiled a leather whip as he drooled from his toothless grin. I used my body to cover Fridrik and protect him; as the whip flayed into my back and cut into my flesh, my blood ran red, but Fridrik was safe in my arms, sandwiched between Eamon and me. I wouldn't let them hurt him. Every slice of the whip tore at my flesh, reminding me what I fought for, but it wasn't silver tipped, and I was thankful for that. The pain sliced into me over and over again.

I heard my mother scream, and I looked up to the gallery to see her shove Father away from her. She leaped down from the gallery like a goddess. Her dress fluttered around her as she landed between the boil-covered man and me. I had never seen her so ferocious and powerful. The vicious snarl that came from her chest was the warning sound only a mother could make. A man charged her, and she shifted into the most beautiful white wolf. Her fur shimmered beautifully as she easily tore his head from his body. She snarled at the others who dared threaten us. A man came running at her and knocked her to the ground. I swung my mace into his face and tore open his cheek, exposing the teeth and muscles in his face. Blood dripped down his neck and chest as his lower jaw sagged unnaturally. I slammed the mace into his face again, crushing his entire skull. I would kill them all for hurting her.

More guards closed in around us again, and Kane jumped down, landing among them. He sank his hatchet into a man's skull, splitting it clean open. Mother's hackles were on end, and her beautiful eyes burned with hate. Three men attacked Kane; Mother bit into the torso of one of them, tearing out his entrails as she tossed him aside to protect us.

Quinn and Father fought guards in the gallery, only two of them to at least ten of our enemy. I was afraid for us all. Our pack was separated into so many smaller groups and outnumbered at every turn.

"I love you, Mother," I said.

I don't know why I said it, but I did. I wasn't even sure she heard me, but after watching her die in my dream, I couldn't stand the idea of her not knowing how much she meant to me. I needed her to know that she made me who I was. If it weren't for her, I wouldn't have survived any of this. It was her unending strength that gave me the strength to survive.

Kane kept the perimeter around us clear. He was ferocious, and he hadn't even shifted yet. I couldn't imagine how strong of a warrior he really was as a wolf. Mother stayed at my side, and I held Fridrik tightly to Eamon's chest as I held my mace with the other hand.

Grey tore into another guard, and he raced back to my side. A guard jumped on his back and stabbed him, causing Grey to shift back into a human. The silver blade took the wolf out of him, but it didn't make him mortal—the Bloodsucker still fueled his veins. Grey turned and killed the man with his bare hands, snapping his neck. My back burned where Grey had been cut, but the poison couldn't affect me.

More men charged out of the tunnel at us, making the kills we'd already had seem insignificant.

Before I could even think what was happening, my father landed as an enormous red-and-silver wolf between Grey and the new guards. He snarled as they leaped onto his back, but he devoured them with the smooth, calculated motions of a killer. I'd never seen my father as a wolf—he was impressive. Quinn landed next to him as a far smaller wolf, and the two joined the fighting.

My pack formed together, and with Father's presence they seemed to fight as a pack rather than individually. Screams echoed in the arena as my pack took the upper hand and killed all of the guards one by one, and we won. I looked at each and every one of my pack. They all had injuries and were covered in blood, but they were all alive, and that was all I could ask for.

Odin came running toward us from one of the tunnels. He was covered in blood and must have barely escaped. He found Kane and Quinn and talked with them quietly. Baran was the only one missing and my heart ached for him. I felt sick, and my stomach was knotted with fear. I couldn't lose Baran; I needed him. Mund, back in his human form, walked over to my side. He was covered in blood and filth.

"Are you okay?" I asked.

"I can't get Baran's scent; it's impossible to track him," Mund said. The frustration and anger in his voice was thick and heavy.

Grey walked over wearing pieces of leather armor he'd collected from the dead. The silver wound in his back had already healed, but he remained in human form. I touched his hand and he smiled. It was incredible watching him fight; even after the silver poisoned him and he'd been turned to a human, he was unstoppable with the Bloodsucker in him. He leaned over and kissed my cheek.

The arena was empty except for my pack and the dead who surrounded us. I looked up to the balcony, where Vigdis looked down on us. The emotionless face she always wore was replaced by malicious hate, and her black eyes were fixed on my mother.

Mother shifted back into a human, and her white cloak dress formed back around her body. Dilara sat on the other side of Mother with her teeth still bared. Dilara was ready to continue the fight, but many of my pack looked beaten.

"What's your next move, Vigdis?" Mother asked as she studied her sister.

"To kill everyone you love," she spat. "To take it all away, just like you took Baran from me."

"You orchestrated this to kill my daughter, but instead you lost yours," Mother said. "Let us end this and call a truce between our families and let Old Mother's love heal our wounds. We don't have to fight anymore."

"I was never one of you," Vigdis said. "I was meant to rule you."

"Stay away from my family, Vigdis," Mother said. Her voice was unwavering.

Vigdis smiled, looking right at me. "Do you love that little whelp of yours? Do you want her to live and breathe and find happiness in this world? Is that what you want? You want me to let you be happy when you've prevented me from ever experiencing the same?" She laughed an evil, melodic tone as she raised her hands. "Kill them all," she said, and her eyes never left mine. We would die here; I could feel it. She disappeared through the doorway.

I wiped the blood from Eamon's face. He was in so much pain, but the love on his face as he held Fridrik was pure. He didn't deserve to die in this game. Fridrik would never know his father because of unnecessary hate. I shook my head, devastated. So many lives lost for nothing.

I heard the scratching and dragging sounds, and I knew what hell Vigdis had unleashed on us. The Draugr were coming to kill us. It was only a matter of time before we were all corpses on the ground. They flooded into the room, filling the balcony, gallery, and all of the tunnels. We were surrounded by the undead. My pack closed in tighter around us, and I could smell their fear. I knew most had never seen these mythical creatures, but it didn't lessen the threat that was about to consume us. They hung from the ceiling like bats, clawing their way to us. They started dropping down all around us, hissing. I shivered and my hair stood on end. We couldn't win this. There were hundreds of them.

30
Stone Wolves

Emil charged at the Draugr with his teeth bared, ready to fight. The rest of my family stood still, terrified. The Draugr tore him apart instantly, feasting on his flesh as he screamed. He never stood a chance. Marcius ran to save him, but it was too late. The Draugr had already stopped consuming Emil, and his blood dripped from their black teeth. They walked slowly over his carcass to attack Marcius. Their hunger was insatiable.

"We're all going to die!" Odin said with a laugh.

My pack started shifting into wolves all around me to fight. Only Mother and I remained human with Fridrik and Eamon. Mother took Fridrik in her arms, and she sang an old Celtic song that filled the room with our sadness. Her words vibrated off the enormous walls. Every word wept with loss, and I felt her pain.

I watched my pack fighting the emaciated creatures. For every one they killed, a dozen more Draugr flooded the room and clawed their way across the ceiling, just waiting for their chance to eat us. I looked at my wrist, wishing Eamon's Bloodmark hadn't faded away. There was nothing left to protect us—we were alone. Dread filled my stomach. We would all die in the worst place imaginable, and by being eaten alive and forced to hear each other scream. My emotions flowed through me, and angry tears ran down my cheeks. I looked helplessly at all of my friends and family. I couldn't protect them.

The creatures pinned Channing down, biting into his arm. He cried out as Mund and Marcius killed the monsters and freed him. I watched in horror as my pack was being slowly destroyed. I knew they couldn't fight forever.

I shifted into a wolf far smaller than all those around me. I looked like a child in a room full of gods. I howled with desperation, letting my voice join my mother's song as I prepared to die. I couldn't face losing all of them. My beloved mother; Mund, who would be leaving a wife and child behind; Baran, lost to the Realms; and my love . . . my Grey. I had failed them. I had failed Old Mother Earth. I failed myself. I howled again, filling the room with sorrow. Nothing could save me from my grief.

The walls began to crack, and stone fell down all around us. The room was caving in. The walls crumbled as the gargoyle wolves broke away from the stone walls and came to life. They leaped to the ground, growling and snarling as they tore into the Draugr. I couldn't believe my eyes. The stone wolves were saving our lives—they were protecting us. I watched their ferocity. The Draugr tried to bite into their stone bodies, but their black teeth shattered and the creatures shrieked as they died all around us.

Mother was in awe as she watched them. "Ashling, you brought the Wolves of Song back to life. You called to them for protection, and they answered you."

The army of stone wolves tore apart our enemies, annihilating the evil that surrounded us. I stared in wonder as our lives were spared. When every last Draugr was dead, the wolves leaped back up the walls. The leader padded forward and bowed to me. His eyes were carved from stone, but the emotion in them humbled me. He howled and we all joined his song.

He leaped up the wall and they all froze in time once again. They were the Wolves of Song, and they had come back to life to protect us, but now they were just a myth.

My pack shifted back into humans. They all looked around incredulously and silently began picking up scraps of armor and the weapons they had dropped.

"We have to leave this place," Father said. "We aren't safe here."

"What about Baran?" I asked. "We have to go after him. We have to save him."

"He's already dead," Father said. "Or will be soon."

"I won't leave him to be murdered and desecrated in this place," I said. "His soul will never be set free—he'll be here for eternity."

"Ashling, it's no use," Brychan said, agreeing with my father.

"You don't know that," I said.

"If we don't get you out now, you'll die here, too," Brychan said.

"Baran is mine to save," I said. "He would go after me."

"We're leaving," Father said. "Now."

"You can't tell me what to do anymore," I said.

"I am your father and your king. You will do what you're told," he boomed.

"Like hell I will!" I screamed. "I'm going to rescue Baran with or without your help."

"Pørr, he's our friend," Mother said.

"And she's our daughter!" Father said. "Do you think Baran would want her to die for him?"

Mother shook her head no, and tears rolled down her cheeks. I was losing. Desperation filled my every thought. I couldn't fail Baran. Not Baran.

"I can't lose him. Please, Father," I begged.

He stared at me for what felt like eternity, but I couldn't read his face. Couldn't he see I needed Baran? He was my friend, my protector, my pack.

"I have to protect you," he said. "Take her."

Brychan picked me up and started running after Father toward the stairs. I kicked and screamed, but his grip only tightened. "I'm sorry, Ashling," he said. But his words were hollow to me.

"You don't understand. I need him."

"There's no other way," Brychan said.

Grey leaped in front of Brychan, stopping him. "Put her down," he said. "Baran is my family, my pack. Ashling and I are going to find him."

"No, you're not," Brychan said. Marcius, Channing, and Odin tackled Grey. It took all three of them to subdue him, but that didn't stop Grey from fighting. Every time he struggled though, Odin punched him, and the pain shot through me. I tried to hide it, but I knew Brychan felt my body shake and tense with every blow. I closed my eyes to hide my weakness, but he knew our secret now. He knew.

"Odin, stop!" I screamed, but Odin kept punching Grey.

Odin looked at me and smiled that slimy, sinister smile of his and punched Grey in the gut. I winced from the pain and curled into Brychan. Odin would pay for this . . . I would make him pay.

"Put me down!" I yelled, finally squirming free. Brychan had always sided with me until now. He was letting Baran die . . . to protect me? Or to please my father? I couldn't even look at him. I chewed my lip as the tears ran down my face.

Grey looked at my tear-stained face and stopped fighting. I could feel his anger, sadness, and guilt. So much guilt. He needed Baran as much as I did, but he let Marcius and Channing drag him out to protect me. He chose me, and the guilt of it seeped into my heart.

I hated Odin, I hated Brychan, and I hated my father. They destroyed my chance to save Baran. Every moment that we wasted was a death sentence for him. My failure would be rewarded with his death.

"This way," Mund said, giving his hand to Mother as they ran. I could feel her anguish. It was much like my own, but richer and deeper. So much sadness flowed through me, suffocating me. I sobbed uncontrollably in my silent sorrow.

Brychan picked me up again and cradled me to his chest, and this time I didn't fight it. We ran out of the Bloodrealms into the eerie red moonlight of the Bloodmoon bleeding in the sky. The humans called it a hunter's moon, but we knew it marked the coming of Bloodsuckers. We were about to become their prey. They were always the strongest on the Bloodmoon. Old Mother's moon would bleed red with our deaths, and the moon would grow darker with each wolf the Bloodsuckers killed. They believed it was an honor to them to kill us under the Bloodmoon.

Brychan ran all the way to the shack without looking back, but I looked back to the entrance to the Bloodrealms. I never thought I would want to go back there, but I longed to be with Baran. I vowed I would go back for him . . . or whatever was left of him. Tears ran down my face at the thought, but I wouldn't leave his body to be forgotten. Even if he was dead, I would take his body and allow his soul to be set free. I would burn his body in his homeland of Scotland and return him to Old Mother. And I would save the people of Fenrir and Stonearch—I owed them freedom. I owed so many for my life. I didn't deserve to live over any of them, but I would honor them all.

Dagny and his guard met us outside the shack. I could smell their fear. They knew what the moon meant, and seeing us covered in blood could only strike fear into their hearts.

"What's happened?" Dagny demanded.

"Verci captured Baran Killian, and Vigdis set the Draugr on us," Father said. "We barely escaped with our lives."

"Double the guard around the shack. Send two dozen men to the east exit, the rest of you guard the main entrance. We need to protect the humans. None of that evil will escape on my watch," Dagny called to his men.

Was he more terrified that the Dvergars would escape or that the Draugr would spill out onto the earth, killing all they saw—every animal, every wolf, and every human, wiping the earth of life? If the Wolves of Song didn't join us again, the Draugr would annihilate the world. Dagny turned and stared at Eamon bleeding in Kane's arms, but didn't say a thing.

"Is Baran alive?" he said.

"I don't know," Mother said. She softly wept; it was enough to make me cry, too. I ran to her, and we held each other.

"I'm so sorry, Mother," I said.

She sobbed in my arms, uncontrollably, and there was nothing I could do to comfort her. My sweet mother was broken. I felt so lost. My whole life she had always comforted me, and now it was my turn to care for her. It was my turn to be her sanctuary.

The frigid look on Father's face could have turned me to stone once, but I wasn't afraid of him anymore. He was just a man, and he couldn't control me. I'd survived more evil than he could ever inflict on me, and now I finally saw him for what he was: scared.

Dagny and his guard escorted us into the shack, and Brychan finally set me down.

"I'm so sorry," he said.

I couldn't even talk. I was so furious with him there weren't words to match my hate. He'd betrayed everything I believed in. Cara, Gwyn, and Tegan with Nia in her arms, rushed over to us. They sobbed with fear. I turned my back on Brychan and walked over to Grey. Odin still had his slimy hands restraining him, and I shoved Odin so hard he slammed into the wall.

"You disobeyed me again," I said.

"No, mi' lady. I protected you," he said, standing up.

I shoved him again, harder. "You enjoyed hurting Grey," I said.

"I only did what I had to, to ensure your royal safety," he said.

He was full of lies. He was always watching, waiting for this moment to attack Grey. And where was he when I was attacked at Castle Raglan? Where was he when my pack fought for their lives in the Bloodrealms? He was always conveniently missing.

"You lie," I said. "Now tell me the truth. You have interfered with Grey since the day you showed up on my doorstep."

"You're confused," he said twisting the truth to confuse me, to make me question myself, but it wouldn't work. I knew the truth. I should have trusted my instinct about him from the moment I met him. He was a traitor. All this time I trusted him and feared Eamon for being different, but I had been dead wrong.

I punched Odin in the throat, making him sputter and cough as he gasped for breath. He stood and growled in my face. I was tired of second-guessing my gut. There was someone inside of him, something he hid, and I needed to know. I couldn't wait any longer for him to kill me in my sleep. Without Baran here to protect me, I had to know.

"Are you challenging me?" I asked.

"I wouldn't think of it," he hissed.

I took a step closer to him, our faces nearly touching. "I warned you not to betray me. Tell me what you did," I said.

My family just stood watching, wide-eyed. None of them intervened on my or Odin's behalf. I didn't care what they thought. I knew I was right.

"You can't save me, little girl," Odin said sadly. "You can't save any of us, but I won't see any more wolves die for this false hope that your birth started. This isn't a revolution—it's suicide. Everyone I ever loved died for the dream of you, and you are nothing more than a little girl."

He continued, "I told you someone would betray you, I just didn't realize it would be me. I believed in you, but you're just a little girl. You're not any stronger than the rest of us," Odin said. Grey charged at him, and Odin slid his blade into Grey's side. The pain burned through me.

I should have let Adomnan kill Odin in the underworld. I protected him then, and he betrayed me now. Mund, Brychan, Channing, and Kane started closing in around us, ready to strike. "I was in your room at Castle Raglan to kill you. I'm the one who locked the gate of the tunnel, and I'm the one who has to destroy you."

"Get away from my baby!" Mother said.

Father closed the distance and stood next to her. "Odin Pohjola, back away from my daughter."

My knees buckled from Grey's pain, which pulsed through me. I could feel him dying. Odin caught my throat in his hand and nearly crushed it as he pulled me back to my feet. My vision flickered from lack of oxygen as I looked at Grey lying on the ground, bleeding.

"Let her go, Odin," Mund growled.

Odin spun me around, putting me in a headlock as he used my body as a shield and backed away from them. I could feel his hot breath on my neck. I recognized his labored breathing from my room at Castle Raglan. I had let an enemy into the heart of our pack.

"Don't worry, Redmund, I only have to kill the half-breed to destroy the prophecy. Look at him, Ashling. He's dying. Neither the wolf nor the Bloodsucker in him can save him now. When he's dead, he can't claim you," he said. "Once he's dead, no one else has to die for the dream of you."

Mund tried to get to me, but Odin pulled his knife under my chin. He could easily kill me, and I knew none of them could get me out of his grasp before he did.

"Redmund, she doesn't have to die. Don't make me kill her. Just step back and let me escape," he said as he pulled me toward the platform. "You may die trying to kill me, but it will definitely not save her. You know Grey's death will save us all. The prophecy must be stopped, and this was the easiest way."

"Odin, take your slimy hands off her," Brychan said.

"Oh, don't worry, Brychan, you can pick up the pieces of her broken heart." Odin sneered.

"Please Odin, let her go," Mother pleaded.

A hatchet flew past me and embedded into Odin's face, splitting it in two. I fell to the ground and gagged for air. I desperately crawled over Odin's dead body to Grey. He clutched his side, trying to pull out the knife.

"No, not yet," I whispered as I struggled to breathe. His pain inside me was blinding. I tore a piece of my dress free and gently pulled the knife from his side. He grunted with pain, the same pain nearly paralyzing me. I forced myself to work quickly. I spit in my hands and rubbed it over the wound to numb it as I began wrapping the fabric around his torso, covering the wound over and over again. I was scared to death, but I couldn't stop to think about it.

"Please don't take him from me," I begged.

Grey groaned as I tightened the fabric, and his blood soaked through the layers. I put my hands over the bandage and closed my eyes and prayed to Old Mother for her mercy and her love to wash over Grey and protect him from evil. Mother knelt and put her hands over mine and began to sing. Tegan, Gwyn, Dilara, and Cara joined their hands on our shoulders, creating the web of life. Our love flowed through us into Grey's wound.

Grey stopped moving, and he didn't make a sound. I squeezed my eyes closed tighter as the flood of tears erupted down my cheeks. I lay my face on his chest and wept. I'd lost everything. I failed everyone. Everything that mattered turned to dust in my mouth. Every decision I'd made was a mistake I couldn't take back. I lost the love of my life, and I lost my ability to protect my family. The prophecy was destroyed . . . and so was my heart. I let my agony take me.

I felt Grey take a breath and mine caught. He touched my face, and I dared to look at him. Was he really alive? His green eyes glowed in the firelight like magic. He smiled that adorable smile that I loved so much. I wrapped my arms around him as tightly as I could.

"Don't do that again," I whispered.

He chuckled. "I'll try not to."

I finally let myself breathe. I knew what I had to do. I had to stop letting other people force me into anything. It was time to shed away the child and become the leader they needed me to be. With Grey and I together, we couldn't lose.

Tegan and Mund melted into each other with Nia sandwiched between them. Gwyn and Quinn were engrossed in each other, and Cara was caring for Channing's wounds. All the emotions around me were overwhelming. I could feel them all. They were my pack, and their needs came above mine, but I couldn't end their fear and pain any more than I could end my own.

Mother and Shikoba cared for Eamon, trying to make him comfortable. I knew he was dying, and there was nothing we could do. I smelled death on him, but I wanted him to have time with Fridrik without my intrusion.

Grey sat beside me and crushed me in his arms. It felt right. I needed to lose myself in his love. The pain in my heart was unbearable. I wept for Baran. I didn't know if he still breathed, but I ached for him. Grey held me tight and cried with me. As we embraced, I felt what seemed to be Baran's pain and fear mixed with Grey's. I couldn't be sure if I was feeling Baran as one of my pack, or if I was feeling him through Grey, but it was tearing me up inside.

"I'm sorry," I said when the tears had finally stopped.

"You have nothing to be sorry for," Grey said. "I'm scared, too."

"Scared for Baran?" I asked.

"He's my pack. Without him, I don't know where I belong," he said. "Baran has been with me since I was two years old. It feels so wrong to have left him behind to die."

"I know. I'm so scared to lose him," I said.

"I'm scared to lose you, too," he said. "You are the only reason any of us are alive. You are the greatest warrior among us. You had the strength to call the Wolves of Song to save us."

"I don't feel strong," I said. "I question myself all the time whether I'm good enough or strong enough."

"Well stop, because the woman I see is strong enough to protect the world," he said.

"Thank you for believing in me."

"I'm sorry I left you in the labyrinth. We should have stayed together."

"Then we both would have died," I said. "And I will never be ready to give you up."

"Death is only our beginning," he said.

"I'd still prefer life and to feel the touch of your skin on mine," I whispered. "Your hot, sweaty body next to mine."

He nuzzled into my ear and whispered. "I love you, my wife."

I couldn't help, but smile. He was the other half of my soul, and I could do anything with him by my side. Together we could save Baran. I just didn't know how yet. Grey went to talk to Mund, leaving me to my thoughts.

I smelled Brychan next to me, but I didn't look up.

"I'm sorry I didn't listen to you," he said.

"I understand why you made the choice you did," I said.

"Can I ask you something?" he said.

I looked up into his blue eyes. "Sure. Why not?"

"Do you know why I yielded my fight with Grey?" he asked.

"No," I said.

"Because I love you enough to see what he means to you. I tried to steal you once, but I see the way you look at him, and the way he looks at you. The way the two of you always found little ways to constantly touch each other. I saw all of the innocence of love in the two of you, and I knew I didn't stand a chance to steal your heart, because you'd already given it away." He smiled sadly. "And I am okay letting go, because I know he's worthy of you."

"Thank you, Brychan. I'm sorry I couldn't love you the way you deserved to be loved," I said. "But I cherish you."

"You are my queen," he said. "You are my dear friend, and you will fulfill the prophecy with Grey by your side. I will always protect you. But I want to know something, Ashling."

"What?"

"You feel his physical pain, don't you?" he asked.

I stared at him with my big golden eyes and said nothing. I didn't know what to say. I couldn't lie, because he already knew the truth. I gnawed at my lip, wishing there was an easy way out.

"I saw it when Grey fought in the pits, but I ignored it, telling myself it was nothing. But when I carried you, and Odin was attacking Grey, I felt your body wince with pain and twist away from the same blows that Grey endured. I know you feel it, but how?"

"I don't know. I feel all of him all the time, as he feels me. We are truly one soul in two bodies. We were bound together before we ever met," I said.

"That's incredible," he said. "And dangerous."

"I know," I said. "That's why you have to keep our secret. We could be destroyed by it."

"I will always keep your secret," he said. "And I will help you save Baran."

Tears filled my eyes at mention of his name. "Thank you." I choked.

Brychan leaned forward and kissed my cheek. Grey walked over with his brow furrowed. "Don't worry, Grey. I never stood a chance." He patted Grey on the back and walked over to where Mund and Tegan sat. Brychan had given us the greatest gift: his love and support and our freedom.

"What was that about?" Grey asked.

"He is supporting my choice in you," I said.

31
Bloodsuckers

The next morning, I left Eamon's side so he could rest. He was quieter in the last few hours. Death was near. Mother carried Fridrik with us to the surface to get some fresh air. I watched as Father was giving orders to the men to scout the terrain.

"So where are we going?" I asked.

"That is none of your concern," he growled.

"It bloody well is my concern."

He studied my angry face. "We will be traveling to Mycenae, Greece, to seek Mother Rhea. She can guide us to find Baran," he said. "Isn't that what you wanted?"

I nodded. I didn't know if he was lying to get me to leave the Bloodrealms, or if he was actually going to help Baran, but I didn't want to risk angering him.

The men all left to scout the terrain for Bloodsuckers, leaving us behind. Mother, Fridrik, Tegan, Nia, Gwyn, Dilara, Cara, Shikoba, and I watched them leave. I walked over to Shikoba as she watched them disappear over the horizon.

"I don't know how to ask this, but how did you die?" I asked her.

She smiled warmly. "I lost my sister and I lost my life to protect my niece, Tallulah. We fought for a better life for her, but I had to die to save her."

"Did it hurt?" I asked.

"Yes, for a time . . ." she said, "But then there isn't any pain anymore. There is only Old Mother's love."

"How is it you're still here? Why didn't Old Mother claim your soul?"

"I'm the last medicine woman of my tribe. I am a healer. So Old Mother offered me the opportunity to stay and heal my people, and in return I would protect you."

"Me?" I said. "You chose to protect me over an eternity in Old Mother's love?"

"We all chose you. That is why you're the chosen one. Not because fate selected you, but because we did," she said.

I had never thought of it that way. Fate hadn't been laid before me to follow, but a series of choices led me to my fate. And not just my own choices, but everyone's. Free will couldn't be contained. We all made the choices that led us to this moment. Every one of them chose me to lead them.

"You lost your necklace," she said.

"I . . . I gave it away," I said. "To a little girl in the Realms who saved me."

She smiled like she knew where it was. Could she see the little girl it now protected? Had she known all along I would give it away to protect another?

"Thank you, Shikoba, for believing in me," I said.

"The winds have changed," she said, pointing to the very top of the tree.

I watched the branches sway in the wind as they invited me to climb. When I looked back, Shikoba had wandered over to Nia, Tegan,

Mother, and Fridrik in the shade of the tree.

I climbed up high into the top branches and rested my head, letting the wind rock me. It was serene up that high in the treetops, where the wind could surround me completely with Old Mother's love. I had always loved the complete freedom of the wind. It was unstoppable.

I caught a Bloodsucker's scent on the breeze and searched the horizon for them. Three Bloodsuckers approached from the north about a half mile away. I recognize them from the Cree lands, and they quickly closed the distance between us. I knew they could see Tegan, Nia, Mother, Fridrik, Gwyn, Cara, Dilara, and Shikoba sitting in the grass below me, but they couldn't see me hidden in the branches high above the ground.

The woman carried a giant silver spear that glinted in the morning sun, and her long brown hair whipped around her in the wind like a veil. She wore fitted pants with silver weapons strapped to them. One of the others carried a crossbow and a quiver of silver arrows.

Tegan growled as she handed Nia and Fridrik to Mother and shifted into a beautiful brown wolf. She lunged forward, snarling at the intruders and warning them not to come any closer. Gwyn and Dilara shifted into wolves, flanking Tegan on each side.

Shikoba stood and walked next to Mother, Cara, and the children. They could easily kill all of us with their silver arrows, but they were closest to Tegan. I was certain the woman Bloodsucker could puncture Tegan's heart with her spear. I knew Tegan had risked so much for the chance to protect Nia.

"You have no place here," Shikoba said. "I suggest you leave with your lives."

"Where is the red wolf?" the woman asked.

"I don't know who you mean," Shikoba said.

"Give that flame-temptress to us, or you will all die with your secrets," she said.

When no one answered, she thrust her spear at Tegan, narrowly missing. Dilara snarled and lunged at the Bloodsuckers. I could smell the fear and hate on the wind. It was the smell of war.

"Where is she?" the woman screamed.

I dropped out of the tree between her and Tegan. She jumped back, startled, her blue eyes wild as nature itself. The wind blew my crazy red hair around my face like a flame hurricane.

"Watching you," I said with a smirk.

"Aren't you going to run?" She sneered.

I laughed. "And who do you presume to be?" I asked.

"Rhonda Jane," she said.

"A Bloodsucker," Cara said.

Rhonda laughed. "Indeed. We prefer to call ourselves hunters, but you can call us anything you want while we kill you."

"What do you want with us?" I asked.

"You," she said. "I only want you."

"And why is that?" I asked.

"To destroy you, of course," she said. "What else would I want with a creature like you?"

Tegan, Gwyn, and Dilara snarled and snapped at them. I felt oddly calm among wolves and Bloodsuckers while this strange woman threatened me. She didn't scare me as much as I knew she should. There was something about her that made me want to comfort her, though I knew she saw me as the enemy.

"I'm certainly not going with you," I said as I took a few steps back. I needed to position myself to protect Mother and the children behind me.

"You either come willingly, or we will kill all of you, including those possessed children. I don't want to kill a babe, but to punish you, I will," she said.

I shook my head in disgust. "What could I have done to you to make you say such unnatural things about a child?" I asked. Was I wrong, or did doubt fill her eyes? I didn't think she wanted to hurt Nia or Fridrik, but I wasn't willing to risk their lives either.

"You murdered our master, Robert Donavan, desecrated his trophies, and you captured and corrupted his son, Grey. We're here to kill you and rescue him," she said.

I nearly swallowed my tongue. She thought I killed Robert. She threatened my family and everything I held dear, and she dared to think Grey would ever be one of them. He wasn't a murderer.

"I didn't kill Robert. Adomnan did."

"So you say," she said. "Do you deny corrupting Grey's soul?"

"What makes you think Grey was ever one of you?" I said. Venom dripped off my words as rage flowed into my soul.

Rhonda took a step closer, and Tegan growled a warning sound so deep that I could feel it vibrate the ground around us. Rhonda aimed her spear at Tegan.

"No!" I yelled. "Don't you dare touch her. This is between us."

Dagny's guard surrounded the Bloodsuckers. "Problem here?" he asked as he bit into a bloody piece of meat. Tegan, Gwyn, and Dilara slowly backed away toward Mother as the guard closed in on the Bloodsuckers.

"More dogs," Rhonda said angrily.

"These Bloodsuckers have come to punish me for the death of Robert Donavan and the corruption of his son, Grey," I said to Dagny.

"Do you want me to exterminate them for you?" Dagny asked me.

"No, not yet," I said, taking a step closer to Rhonda. "Do you actually know Grey?"

She lowered the spear and studied me. "I understand you think you love him," she said. "Do you think your spell over him will last forever?"

"You can't control love. It is as wild as the wind," I said.

"You'll never understand what he is to us."

"Explain it to me," I said.

"He is Robert's successor. Our master."

"He doesn't want to be one of you," I said.

"Only because you brainwashed him against his own kind to be your pet," she said.

"He's a wolf, Rhonda. He can never be one of you," I said.

She looked confused. "That is a lie!" she hissed.

"His mother Brenna was a wolf, and so is he," I said. She swung her spear at me, but I didn't flinch. I stood my ground with the silver point only inches from my heart.

"No, he's not," she said. "He's one of us, you succubus."

The guards all lunged closer to the Bloodsuckers. Dagny chucked his food into the grass as he shifted into a wolf, adding his hideous growl to the pack. The archer aimed his crossbow at Dagny, and fear filled me. One wrong word and we could all die—them, us, everyone.

"Ashling," Mother said. I could hear her unease in the way she spoke.

I had to get through to Rhonda; I had to save her. There was something beautiful inside her. Something worth saving; I could feel it in my bones. "I can't change the truth, but I can help you see your life is worth more than a broken promise of your father's clan. You still have a choice," I said.

"What choice? To let a murderer live?" she said.

It was laughable how afraid they were of us and we were of them. And neither side could see the fear and sadness in the other. We only saw a soulless enemy, but I saw Rhonda's soul. I could feel her. She was different than Robert.

"The choice to make your own path," I said.

Angry tears filled her fierce eyes, and she stared at me. "What do you want from me?" she screamed.

"Your trust," I said, "and your friendship."

She laughed as she wiped away her tears. "Never," she said.

"Rhonda, your heart beats in your chest. I can hear it; don't give up your life so easily for someone else's orders," I said.

"You think I'll lose?" she said.

"I think you will kill some of us before you die, but you are outnumbered seven to one. Don't throw away the life you were given. Don't give up your dreams," I said. "Put down your spear. We share a common enemy."

"You are my enemy," she said.

"No, I am not. I have never been your enemy, and I'm the only friend you have right now," I said. "We both live our lives trying to protect the humans. Let's do it together."

"You eat human flesh!" she screamed.

"Most wolves protect humans and eat livestock or wild game. Only the few forsaken wolves murder humans. You and I were both created to stop them, and together we could finally succeed," I said.

"I want to believe you," she said. The weariness was clear on her face. "I need to see Grey Donavan. I need to know he's alive before I will trust you."

"He's away at the moment. Dilara, would you mind seeking Grey for me?" I said. "Tell him we have a guest."

"What makes you think you can trust me?" Rhonda asked.

I smiled. "I can smell it on you."

She laughed. "I think you're mistaken." But she gestured to her companions to lower their weapons and cautiously sat across from me in the waving grass. "I don't understand. What are you?" she asked.

"A werewolf," I said, smiling. "My name is Ashling Boru. I am a princess of the Irish Boru pack. And my purpose is to protect humans, even you."

"I don't need your protection," she said.

"I believe you."

Shikoba and Gwyn walked over and sat next to me and studied Rhonda. I could feel their uneasiness. I was thankful the others kept their distance. Dagny stayed close enough to kill Rhonda in a heartbeat, but the other guards had stepped back to make Rhonda's companions more comfortable.

"Why are you hunting us?" I asked.

"I came looking for Grey, but I found his home empty, Robert slain, and all the skulls burned. I vowed to hunt you down and kill you myself."

"And now?" I asked.

She shook her head. "I don't know."

"Why do you believe we are all killers?" I said.

"We are taught that all of you live on human flesh, and you are all evil, and the clan must protect humankind by killing all of you," she said.

"Why do you drink our blood?"

"We need your blood to absorb your power, so we can hunt you," she said.

I shuddered. She was so matter-of-fact. No fear. No hesitation.

"And what do you think of us now?" I asked.

She looked from me to my family. She watched Nia and Fridrik squirming in my mother's arms and smiled. "I see a family," she said.

"We aren't evil, Rhonda," I said. "We are just like you."

The more I talked to Rhonda, the more I trusted her. Her companions still scared me a little, but I imagined they felt the same about Dagny and his guards.

Grey came running across the hill to me. He was far faster than a werewolf and a Bloodsucker. Rhonda's eyes grew wide as he approached with Dilara, Mund, Quinn, and Kane trailing behind. They were like living gods.

"Grey," I said. "I'd like to introduce you to Rhonda."

"I hear you tried to kill my love," he said.

She just stared at him. Though I couldn't blame her; he was handsome. His messy hair, sideburns, and intense green eyes made my body burn. I desired everything about him, even in these tense circumstances. Grey sat down and held my hand.

"I did," she said, studying him. "I saw you in Canada; you killed Caleb. I didn't realize that was you. I would have killed you then."

"He attacked me; I protected myself and my pack," he said. "But yes, I killed one of yours, and I'm sorry for your loss."

She stared at him with so much concentration, but her face was unreadable.

He smiled. "Do you know what I am?"

"A wolf," she said uncertainly.

"Are you going to kill me?" he asked as he licked his lips. The action was so distractingly delicious.

"I don't know what to believe anymore," she said.

"I suggest you go with your gut," he said.

"You were meant to lead the clan. You are the master," she said, shaking her head.

"I won't be leading a clan to kill wolves," he said.

"I can see you have found your place," she said, studying my pack and me. "I don't understand it, but I can see you love one another."

"She is my equal." He squeezed my hand. "What do you want of us now?"

She just stared at us with her wide blue eyes.

"You just have to say it," I said. "What do you want of us?"

"If you are what you say you are, then we share a passion for protecting life," she said. "And we share an enemy. I would join you."

"How can we trust you?" Mund asked.

"The same way I'm trusting you," she said. "It's blind faith."

"Whatever our fathers taught you was a lie. These are our people," Grey said.

Grey held out his hand to shake Rhonda's; when she did the same, he grabbed her hand and pulled her closer to us. "If you think you're going to kill us in our sleep, you better be ready to die," he said.

"She won't," I said.

Mund whispered in my ear, "Are you certain about her?"

I glanced back at Rhonda. "I'm certain of no one, but she has a good heart. I can feel it. But they have to earn their place with us."

Mund nodded.

"I will have to take your weapons," I said. I couldn't have them hurting my pack. Rhonda looked wildly around at all of the wolves that surrounded them. "I know it is a lot of trust to ask of you, but you also have to realize that I've already given you my faith by not killing you on sight, and my first obligation is to protect my pack."

She frowned as Mund laid out a tarp.

"Please place your weapons on the tarp. It is only for now," I said.

"I would do the same for my clan," she said, reluctantly setting her spear on the tarp, followed by five knives, and then she twirled a silver ring on her finger. I recognized the Bloodsucker's symbol that was tattooed on Grey's wrist. I shuddered looking at it. "And this." She set the ring down on the ground with all her other weapons. It was such a simple ring, but no less dangerous than the knives next to it.

She ordered her companions to do the same. I couldn't believe how many pieces of silver they carried on them. Mund wrapped the weapons in the tarps and bound them tightly. I could feel everyone breathe easier with the silver locked away. Kane picked up the bundle and carried it on his back. Her other companions were terrified. The potent scent of their fear filled the air, but I was excited to create peace between our people. This rivalry had gone on far too long. This would be the beginning of a new era, an era of love. I just had to teach them to see each other.

I saw Father, Brychan, Channing, and Marcius approaching. I could only imagine how angry Father might be, seeing these three Bloodsuckers among my pack, but I would find out soon enough the depth of his wrath. Father stalked toward me with his furrowed brow and bulging veins.

"Hostages?" he asked Mund.

"Allies," I corrected him.

"Bloodsuckers aren't our allies; they are our most hated enemies. And we kill our enemies," Father said.

"I spared their lives," I said.

"What makes you think you can spare their lives?" he said, grabbing my upper arm and pulling me farther away from Rhonda and the others. His fat fingers dug into my soft flesh, and I smelled Rhonda's fear.

I reached up and flicked him right in the forehead. *Thwapp.* Right between his eyes. He winced and looked utterly stunned.

"And what makes you think I gave you a choice?" I said.

"You dare to strike me?" he boomed.

I laughed. "I didn't strike you; I flicked you. You'll be just fine, I'm sure. Now take your hands off me. This is my pack. And though I respect your counsel, I will not be threatened. And you will not touch me again."

The cold look on his face made me want to cringe away. I wasn't sure that he wouldn't strike me down for my insolence, but I held my place. He let go of my arm, and I felt the blood rush back into it. His grip was murderous.

"You mean to take my throne?" he said angrily.

"No. You are legendary King Pørr Boru of Ireland, and I need you to hold that throne and protect our people, but you answer to me now," I said. "I am taking my rightful place as your Crimson Queen."

"You are meant to unite the packs on your eighteenth birthday, when you're claimed at Carrowmore. Until you fulfill the prophecy, you belong to me," he growled.

"I don't belong to you. I belong to the entire pack—I belong to Old Mother," I said. "And I will not be threatened by you. I will lead our people, and I will protect them all."

He stared at me for a long time with the blood pulsing in the giant vein in his forehead. I could only imagine the turmoil going on in his mind. "Then where are we going?" he said, challenging me.

"Did you not give me counsel that we should seek Mother Rhea before attempting to follow Baran into the Bloodrealms? Is that still your opinion?" I asked.

He clenched and unclenched his teeth over and over again, and finally his eyes fixed on me again. "She's the only one I know who can help us find him," Father said. "If you want to save him, we need her."

"Then we go to Mycenae to find Mother Rhea," I said.

He stood quietly next to me. I could feel his mood shifting between anger and something lighter. Mother wrapped her arm with his, and they walked away talking quietly. I didn't bother to try to listen.

Dilara walked next to me, well within earshot of Rhonda. "Are you sure we should trust the Bloodsuckers?" she said. "She sure flipped sides pretty easily."

"It is always easier to say the words, far harder to take action and protect those you once killed, and kill those you once protected," I said to Rhonda. "Your time will come, and you will have to choose: do you kill my people, or do you protect them?"

Rhonda nodded. "I hope I make the right choice," she said.

"As do I," I said. "So, who are your companions?" I asked.

"This is Jamal and Paul," Rhonda said.

"How do you find each other?" I asked.

"Our fathers induct us and we live the life. I was the first woman allowed in as my father's only child."

"Did they treat you differently?" I asked, thinking of my own life.

She laughed. "Always. Some wanted to protect me. Others thought I was a burden." She looked around at my pack. "You're lucky."

"Sometimes you have to take respect, because it isn't always given freely," I said.

"So this is your revolution?" she asked.

"No, this is my rebellion," I said.

Brychan and Quinn were talking with Jamal and Paul behind us. They started to relax a little, but they were clearly uncomfortable. I watched my pack with the Bloodsuckers, and I was filled with hope. It was a dangerous alliance, but a necessary one if we wanted to win against Verci and Vigdis. I couldn't take Rhonda's life; when I looked at her, I saw pieces of myself.

"Rhonda, how many more are there?" I asked.

"Three," she said. "Our fathers."

"I doubt they will be happy about our alliance."

She laughed. "No, not at all."

"My father nearly had a stroke." I glanced back at him. He was struggling to learn his new place in my world, but I had faith that he would make the right choices, with a little guidance.

"I think they'd get along," Rhonda said. We laughed.

"What will you do now?" I asked.

"Now that I have betrayed my clan and my own father? I don't know. What would you have of me?"

"Your loyalty. A war is coming for the fate of humankind. Verci and Vigdis Dvergar are seeking blood. I need strong fighters by my side to win this war against their evil," I said. Vigdis wanted my mother to suffer, she wanted me dead, and I didn't know yet what Verci had in store for Willem, but I feared for his life. Baran was their captive. I knew Vigdis would punish me for killing her daughter. "And from what I have seen of you, you already scare the shit out of me," I said.

"Strange . . . I'd say the same of you," Rhonda said.

I liked Rhonda and Dilara. I was proud to have them as part of my pack. The people I surrounded myself with would determine my fate now. Their love or their betrayal was all that stood between me and surviving.

"Eamon's dying," Cara said.

Sadness filled me as I picked up Fridrik and brought him into the shack to his father. I knelt down by Eamon while I held his son in his arms. He was too weak to hold Fridrik on his own. Eamon's eyes were barely open, and his breathing was shallow. I knew Eamon was dying, but he just continued to smile at his son. Watching their bond was heartbreaking. I knew he didn't have much time left.

"Eamon?" I whispered. "Don't die."

I couldn't help but look at Fridrik and want to cry for him. He was losing his father and possibly even his mother, Grete. It was a senseless tragedy. No child should have to grow up without parents.

"We all die," he said.

He tapped his pocket, and I slipped my hand inside and pulled out an amulet in the shape of the Tree of Life. I studied it, remembering him hiding something in his pocket when I ran into him at the festival. "You'll need that to win."

He started to gag on his own blood, and it bubbled out of his mouth. I cried as I held his limp hand. The pain of his touch was nothing to the pain in his eyes. He was losing everything. I'd been so stupid; I let this all happen. He was dying because of me. I had thought Eamon was my enemy, and all this time he was risking his life to protect his mate and child from an enemy who fed on my destruction. The faces of evil are never what I expected. He had been one of us, and I couldn't see it—I didn't protect him. I felt like I was drowning.

"I'm sorry I didn't see the real you," I said.

I cried as I watched his life flowing between my fingers, and there was nothing I could do to stop it. He was too far gone for even Old Mother's magic to save him. Now all I could do was watch him die.

"I love you, Fridrik," he said, and he kissed him on the cheek. "Ashling, do something for me," he whispered.

"Anything," I sobbed.

"Destroy them."

Don't miss *Bloodmoon*,
the next book in the Bloodmark Saga.

bloodmarksaga.com

Bloodrealms

Blooderalms,
Norway

Mycenae,
Greece

Dverga Castle,
Iceland

Rock of Cashel,
Ireland

Netherworld,
Canada

Maine,
United States of America

©2014 Jennifer Rich

Pack Reference

Boru – Ireland
Ashling Boru
Bridgid Boru
Cadence Kingery-Boru
Donal Boru
Felan Boru
Flin Boru
Mund Boru
Queen Nessa Vanir-Boru
Niamh Boru
King Pørr Boru
Quinn Boru
Ragnall Boru
Tegan Kahedin-Boru

Costas – Spain
Selene Costas

Cree – Canada
Kaneonuskatew (Kane)
Shikoba
Tallulah

Kahedin – Wales
Lord Beldig Kahedin
Brychan Kahedin
Gwyn Kahedin

Dvergar – Iceland
Adomnan Dvergar
Bento Dvergar
Crob Dvergar
Eamon Dvergar
Fridrik Dvergar
Uaid Dvergar
Vercingetorix (Verci) Dvergar
Vigdis Vanir

Kingery – Switzerland
Cara Kingerly
Channing Kingery
Emil Kingerly
Marcius Kingerly

Killian – Scotland
Baran Killian
Grey Donavan
Khepri Killian
Willem Killian

Tabakov – Russia
Dilara Tabakov

Vanir – Greece
Calista Vanir
Lady Faye Vanir
Mother Rhea Vanir

Norse Lands – Finland
Odin Pohjola

Bloodrealms – Valhalla
Æsileif

Glossary

Aconite
A flower that cures werewolves from silver-poisoning. Also known as Wolfsbane.

Barghest
Werewolves that consume wolf-children, foresaking Old Mother. Their skin becomes toxic and burns the flesh of other wolves and their offspring carry the same skin toxicity.

Battle of Asgard
The battle against the Barghest in the home land of the Pojola pack.

Beltane
Gaelic festival halfway between the spring equinox and the summer solstice ruled by the Irish Boru pack on Old Mother's Lunar Calendar.

Bloodmark
A pack symbol tattooed in blood.

Bloodmoon
A red moon that comes once during each season.

Bloodrealms
Underground fighting world beneath the Seven Sisters Waterfall.

Bloodsucker
The clan of humans that hunt werewolves.

Carrowmore
Carrowmore is one of the passage tomb cemetaries in Ireland. In Bloodmark they are the resting place of the humans in the battle of 4600 BCE.

Crimson Queen
The prophecy foretold by Calista Vanir, of the Crimson Queen who would unite the packs.

Draugr
Undead, human-like creatures that blindly consume all living creatures.

Elder Gods
The original werewolves.

Fenrir
A junkyard city under the Bloodrealms.

Foresaken Packs
Werewolves that broke their vows to Old Mother.

Garm
A pack of wolves that no longer are able to shift to human, and prowel the Bloodrealms looking for flesh.

Hills of Tara
Location of the Vanir and Dvergar battle commemorated by ancient monuments in Ireland.

Lughnasadh
Festival marking harvest, ruled by the Scottish Killian on Old Mother's Lunar Calendar.

M' eudail
Gaelic for 'My dear'.

Netherworlds
Underground werewolf city in Canada.

Passage Grave
Ancient graves of stone for Old Mother's preistesses.

Samhain
Gaelic festival marking the end of summer and the beginning of winter. Ruled by the Dvergar on Old Mother's Lunar Calendar.

Stonearch
A steampunk mobile city under the Bloodrealms.

Tha gaol agam ort
Gaelic for 'I love you'.

Tree of Life
The symbol of the Crimson Queen.

Winter Solstice/Yule
Gaelic festival for winter solstice and celebrates the rebirth of the sun.

Wolves of Song
A song of mythological wolf warriors said to have been trapped in the Bloodrealms.

Yew
The skin of the yew plant can be used to bring someone out of shock.

Ylva
She-wolf.